RAPTURE

THE DEVIANT HEARTS SERIES

N. N. BRITT

Cover Design by Cat at TRC Designs

Cover Photography by N.N. Britt

Cover Model: Anthony Montemarano

Edited by Loredana Elsberry Schwartz at www.elfwerksediting.com and Megan McKeever

Copyedited by R.C. Craig

Proofreading by www.judysproofreading.com

Due to strong language and sexual situations this book is intended for mature audience only.

Dear reader,

This book comes from a dark place and covers a number of sensitive topics that include loss of a loved one and substance abuse due to depression. Therefore, I advise caution as you may find some content triggering.

While I always take great responsibility to research certain aspects I want to discuss in my work, I understand that every journey is unique and I simply hope, as a writer, I'm able to portray this one with justice it deserves.

Thank you so much for buying an authorized edition of this book. Your support allows the author to keep writing for you.

If you obtained an illegal copy of this book, consider donating the money to one of the following organizations.

https://www.alportsyndrome.org
https://www.heart.org
https://www.stjude.org

Sincerely,

N. N. Britt

For Mom

"The path to paradise begins in hell."

DANTE ALIGHIERI

1 HAZEL

I hate numbers.

I hate how uniform and indisputable they are.

I hate how they have taken over my once colorful life completely. How they've turned every neat stroke of baby blue into an ugly blob of infinite black. The black I've been waking up to for the past two years, one month, and twenty-six days.

Guilt and hunger twist my stomach as I struggle with the stubborn luggage that doesn't want to come out of the trunk of my Prius—a farewell present from Owen, my soon-to-be ex-husband on paper, although he hasn't actually been a husband in over two years.

Once the heavy bag makes it to the ground, I smooth my burning palms over the fabric of my winter coat and give myself a few seconds to process the view in front of me—a small private lake house hiding behind the multicolored line of trees, their wind-tortured tips desperate for the attention of afternoon sun. The golds and the reds up above, so typical of fall in Tahoe, look almost lost amidst the heavy gray clouds racing across the November sky.

Agreeing to my friend Rayna's house-sitting arrangement didn't seem like a bad idea when she offered. It does now. Besides, she and her husband never needed a house sitter in Tahoe before.

The blanket of dead leaves shielding the cold ground rustle beneath my boots as I shuffle my feet to the front door.

Painful memories of the happy moments spent here with Owen cause my chest to stiffen.

Life doesn't end at twenty-six, does it?

For some, like my son, River, who was diagnosed with congenital leukemia only two days after his birth, it ends at four.

Here we go—numbers again.

My fingers are numb, just like the rest of my body, when I thrust my hand into the pocket of my pea coat and fish for the key. As soon as I step inside, the faint smell of pumpkin traps me in a bubble of more memories. The time of my life before River. When things were simple. When it was only Rayna, Clay, Owen, and me. And our wild Tahoe weekends.

The cabin looks exactly like it did years ago, unaffected by the storms in our lives. Its vintage rustic interior is warm and inviting. There are lots of carpets, artwork, crafts, and plenty of windows over-looking the lake, its glassy surface almost taking my breath away. But the hint of a feeling lasts only a fraction of a second.

I drop the luggage and cross the living room, my eyes zeroing in on the glimmer of the stainless steel appliances peeking out from the kitchen. Walking over to the fridge, I pull the door open, only to find a package of turkey and a lonely can of tomato juice on the top shelf. My phone buzzes in my pocket when I'm searching for bread. *And possibly wine or beer.*

"Hey, hon." Rayna's voice is hesitant and somewhat uneasy on the line. "How was the drive?"

"Long and boring." I walk back to the island with a stack of the paper plates I found in one of the cabinets. "How was your flight?"

"Clay almost went crazy. Eleven hours on a plane." Rayna forces a laugh. I wish she hadn't, though. Not for me. "Are you settling in okay?"

"Yep. About to make a sandwich."

"Oh God!" She gasps. "You're not going to use the turkey in the fridge, are you? It's been there since Labor Day. I told my cleaning lady to get some groceries for you. Her name is Ester and she usually comes on Thursdays or Fridays. She has her own key."

"Okay, thanks." Looking around the spotless kitchen, I realize today *is* actually Friday. And if Ester was here earlier, she probably didn't get any groceries because Rayna didn't even know I was coming until I got in my car this morning and took off.

I need to eat something, but the thought of going out to a store on my own sends a cold shiver down my spine. Part of me ached to escape L.A. because of the holiday crowds. People are overrated. Most people, anyway. "What's your first stop?"

"Paris."

Owen and I never traveled farther than Arizona, where we went to see his family. "Send me some photos later?"

"Of course." She pauses. "Clay told me you guys are calling it quits… Is it true? Did Owen file for divorce?"

"It was bound to happen sooner or later." I lean against the kitchen island; my tired body is starting to fail me. Being trapped in a car on a lonely highway for eight hours will do that to you. "I guess it wasn't meant to be." I can't believe I'm saying this. Ten years ago, when Owen crashed into my life, I didn't think it was possible to fall for someone harder than I fell for him. But look where we are now. Instead of falling for each other even more, we're just…falling apart.

The doom of my divorce suddenly hits me hard, fast, and repeatedly. The shadow of my marriage has been slowly suffocating me from the inside out for over two years. We don't do anything together anymore—we don't have dinners, we don't watch TV, we don't even talk. Truth be told, I wasn't surprised at all when Owen brought up the divorce. I'd thought about it too but didn't have the heart to tell him. It's been so long since he's shown any affection that I've forgotten what it feels like to be hugged, kissed, or simply touched.

Not that I need or want any of that.

"Hazel?" Rayna's voice jolts me back to reality.

"Sorry." I hold my breath as a painful spasm attacks my stomach.

"I know you hate when I do this, but you need to start getting out. At the very least, do some shopping or get a haircut. You can't spend the rest of your life locked up in your room. You're twenty-six. Not sixty-six. You need a change. Please, just do it for me."

After I tell her that I'll try, we wrap up our phone conversation, I toss the expired turkey and tomato juice into the trash can, dispose of my coat and boots, and haul my luggage to the guest room. Being in this house by myself feels strange. Owen and I used to crash here almost every weekend. His parents hated the fact that he was dating an aspiring painter just as much as my parents hated the fact that I was dating the school's biggest troublemaker. Who knew Owen would eventually settle down and make his dream of getting his real estate license come true?

Part of me wants to turn around and run like a scared little girl, away from the memories, but part of me knows that running won't make any difference. It'll still hurt.

I kneel in front of my luggage, unzip it, and absently look through my things. Seven years of marriage and four years of motherhood stuffed into a leather Kate Spade suitcase as if those parts of my life never existed. After setting aside some of my clothes and bathroom essentials, I pull out a stack of photos from the side pocket and study them one by one—the photos of my little boy, the photos Owen didn't want to keep, the photos that used to decorate the walls of our Encino house. When tears start pricking my eyes, I put all the mementos away and head to the bathroom.

Rayna may have done a shitty job of stocking up her kitchen, but she's made sure there are enough beauty products to host a pageant. And while I try not to look at my reflection in the vanity mirror as I undress, my eyes stare anyway. Even though they don't like what they see.

It's your own damn fault that Owen wants a divorce, Hazel. Look at you. Why should he care about you when you don't?

Shaking off the unsettling feeling, I turn on the water to fill up the tub, adding some vanilla oil from what Rayna left for me. I grab my hairbrush and run it through the strands of my once beautiful golden locks. After a few minutes of fighting the tangled mess, I give up. New hair isn't going to make Owen change his mind. I don't even want him to; it's too late. Our marriage can't be salvaged.

Tossing the hairbrush aside, I carefully lower myself into the tub and rest my head against the ceramic wall in an attempt to relax, but my mind is still reeling from the long drive. Anxiety, fear, and an empty ache—all mixed into one weird, dull sensation filling the hollow parts of my heart isn't letting go of me. All I can think of is River, about what he would look like today, what he would be wearing, what he would be eating for dinner, what he would be asking for for Christmas. Even the flowery scent of the body wash reminds me of the bubble baths I used to make for him.

I'm not sure how much time passes before I finally snap out of my daze, the now lukewarm water almost reaching my mouth, and I can't help but wonder how much time it would take for someone to discover my body if I were to drown while taking a nap.

I hate being awake and sober.

The second, more thorough, kitchen raid leaves me with one twelve-ounce can of Diet Coke. If I wanted to drown my sorrows, that's not enough and definitely not the drink I'd choose. Frustrated and thirsty, I stomp back to the bedroom and pick out a pair of skinny jeans and a sweater from my suitcase. Does Rayna really think a haircut and some shopping will make a difference?

Try it, Hazel?

"Fine, you win," I tell myself after retrieving my tiny makeup bag. I haven't opened it in ages. Not since before River's funeral. What are the chances that the contents haven't dried up or broken?

Surprisingly, when I look inside, my eyeliner, mascara, and eyeshadow kit are still intact.

I walk over to the bathroom and plant my feet in front of the vanity. The zombie staring back at me from the mirror is about to get a makeover.

2 JUSTICE

FAME CAN BE A TWO-FACED BITCH. More often so lately than back when I was in my twenties.

Running my palm over my scruffy cheek, I drink in the crowd packing The Black Lagoon. I don't hate shaving per se, but I do hate the fact that I have to do it religiously day after day when I'm on tour.

Ditching the ritual for a few weeks feels good. Makes me feel... more human.

"Back to the studio in January?" Tony, one of the bouncers working for Marvin, grins at me from his spot across the table, then shoves a handful of onion rings in his mouth.

Marvin, the owner of the joint, went all out when I told him I was going to stop by to see my nephew, Jake's, band. He called in extra security and loaded our table with every item on his menu. Not that it's that big of a menu. The Black Lagoon is no Spago. Either way, I don't have much of an appetite. I'm still on European time.

"You know what they say. No rest for the wicked." I nod, watching Jake talk to his bandmates. Reminds me of my own first show here. Back when I somewhat worshipped my famous jerk of an uncle, Elijah, when his opinion about my music mattered to me, when my best friend, Chance, was still clean and sober. When we were merely a couple of local guys full of dreams, ready to kick ass, ready to rock 'n' roll. We had no clue our first EP would blow up the Billboard charts a few years later. We just wanted to play music. Dirty, loud, and unapologetic music.

"You need a break, man," Tony says, shaking his head.

Tonight he's undercover, sporting a blue Dodgers jersey, jeans, and a pair of sneakers.

TMZ rarely stalks me all the way to Tahoe, but since a leaked copy of my divorce papers is the hottest Twitter trend at the moment, having extra security by my side can never hurt.

At the start of my career when I changed my last name, my publicist hired a few computer wizzes to clean up my presence on the net. The things money can buy. Elijah isn't listed as my uncle anywhere. Not on my Wikipedia page, not in any of the fan clubs or socials. Press isn't allowed to ask about my relation to the infamous Hale. Fuck that asshole and fuck The Gates of Hale legacy. I made it okay on my own.

"It's time to write another album, brother," I say, watching the crowd.

It's not that I disagree with Tony—after over a decade of nonstop touring, I could definitely use some rest. But the short breaks we've taken in between have always been deliberate, always coinciding with our longing to be back in the studio. It's become as routine as brushing our teeth. The question is whether we need another album right now. We've got six of them. All platinum.

Ready to turn my thoughts elsewhere, I take a sip of my beer that I've been nursing for almost ten minutes. Alcohol doesn't have the same hold on me that it does on my soon-to-be ex-wife. Nikki has been to rehab more times than she's done the red carpet. I consumed my fair share of booze and drugs in my twenties, but a sense of self-preservation kicked in after my first and only overdose. A wake-up call like never before. After that, the desire to keep getting fucked up dulled down on its own. I can still have a drink or two and be able to stop if needed, which makes me think that maybe I was never into that shit in the first place. Everyone in the band was doing it because it was cool, because that's what a bunch of dudes with tons of cash coming in do when they're on tour.

Play a show. Get fucked up. Bone some chicks. Pass out. Wake up. Repeat. Week after week. Year after year.

Until someone slips.

Chance was the one who slipped.

Tony's voice pulls me out of my reverie. "You've been on the road for two years now."

"I'll rest when I die," I mutter, relaxing on my bench.

The booths weren't here eighteen years ago. Marvin's remodeled since then. The Black Lagoon isn't simply a dive bar now, it's a dive bar with class where rich assholes like me can hide out in so-called *VIP* sections. I laugh internally at Marvin's idea of VIP. It's just a fucking booth. And despite my pleas to not bring attention to my spot, he still put two extra bouncers nearby…in case anyone wants an autograph.

Pulling the hood of my sweatshirt over my head, I close my eyes and inhale the sharp smell of alcohol, cigarette smoke, and sweat—the smell of live music. People are fools for thinking being in a rock band is glamorous. It's anything but. The only glamorous thing about The Deviant is the posters. We're bad motherfuckers in full gear, with our war paint and our stage costumes. Women all around the globe, and I suspect men too, want to lick us from head to toe. Sex appeal sells. And we're going to keep selling it for as long as we can.

The first sounds of music blast through the bar like a merciless tornado. I can hear every mistake the mixing board guy is making, but I don't think this crowd can tell the difference. They don't know what a good sound engineer can do in a place this small if they haven't worked with mine.

Jake has always been into more aggressive music. He's breathed Metallica since he was a toddler. If he wants to scream his guts out on stage, it's his call.

My eyes drift open when the first song comes to an end and I take in the sight of the raging mass. They seem to enjoy the music. I do too. I like the rawness of the sound.

Tony moves his head to the beat. "Jake is killing it."

I agree.

The thought of posting a short video on my Instagram crosses my mind, but deep down, I know this can lead to a potential disaster. Any other time of the year, sure. But not right now. Not three days into my vacation. This tour cycle has been brutal. The only human interaction I can bear tonight is with Tony and Jake.

I film a few segments with my phone and send them over to May.

She texts me back before I finish typing my note explaining that it's Jake's band.

May: What's this?

Justice: My nephew's band.

May: Are you in Tahoe?

Justice: Yes. Post this on my Instagram in two hours.

May: Why are you in Tahoe in the middle of the divorce clusterfuck?

Justice: Your point?

May: The press is crucifying you.

Of course, TMZ got their hands on the divorce papers before my soon-to-be ex-wife was served.

Justice: Tell me something I don't know.

May: This? https://www.tmz.com/2017/1/2017/nikki-deville-says-hubby-justice-cross-has-a-short-fuse/

I clench my jaw and click on the link I receive from May. Blood starts pounding behind my ears as my eyes sweep over the text. Fucking Nikki. She's always been a drama queen, but calling me violent is a new low. I swallow hard and shove my phone into the pocket of my jacket. How the hell did the two of us stay married for seven years?

Lesson learned, Justice. Don't ever date an actress!

The music is suddenly too loud and too heavy, and I feel like someone just shoved a hammer at me to crack my head open. I suck in a breath through my teeth and glance at the crowd. The white clouds of fog spilling from the tiny stage mist the floor. The bodies twitching to the drumbeat give the place a dark, horror-movie-asylum feel. I like chaos, but not when it takes over my life completely. Like when Chance died or like right now when my soon-to-be ex-wife's ongoing domestic abuse allegations are starting to become unnerving.

"You alright, boss?" Tony yells at me from across the table. His voice drowns in the music blasting through the bar.

"I'm good." I nod, reaching for my phone in my pocket to text May back. When I pull it out, a dozen messages are flashing at me from the screen.

May: Justice? I'm preparing a press release. Tell me something.

Funny thing, but at the beginning of my career, I practiced one simple rule when it came to my personal life. No comment. After I married Nikki, everything changed. Any gossip not contained in a timely manner turned into a fucking abomination.

For a second, I slip into a world of denial where ignoring the TMZ article seems like the best option, but the lie gets under my skin. I've never hit a woman in my life. Not unless she begged me to. If Nikki considers my spanking her in bed those two times we tried to get overly creative a case of domestic abuse, then I'm a fucking ballerina.

Justice: No comment. Just do your magic.

May responds with a thumbs-up emoji, which is her way of letting me know she's pissed because I don't want to personalize the messages she posts for my fans.

Fuck it. I don't owe any explanation to anyone for something I didn't do.

I put the phone away and absently stare out at the hazy floor. A smile touches my lips as my eyes take in the sight of the drunk, care-free crowd. They love the band. I can see it written all over their faces, even through the cloud of fog and lights. The frenzy. The desire to hear more. The longing of a release. Hale blood running through Jake's veins is no coincidence. I've been doing this way too long not to know when a set is a success. The ability to read people is a gift, something every performer needs to possess. It's a vital part of the magic called making music.

That's when the streaks of gold enter my line of vision. She's small and slender, moving through the wall of fog and dancing LEDs, and her hair sparkles in the thick club mist like a star from another galaxy. All I need is a fraction of a second to determine she doesn't belong here. It's not even the funny-looking sweater and the lack of heavy makeup. She has this strange, almost desperate look on her face, but not desperate for a one-night stand or anything of that sort. It's the kind of desperate that says she doesn't want to be here. And I love the color of her eyes. Amber, like fire.

"If you want to leave, boss, just let me know!" Tony yells at me, chewing on his onion rings. I shift my gaze and give him a nod. Two seconds later when I look back at the crowd, the woman with the golden hair is gone.

3 HAZEL

I DRIVE without any sense of direction. My mouth is dry and my hands are shaking. *I need a drink.*

Shifting in my seat, I crane my neck and try to read the blurry neon sign over where a group of people are gathered outside an industrial-type building. My fingers tap-dance against the smooth leather of the steering wheel cover. Eight hours on a lonely highway turned me into a neurotic mess, and the thought of driving myself into the nearest tree to end the torture once and for all crossed my mind. However, the rational part of me stopped the sadistic one from doing such a stupid thing. Sometimes it feels like I'm two different people who are fighting each other over my sanity, because some days I know what I'm doing and some I don't. Today is the latter.

I circle the block, thinking about getting a drink in the bar I just passed. Owen and I partied hard before River came along. I had my first fake ID at seventeen, so being in loud places with hundreds of strangers has never made me uncomfortable. There was simply never a shortage of wine and liquor at home after we buried our baby, and lately, I haven't had a reason to go anywhere of the sort.

After the third loop, I pull into the busy lot and park my Prius between two SUVs. My heart thumping inside my chest threatens to demolish my rib cage as I shut off the engine, roll down the window, and take in the sounds of rock music blasting from inside the building.

Owen and I used to go to lots of concerts before my pregnancy. We went to see Coldplay, Foo Fighters, Linkin Park, My Chemical Romance, and Disturbed. My husband had a soft spot for loud, angry, unconventional music. But all that stopped when River was born and we were suddenly buried under a pile of medical bills and insurance paperwork. There was very little time left for entertainment.

The moment I step outside, cold air crawls under the sleeves of my sweater. Trying not to pay attention to the catcalling and the stares of the local crowd, I clutch my fingers around the straps of my purse and make a beeline for the entrance. The bouncer's face gives away no emotion as he studies my driver's license. My outfit doesn't seem to bother him nearly as much as it does the guys on the sidewalk who won't stop the immature whistling. For a second, I think wearing the skinny jeans was a mistake. *Or coming here was a mistake.*

"The cover is twenty," the bouncer barks, returning my ID.

"To get into a bar?" I ask, glancing at the neon sign above his head as if the answer is going to magically appear there. "Is this male strip-tease night?"

"Live music."

Drawing a deep breath, I search my purse for some cash and hand it to him. Unbelievable.

Inside, the floor is packed, clouds of white smoke consuming the sweaty bodies that are ramming against each other to the wild beat of the song. The place is dark and moody. I slowly make my way to the bar and take one of the only two empty seats left. The music blaring from the vicinity of the stage is aggressive and vulgar. Not my first choice if I were looking for a live band to see, but I don't care. The desire to escape for a while is stronger than my aversion to the offensive lyrics that make no sense.

The bartender approaches me with a lopsided grin. After requesting a shot of tequila and a food menu, I take a minute to study the anarchy on stage. The singer's longish dirty blond hair sticks out in all directions as he violently shakes his head like he's been possessed. He's young—nineteen, maybe twenty—wearing a simple black t-shirt and a pair of jeans. I find his performance, particularly his gut-wrenching screams, somewhat disturbing, but I suppose if the place is this busy, the band must be popular.

The bartender is back with my drink shortly. Wrapping my fingers around the shot glass, I scan the list of food items on the menu. It's strange that hunger is the first feeling that has awakened in me after two years of complete numbness.

As soon as the song comes to an end, I use the opportunity to order a burger and fries, then down my shot and ask for another. By the time my food comes, a familiar lightness has already taken over my body and mind.

The band is about to wrap up their set when someone very unsteady snatches the stool next to mine. Slamming his massive hand against the counter, the stranger demands a drink. His slanting body invades my personal space as his elbow starts making its way in the direction of my plate.

Moving my food aside, I finish the rest of my drink and send a few fries into my mouth to soften the burning in my throat caused by the tequila. I like being numb. Because that's when I don't remember. Although the emptiness always consumes me the next morning, hitting even harder than the night before. But I'm too tired to fight. Too tired to think. Too tired to live—right now, I just want to forget.

My peripheral vision catches the crew disassembling the mount of amplifiers on stage. The singer jumps into the crowd and makes a few rounds, shaking hands and taking photos before he disappears in one of the booths that's conveniently tucked in a dark corner on the oppo-site side of the room.

The asshole next to me slides his stool closer to mine. "Sooo, whazza guy gotta do around here to get the attention of a pretty lady like yourshelf?"

I play dumb. "Excuse me?"

He doesn't beat around the bush. "You wanna go back to my place and have some fuun?"

"No, thank you." I return to my food.

He thrusts his knees into my thigh and slurs, "Youuu look like you c-could usha good time, suuugar. Come on...I can show you a good time."

Anger simmers beneath my skin. I silently move my chair and ignore his remark.

He doesn't get that I want to drink my alcohol and eat my food alone. "Whassit gonna do, sugar?" His hand goes for my thigh.

"Get off of me!" I raise my voice and push him away. My first night of what's supposed to be a trip to rediscover myself is being ruined by some asshole. Just my luck.

"Come on, sugar." He moves closer, trapping me against the counter with his body, his rancid breath in my face.

"I said, get off of me!" I shove both hands at his enormous chest. "I don't need company."

"You deaf, bud?" The new voice drifting in from the dark has a hard edge and a hint of raw power. Then a male silhouette that's lingering among the bar crowd slowly swims into focus. He's tall and lean, but the hood of his sweatshirt that's thrown over his head hides his face. "Didn't you hear the lady? She doesn't want company."

As if on cue, a bulky guy in a Dodgers jersey appears and retrieves the asshole from his spot. The ease with which he does so startles me, and the bar-goers cheer him on. Two seconds later, the idiot who almost drunk-drooled into my food is ancient history.

The mysterious stranger in the hoodie moves closer and gestures at the empty stool. "Hey." His voice softens. "I hope you don't mind. I promise to behave."

"Sure." I nod, drinking him in. He looks handsome and sober. Not that his looks, or his toxicology report, matter.

My pulse starts to race when he leans in and whispers into my ear, "Do you mind if I buy you a drink?"

"I thought you said you were going to behave?"

"Consider it a peace offering." His eyes meet mine. They're silvery gray, big and bottomless.

I don't know if it's the alcohol or him, but my stomach does a few unexpected flips. Something I haven't felt in over two years.

"Okay." I nod again, examining his slightly-out-of-focus—one may even say stunning—face. He's a little older. Looks to be in his thirties, but the good side of them, the youthful and more sensual side. A few silky strands of black hair sticking out from under his hoodie curl chaotically over the collar of his leather jacket.

The big guy in the Dodgers jersey materializes behind us and rests his hand on the stranger's shoulder. There's an inaudible exchange of stares and cryptic gestures between the two, then Dodgers guy gives the mystery man a pat on the back and disappears into the crowd.

"What are you drinking?" Mr. Tall, Dark, and Handsome inquires, keeping his distance, just as he promised.

"Tequila."

"Wow, you're not kidding around." A quiet chuckle leaves his mouth.

"Nope." I take a deep breath and break our eye contact.

"What's your name?"

I tilt my head and stare at the man. The hoodie he's hiding under is distracting, but the longer I study his features, the more I'm convinced I know his face. The brooding eyes, the elegant curve of the lips, the sculptured cheekbones, the thin fringe of stubble on his chin. Even the letters tattooed on the fingers of his left hand.

"Is this some sort of interrogation?" I ask carefully after a few failed attempts to read the word this man chose to imprint on his body forever.

He shoves the hand into the pocket of his jacket and says, "No. I thought it'd be easier to communicate if I call you by your name instead of *babe*."

Yeah. Definitely not that. I cringe at the silly nickname. "Hazel."

"Hazel?" The corners of his lips perk up. "I like that."

"Your turn."

"Daniel."

"Nice to meet you, Daniel." I feel somewhat disappointed. He doesn't look like a Daniel. The obvious bad boy thing this man has going on—the leather jacket, the boots, the hand tat—would probably work better with some cool, exotic, never-before-heard name.

"You don't like my name?" The blue lights dancing in the gray pools of his eyes as he narrows them at me make me giddy. I haven't sat this close to another man in years. And right now, the two tequilas I had and the mess in my head are causing me to feel weird things.

"I just expected something a little more...provocative," I say, sipping on what's left of my second drink.

"Provocative?" He leans closer. "How provocative?" I like the way he smells. His breath is minty and I catch a hint of clean ocean breeze and spice. His voice is suggestive, but not over the top.

I roll my eyes, maybe a bit too dramatically. But I have an excuse—I can blame the theatrics of everything I do and say right now on alcohol.

Daniel orders another tequila for me and a beer for himself.

"Are you in hiding or something?" I dip my French fry in the container of ketchup.

"Why would you think that?" He places his elbow on the counter and props his chin with his hand. The sleeves of his jacket slide down a little, revealing some more ink designs, but I still can't read the letters on his fingers. It's almost as if he doesn't want me to. Fine, that can be the challenge of the night.

"Because of...all this." I wave my hand in front of his face. "But you forgot the sunglasses."

"I'm at a bar." He smiles again. "I'm trying to blend in."

"Well, it's not raining here."

He shakes his head and laughs inaudibly.

The bartender returns with our drinks.

"You either don't want to be recognized or found." I let him in on my theory.

"Maybe I just have a bad haircut," he counters.

A man this gorgeous can't have a bad haircut. Even with his head shaved, he'd probably still look like a god.

Yes, Hazel, you're officially drunk.

"Figures." I sigh, reaching for my tequila.

We silently clink our drinks. He takes a slow sip from his bottle while I down the shot in one go. The buzz in my head intensifies.

"So are you going to tell me who you're hiding from?" I ask, chewing on my tasteless fries.

"My ex."

"If she's your ex, then why the hiding?"

"You know, she's one of those who doesn't get that it's over when it's over."

"Ahhh...I see." His beautiful face is starting to turn into a blob. What a pity. I liked looking at him. "You want my burger?" I slide my plate in his direction.

"I'm good."

"Suit yourself." I shrug.

"What about you?"

"What *about* me?"

"What are you doing here on a Friday night alone?"

"Drinking."

"I can see that." He brings his stool closer to mine. "Do you want to tell me why?"

"What if I don't?"

"I mean, I'm not going to force it out of you." He takes another sip of his beer. "But isn't that the point of doing this?"

"Doing what?"

"Going to a bar, getting drunk, talking to a complete stranger about your issues, and then never seeing each other again? Kinda like going to a shrink but for free."

"You do that a lot?"

"Actually, no. I just go to a regular shrink, but I wanted to try this since the regular shrink doesn't do any good." He smirks again. Damn him. I don't know if it's the alcohol or if it's me, but I want to keep talking.

"Sooo..." I drawl. "You have a regular shrink?"

"Is that a problem?" He cocks a brow.

"Not...not really." I blink a few times to bring his face back into focus. "The way things in this country are going, everyone will have to have a mandatory shrink soon."

"That wouldn't be so bad, would it?"

"Guess not." I change the subject. "So...wanna tell me about that ex of yours and why you're hiding?"

His lips touch the rim of the beer bottle again. *His lips are...fine.* "She's been served."

It takes me a good minute to get what exactly he's talking about. "Oh." My heart shrinks at the thought of my own divorce. "Did she not take it well?"

"Not really."

"Did she not see this coming?"

"I don't know." He shrugs. His eyebrows pull together as he runs his hand over his unshaven cheek. "Is this some kind of interrogation?" A smile.

"Youuu started it," I slur, fighting the unexpected laugh rippling through my chest. "I'm just trying to be a good bar shrink."

"You're doing an excellent job, babe." His hot breath makes my skin prickle as he whispers it into my ear.

If I were sober, I'd probably tell him off and ask him to leave, but the fuzziness in my head, the strange pulsating sensation in my stomach, and the fact that I no longer owe anything to Owen indicate that it's okay to keep this conversation going. I find Daniel intriguing, a little different, cocky even, but interesting enough to distract me from the depressing thoughts in my head. Maybe Rayna is right after all. Maybe I just need to get out more.

"Do you call every woman you meet at a bar babe?" I ask, doing a ninety-degree spin on my stool to face him. "I thought we agreed on my name." I have to lean against the bar to prevent myself from falling off. Having three shots of tequila with only a few fries is making me lose control over my own body. But I do know I don't want to end up on the floor.

"Right." He nods, also shifting on his stool, his knee connecting with the legs of mine. "I'll do my best to keep my word."

"Hey." I wave at the bartender again, wanting shot number four.

"You got a ride home?" Daniel asks after I order.

"I thought this was a no-strings-attached situation?" I mumble, my tongue barely moving in my mouth. Then I down my tequila while the plate of fries, now stale and cold, remains in front of me.

"It is. I just want to make sure you get home safe," he says. "I promise I won't follow."

"Pfff." I try to suppress a hiccup. "That would be considered breaking the rules of bar therapy."

"Sounds like you're a bar therapy pro."

"Not really... I don't typically..." I have to stop for a second to think about what I was going to say. Everything in the bar, including my plate, is spinning. My fingers miss at least twice while trying to find the little container of ketchup. "...go out and get drunk in a bar on a Friday night. I'm a stay-at-home type."

The silence between us becomes weird. I avert my gaze, make another ketchup-dipping attempt, and bring the fry toward my mouth. But, of course, I miscalculate and the runny substance, which seems to have a mind of its own, ends up all over my sweater.

"Shit." I rub my fingers against the fabric. Why didn't I wear something black? Black is nice. It's the color of my life.

"Here." Daniel hands me a stack of napkins and waves at the bartender. Two seconds later, a wet towel is being shoved at me. My attempt to clean off the ketchup turns into a disaster. My fingers aren't listening, and I keep dropping the towel on my jeans. My sweater looks like one huge red blur.

Bottom line: Drinking at home would have spared me the embarrassment.

"You mind?" Daniel slowly pulls the towel away. I can feel his hand grasping my shoulder to steady me while his other one slides across my chest, up and down....up and down. His face is an even bigger blur, the music is muffled, and the lights dancing in the back are fading in and out. How did I get here? What am I even doing? My son is dead, my husband and I are getting a divorce, and I'm drunk out of my mind, letting some stranger in a bar grab my breasts.

"Hey…you okay?" His voice pulls me back to reality.

"I'm fine," I say breathlessly, sliding from my stool and waving at the bartender. "I'm...going home..."

Daniel wraps his arm around me. "How are you getting home? Someone picking you up?"

"I need to close my tab," I blurt out at the bartender, trying to ignore the fact that Daniel's hand on my waist doesn't feel too bad. On the contrary, it's strong, nice, warm...and muscular. Even with all those layers of leather and material rubbing against my sweater. I'm sure it's because Owen and I haven't been close for a very long time and it's simply a normal physical reaction. Nothing more.

"Hey, why don't we get you a cab, huh?" he mumbles in my ear, giving some silent signals to the bartender.

"What am I supposed to do with my car? Just leave it?" I huff.

"Listen, you can't drive like this, babe. I'll get you a cab or an Uber, alright?" he insists.

"I don't need you to get me a cab or an Uber... I...can...takare of myshelf." I slam my hand against the bar and switch my attention to the bartender, who keeps ignoring my requests to close my tab. Summoning all the strength left in me, I shout, "Anyone working here?!"

"I already took care of the bill. Come on." Daniel hooks his arm through mine.

"I didden ass you to," I growl, jerking my other arm, which causes his beer to fly off the bar. I can see it traveling down in slow motion, the bubbly contents spilling on my sweater and jeans like a well-deserved punishment for getting wasted.

"Fuck," I blurt out as the bottle shatters right next to my feet, splashing the leftover liquid all over my boots.

"Just put it on my tab, man." I can hear Daniel's instructions right before he walks me toward the entrance.

Then there are a few blank moments; I don't exactly remember how my purse ends up on my shoulder, but I can feel it bumping into the bodies of strangers as we rip through the crowd.

The air outside is ice cold. My lungs start shrinking as I take a deep breath when we step into the parking lot. Correction: when I get dragged into the parking lot.

"What's your address?" Daniel asks, tapping the screen of his phone.

I sway on my feet, back and forth, trying to keep my balance while I watch the thick clouds coming out of my mouth as I attempt to produce a coherent sentence.

"No srings attashed, remember?" A quivering combo of mumbling and slurring comes out of my mouth on the third try. My body begins to shake, my stomach is churning, and I can't keep my eyes open. This isn't good at all.

"Look, I'm only trying to help, okay? You can't even hold yourself up. How the fuck are you going to drive?" Irritation is evident in his voice.

"Whadyou care?" I whisper, fighting gravity.

"You're right. I don't. But I'd be an asshole to let you get behind the wheel in this condition."

I blink a few times, trying to focus on the letters on his fingers as he runs his hand across his forehead, pushing some of the hair back under the hood.

FAITH

"Juss leave me alone," I choke out, fighting the twister in my head. What happens after that, I'm not sure. I black out.

4 JUSTICE

I DON'T KNOW what's worse—dealing with my soon-to-be ex-wife or drunk women. Nikki Deville will drive a person crazy even when she's sober and on her meds, but right now, the woman with golden hair is leading the female-disaster-of-the-year competition.

"Hey...Hazel?" I mutter with both feet rooted to the wet asphalt and my arms wrapped around her tiny frame. This isn't what I had in mind for tonight. "Hazel...Wake up."

No reaction. She's out cold.

"Shit." I scan the parking lot. The brilliant idea of trying to find her car keys inside her purse and leaving her in her vehicle crosses my mind, but the rowdy bunch near the bar entrance is making me uneasy. Better get out of here and fast before someone figures out who I am.

I take a deep breath, readjust my grip, and carry the woman to my Jeep. Thank God she's small, but getting her into the passenger seat is a fucking pain anyway. Her arms and legs don't want to cooperate, and I'm pretty sure the ketchup from her sweater traveled to my sweatshirt. I'm still not sure why I'm doing it when we leave the parking lot.

For Chance. You're making sure this person doesn't end up dead. Because that's what you do. You're becoming a better man, Justice.

When we stop at a light, I glance over at Sleeping Beauty and mentally curse myself. What the hell am I going to do with her if—when—she figures out who I am? She didn't seem to know when I approached her at the bar. I shouldn't have, but I hate seeing drunk douchebags hitting on women. Something about her made me step in. Part of my rehabilitation process maybe.

By the time I get back to the cabin, it's almost one. With the engine still running, I sit in my driveway and think for a few minutes. Leaving her in the cold wouldn't be cool. Taking her inside is an invasion of my privacy. I never bring anyone here, let alone a drunk female I just met at a bar. The only two people who are allowed to be in this place are Aiden and Nikki. No, scratch that. That conniving bitch doesn't have a right to come here anymore, which reminds me that I need to make sure to ask Dom—my manager/personal assistant/nanny—to change the locks and the access codes. I don't want my ex anywhere near my family's property. Especially after she started fucking remodeling without checking with me first. The Malibu house is more than enough of a parting gift.

I shut off the engine, circle around my car, and swing the door open. The jet lag is kicking my ass big time. My body and mind crave sleep, but instead, I'm stuck here with a woman I barely know. My eyes sweep over her, snug in the passenger seat of my Jeep. She looks small and almost peaceful, as if she wasn't the one drinking herself silly back at The Black Lagoon. There's a hint of despair on her face, the same look she wore earlier when I first saw her at the bar. Something tells me leaving her here would go against my better-man beliefs. I pull her out of the car and carry her inside, hoping she wakes up before we get to the guest room, but she's out cold, like after taking a bottle of Ambien.

My feet trip over my unpacked suitcase as I'm crossing the living room and the gravity starts pulling Hazel's body toward the floor, but I quickly regain my balance.

"Fuck." Drawing her closer to my chest, I kick the suitcase in annoyance. The silence that follows next is razor sharp, and I swear I can hear her faint heartbeat shadowing the pounding of mine while we move through the house. For a small person, she sure is giving me a hell of a workout.

I push the door of the guest room open with my shoulder and take a second to digest the view of the mattress, which is covered in plastic. Apparently, parts of the house are still being remodeled. Or *upgraded,* as Nikki called it. Even though I instructed Dom to cut this shit out.

"Upgrade my ass," I mutter, inhaling deeply as frustration and anger begin to choke me. Nikki and Aiden have spent a total of five days here since he was born. She never liked bringing our son here. This place isn't child-friendly, according to her. Too ancient. Too quiet. Too far from civilization. Doesn't matter anymore. Soon the little guy will be old enough to know not to stick his fingers into the outlets.

The bitter asshole in me is tempted to leave Hazel in the guest room, but I know I wouldn't want to wake up in a strange house on a mattress without sheets or blankets. But hey, there's always the couch.

The moment I turn around to take her back to the living room, an inaudible slur leaves her mouth.

"Hazel?" I whisper, in hopes that she'll wake up so I can get her address and send her back to her place.

"I f-feel s-s-s," she coughs into my sweater.

"You're what?"

"Feel siiick." Another slur.

I freeze in the middle of the hallway like a fucking deer in the headlights, trying to figure out the fastest route to the bathroom.

"I think I'm go-mm to th-throw up." She wiggles in my arms.

Hell no! Not happening. "Not yet, Hazel," I say, pushing my bedroom door open with my foot, and dart to the bathroom before things get really messy.

We cut it very close but make it on time. She falls to her knees and empties the contents of her stomach into the toilet while I hold her up.

Just pretend this is a bad dream, Justice.

After she's done puking, we sit there for a few minutes to make sure that's the last of it. She's quiet and reminds me of a rag doll, and the fact that I can't get the address out of her pisses me off because I don't want some drunk woman I know nothing about in my sanctuary.

"Can you get up?"

She shakes her head and her body begins to slant. Sending her home in this condition without an escort probably isn't a good idea anyway.

"Fucking hell," I grumble to myself, lifting her up. My attempt to help her clean up at the sink turns into a wet adventure. Her head doesn't want to stay up, and her arms and legs are like rubber. After fighting over the paper towels while I try to dry her off, we walk to my bedroom and I sit her on the edge of my bed. "If you're going to spend the night, you can't sleep in this," I say, brushing her hair away from her damp cheek.

"Mm-kay." She attempts to grab my left hand. "What doesh umm-m tattoo say?"

"Huh?"

"Whashur t-tattoo say?"

I ignore her question. "I'll get you a t-shirt. You're not sleeping in this." I point at the ketchup stain on her clothes.

Her eyes are hooded when she starts pulling her sweater over her head. It's both funny and painful to watch and since the sight of her bare skin stirs something inside me, I choose not to.

After I tear my gaze away from her poor attempt at undressing, I walk over to my closet, cursing myself yet again for bringing this woman here. Then my jaw drops to the floor when I turn around and see her splayed on my bed in only her bra and her jeans that are pulled halfway down her legs. Apparently, she passed out somewhere around the time she tried to get them off.

Are you fucking kidding me? "Hazel?" I dart back to my bed and give her shoulder a light squeeze. "Come on. Wake up! It'll only take two minutes. I promise. I need you to be up when we do this."

I'm dead if this woman pulls a Nikki on me tomorrow morning and tells the paps that I did something to her.

Hazel doesn't respond, which complicates things greatly. I don't want to touch her while she's unconscious, but I can't leave her here like this, half naked and smelling like a dive bar. I've done all sorts of shit to women, but it's always been consensual. And right now, I'm stepping into a very dangerous territory, especially with Nikki calling me names in public.

My traitorous eyes scan her body, taking in every little detail. Hiding under a thin layer of black lace, she has the most amazing set of breasts I've ever seen on a woman, not too big and not too small—just the right size to fit in the palm of my hand.

We could've had a good time if she wasn't so clumsy and drunk.

Remember, you're working on being a better man, Justice.

"I bet you give one hell of a blowjob, sweetheart," I mumble under my breath, studying her mouth. Not that I really need one right now or even when she wakes up. For that, among other things, I have Rachel. Rachel sucks just as good as she does makeup. Yeah, I know, I can be a sick fuck. I say crude shit like this even if I don't mean it. Old habits die hard.

The egoistic afterthought that most women would kill for a chance to spend a night in my bed leads me to believe that what I'm about to do isn't going to create a problem. Because I really don't want Hazel to wake up in a bra and a pair of jeans that are pulled halfway down—it would look worse than a clean t-shirt. It would smell worse too. Besides, she probably won't remember any of it tomorrow. So with that, my decision is made.

Don't fucking stare at her breasts, Justice.

Why not? They're real. I haven't touched real breasts in over a decade.

Sticking to my quest to be a better man, I listen to my first thought, and focus on Hazel's face as I get her into one of my t-shirts. Then I take off her boots and her jeans, grab the rest of her clothes, and leave the room before my satin sheets start smelling like the dumpster behind The Black Lagoon.

The roar of an engine in my driveway catches me off guard when I'm in the laundry room.

"Justice!" My soon-to-be ex-wife's voice coming from out on the deck startles me.

Cursing myself for not changing the access codes to the property before filing for divorce, I rush out of the laundry room to shut the bedroom door before Nikki discovers Hazel.

The click of her heels and the scent of her fragrance plague every part of the cabin when she lets herself in, and after I meet her in the living room, we square off.

"I know that Mexican bitch of yours leaked it!" She tosses the stack of papers at me.

"May is Puerto Rican," I say matter-of-factly, trying to keep my voice down.

"Who cares?"

My pulse begins to race. For someone who's so hell-bent on making the world a better place for women of all ages, sizes, and skin color, Nikki's quite a hypocrite. The female activists supporting her massive Twitter campaign would throw stones at her for calling my publicist names. "What the hell are you doing here?" Isn't she supposed to be on set of whatever the hell Hollywood blockbuster she's starring in right now?

"What's this?" She gestures toward the papers and peers at me with contempt.

"I thought you knew how to read, babe." Lately, I've been wondering why the fuck I married her. The only logical explanation I can come up with is whatever drugs I was doing at the moment. Must have been acid or some other hard shit, because I hardly remember proposing.

"You seriously think I'm buying this crap? I know you like the back of my hand. There's no way in hell this was leaked to the press before I got served. It wasn't a fucking accident. You and your minions did it." Nikki throws her famous femme fatale look at me.

No, sweetheart, this doesn't work anymore with me.

"Well, I found out from TMZ that I'm an abusive husband. That's not cool. Have I ever laid a finger on you that you didn't ask for?" What's ironic is that the sick part of me wants to wrap my hands around her throat and squeeze really hard so she'll stop screaming, but that's not what I do. "Or was it not the way you liked it?" I have no idea why I'd say that shit to her—sometimes I feel like I'm programmed to turn every question directed at me into an innuendo. But it's hard not to when ninety percent of my lyrics are soft porn. Making sexual comments is part of who I am. I just don't know why I do it with her. She and I haven't slept together in over five months. The last time it happened, it was just another angry fuck. Us trying to work it out. Yet look where we are now.

She narrows her steel blue eyes at me. Aiden has nearly the same eyes. Blue, but not winter ice. His are summer ocean blue. Warm and fuzzy. Sometimes I wonder how a heartless woman like Nikki could be a mother to someone pure like Aiden. "You want war, Justice?" She throws both hands in the air. "You got it."

"I just want a divorce, Nikki," I retort.

"You play dirty, I play dirty too."

"Just sign the goddamn papers and let's get it over with." I grit my teeth, still unsure why the hell she just can't do what we should have done a long time ago. We don't even live together anymore.

"You really expect me to just sign them?" She flips her platinum blonde hair and gives me another if-looks-could-kill stare.

"Yes, I expect you to sign so that we can both move on," I say, hoping Hazel is still asleep.

"I'm going to have my lawyers review these, Justice," Nikki hisses heading for the door.

"Have at it." I doubt her puppets will find anything interesting. I'm already giving her the Malibu villa. Not because I'm a nice guy, but because I don't want to yank Aiden out of his home.

"Oh." She spins on her heels to face me one last time. "And you can forget about joint custody, Justice. I promise you, you'll never see Aiden again. I'll make sure of it."

"How? I'm not the one on antidepressants and in and out of rehab, Nikki. You'll never be able to do it," I say, doing my best to keep my calm, but rage is starting to swallow me.

"Watch me," she huffs, walking off into the cold Tahoe night. The front door is still wide open when she gets into her Porsche.

There's no way she's going to take my son away. Not with her track record and her number of trips to the Betty Ford Clinic. Not happening. My lawyers aren't cheap for a reason.

After shutting the front door, I circle around the cabin for a few minutes, then drop down on the couch and call Dom.

"Do you know what time it is, Justice? Aren't you on vacation?" He doesn't sound happy.

"Nikki was here," I say, ignoring his questions. He'll get over it. That's what I pay him for.

"In Tahoe?" he asks.

"Yeah."

"Shit."

"You don't say." I stare out the French doors at the dark, gloomy surface of the lake as it glistens in the fading moonlight. I can tell by the faint tremor of the water that it's drizzling outside. "She's trying to pull this custody crap."

"Is Aiden with her?"

"No. He's staying with my parents," I explain. "Can you get someone to change the codes and look at the security system first thing tomorrow morning?"

"Yes." Dom clears his throat and pauses for a second. "You're sure you're okay?"

"I'm fine." *Am I really?*

"Alright. Don't stress. Spend some time with your kid. I'll hold the fort for as long as I can."

"Thanks. Later." I end the call and toss the phone on the table. There's nothing Nikki can do about the joint custody. I'm a good father, no matter what she or anyone else thinks. I stopped doing drugs, I hardly drink, I don't publicize my affairs. I also spend as much time with Aiden as I can when I'm off tour. Tomorrow, once I deal with Hazel, I'm going to my parents'.

Sounds like a solid plan.

I sink deeper into the couch, lean my head back, and close my eyes, letting the rhythmic lapping of the lake lull me to sleep. Damn jet lag.

5 HAZEL

Two years. One month. Twenty...seven days.

The slight uncertainty that creeps up on me when I count out another day in my pounding head makes my heart jolt.

I miss you so much, my sweet baby.

The gentle sound of the rain beating against the glass somewhere up above distracts me from my thoughts. Ripping my eyes open, I blink a few times and try to figure out why I'm in the master bedroom of Rayna's cabin. Because the vaulted ceiling with skylight is definitely not something my room has.

On second thought, I don't think Rayna's cabin has vaulted ceilings at all.

I stare at the tiny blurs of raindrops sliding across the glass above me for a few minutes and give my throbbing head some time to piece together yesterday's scattered memories.

Shit.

The last thing I remember from last night is talking to some tattooed stranger about his ex. At a bar.

Uh-oh. This can't be good.

My headache is beyond excruciating. I don't think I've ever gotten *this* drunk before. The sturdy mattress tips slightly under the weight of my sore body as I shift beneath the smooth satin bedding.

The faint scent of spice and lavender hits my nostrils when I breathe in, but then panic grips me when I pull back the sheet and realize I'm wearing something entirely different from what I had on when I left Rayna's cabin. Did I sleep with a stranger? After being faithful to one man for over a decade?

As if I don't hate myself enough already for being a shit of a mother who refuses to visit her son's grave this holiday season.

Besides, the guy wasn't even my type. What was his name again?

Ahh, Daniel... Tall, mysterious, cocky. He didn't seem like a Daniel. And although there was something oddly familiar about him, I knew I'd never met him before.

Drawing in another shaky breath, I force myself to sit up and swing my legs over the edge of the bed. My eyes try to make sense of the enormous room that's furnished with an exquisite rustic walnut hardwood dresser, a matching armoire, and two nightstands. The wall-to-wall window right across from me overlooks the lake, just like the one in Rayna's cabin, but the view is a bit different, more intimate. There are no signs of other houses or boats anywhere on the horizon. It's just the gray rain-rippled surface, stretching far away into nothing.

After a few minutes of sorting through the black holes in my memory, I slide off the monstrous field of the bed to the soft fluff of the carpet and slowly make my way to the only door I see, hoping it leads to the bathroom. Meanwhile my eyes are searching for my clothes, which are apparently not here.

The sudden urge to feel some cold water on my face and get rid of my horrible breath reminds me again of how stupid it was to let myself be brought here instead of Rayna's cabin. The worst part is that I don't even remember how it happened.

Once at the door, I stare down at my floating feet. My socks are still on. Now that I think about it...my bra and my panties are still on too. Maybe I didn't have sex with the stranger after all. I sure hope not— my divorce isn't even finalized yet.

It's not cheating if you and your husband are no longer together, Hazel.

Living under the same roof doesn't necessarily mean you're a couple. You stopped being one after River died.

After I push the door open, it's clear my calculations are way off. Instead of the bathroom, I find myself staring at a wall with a framed silver record hanging on it. I narrow my eyes in an attempt to read the signature, but all my throbbing brain can grasp are the tiny crosses scattered under it.

Oh my God, I hope he's not a priest.

Then I hear some muffled voices coming from somewhere inside the house, and as I strain to listen, they grow louder.

Voice number one, which sounds very familiar, drifts to me from the opposite end of the hallway. "...she's lying! I never put a finger on her. For all you know, she slammed her head into the tree outside my house to make it look like I did it! She's an actress, for God's sake!"

These are the first words I can actually understand, and I don't like what I'm hearing. In a panic, I bring my hand to my face and feel around, hoping I'm not the woman who accidentally assaulted the tree.

"That's why we're here, Mr. Cross. To get your side of the story," voice number two says. It's calm and reserved with a hint of ice. *And that name—is that what's with all the crosses?*

"My side of the story is that I did *not* touch Nikki. She came in here last night, yelled at me like a demented bitch, and then left."

Why don't I remember any of this?

My mind remains in a half-drunken zombie daze as I wander into the room and see three men standing in the middle of it, one with his back to me and the other two standing opposite him. Despite all the clouds covering the sky and the rain pounding hard against the house, the daylight blinds me. There are too many windows. Too much water. Too much everything. Thank goodness my consciousness is still in the dark, the comfort of which feels like home.

The two men facing my direction look official. One, who looks to be in his fifties, is bulkier and has an irritated expression on his tanned, wrinkled face. The other is probably in his late twenties or early thirties, is fit, and has both hands buried in the pockets of his dress pants, giving me a perfect view of his badge.

Police?

My breath catches in my throat. Then as the two pairs of eyes, which definitely belong to law enforcement, slowly divert to me, I, on the other hand, can't stop staring at the back of the man they're questioning. Or, to be more precise, the massive tattoo in the shape of a cross that's inked into his skin. All the little pieces of the déjà vu puzzle start coming down on me harder than the rain raging outside.

I remember where I've seen him before.

I was six months pregnant when Owen took me to see the new Nikki Deville movie. She was a fresh Hollywood flame—scandalous, beautiful, and undeniably talented. We walked out of the theater with dropped jaws, raving about her acting skills all the way home to our one-bedroom apartment. The next day, I googled the rest of the cast, including the cute guy with the cross on his back who was in only one scene. He was Nikki's boyfriend at the time and they married shortly after. Apparently, TMZ hired a helicopter to fly over their Malibu mansion to get the shots. Tabloids were buzzing about it nonstop for weeks. Funny thing, Owen and I had seen his band live a year before his movie cameo.

Yesterday, I didn't recognize him without the makeup.

I'm not sure whether it's due to the shock factor or the amount of alcohol I consumed last night, but I can't remember his name, even though I just heard it a minute ago.

The younger policeman comes to the rescue. "Mr. Cross, we'll need you to come down to the station with us." He clears his throat and his gaze shifts to me, as does his partner's.

"Excuse me—" I force out, blinking rapidly while still staring at the tattoo. The cross, the vines, and the other ornaments twirling up the man's back and around his sculpted arms fascinate me. Owen has a couple of tiny tattoos that he got when he was still in high school. They were a huge negative in the eyes of my father. He despised my future husband with a passion. I think he would have despised him even more if I had gotten a permanent stamp on my body too, but I just never found the time. Now that I'm three feet away from this intricate web rooted into the skin of an international rockstar, I regret not having the time for body art, because it's truly beautiful.

Ask for your clothes and leave.

Nikki's husband glances at me over his shoulder, and his eyes seem to eat me alive. "I'm not going anywhere." He turns back to his guests. "I didn't touch Nikki. She stormed in here last night, scared the shit out of me and my lady friend. After she left, we resumed our adult activities, gentlemen… If you know what I mean."

"See, here's the thing, Mr. Cross," the older officer says. "Your wife didn't mention your…" His eyes jump to me. "Lady friend."

I want to scream, run, and puke all at once. What is even going on?

"I'm not really into sharing my current dates with my ex-wife. She was in the bedroom when Nikki showed up."

"It would save us a whole lot of paperwork, Mr. Cross, if you were to cooperate," the younger policeman explains.

"Okay," Nikki's husband says. "I'll get in touch with my lawyers and we'll arrange something. How does tomorrow work for you, gentlemen? Let me walk you out. My friend and I would like some privacy. I'm due for my morning blowjob and it's almost noon."

He did not just say that.

My heart is riding the wildest roller coaster ever, exploring every part of my body from head to toe.

"Have a good day, gentlemen." The door slams shut.

"Blowjob is not happening," I choke out, fighting the horrible dryness in my throat.

"Relax, babe." Nikki's husband lets out a loud sigh of relief and makes his way across the room and into the kitchen. "Nothing's happening unless you ask for it."

"What?" I follow him.

"Coffee?" He smirks, yanking the carafe out of the massive state-of-the-art stainless-steel coffeemaker. Actually, everything in this kitchen is state-of-the-art. Done mostly in earthy tones, with lots of wood, artwork, and exquisite décor. Just like its owner.

The words start spilling out of me like puke. "I don't want coffee… or a blowjob…or anything else you have to offer. I need my clothes back and I need to go."

"I'm not offering a blowjob." He cocks his brow. "Unless you have a dick, which you don't... Even if you did, I wouldn't give you any. I don't swing that way."

"Just stop!" I squeeze my eyes shut and shake my head. The mouth this man has.

"I take it you're not a morning person?" His eyes catch my gaze as he leans against the marble countertop. The carafe is still in his left hand, midair, which creates a perfect curve of his arm, making it impossible to ignore the muscles contracting under his partially inked skin. The word *faith* on his fingers evokes a strange feeling of déjà vu in me.

The fact that he's wearing nothing but a pair of faded jeans that sit invitingly low on his hips makes matters even worse.

"Can I get my clothes back, please?" I sniff, ignoring his remark. This stupid shirt is barely covering my ass.

"I doubt you'd want to wear dried-up ketchup and beer."

"I'm serious. Can we please stop playing games?" I fold my arms across my chest, slowly shrinking under his drilling gray gaze.

"Your stuff is in the laundry room. Sorry. My cleaning person hasn't been here yet." He shrugs, his voice warmer this time.

"Why is my stuff in the laundry room?" I ask, rubbing my toes against the kitchen floor tiles.

"You don't remember the beer and ketchup incident back at the bar?"

"No."

"What about throwing up in my bathroom?"

"Say what?"

"That's what I thought." He shifts his body, pulls out two mugs from one of the cabinets and fills them up with fresh coffee.

Embarrassed doesn't even come close to how I feel right now. "Tell me you didn't hold my hair. Because you didn't have to…you know," I croak, watching him. Famous people doing regular things is fascinating.

He lets out a soft laugh. "Cream? Sugar?"

"Both." My brain is trying to put together a coherent sentence while my possible one-night stand is making me coffee. "Ummm…can I ask you something?"

"The answer is no." He closes the distance between us in two wide strides, his height towering over me as he hands me the mug.

"You didn't even hear the question," I fume, taking the coffee.

"Let me guess. You were going to ask me if we fucked."

"Fucked isn't the word I was going to use." I'm turning all shades of red. I really wish he wouldn't stand so close. "But yes, I wanted to know if things got physical."

"Don't worry. You passed out when we were in the parking lot before I could get you a cab. I'm an asshole, but I'm not going to leave a drunk woman outside a bar if she has no one to come and get her."

"Okay...thanks, I guess." I take a small sip to see how the coffee tastes. A little sweet yet rich and bitter. Just the way I like it.

"My turn." He runs his hand through his disheveled hair and pushes some loose strands off his face. I'm still trying to get used to the idea of seeing him without makeup.

"Sure." I let the hot liquid drip down my aching throat.

"How much do you want for helping me out? Name your price."

"Helping you out with what?"

"Backing up my story."

"What story?" My head's starting to hurt twice as much as it did when I woke up.

"I need you to tell the police that you and I were together last night when my psychotic ex stormed in here making threats."

"I don't remember anything," I tell him.

"They don't know that and neither does Nikki. All you have to do is tell the police we hooked up at the bar, came back here, then my ex showed up. You never saw her. She never saw you. You were in the bedroom and heard her threats. When she left, we fucked. It's that easy."

I can't stop cringing while he reveals his plan to me. My hands, wrapped around the hot mug, are shaking. As if I don't have enough shit to deal with, I've somehow gotten caught up in this petty, very high-profile couple fight or whatever they're having at the moment. I wouldn't be surprised if it's just a publicity stunt. If my memory serves me right, they were a rocky item from the start. I haven't been following much of anything since River died, but Owen still has some of the band's CDs.

"Can you just slow down a little?" I mumble under my breath. "I don't remember anything. We did not *fuck,* as you just said. Besides, I really have a lot going on of my own."

"Look. It's just a fucking favor, okay? No big deal. You were here. I'll fill in the blanks." He slightly raises his voice, desperation and anger spiking. His eyes lock on mine. "I could have left you out there in the parking lot alone and passed out last night...and you might have gotten robbed, raped, or killed. You can't do one thing for me in return? I'll pay you."

"I'm sorry. As I said, I already have a lot going on," I repeat mechanically.

"Fine." He grabs my hand and silently pulls me through the kitchen, into the hallway. My coffee is spilling from the mug as I get dragged into the laundry room, and I'm too dazed to put up a fight.

"Your clothes," he growls, releasing his hold.

The door of the laundry room is still wide open when he walks out.

What an ass! Who does he think he is, talking to me as if I'm one of his groupies?

I find my clothes on top of the dryer, and my boots are sitting on the floor. I put the mug down on the washing machine and pick up my sweater, examining the red ketchup stains from last night's bar debacle. I don't remember getting beer on my clothes at all, but it definitely smells like it.

My mind is cooking up a list of shaming expressions I could throw back at him on the way out as I put on my stained clothes. The distant sound of a phone's ringtone mixed with his voice echoing through the hallway disappears behind one of the doors after a loud slam.

He is pissed at me because I don't want to lie? What kind of logic is that? And I never asked for any of his damn help. He could have just left me there last night and not bothered.

Once fully dressed, I step out of the laundry room and stare at the vinyls decorating the walls. It's probably best to leave quietly while he's on the phone. Less drama.

I'm determined to walk out of this house without a single word and forget this morning ever happened when I remember my purse. I'm positive I had it with me last night at the bar.

The man's voice, now frantic, drifts from behind the closed door of the room across from the bedroom.

"...the cameras were fucking off! Why?" Pause. "Cheating on your wife and beating her bloody are two different things, Dom. She fucked me over dozens of times. It's been all over the internet since we separated... It won't make any difference in court if I tell them I was with another woman—she's been cheating on me for years. But she can't go around and tell everyone, including fucking TMZ, that I hit her when I never did. You know she's doing it to keep me away from Aiden...and I can't let that happen..."

He is too busy talking to whomever he's paying to listen to his complaints. He won't notice if I go get my purse. I tiptoe across the hallway and slip into the bedroom to look for it, but after a few minutes of frantic searching, I give up.

Crap. The moment I step back into the hallway, the door across from me flies open and a pair of angry gray eyes drill into me.

"What the fuck are you doing?" He moves closer, his phone still clutched in one hand. I want to say something but my mouth won't open. A light spasm grips my chest at the sight of the baby blue wallpaper with teddy bears decorating the walls of the room he was in. There's a pile of toys, a tiny desk, and silver star-studded letters glued to the wall above the bed that spell out *Aiden.*

He has a little boy.

I don't know why I didn't put it together earlier during his phone tirade. I haven't been keeping up with all things famous for quite some time. I had no idea they had a child. River's last year was hard. We were in and out of the hospital. There was no time for the movies or celebrity news. There was just River...slowly fading, and I wanted to spend every second of every remaining day with him.

"How old is your son?" I ask, still standing in the middle of the hallway, in my beer-smelling boots and ketchup-stained sweater. My heart is beating so fast that I'm scared it's going to run away.

"Please just leave." He points in the direction of the living room, face gloomy. "I'm in deep fucking shit right now and if you aren't going to help me, then you need to leave."

"Did you ever do what she's claiming you did last night?" I ask meekly.

He folds his arms on his chest and this is when I see it, his son's name tattooed on his left pec.

"Can I think about it?"

He tilts his head in question.

"About your offer," I explain, my voice barely above a whisper. I'm still not completely sure what to believe—there's not a single scratch on his hands, yet a man beating the shit out of someone would have a couple of marks, right? God, I'm so confused.

"How much time do you need to think about it, babe?" he asks, his eyes boring into mine as if he's ready to swallow me whole.

I take it back. I'm not confused. I'm terrified of everything that I've felt today since the moment I woke up in his bed. Too much, too fast, too complicated. And somewhere among all this mess, there's a little boy, and his mom and dad are about to rip each other's throats out.

"I just really need to take a shower and change," I whimper, trying to keep my calm but on the inside, I'm screaming. "I don't even remember your name. But I know it's not Daniel."

A smirk tilts the side of his mouth. "Justice."

"What?"

"That's my name."

"Oh right." I feel stupid for being so uneducated when it comes to celebrities and tabloids.

"Is that provocative enough for you?"

"Yeah." I avert my gaze from his muscular chest. "Have you seen my purse by any chance?"

"It's in my car. Give me a second. I'll drive you back to yours."

"You don't have to. I can take a cab or an Uber."

"I insist."

"You really don't have to, Justice."

"Just shut up and give me two minutes to put some clothes on." He breezes past me into the bedroom.

Yes, good idea. Please put some clothes on, because your abs are distracting me.

6   JUSTICE

AW-fuc-K-ing-WARD isn't even the worst word I'd use to describe this morning. The woman in the ketchup-stained sweater who's occupying the passenger seat of my Jeep is both pissing me off and giving me hope regarding fighting Nikki over these ridiculous charges. I knew my ex was a selfish bitch, but I never thought she'd pull this abusive husband crap on me just to make sure I don't get to freely see my son whenever I want. And to think I was going to be kind and not bring her rehab trips into the picture unless really necessary.

But now, what I hoped would be a simple divorce with minimum press drama is turning into a tabloid nightmare. I had no idea Nikki was this much of a schemer. The photos of her face all bruised and bloody that are flooding social media make me sick.

Hazel's quiet. The tired look in her amber eyes causes me to rethink my strategy. Maybe I was a bit too pushy when I demanded she cover my ass.

"How long have you and Nikki Deville been married?" she asks after a few minutes of uncomfortable silence.

"Too long." I try to keep my wandering eyes on the road. "Seven years."

"That's a long time in celebrity years. It's like the equivalent of four-teen years of my marriage."

It's my turn to be surprised. I somehow missed a wedding band on her finger last night when I was undressing her. My eyes want to glance at her hands again. Honestly, I don't pay attention to shit like that. Details. Half the women I've fucked have been married. Only, Hazel doesn't seem like the marrying type. Too young, for starters. She doesn't look a day over twenty-five. And who the hell marries at twenty-five? Or maybe I'm losing my touch at reading people.

You're getting old, Justice.

Thirty-four isn't old, I counter myself.

"It was a disaster. I don't think anyone would want to stay married to Nikki Deville that long," I scoff, giving my full attention to the road again. The light November drizzle starts turning into a wall of raging rain again.

"Is she that bad?"

"You follow the news at all?"

"Ummm..." Her voice trembles. In my peripheral, I see the rigid movements of her hands as she clutches them around the strap of her bag. "I've been away from the scene for a while."

"Away? Like on vacation or something?"

"No...not that. We just had a lot going on."

"I see. Well, Nikki's been in and out of rehab more times than I've been out of the country, which is why I have to have joint custody. I don't want to wait for my fucking turn to spend time with my son. I mean, she's an okay mom and she loves Aiden, but she loves her career more. And if she goes into one of her episodes again where she needs to fucking do rounds of coke for three weeks because her next role is a junkie hooker, I want to be able to just take my son away from that house without a court order."

"She did that?" Hazel gasps, her head snapping in my direction.

"She's into the *method acting* shit. I'm an artist. I get it, but when you're a parent, it's different. It's not fucking okay anymore when you have a three-year-old." I can almost feel the smile that breaks on her lips. "You and your husband have kids?"

She shifts in her seat. "My husband and I are getting a divorce."

"Shit." Now that explains why no wedding band. "You and I...we're in the same boat, babe."

"I suppose so."

There's reluctance in her voice. She isn't ready to talk about her life. Fine. I'm not going to push her. I honestly don't care. I just want her to agree to help me.

"Why the makeup?" she asks after another long pause.

"What do you mean?"

"Why do you wear the makeup when you're on stage?" Her voice is laced with genuine curiosity.

"I take it you're not in my fan club?"

"Does that hurt your ego?" She lets out a soft laugh. "Don't answer a question with a question."

I tighten my grip around the steering wheel. "It's not just a band, it's more of a concept. An ongoing project. Like a comic book or a series with every album being a new edition. Think about the band members as the characters. Each one of us has a story to tell."

I pause for a second. My mind jumps back in time to the last year of high school when Chance and I came up with the idea. We didn't care that people would call us KISS or Marilyn Manson or Avenged Seven-fold knockoffs. We wanted to be bold and revolutionary and we thought we were being original. Elijah was furious. He called us a bunch of posers and a disgrace to the rock music community. When you have a legend for an uncle who was inducted into the Rock & Roll Hall of Fame during the first year of eligibility, you can't really argue with his opinion. You suck it up, change your last name, and pray to God you have what it takes to make it on your own just to prove the asshole wrong.

"So like superheroes or something?" Hazel inquires.

"Not exactly. We're not sporting capes or anything."

"Why all the religious references?"

"Because I'd like to believe we're going somewhere after this," I reply, eyeing the black letters inked on my fingers. I needed to have faith in my idea when I was starting out. I wanted to detach myself from the name Hale and do my own thing, without people saying behind my back that I was getting a free pass because of my uncle's connections.

She points at my hand. "Is that why you have this tattoo?"

"Yes."

"And the cross on your back? You don't strike me as a very religious guy. Do you even go to church?"

"Sure I do. I'm a missionary who spreads love for all things sexy and twisted across the planet." My side vision catches Hazel fidgeting in her seat. Her cheeks are inferno red. "You asked." I laugh.

The silence that falls between us goes on for a while. The rain hitting the windshield of my Jeep is ruthless, and the road ahead is one huge, messy puddle. I have to turn on the high beams to be able to see where we're headed.

"My husband..." she stutters. "My ex...took me to see your show once. I think it was 2010—I'm not sure. We used to go to a lot of concerts."

"Did you have fun?"

"It was really weird. I felt like we'd been summoned to a church to join a religious cult at first."

"That's the idea, babe."

"Do women really fall for all that?"

"Yeah, they kinda do. Men too."

"I thought I'd slept with a priest when I woke up." She snorts.

"So you're open to kinky stuff?"

"Shut up. It was freaking creepy."

"It's only creepy at first. Most women embrace the concept pretty quickly. I bet you'd like it if you gave it a try." I can't resist goading her.

"Really? Is everything with you always about sex?"

"I'm just trying to keep the conversation going."

"You don't need to throw in remarks like that every other sentence to impress me."

I can feel her gaze on my cheek and part of me wants to look at her, dive right into those amber eyes, but I'm not going to risk driving us into a tree. Roads here are shit during the rain.

"Does it make you uncomfortable?" I hit the brake once we pull up to the empty intersection. As soon as my Jeep comes to a stop, I turn to face her.

"I'm not your groupie, so you don't have to speak to me as if I am." She stares at me like a teacher when one of her students has done something horrible in front of the class. "And I didn't appreciate you yelling at me earlier and demanding things as if you're entitled to getting what you want just because you're famous."

"What if I say I'm sorry?" Not exactly a phrase I like to throw out there, but maybe it's one of those rare cases where it needs to be done.

She takes a few moments to evaluate my truce offering. "Okay. Apology accepted."

Well, that was easy. Now I just need to seal the deal.

"Look, I really mean it. I'm sorry I went off on you. It's just..." The words get stuck in my throat. What the fuck am I even saying? "I can't have my psycho ex raising my son all by herself. If you could help me out by telling the police that you were with me and nothing happened between me and her and I didn't hit her, I'd be forever fucking grateful."

There, I said it. Or more like begged.

We stare at each other for a few moments until the light changes to green.

"I'm still married. Remember?" she says in a low voice.

"You're getting a divorce." I hit the gas.

"It's not going to affect me in just one way. It's going to affect my life in many ways. And I have a lot going on right now."

"You already said, and I'm willing to compensate you. Name your price. The faster we get it over with, the sooner you can return to doing whatever the fuck it is you're doing here," I mutter, trying to hide my frustration. Who turns down easy money?

"I wish you had just fucking left me in that parking lot." She sighs.

Despair and irritation in her voice make my heart shrink in my chest. Why can't she just stop being so fucking difficult? What does she have going on that money can't fucking solve?

All this is on the tip of my tongue, but instead, I say what a person who's trying to be a better man would. "Look, Hazel." This is the first time since she woke up that I'm actually calling her by her name. I like the way it rolls off my tongue, like the lyrics of one of my old songs. "I get it. I really do. Divorce is fucking depressing. But I can help you deal with some of the shit. If you've got any bills to pay or you need help moving to a new place or whatever, I can take care of it. It's not like I'm asking you to fucking kill somebody."

"You're asking me to lie," she whispers, looking away.

"My lawyer will make sure there's as little press as possible and your name stays out of it. I just can't control what my wife says or posts on her social media. Today she publicly called me a deranged, abusive psycho. I don't want my son to believe that's who I am because I'm not."

"I need to take a shower and brush my teeth. Can we talk about it later? Maybe on the phone when I can actually think straight?"

Last resort. "Will it make it easier if I fuck you or something? You seem tense."

"Please don't." Her hand flies into the air as a warning sign.

"Had to ask, babe. Sometimes it works when I really want something."

"I'll pretend I didn't hear the last question."

"Alright. Here we are," I mutter, pulling into the parking lot full of puddles and trash. Looks like last night was a full-on party. "Which one is your car?"

"The Prius."

Somehow, I knew that.

"What's your number?" I fish for my phone in the console once we park. She looks at me all confused from under a layer of long lashes. "So I can call you later and we can discuss it," I explain. If she hadn't been so drunk and difficult yesterday, I definitely would have fucked her. Besides, her tits are real.

"Right," she says breathlessly, and as she recites her digits, I punch them into my new contact window, ignoring the long string of notifications from Dom, May, Zander, and the rest of my crew. I fucking hate Nikki for stirring this shit up. I don't even want to know what people are saying about all this anymore.

"I'll call you later?" I yell as she pushes the door of my Jeep open and jumps into the pouring rain.

"Sure. Thanks for the ride. Drive safe," she replies before disappearing into her light blue Prius.

I fall back against the seat, close my eyes, and try to breathe. My heart is bouncing in my chest like a ping-pong ball. What if she gave me a number that doesn't exist? What if she doesn't agree to help me? What if Nikki ends up taking my son away for good? So many fucking possibilities.

The rain is still heavy, the wipers swaying back and forth, fiercely splashing water around. I almost find it calming watching those motherfuckers working like crazy. The phone, still on my lap, goes off when the Prius starts backing up.

"Did you see the damage?" May asks as soon as I take the call.

"I saw her Facebook." I refer to my wife's new portfolio her PR reps posted on her official page at four in the morning. Along with the photos. I wonder if she hired someone to smack her around or did it herself. Or her makeup artist is better than mine.

"Why are we still waiting, Justice?" my publicist demands.

"I didn't hit her."

"I know that, but I need to give something to the press. Did you read the press release I sent you for approval?"

I was busy dealing with the police and a drunk woman I picked up at the bar last night. "Did you post Jake's video?"

"Are you serious, Justice? No one cares about your nephew's band right now."

"Yes, I read the press release." Total lie. More like skimmed. "The cops were at the cabin a little while ago asking questions. Fucking cops! In my home. I need to get everything straight before I can give you a better explanation. Just post what you have."

My eyes are glued to the rearview mirror as the tiny light blue car leaves the lot. If she lied about the number, I'm screwed.

"Your fans are fucking crucifying you right now." May keeps assaulting my ear. "It's been almost eight hours and you don't have anything else to say? The reporters are already camping outside your Malibu residence!"

The way my wife is butchering my reputation, I'll soon have the paparazzi here—the only place no one knows about. At least not before last night.

"Justice, are you there?"

I have a love-hate relationship with my publicist. Not that kind of love. May Santos is probably the only woman in this business I never fucked and never will. She can be brutally honest to the point where I want to fire her ass and get someone less jumpy, but I've been saying this for the past ten years and the lady is still around.

"You hear me, Justice?" she cries out as I watch the Prius vanish into the rain.

This is not stalking...

"I'll call you later," I snap, dropping the phone onto my lap, and hit reverse.

Whatever the fuck happened to being a better man, Justice? Are you going to follow this chick to her house to try and get the answer you want? You know you can't make people do anything they don't want to.

Suddenly, I feel like a trapped animal. The world starts to slowly close in on me as my Jeep pushes through the wall of rain, my eyes never leaving the Prius melding with the light traffic ahead. I've never hated anyone in my entire life as much as I hate Nikki right now. It was supposed to be an easy divorce, but she wants to make it a fucking spectacle.

I grab my phone and hit the first number on speed dial, then switch to speaker before some stickler cop who has nothing better to do in this weather pulls me over for talking on the phone while driving. Normally, I'd give zero fucks about getting a ticket. I've got a long string of those on my record. All paid, but still. But I'm too fucking obsessed with the golden-haired woman in the Prius. If I don't get her to help me, I'm out of options.

"Mom?" My voice doesn't sound as calm as I want it to.

"Justice," Gladys interrupts. "Your father and I have been calling you all morning. Why aren't you picking up?"

"Let me talk to Aiden."

I'm glad I took him to Crystal Bay. At least he won't be seeing his mother's face and hearing her stupid stories about me being the one to hurt her.

"Nikki picked him up hours ago."

"What?" I can feel my heart breaking all my ribs one by one. "Why did you let her take him?" I dig my fingers into the steering wheel so fucking hard that it hurts.

"I'm sorry, honey. Your dad wasn't home. And she was screaming and throwing things, threatening to bring her lawyers."

"Fuck!" I don't know what else to say.

"Don't talk to your mother like that."

"Well, what do you want me to say? Why didn't you call the police? It's kidnapping."

"You're still married to her, Justice. Remember?"

"Just so we're clear. The paint job on her face isn't mine."

"Don't you think I know that? I raised you."

At least someone believes me. "Mom, I gotta go. I need to call my lawyer."

"Okay, please let him handle everything and don't do anything rash, honey."

I end the call and speed dial my lawyer's number. If Nikki wants to play hardball, I can play it too. Our conversation is brief. It's mostly me screaming, but I'm pretty sure the five-hundred-dollar-an-hour rate covers a client's meltdown.

My mind is still racing when the Prius swerves into the driveway of a small cabin by the lake. I pull up to the curb a little farther ahead, right next to the mailbox of the neighboring property, and wait for a while. Going after her would be a dick move. She doesn't seem to do well under pressure.

Besides, I've got bigger problems now. My vacation was just cut short by my ex. After making a U-turn, I pin the location on Google maps in my phone.

The drive back to my place is stressful. I'll call Hazel in a few hours and see if we can come to a mutual agreement. There's no way she's going to refuse money.

By the time I'm done with all my phone calls, it's late afternoon. #JusticeCross and #NikkiDeville are trending across social media. Cringing, I skim through Facebook and Twitter, both packed with the photos of my wife's bruised face. Somewhere deep inside me there's still a bit of compassion left; part of me hates seeing her all banged up. She's the mother of my child. We had some good times, and once upon a time, she made me happy. You don't need to be an expert to see that those bruises are from some hard blows and not just a makeup parade, but mostly I'm pissed because of how well she can manipulate the public, including my own fan base.

All I wanted was a few weeks off before going back to L.A. to work on the new material. Now it's turning into a holiday nightmare, the biggest charade of the year. And I despise it with all my heart because Aiden is going to be collateral damage.

Around six, I decide to make the phone call. After a few rings, it goes to voicemail. I hang up. Ten minutes later, I dial again. Nothing. By six forty-five, my patience runs out. I grab my car keys and my jacket and head out.

7 HAZEL

I'M HALFWAY through the recently posted TMZ article about a new development in the Nikki Deville and Justice Cross scandal when I hear the doorbell ring. Must be my Chinese takeout. Pretty fast for nasty weather like tonight.

My mind is still suffering from mild post-traumatic stress after waking up in the bed of a man who allegedly kicked the shit out of his wife while I was passed out in the next room. Lying to the police for money seems like the worst idea ever. Even if it's going to help a father to be close to his child. My family and I will be dragged through the mud by the tabloids if things don't end up being as contained as promised. And I'm still technically married to Owen, so the whole planet will think I'm a cheater. Doing this in the middle of my divorce is stupid.

I set my iPad aside, grab the last twenty from my purse, and rush to the door to get my food. My mouth falls open when, instead of the delivery person Justice's face invades my line of vision. He's on my porch, well-dressed, and from the look in his eyes and the way his lips are clamped tightly together, he doesn't appear to be in the best of moods.

"What the hell are you doing here?" I recover immediately. Mixed emotions are stirring inside me, but at least I'm wearing a pair of sweatpants and a shirt this time. "Did you follow me here?"

"You didn't answer your phone." He shrugs, brushing past me. The obvious disregard for my feelings baffles the hell out of me. He's tall, strong, and apparently doesn't take no for an answer. The fact that he's forcing himself inside makes me wonder if Rayna and Clay have a gun stashed somewhere.

"Because I just woke up," I explain, watching him pace around the room, his soggy boots leaving small, dirty puddles on the floor. My mind is struggling with the idea of rockstar Justice Cross stalking me to Rayna's cabin. "You've got some nerve showing up here."

"How much do you want?" he asks, pushing the wet strands off his face, a hint of panic in his voice.

"It's not about money." I shut the front door before we both catch pneumonia. It's obvious he's not going to leave until he's ready.

"Then what is it?"

I bite my bottom lip and look down at my slippers. It's everything and nothing all at once, but it's mostly my desire to be left alone and grieve River in silence.

"I came here because I need some time to sort through some stuff in my life," I breathe out, wrapping my arms around my waist as my eyes search his. "Getting involved in a...high-profile mess like the one you're in right now might not be something I can handle, Justice. That's the honest truth."

"I already talked to my lawyer and my publicist. If you agree to help me, it will all die down in a few days. Then you can go back to being depressed. I'll make it as painless for you as possible, Hazel." His voice is calm and reassuring. I wonder if he's as good of an actor as his wife or maybe he's simply desperate and doesn't want to lose his son.

"Okay." I nod slowly. "As long as you can keep it out of the press, I have one condition."

What the hell am I doing?

"Fine." He takes a step in my direction. "Lay it all out, babe." He smirks.

"If we do this, I need you to stop making sexual comments. It's impolite and disrespectful. And I don't like it," I say firmly. "I don't need the money."

"Deal." The corners of his lips curl up. He looks almost innocent with this endearing smile on his face. A lot like his three-year-old son, whose photos I googled earlier.

Sadly, deep inside, I know Justice just worked me like one of his fangirls and I let myself fall for it.

"So let's talk details." I stroll into the kitchen and point at a chair at the table. My empty stomach flips as I watch him sit down, his arms crossed over his broad chest. The lead singer of The Deviant is in my kitchen—okay, in Rayna's kitchen, but that's only a technicality.

"I think we should stick to the bar meeting and not twist anything there," he says, waiting for me to sit down. His gray eyes lock on mine while I attempt to study his body language.

"I agree." I fiddle with the hem of my shirt. Suddenly, I'm way too aware of my outfit, an old faded top, black sweatpants, and ridiculously huge purple slippers. It shouldn't bother me, but it does, especially since he's oozing masculinity with his expensive leather jacket, designer jeans, and lavish cologne. Thankfully, his shirt is buttoned up —I don't think I could handle much more.

Naked. That's how I feel under his piercing gaze.

"Cool. I'm Justice, by the way." A tiny raindrop rolls down his cheek as he flashes me a half smile.

"I'm Hazel," I respond, taking my seat across from him. "I'm not sure at what point I blacked out."

"When I was about to get you a cab."

"In the bar?"

"In the parking lot."

"Are we including the puking incident too?"

"I think we should skip that."

"Okay. Just so you know, Justice." I take a second and plug in his name. I like saying it, for some reason. Maybe because every time I do, something inside me clicks. "This isn't something I do on a weekly basis. I mean going to a bar, getting wasted, and passing out in front of a stranger. It's just... How shall I put it?" I sigh loudly while he watches me. "I'm not having a good year."

Pathetic explanation, but I can't bring myself to talk about River. Those are my private memories and I plan on keeping it that way.

"It's all good, babe." He shrugs. "We'll keep it simple. You were too hammered to remember the details, but let's just say my ex was loud enough for you to hear her cursing up a storm. For the record, she was at the cabin for about five minutes threatening to take my son away and then left. I did *not* hit her."

"I believe you." My stomach flutters under his hypnotizing gaze. No wonder he's famous. The ability to mesmerize a person with one stare isn't something most mortals can do. This man is gifted.

"Thanks." He half smiles at me again, running his left hand through his wet hair to slick it back.

"Do we have to say we had sex?" I ask, averting my gaze. I'm still legally married to Owen. Technically, that'd be cheating and even though we haven't been close in over two years, letting him go has been hard. He was my first everything.

"Well, if we say we slept in one bed and nothing happened, it'll definitely blow my cover." Justice snorts.

Well, shit. He just virtually robbed me of my celibacy. I'm pretty sure I'm redder than a beet. How is it possible for a man to make you feel as if you've had sex with him by simply talking about it?

It's has to be hormones, Hazel. You and Owen haven't been close since before River died. It's completely normal.

"Okay. Can we not get too detailed then?" I croak. My mind is thinking otherwise though, imagining things it shouldn't. "I was drunk, so let's leave it at that."

"Sure." He nods, leaning forward, his eyes searching mine. "I'd offer to practice, but I'm respecting your condition, so I'm just going with the flow here."

He can't stop with the innuendos, can he?

"Yes, please do...or the deal is off." I stare right back at him, and my heart is thrashing like a little bird. I'm curious, flattered, and scared all at once.

"Something on your mind, babe?" He slides his chair closer and lays his hands on the table.

I clear my throat. "Hypothetically speaking...Was I even good?"

A hint of a smile breaks on his lips. "*Hypothetically*, yeah. I loved your tits."

"How do you know what my tits are like?" I cry out, feeling even more violated than I felt this morning.

"You have my word that I didn't take off your clothes." He raises his left hand defensively. "You started it and I had to finish because where you left off... Let's say it didn't look very good. But I swear I didn't touch you inappropriately."

I sigh with relief. "Okay." *Does this mean my 32 Cs are better than Nikki's?* God, am I still drunk?

By the time we're done going over the details of our alleged night together, it's almost nine. My stomach is miserable from hunger and I desperately want a drink. The sound of the doorbell has never made me happier.

"Food delivery," I explain when I catch the expression of worry on my guest's face. Being seen here with me is probably not part of his plan.

After paying for my goodies, I return to the kitchen and set the bag on the table. "I'm sorry. I wasn't expecting anyone." The polite host in me takes the initiative. "Do you want some? I'm sure there's enough for two."

"Smells dangerous." He shakes his head, watching me while I retrieve the containers from the wet plastic bag.

"It's Chinese. It's meant to smell dangerous."

He cringes.

"What?" I give him the side-eye. "It's the only place in town that delivers after six."

"You're not much of a cook, huh?" he asks matter-of-factly.

"When I'm in the mood." The truth is, I haven't been in the mood to do anything around the house for a while. I used to be a model wife. I cooked, cleaned, ironed Owen's shirts, even helped him with our taxes. All while taking care of a child with cancer. But right now, cooking doesn't feel like something I'd want to resume, mainly because eating all by myself in silence doesn't make the food taste any better.

His phone goes off when I'm about to inspect my chicken and veggie plate.

"Sorry. I have to take this," Justice mumbles, getting up from the chair.

My stomach flips again as I watch him strut around the living room with his iPhone pressed to his ear. I'm still having serious doubts about my decision to help Justice Cross execute his plan, but the terror in his voice is genuine as he keeps throwing questions at the person at the other end of the conversation.

"So what? Are they gonna subpoena me or something? You know this is fucked up, right? She can't do that. I didn't hit her... Yeah, yeah, okay... I'll see you tomorrow morning."

The moment he ends the call, his eyes go from gray to black. He stops dead in his tracks, clenches his jaw, and stares at nothing in particular, his chest rising and falling each time he takes a deep, loud breath.

"Is everything okay?" I squeak from my spot at the table.

He rubs the back of his neck and strolls into the kitchen. "Nikki filed a restraining order."

"Oh."

"She picked up Aiden from my parents' this morning and I'm not allowed to be anywhere near her, meaning I can't be anywhere near my son either until my lawyers fix this."

"I'm sorry," I mutter, pulling the lid off the container.

"I need you to come with me to the station tomorrow to talk to the police. Please."

"The police station?" I ask, eyeing the fried pieces of peanuts scattered all over my food.

"My lawyer will do all the talking. You just have to show up."

"Will your wife drop the charges after we do this?" *Fucking peanuts.*

"She can't prove that I hit her if I have an alibi, can she?"

"Right." I nod absently, still fuming internally over my messed-up dinner.

Another awkward moment of silence with nothing but the sounds of the rain lulling me into a dreamy haze. Something that's been happening to me a lot lately. As if my mind wants to take a random vacation and check out. It's a good kind of haze, numb and dark, where nothing can bother me, but right now, the void is filled with questions. How the hell did I end up agreeing to this? What if Owen finds out? *Of course, he will. He's always on his phone. I'm sure he still checks Facebook and this is going to be in the tabloids.* What if I don't sound convincing enough? What if I end up making it worse?

"What's wrong?" The deep, low voice comes crashing at me out of nowhere, slowly dragging me back to the real world.

"I'm allergic to peanuts." As I slide the container to the middle of the table, I realize that the last time I actually ate was yesterday at the bar.

"Well, shit." He stares at the food for a few seconds, then back at me. "Okay. Why don't you get dressed? We'll go grab something out. I know a good place not far from here."

"No, thanks," I reply dryly.

"It's just dinner. I'm not taking you back to my place, babe," he insists.

"Aren't you paranoid about being seen in public?"

"It's not that kind of place. I know the owner; he's a friend of my father's. Come on, cut the crap. You look like you're about to faint. Let's go."

"If that's your way of complimenting a woman, you need to brush up on your skills," I scoff, folding my arms on my chest. This man really has no manners, and as much as it bothers me, it also feeds my sudden curiosity.

"I'm only trying to be nice and get some food in you, Hazel. Okay? Will you please do me a favor and change into something more appropriate so we can go eat?"

"You don't like what I'm wearing?"

"Fuck." He groans, closing his eyes for a second. "You're going to give me a coronary." His jaw clenches again as he rocks on his heels, waiting anxiously.

The soon-to-be-divorced, depressed, reclusive woman in me wants to kick this man out and go back to sleep, but the hunger and anxiety are telling me to do something completely opposite of what my heart desires at the moment. Maybe this is what Rayna meant by making changes in my dull life.

You can't be sad forever, Hazel.

"Okay," I mumble under my breath. "Just give me a few minutes."

I'm already regretting my decision by the time I make it to the guest bedroom. The first thing that comes to mind as I rush to my still unpacked luggage is to go back, apologize, and ask Justice to leave. All the insecurities I just sort of pushed to the back of my mind some years ago are now starting to swallow me like a black hole. He's an internationally acclaimed singer with the looks of a model, and I'm a college dropout who hasn't been to a hair salon in over two years.

I'm not even a mom anymore!

After rummaging through my stacks of folded clothes with tears in my eyes and a throbbing pain in the back of my head, I choose a black knit top and a pair of dark blue jeans. Casual, conservative, and…boring.

The impatient stomping of boots out in the living room isn't helping my anxiety. Geez, could he stop circling?

"I'll be right out!" I yell before locking myself in the bathroom. The smell of burned hair fills the air in a matter of seconds as I clumsily work the settings of the curling iron. When was the last time I actually fussed this much over a dinner? What's wrong with me?

"That'll do it," I tell my reflection, clicking the curling iron off and tossing it back on the counter. It's not like I'm going on a date. We're not even friends.

Black knee-high boots and a dark blue pea coat complete my outfit.

"Let's go before I change my mind," I croak, flying past Justice to the front door.

8 JUSTICE

Hazel is definitely one of the strangest women I've ever met.

And I've met a lot of women.

"The shrimp curry is pretty good." I throw out another recommendation, lifting my eyes from the menu, the heel of my boot tapping the floor impatiently. She's been staring at the appetizer section for ten minutes, half a glass of wine already gone. For a woman who missed supper, Hazel sure as hell takes an eternity to order.

Deep inside, I'm already regretting bringing her to this place, but the better-man shit I'm working on is forcing me to stay put. Worst of all, Joe was still here when we arrived. He's not used to me bringing random female guests to his restaurant. This is where I used to take Nikki before things went to shit. This is where Dom and I eat. Sometimes May joins us. Every so often, I come here with my parents or my sister. But I never bring women I met at the bar.

"How do people even eat oysters?" Hazel scrunches up her nose, flipping the menu page.

"Is that a trick question?" I ask, studying her face. She doesn't wear a lot of makeup and I can tell this is her natural hair color. She's beautiful in her own way. Not bombshell take-your-breath-away hot, but more of an exquisite enigma. Small and slender, almost invisible, but at the same time bright and radiant like a star.

"No." She finally lifts her eyes from the menu and stares at me. "I'm just curious. They don't look very appetizing."

"Don't judge a book by its cover." I take a deep, long breath.

God, give me the strength to get through this dinner.

Shaking her head, she gives me a massive eye roll and resumes scanning the menu. By the time she finally makes up her mind and orders, I'm on the verge of having a fucking breakdown.

Once the waiter is gone, an awkward silence follows. I'm doing my best to stick to my part of the deal and keep my mouth shut. Most women like my sex jokes. Hazel finds them disrespectful. How the fuck am I being disrespectful? I complimented her tits. I don't even do that to some of the women I *sleep* with. She should be flattered.

"So how do you know the owner?" she asks after a few long moments of studying the interior of the dining room. Her amber eyes keep jumping from table to table as if she's trying to memorize every tiny detail.

"Joe is my father's friend. They used to jam together when they were young," I explain briefly. My personal information is only given out on a need-to-know basis. And there's no need for Hazel to know more.

"*Jam* as in with a band?" she asks, her fingers now playing with the napkin. Her glass of wine is almost finished.

"Yeah."

"Was your father a famous musician like you?"

"No. He just played for fun. Small local band."

"Did you always want to be in a band?" She leans forward and gives me an inquisitive look. Her golden strands slowly fall over her shoulders and down her chest, sweeping the edge of the table.

"Yep. All my life."

"What did your parents say when you got your first record deal?"

"You sure do ask a lot of questions, babe." I try to dodge them, but she's already finished with her drink, and if my memory serves me right, she gets a little loose when she's buzzed. That explains her sudden curiosity.

"I'm just trying to keep the conversation going."

"My parents were stoked when my band got the record deal. Happy now?" I shoot her a glare.

"They sound like cool parents then."

"They are."

She sniffs, falling back in her chair. "I wish my parents had been cool about it when I married Owen."

"Is he an asshole or something?"

"No. Not really." She grabs her napkin.

"Then why were your parents not happy with you marrying the dude?"

"I don't think getting married at nineteen is something most parents see as a bright future for their only daughter." She looks out the window while torturing the napkin between her forefinger and thumb. The lost expression on her face is making me curious.

"Did he propose to you in high school or something?" This woman is full of surprises. First she doesn't want to sleep with me, and now I'm finding out she wasted the best years of her life being tied to some douche named Owen.

"No. A few weeks after we graduated high school," she says, mustering up a smile. "Owen was a year older and he was trouble...or at least that's what my parents thought." She shrugs. "They hated him."

"Trouble? Like in a gang or something?" Hazel doesn't strike me as someone who'd be married to a criminal. She looks like a straight-shooter, with all those fucking sweaters and coats. I wouldn't be surprised if she were a teacher. A hot one at that.

"No." A soft laugh escapes her lips. "He had some friends like that, but no. He wasn't in a gang."

"What does he do now?"

"He's in real estate."

"Sounds like he's got it all figured out."

"Yeah. He likes it. It keeps him occupied and it pays the bills."

"So you've been with this dude since high school. Why are you two getting a divorce then?"

"We just grew apart." Hazel's hand releases the napkin and her voice grows quiet, which makes her explanation sound very unconvincing.

"Did he cheat?"

"No. We stopped being in love...I think. It's complicated."

"Yeah, sounds like you shouldn't have married him at nineteen." I give my opinion.

"Aren't you the expert?" she says sarcastically.

"I never claimed to be an expert, babe. But at least sample some merchandise before making a purchase, if you know what I mean."

"I'm not into sampling." She cocks her head, giving me a half-smile.

Who the fuck wouldn't be into exploring the possibilities? Don't go there, Justice. Just don't. But the sex addict in me can't fight the curiosity.

"So you've been with one dude all your life?"

"None of your business," she whispers after a short pause, her amber eyes intensely staring into mine, her lips pursed together.

The answer is definitely a yes, I think to myself as I watch a tiny vein pulsating on her forehead. Fuck, I really enjoy pissing this woman off. She gets feisty, which I find sexy.

What the fuck is your problem, Justice? She isn't even your type. And too fucking skinny. And since when are you interested in all-fucking-natural tits?

The truth is, I'm confused. I haven't gotten laid in over five weeks. The last month of the European leg of the tour was a nightmare. Zander was constantly up in my face sharing his absolutely ridiculous ideas for the new album. For a second there, I thought he was back to doing coke, because that's when he and Chance were the most productive. The label was pushing us into doing more press than necessary to promote the upcoming record that wasn't even in the works yet. All we had was bits and pieces. Tyler kept on bitching about our sound engineer fucking up during his solos. Cruz was having a phone feud with his wife almost every night, which always resulted in me consoling him. The whole thing was a mess and I didn't really have time for Rachel and our games.

And with her going out of town and me being tied up in a messy divorce, sex hasn't seemed like a priority. Not until Hazel walked into Marvin's bar. With her natural hair, porcelain skin, and crappy attitude. She confuses me. It's like lowering society's fucking bar, which I rarely do. The world doesn't accept Justice Cross fucking someone who doesn't wear makeup and doesn't have at least a D cup.

Hazel and I keep to ourselves for a few minutes. She gets a refill on her wine, I get another water. Then when the food finally comes out, we eat in silence while listening to the rain and exchanging occasional glances. My hand is itching to dial Rachel to see if she's still in L.A., but I refrain from being a total ass in front of the woman who's going to lie to the police for me.

"So..." I put my fork aside after finishing the lobster. "Are we good?"

"Honestly"—Hazel stops chewing and gives me a long pondering look—"I'm having second thoughts."

"It'll be over quickly. I promise."

"I don't need to sign any agreements or anything, right?" She bats her eyes at me, placing her utensils next to her plate.

"A paper trail would get us both screwed. This is just between me and you. You don't tell a soul. Not even your priest when you go for your confession or whatever."

"You and priests." She snorts, averting her gaze, which I find...weirdly cute.

"No one can know, okay?" I repeat. "You understand?"

"I understand." She fiddles with her napkin again, and I notice that the shadows beneath her eyes seem even bigger than yesterday.

"You want something else? Dessert?" I ask, ignoring her obvious inner turmoil that's breaking through. Yeah. I know I'm an ass who has no regard for the feelings of other people.

"No, thanks. I'm full."

"No problem. Taking a woman I allegedly fucked to dinner is the least I can do, right?" The cocky bastard in me wants to crack another joke, but the amber eyes pinning me to my chair as soon as the stupid shit leaves my mouth make me swallow it back. "Sorry," I croak. "I forgot we're on a strictly no-sexual-innuendo level."

"That's right," she says firmly, her gaze burning right into my skull. The alcohol and the anger coloring her cheeks. Pissed suits her.

When the waiter comes back to check on us, Hazel attempts to ask for a third glass of wine, but my common sense tells me to cut her off before I end up repeating yesterday's clusterfuck. Hauling her drunk ass back home is not what I have in mind. My plan is to get Rachel here and fuck her silly. Great for stress relief.

"We'll just have more water and the check." I send the waiter away and turn my attention back to Hazel, whose eyes are shooting daggers at me. "Look, we have a hard day tomorrow. Both me and you. Why don't I take you home, and after all this is over, I'll buy you a case of wine and you can drink all you want?"

She blinks a few times, lips pursed, expression sour.

"I don't want you to be hungover when we do this. That's all."

She sniffs, folding her arms on her chest. "Fine."

"Good." I open my wallet and pull out my American Express. Joe doesn't like it when I pay for food here, but what's another two hundred bucks for someone like me, right?

After the bill is taken care of, I walk Hazel to the back of the restaurant.

"Is this how you always come in?" she asks as we stroll past the storage area.

"Pretty much," I say.

"Is it hard...to constantly be in hiding?" she stutters, and her voice starts falling back behind me.

"It's not a lifestyle for everyone." I slow down a bit and wait for her. When she catches up, I hook my arm through hers and pick up the pace.

"You ever want to just be normal?" The clacking of her heels bouncing off the floor is like a percussionist's nightmare. She either misses a step or finds a way to trip over nothing at least ten times before we reach the exit.

"Why?" I ask, pushing the door open to let her go first.

"I don't know." She shrugs, stumbling outside into the late-night November mist.

"You have to sacrifice some things if you want to be successful, Hazel."

"Like freedom?" She takes a few shaky steps forward, spins on her heel, and tilts her head. Her amber eyes peer at me from under a thick layer of long, dark lashes. The door slowly shuts behind me, leaving just the two of us in this small back lot with a few employee vehicles and my Jeep parked across the way.

I don't know why I've never really noticed how expressive her eyes actually are. I've definitely over-evaluated and compared her tits to those of every single woman I've fucked. But right now I can't stop staring at the tiny fragments of all the shades of gold in that gaze that are piercing right into my soul. Standing here across from her with the yellow pole light illuminating her face, I'm seeing the things I failed to spot during our first encounter. Like the way her forehead stops right at my chin and how her hair falls over her shoulders in messy cascades of gold.

Funny thing, but I gather all this in the fraction of a second that she's waiting for my answer to a question I don't even remember.

"You really like hiding out, pretending to be someone else, sneaking into restaurants through the back?" She keeps rocking on her heels back and forth, with her hands now tucked into the front pockets of her petite dark blue coat. "Sounds like a nightmare, not a sacrifice."

"It's worth it. I get to do what I love for a living. Not many people can say that."

"Is it worth having your son yanked from parent to parent whenever one of you feels like it?" Her voice is lower than a whisper.

There's a harsh sting in my chest. "You don't know anything about my family," I say quietly. "Let me be the one to judge my own actions, okay?"

"That's right." She inhales deeply, and I can see the pain in her eyes as her head sinks into her shoulders. "The thing is...I don't know if I can do this..." Her lower lip begins to tremble. The words send a cold shiver down my spine.

"Look"—I take a step forward to close the distance between us —"I'm also getting a fucking divorce, and I'm not having a good year either, Hazel."

She bites the inside of her cheek and gives me a defeated look, the kind that makes me want to fucking cry.

"Hey, listen." My brain is working overtime. It's been a long time since I've had to handle a woman having a meltdown, which Hazel seems to do quite often. Under different circumstances, I'd just run for the hills, but we're in the middle of my battle against Nikki. "It's gonna be alright. And I promise it'll be over before you know it." I bring my hand to her cheek and cup it gently, something I haven't done to anyone in ages. Lately, when I'm with a woman, it's just wham-bam-thank-you-ma'am.

"Okay." She nods lightly with her cheek still pressed to my palm. The way her soft skin feels against mine makes my blood rush with all sorts of sensations throughout my body, some lustful, some tender. Without giving it much thought, I lean forward and plant a kiss on her forehead.

The taste of coconut is still on the tip of my tongue as we silently walk back to my Jeep. Neither one of us knows what just happened, so the drive to her place is quiet with the rain being the only soundtrack. When I let her out, she tells me thanks and waves goodbye before I watch her go inside. Then by the time I get to my cabin, it's way past midnight. The thought of calling Rachel doesn't seem appealing anymore. Instead, I take a shower and go to sleep.

9 HAZEL

WHEN MY ALARM GOES OFF, I'm already wide awake, mind racing, body shivering, and a sticky, cold sweat breaking under the flannel shirt I slept in. Actually, I don't believe I slept at all. More like tossed and turned all night, regretting my decision, thinking of all sorts of shit scenarios Karma is going to throw my way after lying to the police. But the funny thing is that I'm not scared of Karma anymore. Everything I had, she took: my son, my marriage, my sanity. I don't even know whether it's for the sins I committed in a previous life or for what I'm about to do. I *am* scared of my parents' reaction, though. And Owen's.

I take a deep, shaky breath and count down another day of my post-River life. Each time I flip the page of my mental calendar, his tiny face is blurrier, his smile is fading, his laughter quieter. I dread the morning when I wake up and no longer see him.

Two years. One month. Twenty-eight days.

You wouldn't like Mommy right now, angel. She's been missing you like crazy and she's making a whole lot of bad decisions.

I slowly sit up and swing my legs over the edge of the bed, the tips of my toes brushing against the soft carpet. The sun beaming into the room through the slim openings between the blind slats is refreshing after what seems like an eternity of nonstop rain. My head is still throbbing from the deadly combination of wine and no sleep, but for the most part, I'm awake. Tired, but ready to get on with this day.

I pick up my phone from the nightstand and lazily skim through the messages.

Rayna: Hey, sweetie! Just wanted to see how you're doing. I hope you got that fireplace started. Please do something fun. Love you bunches. Clay says hi. Call me or text me if you need anything. And I mean ANYTHING!!! XOXO

Mom: Hi, Hazel. Dad and I are worried. We haven't heard from you in over two weeks. Call us when you have a moment. We love you. Bye.

The last message is from the number I haven't programmed into my phone yet.

Unknown: Pick you up at 9. ✝ ✝ ✝

Asshole has his own emoji?

My heart skips a beat as last night's memories crawl into my fuzzy brain. The soft touch of his lips on my forehead felt oddly comforting.

I promised myself not to read anything related to the Nikki Deville and Justice Cross press battle, but somehow I end up googling the recent updates and developments, most of them consisting of Nikki publicly trashing Justice. By the time I'm done studying the headlines and the photos of her injuries, I'm suspicious of Justice again. Doubts begin to stir up in the pit of my stomach. The turmoil over the possibility that Nikki's claims are not just a product of her imagination send cold shivers down my spine as I iron the only pair of dress slacks I packed for this trip.

The scared-to-death excuse of a person in me is absently working the toothbrush when the sound of tires in Rayna's driveway breaks the silent monotony of my morning. Cursing under my breath, I spit the rest of the toothpaste into the sink and head for the front door. My hair still isn't done and my makeup will probably be taking a back seat for the day.

"Hazel?" A tall forty-something man in a green winter jacket and a pair of dark blue jeans eyes me with curiosity when I step out on the porch.

"Yes." I peek over his shoulder at the shiny black limo parked right next to my Prius.

"I'm Dominic. Justice's manager." He walks toward me and extends his hand for a shake.

"I'm not ready yet," I mutter, silently questioning the need for the limo and wondering if the streaks of gray in Dominic's slicked and tied-back hair is the result of working for the biggest asshole in the music business.

"We'll wait in the car." He nods, his hand still midair, waiting for that handshake I'm contemplating. My eyes jump back to the limo, hoping to get a glimpse of the man whose unexpected entrance into my dull life has been making me feel some strange things. Like the flutter in my lower stomach right now. Part of me suddenly starts regretting my earlier no-makeup decision.

Finally, I give Dominic the handshake he's been waiting almost forever for. "I'll be out in ten minutes."

Once inside, I rush back to the bathroom and put finishing touches on my hair by tying it into a simple bun.

There. The woman staring at me from the mirror above the sink looks honest enough. All she has to do now is make sure she keeps a straight face while lying to the police. Piece of cake, right?

After giving my reflection a mini pep talk, I toss my phone into my purse and head out. The limo occupying the driveway is like a misplaced spaceship, ready to eat me alive. The only other time I rode in a limo was on my wedding day. Feels like a lifetime ago.

The moment I slide into the back, Justice winks at me and pats the seat, signaling for me to sit right next to him. Part of me hates his asshole demeanor, but with two other people inside, arguing seems silly. I save the unnecessary debate for later and take the spot.

"Hey." He turns to face me. His eyes travel down to my breasts. The man has no shame!

"Hi." My speech is on the verge of incoherence, my knees are all wobbly, my stomach jumping.

I take in the other occupants of the limo. Dominic is across from us, and a short brunette is sitting next to him, her age hard to determine because of the amount of makeup covering her face. Not that it matters, but my best guess is that she's at least forty, which makes me feel disconnected, like a high schooler. I remind myself that Justice is also fairly young, just eight years older than me. Actually, if I hadn't purposely googled his age, I wouldn't have thought he was more than thirty. The man cleans up well, despite his past addictions. And, yes. I took the time to read his history. A couple of DUIs in the early twenties, an overdose at twenty-six, one trip to rehab shortly after that. Nothing hinting at him being an abusive husband. Of course, trusting everything that's on the internet is like playing Russian roulette.

"This is May. She's my publicist," Justice says. "And you already met Dom." He tips his chin in the direction of his manager.

"Pleasure, Hazel. How are you doing?" May asks, giving me a forced half-second smile while typing away on her iPad. I assume she doesn't really care how I'm doing since she's clearly busy and can't be bothered with waiting for my response.

"You want something to drink? Juice? Water?" Dominic points at the mini bar."

A shot of tequila would be good right now.

"No, thanks." I swallow hard. My head snaps back to Justice. "What about your lawyer?"

"His plane just landed. He'll meet us there."

The limo starts moving.

Clasping my hands together on my lap, I try to breathe. The silence surrounding us is heavier than a truck full of rocks, and occasional glances from Dominic and May make me uncomfortable.

"You okay?" Justice asks, and I see a spark in his eyes.

"I'm fine," I reply dryly, dodging another stare from the publicist. She seems tense. I wonder if the rockstar ever offered her his solution to fix that.

The leather squeaks under the weight of Justice's body as he slides closer. Suddenly, I'm too aware of his presence. He drapes his arm over my shoulder, whispering into my ear, "What the fuck are you wearing?"

"Excuse me?" I mouth at him, not sure if Dominic and May are supposed to hear this conversation. The humming of the engine doesn't provide much of a cover.

"No one is going to believe I banged you if you dress like an elementary school teacher." He closes the remainder of the airspace between us. "Not even my publicist." He rasps in a low voice.

"I can wear whatever I want," I come back instantly, forming my hands into fists.

"Listen, you look really nice." He licks his lips. "Just not my type." His eyes, pinning me to the leather seat, grow darker. His thigh is now pressed to mine.

"What does it matter?" I shift in my spot nervously.

"Well, it would be good to make it at least somewhat believable, babe," he says in my hair.

"Is that what we're doing right now? With you all over me? Making it believable in front of your manager and your publicist?" I cross my arms over my chest.

He lets out a soft chuckle.

"This is against the rules," I murmur, peeking at May and Dominic out of the corner of my eye. Thankfully, they found something to talk about and are no longer paying attention to what we're doing, which leaves me to be one-on-one with the man who finds enjoyment in invading my personal space.

"Sorry." He sighs, pulling back a little, his arm still on my shoulder.

"Can you please keep your hands off me?" I whisper through clenched teeth, though the feel of his rock-hard muscles rubbing the back of my neck makes my stomach twirl.

"Now I see why you're getting a divorce." He snorts out a muffled laugh.

"Don't go there."

"Sorry."

"You don't need to apologize every three seconds, especially if you don't mean it, Justice."

"I don't say sorry if I don't mean it."

I can't think of anything intelligent to respond with. Instead, I just roll my eyes.

We drive in silence for a while, then the question that comes from Justice next catches me off guard.

"What do you do?"

"What do you mean?"

"What do you do for a living? I never asked you. We allegedly slept together and I don't even know what you do."

I secretly wish he hadn't asked me that. "I'm between jobs." The best way to explain to a stranger that you don't work. Haven't worked in a while, or ever actually, but Justice Cross doesn't need to know any of that, or about my failed attempts at college, or my junior-high artistic aspirations. Seems like a lifetime ago.

"I see." He nods.

"Why do you care?"

"Just curious." He shrugs. "Any interesting hobbies?"

I roll my eyes again. "I only signed up for one interrogation today."

"Someone's in a mood," he mumbles to himself.

Jerk.

I don't say anything for the remainder of the trip, using most of my willpower to keep it together. Once we're at the station, I hang my head low and silently trail Justice through the brightly lit hallway of the local law enforcement establishment, my mind still refusing to believe I'm going through with this farce. May and Dominic follow like obedient puppies.

We're escorted into a small room with no windows where a bulky guy in a gray suit and absolutely no hair is already waiting for us with his briefcase wide open and a stack of papers out on the table. Talk about coming prepared.

"Gary Schmidt. How are you?" He extends his huge hand for a shake after saying a brief hello to Justice and his entourage.

"I'm fine. Thank you. How are you?" I reply mechanically, returning the gesture while sinking into a cold metal chair Dominic pulls out for me. Well, at least *he* has manners, unlike his boss who's relaxing to my left.

"Let's go over the timeline again," Gary barks out. His narrow eyes hiding under a thick furrowed brow jump from me to Justice and back, making me slump deeper and deeper into the chair.

"I was drunk," I blurt out. "I don't think I can follow the timeline."

"That's okay, Hazel. Being drunk is only illegal if you're driving. No one says you can't have sex while intoxicated, unless you're a minor."

At least he has a sense of humor.

The three minutes I spend with Justice and his lawyer going over my fake memories of the night we allegedly slept together are nothing compared to the actual questioning by the detectives that follows right after. Thankfully, most of the talking is done by Gary.

"My client came to you on his own. There's no need to get all crazy. Everyone knows Mr. Cross and his wife are separated and have been seeing other people for a while now. There is nothing wrong with him having a friend over. Ms. Deville didn't spend more than five minutes inside his residence. The injuries she received are not the result of my client's doing. Take a better look, gentlemen. Do Mr. Cross's hands look like he was engaged in any kind of fighting at all? It's obvious he was not the one who assaulted Ms. Deville the other night."

His words are pounding in my head like a sledgehammer, each new swing causing my skull to crack open more and more. I think by the time we're done here, my brain might be one huge puddle of melted gray matter on the floor.

The room starts closing in on me somewhere around the time both detectives are trying to discredit my words. It's not even the fact that I don't believe Justice. I do, despite my earlier doubts. Otherwise I wouldn't be here. But I'm scared shitless, scared of paparazzi, and scared of Owen seeing my name in the tabloids. My eyes jump from Gary's briefcase to May's iPad and finally freeze on the tattooed letters inked on Justice's hand as his fingers do a little dance on the tabletop to my left.

Tap...tap...tap...

I run my sweaty palms over the fabric of the poorly ironed slacks and clasp my knees. The air feels hot and heavy, impossible to breathe in. And the soccer ball sized lump in my throat isn't making it any better.

This will be over in a few minutes, Hazel. Just don't have a meltdown in front of the detectives.

Easy to say, not easy to do with six pairs of eyes gawking at me. I release my knees and slowly lean back in my chair, my vision blurring, my fingers shaking, my heart racing like an express train. *Oh my God. I have early Parkinson's!*

This is when "faith" carefully slides under the tabletop and takes hold of my hand. The soft fingers laced with mine feel soothing, almost encouraging. The warmth of his touch spreads through my body like a shockwave as I sit there, completely undone, butterfly-like sensations taking over my insides. The last time I felt something close to this was years ago.

I don't know if anyone in the room realizes Justice Cross is holding my hand while we're finishing up with the questions, but I almost don't want him to let go once we're done. All my cells are reacting to his presence in a very strange way, making me hot one minute and cold the next.

I'm still in a daze as we walk back to the parking lot, Gary talking to Dominic with May on the phone right behind them, their voices all booming somewhere in the back of my head.

"You okay?" A soft whisper reaches my ear once our procession has made it halfway to the limo. The driver is already flashing a smile and has the doors wide open, ready to take me back to my dark and lonely existence.

"I'm fine." I clasp the straps of my bag. *I could really use a drink right now.*

"You were flatlining in there, babe," Justice murmurs, leaning in, his hand pressed against the small of my back, his shoulder rubbing mine as we stroll toward the vehicle.

"I'm not a very good liar if you haven't noticed," I hiss through clenched teeth, trying to ignore the fluttering in my stomach. Why is he making me feel this way?

"You can say *that* again," he snorts, shaking his head.

"You know I hate you, right? You just made me do the most dishonorable thing in my life."

"Is that so?"

"If you don't hold up your part of the bargain and my family ends up reading about this in the tabloids, I'll never speak to you again."

"I promise that May will contain this to the best of her abilities."

"Take me home, please," I request coldly.

The drive back to my place consists mainly of Dominic and May discussing The Deviant's new album and the tour plans for next year. They could be speaking Chinese for all I know. Their business talk sounds just as confusing. The rockstar himself, barely engaged in their banter, thankfully makes no attempts to hold my hand, which is good because going from ice-cold to scorching hot in under a second isn't something my body can handle at the moment. What I really want is my bed and a glass of wine.

When we arrive at Rayna's, Justice starts to get out, but I tell him no, and our goodbye is dry and brief. The moment I get inside, hot tears start spilling down my cheeks. I close the door and, needing a few minutes to pull myself together, I lean against it and try to breathe as I listen to the purring of the engine disappear. My mind is beginning to shut down when I drop down on the couch, still in my coat and my boots, and sleep takes over in an instant as I cuddle one of Rayna's decorative pillows. The numbness feels nice, comforting, like home. I've been numb for so long that I'm not sure I want to be anything different. I just don't know how anymore.

When the phone wakes me up, it's already dark out. My neck hurts from the uncomfortable position I slept in, my mouth is dry, and my drool is on Rayna's colorful pillow. After replaying the morning's events in my head at least a dozen times, I fish for my phone in my purse. The missed call is from Owen, and I immediately call him back. Not because he's still my husband and deserves the luxury of knowing how I am. It's more of a habit. A reflex really. And it pisses me off. I want to stop thinking about him and the past ten years of my life I gave him. I want it to stop hurting.

"Are you all settled?" he asks dryly.

"Yeah. I'm fine."

"You sound sick."

"I was sleeping." I bite back a yawn.

"Did you get a chance to look at the divorce papers yet?"

He can't wait to get rid of me. I wonder if he's seeing someone. "I'll look at them tonight, Owen."

"Please do."

"I'll look at the papers tonight. Promise," I repeat and end the call.

After sulking over the shit that my life has become, I open the browser and scan the celebrity gossip headlines.

Rock Singer Justice Cross Responds to His Wife's Accusations.

The Deviant's Singer Finally Breaks His Silence.

Nikki Deville's Accusations Are False.

I find myself cringing at some of the articles while scanning the press release quoted off Justice's official Facebook page two hours ago. Looks like it was posted when I was drooling all over Rayna's pillow. May is definitely a great publicist. She made his infidelity sound way cool. But then again, those two have been separated for quite some time. I wouldn't hold it against him if I was a fan of the band. Still better than being an abusive husband. No one would let him anywhere near his son if that were the case.

I absently click on a few more recommended links. Some of the headlines are starting to sound ridiculous, and the ones calling Nikki's performance Oscar-worthy are making me laugh until I come across one that I don't like at all.

Justice Cross and His Ladies: Who's the New Secret Flavor of the Week?

I blink a few times and bring the phone closer to my face. Right below the headline, there's a photo of him leaning into a woman near the back entrance of the restaurant we went to last night. Not the greatest quality, but it's definitely him.

Shit.

I nervously slide my fingers across the screen, trying to zoom in the photo.

Shit. Shit. Shit!!!

The woman is me.

10 JUSTICE

"This is me! This is fucking me, Justice!" she screams into the phone, her voice ripping me to shreds. Having her on speakerphone is painful. Even when she's done howling, her echoes are still bouncing off the walls of my bedroom for a few brief moments as a reminder of how much of a dick I actually am.

The better-man shit isn't progressing, huh?

I narrow my eyes and stare at the stupid photo and the headline she texted me right before calling. My mind is trying to grasp the seriousness of this article. Another shit magazine fishing for stuff that's not there. Who even cares who I sleep with, right?

Get a grip, Justice. The whole damn planet, that's who.

"Just take it easy, babe," I mutter, looking at the photo again. Fuck, someone must have followed me around all day, because this is the shit paparazzi live for. The asshole with the camera probably sat there outside the restaurant waiting for us to leave so that they could capture the exact moment of me trying to fucking console this woman. And now she's all pissed and manic like she's on fucking speed.

"Take it easy? You want me to take it easy when the photo of you all over me is out circulating on the internet?" She laughs hysterically. "I'm not even divorced yet."

"Neither am I. Besides, you can't even tell that's you. And I'm not all over you." I keep staring at the screen, unable to take my eyes off the headline.

"My husband will recognize me, and my parents, and my...my friends too, Justice!"

I like the way she says my name. It sounds different coming out of her mouth, not all fake like the way most women say it.

"The quality's not that great anyway." I make another attempt to calm her down. "And you can't even see your face; my shoulder's in the way. You're overreacting, Hazel."

She goes quiet.

"Hazel?" I say. "It's not as bad as it looks. Seriously." We didn't even fucking kiss like normal adults. All I did was touch her forehead. *With my lips.* It's not like there's a sex tape out there now.

"It's me, Justice. And you are very much in my personal space."
Ouch!

I don't really know what her problem is. No woman ever complained about me being in her personal space before. I'm practically certain she's secretly a lesbian. That's the only explanation for her odd behavior, divorce included. Maybe she's just coming out right now. Because let's face it, if she doesn't want me to touch her, then why the fuck would she give it up to whatever-his-name-is that she's been married to half of her life? Maybe she doesn't like dick and she's just figuring it out. Some people are slower. Takes them a lifetime.

I'm almost content with my brilliant discovery, but somewhere deep inside, there's still doubt. It's stupid, but I liked holding her hand today at the station. Not that I wanted to get all sentimental, but her face was whiter than a piece of paper, and she was about to fall apart in front of everyone. It was a rare opportunity to show her that I still had control, although surprisingly, it felt nice, warm and feminine, and just exquisite. It was a little shaky, but I could understand why. I haven't touched a soft hand like hers in a long time.

"It's not like we're making out, okay?" I say, my voice calmer.

"It looks like it," she whispers. Thank God, no more screaming.

"No, it doesn't." I clear my throat. I've been caught on camera doing worse.

"Can you make it go away?"

"Go away? What am I, an eraser?"

"Can't your publicist do something about it?"

"May can do a lot of stuff, but she's not a magician. It's already out there, babe. I'll ask her to keep tabs on it and see if she knows how the photo got leaked to the press, but once it's there, it's there."

I hear a loud sigh of disappointment. "But you promised."

"It'll go away tomorrow when my ex comes up with another lie."

"Are you sure?"

"I'm pretty sure."

Pause.

"Is she going to drop the charges at least?"

"My lawyers are on it." My eyes dart to the suitcase I started packing. There's no way I'm staying here and waiting for the restraining order deal to be sorted out. Tomorrow, I'm going back to L.A. to see my son.

"Okay...at least I didn't fuck that up," she mumbles into the phone.

No, I don't think so. On the contrary, she did really well. Except for that one moment of weakness when she almost passed out. But I won't hold it against her.

"Will you ask your PR shark to please keep those stupid websites from posting anymore photos of me on the internet?"

"I promise I'll do the best I can. So are we good? You need anything? I can have Dominic there whenever. He's available tonight and tomorrow morning." Her empty kitchen comes to mind. I wonder if she ever got groceries or if she was going to order that Chinese crap for dinner again.

"I'm a big girl. I can take care of myself, Justice." She lets out a wry laugh.

"Right. I forgot most people aren't spoiled assholes like the one you're talking to right now."

"Just stop it. Goodbye."

She hangs up before I even get a chance to respond. That husband of hers must be doing jumping jacks around their house right now, because it doesn't take an expert to see that being married to Hazel is a fucking nightmare.

As soon as I end the call, I notice an unread message from Rachel.

Rachel: Are you banging a teacher or is your new friend into cosplay?

I'm torn between ignoring the text and asking her to come out to Tahoe. She doesn't do drama, but she gives one hell of a blowjob. Among other things. Rachel is the girl who loves to experiment. She never says no to anything.

I circle around the bedroom for a few minutes, trying to figure out why I'm not in the mood for sex. Usually I always am, with the exception of the show and studio days. That's when all my energy goes into music. Fucking a woman before a performance in front of fifteen thousand people is a huge no-no. It's like eating a dessert before an entree. Same goes for the album recording. There's no room for sex when the band is on a hot streak. It distracts me from hearing the music and messes with my creativity. And I can't have that.

Right now, I'm supposed to be on a break. Two and a half months of nothing before we go back into the studio to work on the new album. I should be enjoying myself, getting laid, eating sushi, doing fucking yoga or whatever else people on spiritual retreats are doing. But instead, I'm dealing with the bullshit my ex is dumping on me, including her sucker attempts to contest joint custody of our son.

When my head starts to spin from all the pointless looping around, I stop in my tracks and text Rachel back.

Justice: None of your business.

Rachel: Since when are you into plain Janes?

Justice: Are you jealous?

Rachel: You know I'm never jealous. I bet she can't do what I can.

Justice: Are you in L.A. right now?

Rachel: Yes. Wanna hang?

She doesn't know I'm in Tahoe. Theoretically, I can Uber her up here and we can meet up in a hotel. But that sounds too complicated right now. I really need to wrap up the domestic abuse crap here and then move on to the restraining order.

Justice: Let me think about it.

Rachel: The teacher must know a few tricks. Since when do you need to think about seeing me?

Justice: I'm going through a lot of shit right now. I'll text you later on and let you know.

Rachel: Sure thing, daddy.

Drawing a long deep breath, I close the iMessage window and call my mother.

"Hey, Mom. Did you get to talk to Nikki?"

"She's not picking up, Justice. I left her two voicemails."

Bitch is doing it on purpose. But I refrain from cursing in front of my mother. Not that she hasn't seen me at my worst, fucked up and all, but the better-man shit needs to shine through sometimes, right?

"Can you try again in a little bit, Mom?" I plead. Part of me desperately wants to call my ex, but that could result in me getting fucked even more. There's nothing else left to do but wait till tomorrow morning and see if my lawyer can at least get the phone calls bullshit resolved.

"I'll try, Justice. Don't worry. I'm sure Aiden is fine."

"He's three years old, Mom! She yanked him out of your house with all that war paint on her face, and now he thinks I did it to her! He'll be scared shitless of me by the time she's done brainwashing him!"

"Honey." My mother's tone changes from the typical bossy to her rare tender one. Having a douche of a rockstar for a son is not an easy thing to handle, which is something I admire about my mom. She's been there for me through thick and thin—OD, rehab, all my early run-ins with the law. Now she's the middleman between Nikki and me. Gladys Hale is one tough cookie.

"Just don't do anything stupid," she says softly into the phone. Her voice is like music to my ears. The special kind, only meant for me. Out of all the women in my life, she's the one constant who I know will always say the right words when I need to hear them the most, even if she doesn't always give me the solution. "It will sort itself out. Let the lawyers handle this."

"I know, Mom. I'm going back to L.A. tomorrow to make sure he's okay."

"He's okay. Nikki might be bat-shit crazy, but she's his mother."

"Did you just call my ex-wife bat-shit crazy, Mom?" I snort, my mind still not sure if what I heard was a figment of my imagination or if Gladys can really be that dynamic.

"Don't tell your dad I said that." She laughs softly. "I picked up a few things from you over the years."

After I'm done expressing my frustration over my ex-wife's stunt in the most antagonistic way that no mother should ever hear, we talk for a few more minutes about less hazardous topics and say our goodbyes.

Three unread messages from Rachel are waiting for me around nine, once I'm done with my daily workout. Still sweaty, I walk over to the kitchen and grab a bottle of water from the fridge, settle at the empty table with my phone out in front of me, and absently stare at the texts.

Rachel: Have you thought about it?

Rachel: I'm free all day tomorrow.

Rachel: ?????

When did it exactly happen? When did the appeal of having a smoking hot woman doing all sorts of kinky shit to me stop tickling my fancy?

In a way, it scares me.

After a few more moments of contemplating, I open the iMessage and text Hazel.

Justice: Hey. Just wanted to say I'm sorry about the photo.

Nothing.

I shift in my chair, pop the plastic cap open, and down half the bottle in one go. I shouldn't feel bad, but I do. My eyes trail back to the screen of my phone.

Still nothing.

"Ah, fuck this," I mumble, getting up to my feet. The one time I actually want to make the better-man shit happen, the woman ignores me. Not like I give out tons of apologies on a daily basis. I don't have an unlimited stack of them.

Disappointed, I finish my water and head for the shower. Having Rachel come over no longer seems like a good backup plan. Sleep sounds like a better option, especially with Nikki making my existence beyond miserable the last couple of days.

Once I'm in my bed and staring at the dark brooding sky above my head, I'm trying to find at least one star hidden behind the thick layer of clouds when the phone chimes on the nightstand and interrupts the silence. I swear to fucking God, if this is Rachel I'm going to put a stop to this relationship once and for all. She knows better than this. No response means I'm not up for it, and she's never been into drama or wanting more than what we have, so right now, she's pissing me off.

Only, it's not Rachel.

Hazel: As long as this is as far as it goes. My friend's cabin is not equipped with anti-paparazzi protection.

I snort out a laugh and my pillow shakes with the movements of my body. A strange warmth envelops my chest, my heart might even skip a beat or two. This woman has a sense of humor when she's in the mood.

I wait for a few minutes, tossing some ideas around in my head, then send her a reply.

Justice: Mine is. You're welcome to come over.

A dangerous game, but since she's texting me this late... Right?

Hazel: You just can't stop, can you? Mr.ICANGETANYWOM-ANIWANT.

I stare at the text for a while, my brain reorganizing the last word to make some sense of it and when it's dissected, it fucking hurts.

Justice: Is that all you think I am?

Hazel: You haven't done anything to prove otherwise.

Justice: I took you to dinner and didn't try to fuck you.

Hazel: I didn't ask you to take me to dinner. Look how that turned out. Photo of you all over me up on all the celebrity gossip websites. And I'm not even a celebrity!

Oh, those exclamation marks. She is definitely pissed. If she keeps that all-caps game, I will flip my shit.

Justice: I apologized.

Hazel: It won't make the photo disappear.

Justice: It's a shit quality grainy picture, no one will ever know it's you.

Hazel: Better not because I'm adding it to your bill then.

Justice: ?

Hazel: I'm just kidding. I told you I don't need your money.

Justice: Don't do this. Just tell me how much you think this whole ordeal is worth and I will compensate your time and effort.

Hazel: My effort? I almost had a heart attack at the police station today. I think if I die from a heart attack, the money is useless.

Justice: I'm sorry it was uncomfortable. Will VIP access to all The Deviant shows for life be a better alternative?

Hazel: I haven't been to a concert in years. I'm not sure it's my thing at this point of my life. But thank you for the offer.

How can music no longer be a thing in someone's life? I would die if I were to go deaf or blind and not be able to write and perform. It's all I know and it's all I ever wanted to do.

Justice: I'd love for you to come to one of our shows. We go back on the road by summer. I hope you're still around.

Hazel: If this is your way of trying to sleep with me, forget about it.

Justice: Who said anything about sleeping?

Hazel: I'm just warning you before you get your hopes up.

Justice: That's not why I texted you. I am trying to do a better-man thing here.

Hazel: Is this another one of your tricks?

Justice: Nope.

Hazel: Okay. I'm going to finish my wine and get back to bed. I'm tired. Good night, rockstar.

Justice: Goodnight, Hazel.

My message still has the "delivered" stamp when I finally toss the phone aside and close my eyes. And as I listen to the steady rhythm of my own heartbeat drumming in my ears, sleep comes shortly after.

11 JUSTICE

THE OMINOUS POUNDING outside my bedroom is starting to get on my nerves. Shoving my face into the pillow, I curse inaudibly. I desperately want this racket to go away so I can catch up on my sleep. It takes me a good moment to come to terms with the fact that I'm not dreaming. Someone is in the hall, needing to see me. And the fucker is persistent.

"Justice?" Dom's voice drifts in from behind the door. "Are you there?"

Sitting up, I let out an exasperated growl. My eyes register the busy screen of my phone, notifications flooding it like never before. And since the band isn't in the middle of a press campaign, all those emails and messages are definitely more stupid shit added to the already existing pile.

I slide from the bed and grab a random t-shirt from the closet. "I'm up."

"You sleep like a rock," Dom snaps as I push past him into the hallway.

Ever since he walked in on me with two very creative Dutch chicks five years ago in Amsterdam, we have this silent agreement—he doesn't come into my bedroom unless I scream bloody murder. Funny, but after that European adventure, the number of times I engaged in threesomes shrunk significantly. The arrangement with Rachel seemed safe and interesting enough, but more importantly, she didn't need to be carded.

"I'm on vacation. Can I get some fucking privacy in my own place or what?" Sliding the t-shirt over my head, I stroll into the kitchen.

"Your face is all over the news again."

"What did Nikki do this time?" I ask, taking a long, deep breath to mentally prepare myself for another blow. Somewhere in my gut, there's a tiny hint of panic. What if she's claiming I hurt our son now since her devious plan portraying me as a guy who likes to kick the shit out of women didn't work? That pretty head of hers is twisted enough to come up with something that sick.

"It's not Nikki."

"What time is my flight?" I ask, looking at the digital clock on the microwave. It's almost noon.

"Ten after three."

"I think I'm starting to hate planes," I mumble to myself.

"They like her," Dom announces, throwing the magazine on the kitchen island, a picture of me and Hazel on the cover. Only, it's not the shitty quality one from yesterday's website. It's a damn good high-resolution photo, similar to the one I saw online, but the angle is slightly different with her face out in the open and me leaning into her, my hand resting on her cheek.

The headline makes me a little dizzy, though.

Justice Cross Has a New Woman: Is This Just a Fling or Is the Rockstar Finally Getting Serious? Find Out Inside.

Fuck.

I walk over to the island and carefully scan the cover of the magazine. These assholes work fast. It's already out in print. Cheap paper and flashy, cheesy headlines. The type of coverage I don't need or want.

"It's a feature too," Dom says sarcastically, flipping the pages and sliding the magazine in my direction.

"Right." I nod absently, staring at the blocks of paragraphs.

It's been a very long time since I've read something about myself in the press. May does that. She's not just my spokesperson; she has pretty much taken on the role of the part of my brain responsible for the stuff my fans get to read in all of my official statements and social media posts. I don't trust my own instincts, whether for making the big decisions that affect millions of people or for posting pictures of my food on my Instagram account. But right now, for some reason, I can't rip my eyes off the flimsy, low-budget magazine page because it makes me feel shitty for letting Hazel down.

A reliable source close to the actress confirms that she dropped the assault charges against her husband. She is still, however, insisting on his infidelity being the main reason for their separation earlier this year. Just a reminder, Justice Cross never denied spending time with another woman the night of the alleged assault, and now that we've taken a closer look at the marriage of the rock singer and Hollywood's hottest leading lady, we can't help but stop and wonder if Mr. Cross has been involved with the mysterious woman longer than he's led us to believe.

Twenty-six-year-old Hazel Tanner-Alexander is a college dropout who married her high school sweetheart at nineteen. The couple's son died due to complications caused by leukemia in September 2015. This might be just a coincidence, but the husband of soon-to-be Ms. Tanner (again) filed for divorce just a few weeks prior to when Mr. Cross's publicist confirmed the rock singer and his wife were officially calling it quits.

"What the fuck is this?" I grate out through clenched teeth. My heart bounces in my chest like a ping-pong ball, each slam hitting harder and harder against my ribs to the point where I can barely breathe through the pain.

Dominic slides his phone to me with the TMZ page already up.

"People seem to sympathize with her. It's all over Facebook and Twitter."

I'm too shocked to think clearly, let alone move a muscle. The idea itself of losing a child is horrifying. The fact that I know someone who's going through this pain is making my stomach churn. What if it were Aiden?

"You think I care if it's all over Facebook?" I toss the phone back to Dom without looking at it.

"No, Justice. I think it's very low to make a spectacle of a person who lost a child, but there's nothing we can do about it. Once it's out, it's out. You know how it is."

"Well, I don't find this crap entertaining!"

"What do you want me to do?" A barely visible line in his forehead deepens as he furrows his brow.

"Call May," I mutter on my way to the bedroom closet. Going back to the old no-comment tactic does seem appealing, but pretending that it doesn't bother me that some cheap, money-grabbing crooks that call themselves publications are printing this nonsense won't make Hazel feel any better.

"Where are you going?" Dom asks as I hurriedly slip into a pair of jeans.

"Out."

"You know there are two guys stalking your place from across the street. They've been sitting there since six this morning."

"Fucking great. Why don't I just invite them in for a cup of coffee and let them sort through my shit while I'm at it." I grab my leather jacket and my phone.

"You have to be at the airport in two and a half hours."

"I know." But deep down I don't care about the flight. There's always another one. It's not like I'm traveling to Cuba. I just can't leave her like this without saying anything, and apologizing over the phone like an insensitive jerk is out of the question.

"Just don't do anything stupid, man," Dom mutters as I breeze past him into the hallway, my heart racing.

"Heard that one before. Nikki will still find a way to make me look bad."

The menacing clouds on the horizon promise another surge of rain, which seems very fitting considering my shitty mood and the overall gloom that has taken over my world since the moment I read about Hazel's son. I hop behind the wheel of my Jeep, start the engine, and head for the gate, my eyes scanning Dom's silhouette in the rearview mirror as he remains still on the porch of my no-longer-secret spot. Maybe I should sell the cabin. Nikki storming through it with the divorce papers that night was bad luck.

As soon as the Jeep comes to a halt at a red light, I connect my phone to Bluetooth and call my lawyer.

"Any news on the restraining order?"

"I'm working on it, Justice."

"I'm going back to L.A. to see Aiden."

"You do understand that you can get arrested if you just show up on her doorstep, right?"

"It's still my fucking doorstep! I own the damn house."

"I know and trust me, I understand how you feel. But we'll fix it. I just need twenty-four hours. Meanwhile, sit tight and don't panic. She has no leverage."

I hate the fact that every single person I know tells me not to panic.

The first signs of rain on my windshield turn into a raging waterfall by the time I finally pull up into the short driveway of Hazel's cabin. The earlier phone conversation with my lawyer has made me jittery, so I sit in my car to collect my thoughts before I have to confront the woman who's been driving me mad these past couple of days. The rain rhythmically pelts against the roof of the Jeep almost in sync with my own heartbeat. It's both peaceful and troubling, like a lullaby that's sending you off into a dream that you know is going to be a nightmare.

All the little things about Hazel, those missing pieces of the puzzle, are suddenly starting to form into a picture, one I can see clearly and understand better now. The excessive drinking, the lack of judgment, the dull expression on her face, the absence of a smile. I hate it to the point that it hurts, even though I don't know how it feels to be in her shoes. At least not the part that's grieving the death of a child. Sure, losing my best friend wasn't any easier, but a child?

Finally, when my brain fully grasps the concept of facing the woman who's lost her son to a horrific disease, I get out of the Jeep and walk over to the front door, ignoring the streams of water falling beneath the collar of my leather jacket.

I press the doorbell a few times and wait. The things I wanted to say gradually disappear into nothing, turning my brain into a rut full of black useless matter that can no longer produce a coherent thought.

The subdued sound of the doorbell echoing against the walls of the cabin isn't very welcoming. My heart skips a beat when I hear her working the lock. She eases the door open, but not wide enough for me to step inside. Her sad amber eyes scan me absentmindedly, as if she's not sure who I am.

"What are you doing here?" The question comes in the form of a slurred whisper.

"Do you mind?" I try to keep my gaze on her face because her naked legs are a distraction when all she's wearing is a t-shirt that barely covers her thighs. "It's a little wet outside."

"Why are you here?" she asks, still guarding the entrance with her body.

"I just wanted to talk."

"About what?" She cocks her head.

"Come on, Hazel. I'm freezing my ass off out here." I push on the door slightly and brush past her into the living room. My eyes register a bottle of wine on the coffee table and another one on the kitchen counter along with a glass. What are the chances she finished them both?

I don't know how to do this. There's no right way to ask about the death of a child, but the question threatens to leave my mouth any second now. "Why didn't you tell me about your son?" I say quietly as she slowly closes the front door.

The silence that takes over the room is agonizing.

"It's none of your business." She exhales sharply, walking over to the kitchen counter to inspect the bottle of wine.

"Look...I—" My tongue is too stiff and the right words are no longer wanting to come out. It's just a jumbled monologue now. Phrases that don't make much sense. "I'm sorry, Hazel. I'm sorry it got out of hand and...I don't know how to fix it, but I wanted you to know that it wasn't my intention."

"It wasn't your intention? Well, what was your intention?" She scowls, pouring the last of the wine into her glass. "My face is all over the internet now. My phone has been going off since six this morning. I've got reporters emailing me, texting me, sending me messages on Facebook. My husband is probably thinking I've been cheating on him for months." She downs the drink in one go and angrily slams the glass against the kitchen counter. I'm surprised it doesn't crack from the impact.

"I'm sorry," I mutter, taking a step forward. The t-shirt she's wearing is too fucking short. The fact that she doesn't have a bra on underneath is even worse. I shouldn't even be thinking about her body while trying to apologize for dragging her into this crap, but the sick part of me, the guy who's used to women throwing themselves at him, keeps wondering what's under there. It's more of a reflex now after so many years of being spoiled, and it's fucking annoying because I can't turn it off.

"You know what, Justice?" She stomps past me into the living room, barefoot, hair flying, totally clueless that she's making it very hard for me not to stare at her the way I shouldn't. Because it's fucking wrong. Obviously, now that I know why she's not interested in me, or men in general, it makes me feel like a total idiot for throwing all those sexual comments at her.

"All I really wanted was a few weeks alone." She stops in her tracks and spins in my direction. "And you fucking took that away from me, and now you think that your rock 'n' roll apology in the form of a fat check is going to make it better." Her eyes darken, and her voice is on the verge of breaking. "So why don't you shove your apology along with your money up your rich ass and leave me the hell alone?"

I swallow hard, still not sure my words are going to make any difference, but leaving without letting her know how sorry I truly am about all the press hustle she's been put through because of me would be the coward's way out.

"Can you just give me two minutes of your time, Hazel?" I ask quietly, taking a cautious step forward.

She keeps nibbling on her lower lip, arms crossed on her chest, eyes peering at me from under her lashes. I can tell she's been crying by that tortured expression on her face.

"I'm really am so sorry I'm putting you through this." My voice is a bit on the shaky side. "I wish you'd told me about your son. I wouldn't have asked you to cover my ass..."

"Don't talk about him, okay?" she murmurs, shuffling her feet.

"I'm not trying to—"

She cuts me off before I get to finish my sentence. "You don't have the right. Just stop it and get out. Leave me alone." Tears start streaming down her cheeks.

I'd be happy to. I don't fucking like this type of drama. That's something I've been trying to stay away from since I came to terms with Chance's OD. Going back into that world of darkness and despair is not a trip I plan on taking, not when I have tons of other issues in my life, like my wife trying to take away my son. Yet, part of me isn't ready to go. It's not okay to just walk out on a woman having a meltdown, is it? Especially if she doesn't know when to stop drinking.

"Hazel."

"I don't want you here, Justice." Her tears turn to sobs. "Can't you see that?"

I take another step forward, thinking that maybe the best thing right now is to ask her to put some clothes on because this place is cold as a fucking tomb and I can clearly see that she's shaking.

"I don't need your pity!" she barks out. "Or your apologies." Her fist lands on my chest when I close the space between us in two strides.

My attempt to intercept her second blow is pathetic. I guess I didn't really expect this much fury from someone so fragile. She's not short, but from what I can gather, the wine dinners and the occasional Chinese food must be the main reason for her being this thin.

"Stop it!" I grab her wrist as she launches her fist at me again. This time the impact is harder, and I can feel my heart wincing in my chest.

"I hate you!" She sobs into my neck as I wrap my arms around her to keep her from hitting me. "Leave me alone."

"Stop it, Hazel. I've got you." I scoop her into a tight embrace.

"You don't have the right to talk about my son. You don't!" she cries out. Her body is thrashing against mine now as she attempts to break free from my grasp.

"Please, just stop...I'm sorry," I tell her, refusing to let go. "Just stop." Her foot lands on my boot.

I let her silently assault me until there's nothing left, until she's quiet in my arms with her face against my t-shirt that's now damp with her tears. The most awkward moment I've ever had with a half-naked woman. I don't know what to say or what to do really. This vaguely reminds me of Chance's OD. The main difference being that right now there's no foam coming out of Hazel's mouth and she's not having a real seizure. So I just keep holding her while I wait for her to calm down, listening to her occasional inaudible sobs and her uneven breathing as I try to ignore the fact that, despite the drunken hysteria, she feels as if she belongs here—in my arms.

After a while, I slowly unlock my grasp, letting my hand cup the back of her head. Her hair is soft and silky, perfect to the touch, and it smells like coconut.

Suddenly I'm lost in the scent and the warmth of her body, a body that's pressed to mine in a way it shouldn't be. Her hot breath tickling my neck and her tiny fingers tangled in my jacket create a strange burning sensation in my chest. I rub my unshaven cheek against hers, and as my hand continues to cradle the back of her head, she thrusts her chin into the crook of my neck. This is the first time in my life a closeness has scared me, because ten minutes ago, she was literally kicking me out, and now our bodies are molded together in the middle of her living room and she's no longer resisting my touch.

I don't know whether it's my desire to have a little taste or simply an impulse, but I gently brush my lips over her temple and wait for her reaction. When she digs her fingers deeper into the folds of my jacket, I feel like my heart is running a fucking marathon, which is both pleasing and terrifying. I trace a slow, barely-there kiss down her cheek and stop when my lips reach the corner of her mouth. There's a moment of deafening silence and the only thing I can hear is leather squeaking as she readjusts her grip and the sound of my own heart-beat pounding in my ears while my blood rushes to the southern region of my body. Fuck.

Then I hungrily cover her mouth with mine as my fingers slide to the back of her neck, pulling her in the direction of the kiss. Her lips are soft at first, unresponsive even, but then she matches the strokes of my tongue almost instantly. Her body tenses and her breath hitches, a soft moan escaping the back of her throat as she tugs on my jacket for balance. I've never heard a sound like it before, a combination of suggestive and pure. As if she just had her first sip of water after a year in the desert.

My mind is far away when she pulls back, her hands shoving against my chest. Then she takes a step back and slaps me. Fucking hard. Not the stars-seeing kind of hard, but it's goddamn unexpected because two seconds ago she seemed to be enjoying my tongue exploring her mouth.

"What's that for?" I choke out, rubbing my burning cheek.

"Get out," she hisses through her teeth.

"I thought—"

"Get out."

Her eyes are two dark pools of anger.

"Fine." I take a deep breath and head for the door, back into the pouring rain, back to my rich-and-famous-people problems.

My cheek is still burning when I pull over two blocks away from Hazel's place. I put the gear in neutral and inhale sharply, my fingers choking the steering wheel as my mind races. The merciless rain beating against the windshield is driving me nuts. I can't think, I can't breathe, I can't fucking drive.

After the initial shock of everything that just happened at Hazel's place wears off, I scramble for my phone and dial May.

"Don't worry about it, Justice," she says, straight to the point as if she just read my mind. "Most likely it's Nikki's hired guns baiting you."

"You want me to sit this one out?"

"Yes, TMZ just interviewed Hazel and Owen's neighbor. Over thirty thousand hits on YouTube already. I think publicly defending this woman on your social media won't look good. Especially right now."

"I don't care what you think. It's fucking low to put someone's life on display like that." At this point I'm not sure if I'm mad at the press or myself. "So I want you to make sure everyone knows where I stand."

"Fine. Talk to you later."

I end the call and just sit with my eyes fixed on the wet road ahead. Not sure for how long. Until the sound of my ringtone drags me back to reality.

"Yeah?"

"You're going to miss your flight." Dom's gravelly voice fills my head.

"Okay."

"Okay what? You want me to get you on the next one?"

"Yeah," I whisper, jerking the gear lever.

Hazel made me fucking late. I should be pissed. Only, I'm not.

12 HAZEL

THE AROMA of the freshly brewed coffee is finally starting to wake me. I walk over to the fridge and scan the empty shelves for some dairy. My growling stomach reminds me that it hasn't seen anything solid in at least two days, maybe more. I haven't been keeping track of time since the self-serving prick of a rockstar fled the cabin, leaving me speechless, mad, terrified, and shaking all at once.

While my eyes are doing another pointless trip around the fridge, my mind pulls me back to the memories of the kiss; his strong arms wrapped about my body felt almost comforting and at the same time completely wrong. Upon the completion of my fridge inspection, I come to terms with drinking my coffee black. At least there's still sugar.

I prop myself against the kitchen counter and look at the pot, my eyes following the dark liquid as it drips into the dense pool of blackness. I find watching the brewing process therapeutic.

A noise at the front door startles me. The first thought that comes to mind is that I'm either being robbed or ambushed by the reporters, but as soon as I see a tiny Hispanic woman enter the cabin, I realize she's Ester.

I take the coffee to my room, leaving the housekeeper to her chores.

Dread simmers in my belly as I sit on the edge of the bed and sip the steaming hot liquid. Part of me wants to stay in the dark, but part of me understands I need to let my parents know I'm alive before they organize a search party or send the police to check on me.

Setting the mug on the nightstand, I retrieve the charger from the drawer, plug it into the outlet, and connect to my phone, waiting for the white Apple logo to come up on the dark lifeless screen.

My mind starts drifting back to the kiss again. Part of me tries to relive the moment because it felt good to have someone hug me like Justice did. Undeniably. Fiercely. The way his body molded to mine was not just eye-opening but also mind-blowing. Owen hasn't touched me that way since before River's death. Actually, no one has ever touched me that way. Not even Owen.

A slight shiver runs down my spine as I close my eyes to recreate the taste of his lips and tongue on mine. Firm and demanding, like a twister, sucking me into whirlwind of repressed emotions and strange hidden desires.

The unexpected vibration yanking me out of my deep thoughts indicates the resurrection of my phone is complete. Now it's all about keeping calm while facing the wrath of the people whom I forgot to remember yesterday because I slept through Thanksgiving.

I take a few more sips of my coffee, set it back on the nightstand, and start reading.

Mom: Is everything okay? Would you call us, please?

Mom: Honey, some people came in asking for you yesterday. They said they were from some magazine. Please call us.

Rayna: OH MY FUCKING GOD, HAZEL! WHY IS YOUR FACE ALL OVER THE INTERNET?

Justice: I'm very sorry. Can you please pick up the phone?

Rayna: HAZEL? IS THIS TRUE? ARE YOU DATING JUSTICE CROSS?

Justice: Can we talk?

Unknown: Hi, Hazel. This is Rich from HotXShotMazagine.com. I would love to interview you for our next issue. Are you available this weekend?

Really?

Dad: Happy Thanksgiving. Call us.

Justice: I'm sorry. Can we talk?

Justice: Are you okay?

Justice: I'm going to make Dom fly back to Tahoe if you don't at least text me back and let me know you're okay. I'm sorry about everything.

Justice: Hazel? Please don't make me send Dom to check on you.

This man is persistent. He really doesn't take no for an answer, does he?

I shift on the bed and skim through the list of missed calls without bothering to check the voicemails. They're all from the reporters, which scares the hell out of me. One minute, I'm a nobody, and the next, every news outlet on the planet wants to talk to me about my affair with Justice Cross.

After finishing my coffee, I head to the bathroom and take a long hot shower. Getting rid of the sticky layer of sweat that's been covering my body for several days feels liberating, almost as if I'm a new person. At least on the outside.

While I stand under the stream of water, I weigh my options to decide who to call first—Owen or Justice. My mind is tired and I don't feel like discussing the divorce and the tabloid stuff with my ex just yet, although I know it's inevitable. The story is out there. I'm a little surprised he hasn't initiated the conversation first.

Once finished with the shower, I blow dry my hair, look for a clean pair of jeans and a sweater, and gather some of my dirty clothes into a basket and take it to the laundry room out back to have Ester wash it.

"Oh, Miss Hazel? You're leaving?" Her head pops up from under the tabletop as I stroll into the living room.

"I don't want to be in your way...I'll go grab something to eat."

"I cook," she says, getting back to her feet with a sponge in one hand and a bottle of cleaner in the other.

"You don't have to."

"It's okay. Miss Rayna pay me." This woman reminds me of Justice. She doesn't take no for an answer.

"I'll eat it for dinner then. That okay?" I sense that refusing the homemade food offer will offend her cooking skills.

"Sí. I make for three days." Ester's face beams with pride. "You eat meat, Miss Hazel, or only vegetarian?"

"Meat is fine." I squeeze out a smile, looking around the living room in an attempt to locate my coat. A huge colorful flower arrangement set up on the table by the window grabs my attention.

How did I not notice that before? "What is this?" I ask, walking over to the table.

"Oh, this came when you were in the shower, Miss. Hazel. I sign for you." She grins, giving me an encouraging nod to let me know it's okay to touch the flowers as I keep eyeing them suspiciously.

"Thank you." I scan the exquisite lush petals of white lilies tucked in between the red roses and pink carnations. This doesn't seem like something my ex-husband, who's requesting I sign the divorce papers as soon as possible, would do. Especially not after the tabloids.

"Very pretty. Looks expensive too," Ester states from back under the table. "Miss Hazel has a new boyfriend?"

I ignore the last remark. Brushing my fingers against the soft blooming beauty, I spin the vase a little and notice a small note tucked behind one of the lilies.

Hazel, I'm very sorry about what happened. I just need to know you're okay. I'm worried. If you can call me or text me and let me know you're fine, I'll back off. Promise.
Justice.

He makes it really difficult for me to hate him. Especially without those silly crosses he used once as a part of his signature. The man's ego is bigger than his fan base, but right now he's finding a way to creep into my heart against my will.

The realization that I picked the worst day of the year to eat out hits me only after I find myself stuck in a huge jammed parking lot at the local shopping center. It had to be Black Friday, right?

I let out an exasperated sigh and hit the gas, my Prius moving forward just a couple of inches. My eyes carefully inspect the cracks and crevices of this vehicular hell in search of an empty spot. People go about their business, talking and laughing, while the huge colorful shopping bags and the happiness flickering in their eyes both seem trivial to them. Watching the holiday madness through the windshield of my car feels like taking a peek into a different dimension, the one I don't belong to anymore.

Loud honking coming from behind me snaps me back to the world of post-Thanksgiving insanity, and by the time I find an empty space, the acidic stinging in my stomach is unbearable and I feel like throwing up. The holiday noise swallows me as soon as I step out of the car, and my lungs constrict from the exhaust fumes filling the chill November air. I feel dizzy and disoriented, not sure where to go next, not sure why I'm here anymore.

For a while, I just wander through the crowds without any sense of direction, staring at the merchandise through the large display windows until one of the stores grabs my attention. I stop in my tracks and take in the sight of the painting supplies neatly set up on the opposite side of the glass wall. My heart starts to race. I'm not sure why I abandoned my watercolors. I loved painting when I was in school, and I was really good. But that was over ten years ago. Hazel Alexander was a different person back then. She was Hazel Tanner. She was happy.

Shaking off the depressing thoughts, I decide to get something to eat.

Once in the restaurant, I ask for a table in the corner, away from the traffic and kitchen noise, away from people. The responsible daughter in me finally musters up enough courage to text back her parents and let them know she's okay. Explaining the Justice Cross gossip to Rayna will be much harder. It can probably wait until we have an actual phone conversation.

The waitress brings out my food twenty minutes later. She smiles politely, asks if I need anything else, and then leaves. After sending a few pieces of the hot cheesy meatloaf into my mouth, I fall back in my chair and let the food settle. It's been so long since I ate real hot, homemade food that I'm not sure my stomach isn't going to send it back up. Of course, this isn't as good as my mother's or my own cooking, but right now it's as close as it gets.

My eyes keep returning to my phone sitting next to the glass of water. Deep down I know this madness needs to be stopped before it turns into a bigger nightmare, but the vision of the fresh lilies and roses is already corrupting my brain. It's nice to feel like a real woman for once.

My hand is shaking a bit when I finally pick up the phone and text Justice.

Hazel: Thank you for the flowers. You didn't have to do that.

The reply comes instantly.

Justice: I wanted to. I feel really bad about what happened on Tuesday. I'm sorry.

Hazel: It's fine. I'm not mad. Just overwhelmed. The reporters won't stop emailing and calling.

Justice: I'm sorry. Anything I can do?

Hazel: Tell them to go stalk someone else? LOL

Justice: I wish I could. Happy late Thanksgiving, by the way.

Hazel: Same to you.

Justice: Did you do anything?

Hazel: I slept. You?

Justice: Aiden and I are hanging out at my parents'.

Hazel: No more restraining order?

Justice: No. We came back yesterday morning.

Hazel: I'm glad it worked out.

Justice: You made me miss my flight on Tuesday.

My heart spasms in my chest. I look away from the screen of my phone and draw a deep breath before getting back to texting.

Hazel: I'm sorry.

Justice: Don't be. I'm the one who is sorry for dragging you into my mess. And I'm sorry for messaging you and calling you like crazy. I just wanted to make sure you were okay.

Hazel: I'm okay.

Justice: Do you want to have dinner with me?

Hazel: You and me in public is not a good combination.

Justice: I mean like friends. No ulterior motives. I will behave. Promise. Besides, half the planet thinks we're dating.

Hazel: I don't think it's a good idea, Justice. Goodbye.

The meatloaf is cold by the time our text marathon ends. My appetite is also gone. Along with the desire to try and be a normal person for at least a few more hours. I ask for the check and politely refuse the offer to take the rest of my meal to go since Ester is going to load the kitchen up with three days' worth of food.

The waitress is back in less than a minute. "I'm sorry, ma'am, but your card has been declined," she whispers, giving me an apologetic smile.

"What?" I stare at my Visa with the receipt attached to it for a few moments. My brain is processing the information, but apparently not fast enough because the woman is already asking for another method of payment while I'm still trying to understand why the credit card that's been working for me for years is no longer cooperating.

"Let me see if I have enough cash. Can you try it again?" I fist the folds of my bag to try to find some money.

"I did. Twice." The waitress forces out another smile, but this time, the frustration on her face is evident.

"Okay." Thankfully, there's a loose twenty in the bottom of my purse. I hand the bill to the waitress and tell her to keep the change.

As soon as I step outside, I call Owen. He doesn't pick up. After two more attempts, I send him a text.

Hazel: Did you pay the credit card bill this month?

No response. Great. He's ignoring me.

I tuck the phone back in the pocket of my coat and step into the human traffic that carries me in the direction of the department store.

You sure know how to pick the time to go out and try to be normal, Hazel. Busiest day of the year is perfect, isn't it?

Despite the crowd rushing me toward the store, I manage to find the perfect pace that gives me an opportunity to stare at all the holiday merchandise on display in the quaint boutiques. How awesome it would be to have River with me now. I can almost imagine his small hand in mine as we walk side by side, wowed by the abundance of colorful lights and ornaments. He loved Christmas decorations. Owen and I never brought him to Tahoe. Not once in his life did my baby see real snow. Fake snow at the mall? Yes, a few times. But not the real stuff that falls from the sky, soft and fuzzy-looking pieces of magic, little crystals that melt once they land on your tongue. I don't know why we didn't bring our son here.

As much as I hate it, I break out in tears when I lay my eyes on the large window of a children's clothing store. Part of me wants to run back to my car and drive off, but my body's suddenly dead frozen. I can't move a finger, let alone step aside at the request of some large, angry woman rolling a shopping cart through the human mass. Seeing the tiny shoes and jackets on display makes my heart hurt, and the warmth in my chest turns into a black hole. I nervously wipe off the tears with the back of my hand and start walking away from the store, my feet carrying me into nothing until I can't fight the crowds anymore. Their voices, all meshed into one irritating happy growl, are making me sick. I duck in the direction of a glass door that leads to a store that seems like an appropriate place to escape because it's free of people.

The chime above my head announces my entry before I even realize where exactly my scattered brain has led me, but the soft music playing in the background and the quiet from the shopping madness are oddly inviting. Two girls wearing all black and a guy in a pink shirt with an Elvis-style haircut gawk at me from behind the reception desk.

"Hi." The girl with short purple hair bats her long lashes at me and gives me a wide smile. "Do you have an appointment?"

"No." I shake my head, scanning the empty chairs and stylist stations lined up along the wall-to-wall mirrors on both sides of the store.

"She doesn't need an appointment, honey." The guy in the pink shirt steps in, first giving the side-eye to his co-worker and then switching his full attention to me. "She needs a haircut and color. Right, babe?" His charming grin isn't the kind one can say no to.

"Sure." I swallow hard. "I guess so."

"Come on." He winks. "We'll princess you up for the holidays."

Princess me up? I take a deep, shaky breath and follow him to one of the chairs.

13 HAZEL

The person staring at me from the infinite mirror wall above the station is now a very vague reminder of what a depressed failure of a mom Hazel Alexander used to look like. Right now, she's the girl with the brand-new golden locks who shed about five or six years of her pathetic life after spending two and a half hours in the salon chair under the masterful hands of Sidney, her new favorite person of the year.

"You look fab, babe." He claps again, and his co-workers nod in agreement as I carefully scan the waves of my reborn hair. Even my face is different. Younger, bolder—I still have those shadows under my eyes, but it's nothing a tiny bit of a concealer can't fix, right?

The question is, who are you trying to impress, Hazel?

Mr. Rockstar? You know he's off-limits and probably not interested in anything but fucking you on a bet with his manager or just to have checkmark next to your name on his sex list.

I exhale sharply and shake off the silly idea. This is stupid. I don't need to impress anyone. The trip is my attempt to make some changes in my life. That's exactly what I just did. Made a change.

My excitement over my new haircut ends, however, when I get the same response from the girl at the front desk as I did earlier at the restaurant. My other card is declined too. I feel both embarrassed and mad. Embarrassed because I don't have three hundred dollars in cash to pay for my new hair, and mad because Owen still hasn't returned my message about the credit cards. Like he wasn't the one demanding me to sign the divorce papers.

"I'm so sorry," I whimper to Sidney, handing another Visa to the receptionist. "Can you try this one?"

"Sorry, this one was declined too," the front desk girl says, smiling. Her smile doesn't reach her eyes, though.

"Are you sure? Do you mind if I just call my bank and see what's going on?" My cheeks and my ears and burning with shame.

The bank has me on hold for over twenty minutes just to tell me that Owen hasn't made any payments yet.

Goddamn you, Justice, and your stupid tabloids.

"I really am sorry for the inconvenience," I mumble apologetically for the hundredth time after an hour of hanging around the reception area. "I promise I'll pay. You can invoice me and as soon as my bank fixes the problem, I will—"

All three workers are giving me the stink eye, probably thinking I walked in their salon determined to get a freebie on purpose. I don't blame them. I blame myself for being so thoughtless as to have this poor guy use all his magic on me while my cards were obviously not good. With a huge frown on his face, Sidney collects my information along with the copy of my driver's license and less than reluctantly lets me go.

My head is spinning on the way back to my car. I'm out of money and I probably need to cut my vacation short and go back to L.A. to look for a job. Then when it rains, it pours. When I try to start my Prius, the buzzing coming from the vicinity of the engine isn't what the car usually sounds like. I turn they key again. Nothing.

"You gotta be fucking kidding me!" I slam both hands against my knees.

After the AAA operator wraps up her dull, lengthy greeting by asking me the number on my membership card, I recite the digits one by one, as slowly as possible for good measure, crossing my fingers it's still valid. I don't even remember when their services were used last.

"I'm sorry, but it looks like the membership expired in August, Mrs. Alexander," the girl says. For a brief moment, I'm not sure what ticks me off the most—*Mrs. Alexander* or the fact that I can't get roadside assistance.

"Okay, can you just renew it with the card on file?" I ask, fidgeting in my seat, sweat breaking under the thick fabric of my sweater.

"I'm sorry. We don't retain our clients' credit card information. Would you like to make the annual payment right now?"

"How?!" I snap, slamming the back of my head against the headrest.

"Excuse me?" The operator sounds a little confused.

"Okay... Can you try this card?" In desperation, I pull out my Visa, the one that was declined earlier in the hair salon, and read the card number.

"Sorry, Mrs. Alexander," the girl says.

After ending the call with AAA, I get out of the car and scan the crowd. Surely someone will have jumper cables stashed in the trunk.

The first victim, an older man with just one shopping bag and a pair of headphones dangling from under his collar, is a no go. The second person simply brushes me off. I give up after the third attempt. People don't seem to be paying attention to anything but Black Friday specials.

I sit in my car for a while, fighting the tears, contemplating if this is the right time to take Justice up on his offer. Yes, egotistic, oversexualized rockstar Justice Cross who sent me a bunch of flowers today.

Part of me hopes he doesn't pick up the phone, but he does.

"Do I hear the sound of apocalypse?" he asks.

"No, just me." I sniff, which doesn't help my feeble attempts at not coming off as too needy. "You owe me, remember?"

"I sure do. You got a number for me?" His voice has this incredible ability to change from deep and clear to low and raspy. The man can sure speak beautifully.

Is that the flowers polluting your brain, Hazel?

"Actually, it's more of a favor," I say meekly. "I'm having car trouble and I need a ride home. My AAA membership expired and looks like my card is blocked, so..."

"Sounds like you're having a shitty day."

"You don't want to know." I shake my head, a smile breaking on my lips for some reason.

"Where are you?"

"I'm at the Plaza."

"Tahoe Plaza?"

"Yes." I feel like shit for disturbing his family time. "In the parking lot across from Macy's."

"I'll be there within an hour."

"No... You don't have to come!" I cry out. "I was going to see if I could borrow your AAA membership."

"I'll be there within an hour," he insists.

"Justice—"

"Just hang in there. Help is on the way." He ends the call before I get a chance to open my mouth.

The knock on my car's window comes forty-five minutes later. I shift in my seat and look through the tinted glass. A black baseball cap with the multicolored X-Men moniker enters my line of vision first. Then seeing the gray eyes staring right back at me from under the visor causes my heart to jump in my throat.

"You didn't have to do this," I say, pushing the door slightly open.

Justice moves to the side and pops his head in the car, placing both hands on the roof. "You look nice. I like the new hair."

"Thanks." God, please don't let me blush. Crap. Too late. I can feel the blood rushing to my face like lava.

"You don't have roadside assistance from Toyota?"

"We didn't buy that feature when we got the car," I explain, taking a deep breath as my heart does summersaults in my chest.

"Alright. Let me take you home." He straightens up.

"What about my car?" I grab my purse and follow him out.

"Dom will take care of it." Justice points at Dominic's head on the opposite side of the Prius, iPhone molded to his ear, a serious expression on his tired face. "Give me your car keys."

My mouth falls open. "You brought your manager too?" I shut the door of the car and hand Justice my keys. He waves at Dominic and tosses them to him.

My body and mind are too aware of the livid crowd and the annoying noise in the parking lot, suddenly hitting every one of my cells. But what really bothers me is how effectively Justice positions himself, his height towering over mine as he places his hands back on the roof of my car, trapping me between his body and the Prius.

"I try not to." He licks his lips. "But if you need a favor, I can't say no, can I?" He smirks, taking a half step forward. Even in this horrible hat, he still looks intriguing, rebellious, and sexy. Something my brain shouldn't be paying attention to, but it does, so the images of us kissing in Rayna's cabin slowly creep back into my consciousness. And I secretly hate that he has this effect on me, because I can't turn it off. I don't know how.

"You don't have to do all this, Justice," I whisper, nervously looking around.

"We're seeing each other, remember?" He laughs a little, this time warmer and without the usual manufactured sex appeal he always injects into his behavior when in public.

"No, we're not."

"Well, that's between me and you, but the rest of the world thinks we are. Might as well take advantage of that. There are two dudes across the lot already filming us on their cell phones. Next to the pickup truck. Six o'clock."

"Are you kidding me?" I gasp, turning my head.

"Don't stare," he murmurs, cupping my cheek and forcing me to look back at him. His thumb makes a circular movement, caressing my skin.

"Seriously, Justice? Are you doing it for the press?" I shove my purse into his groin area. Letting him touch me the way he does is not going to end up well, and falling for his trap in a public place is the last thing I plan to do.

"Ouch." He groans but doesn't back down. "That was low, babe."

"I didn't even hit you that hard." I put my other hand on his chest and apply some pressure.

"Sorry." He inhales sharply and steps back some, the perfect opportunity for me to wiggle my way past this blockade.

"I have second thoughts about accepting a ride from you now."

"Come on. I'll take you home. I'm sorry. I'm an ass." He hooks his arm through mine and pulls me away from the Prius and right into a group of teens, causing an unexpected commotion next to my car. I start to believe he's accidentally stomped one of the passersby to death, because the shriek that emanates from the crowd is downright scary, but the one that comes right after is definitely a cry of adoration, which in my book is even worse.

"Oh my God! Are you Justice Cross?" The girl's scream causes a wave of shock among the shoppers. Two seconds later, half of the parking lot is headed in our direction, girls and guys of all ages swarming like bees. Dominic is off the phone, fighting his way in.

"I'm so in love with your last album! "Sin with Me" is my favorite song!"

"Can you take a photo with me and my friend, Justice? You're the best rock singer ever!"

His arm is no longer wrapped around mine because he's busy posing for the selfies while I'm being sandwiched by a group of teens.

"Can you do one without the hat?"

Oh, God, these fans are demanding! I think to myself as I watch him throwing the devil's horns up for the camera. Then I notice that someone is pulling on the sleeve of my coat.

"You're Hazel, aren't you?" a pink-haired girl who's probably about my age asks as I spin around on my heels. Her baby blue eyes are eating me up.

"Excuse me?" An incoherent insult escapes my mouth.

"I read about your little boy. I'm very sorry for your loss," she says, her voice vanishing into the ruckus of all the others.

I'm not sure how to answer that, but I know I don't want to be surrounded by a crowd of raging fans ready to rip out each other's eyes for a photo with the singer who made it to number twenty-four on *People* magazine's Sexiest Man Alive list.

"I'm shipping you two. Do you have a Twitter account?" the girl asks.

"Twitter?" My tongue refuses to do what my brain thinks it should.

"Yeah, you need to sign up if you don't have an account. Look up hashtag *Jazel*. It's been trending all week." The girl's grin is bigger than her whole face.

"What's Jazel?" I ask, feeling somewhat lost in her explanation.

"That's your ship name. You and Justice. I hope you guys are together for good. Nikki Deville is a bitch."

"Right." I nod absentmindedly, my heart racing.

"Hey, nice to meet you, Hazel." The pink hair tips her chin. "I'm gonna go get a photo with your man. Can't fucking wait for the new album."

Before I get a chance to take the Twitter information in, another girl about the same age jumps on my pink-haired fan and says, batting her fake purple lashes at me, "You're pretty. Justice will make you a cute baby. Have you met Aiden? He's adorable."

My body begins to shake violently as anger and frustration take over my world. I'm two seconds away from screaming when Dominic pulls me from the crowd. Hot tears are streaming down my cheeks, and I don't really care that people can see me crying. My face is all over the tabloids anyway.

"Let's go," he mutters, protectively throwing his arm over my shoulder. "His fans are a little nutty."

"You don't say." I sniff.

"Come on, the guy writes songs about having oral sex in a church. Normal people don't listen to that."

"Oral sex?" I ask in disbelief, trying to think of which track that might be.

"What did you think "The Temple of Love" was about?" Dominic chuckles, opening the passenger door of the Jeep that's shamelessly occupying the curbside to-go parking spot.

"I wish I could un-know that," I mumble, getting inside. Right now, my shit is a thousand different things but together.

The impromptu autograph session is over ten minutes later. By that time, I'm on pins and needles, wanting to get out of this parking lot before gossip and celebrity-selfie-hungry people start attacking the Jeep. I can already imagine this mall trip turning into an episode of *The Walking Dead*, with The Deviant admirers trying to break the windows to get a little piece of Justice Cross. Nikki Deville must be just as crazy as his fans if she married the guy.

"I'm really sorry about that, Hazel." Justice gets behind the wheel and starts the car.

"Did you know that we have a ship name?" I ask with a straight face as he slowly backs up into the traffic. "Apparently, we're hashtag Jazel on Twitter."

"That's an ugly name for a ship." He laughs softly.

"I don't want us to be a ship, Justice. I'm sure my husband cut off all my credit cards because he thinks you can now buy me my AAA roadside assistance."

"That's a douchey thing. I'm leaving my wife our Malibu mansion and your ex is screwing you over forty bucks?"

"I haven't even paid for this stupid haircut yet," I cry out, fighting the urge to hit something.

"How much do you need?"

"I don't want your money and I don't want your crazy fans to make us into a ship! The only ship name that works for us is the fucking Titanic!" My raised voice cracks as I keep propelling all my frustration at him. Probably not a good idea while trying to merge with the traffic, but my patience is running thin after the cute baby comment from one of the girls.

There's a long pause filled with nothing but the humming of the engine and hushed sounds of the outside noise. I press my forehead against the cold tinted window of the Jeep and stare at the hordes of shoppers disappearing on the horizon as we leave the Plaza.

"I'm sorry about the little hiccup in the parking lot," Justice says, his hand reaching out for mine.

"That's okay," I whisper under my breath. Part of me hates his touch, but not because it's unpleasant. On the contrary, it's like a security blanket, warm and comforting, luring me into the abyss of wanting more. It's all I think about until we get to the cabin.

"Thanks for the ride." I grab hold of the door handle as soon as the car comes to a stop.

"Anytime, babe." He grins.

"I appreciate the roadside assistance."

"Justice Cross Auto Repair and Towing at your service twenty-four hours a day."

I can barely hold back a giggle. "Are you trying to be cute to impress me, Mr. Rockstar?"

"I'm trying to make you smile, babe." His gray eyes lock on mine.

"Looks like it's working." I tighten my fingers around the handle.

"Hey... Do you mind if I use your bathroom?" he asks, shifting in his seat. "It's a long drive back to my place."

"Okay, sure," I say, hoping Ester is done with her cleaning by now.

In silence, we walk up to the porch. I fish for the keys in the folds of my purse and unlock the front door. Just as expected, the place is spotless with the soft pumpkin aroma in the air, and the flower arrangement is now on the table in the breakfast nook.

"It's the last door on the right." I point in the direction of the bathroom while trying to find my iPad. The fact that Owen didn't even give me a warning about the credit card being cut off is bugging me.

When Justice walks back into the kitchen, my heart is still racing, but mostly from all the hand-holding earlier in the car rather than the online banking fiasco I'm trying to figure out. I shift on my stool and clear my throat. The screaming episode made my vocal cords stiff and scratchy.

"I wasn't sure which ones you liked," he says, rocking on his heels, hands tucked in the pockets of his jacket. My guess is this is one of his stalling techniques.

"What do you mean?" I ask, looking up from the iPad. My mind is struggling with the accounting tasks. I never was good with numbers. So much for having an accountant for a father.

"The flowers," he explains. "I wasn't sure which flowers you liked."

"They're all very pretty. Thanks. You really didn't have to do that." Who am I kidding? I loved it. No matter how much I try to resist the charm of Justice Cross, it's simply impossible, especially with him being...almost normal.

"Look, I feel like shit...for the tabloid stuff," he stammers, locking his gaze on mine. "And I don't normally feel like shit. Ever."

"Because you're an ass?" I bite back a smile.

"Pretty much."

"Ummm..." I have to look away for a second because I'm suddenly drowning in those gray pools of his eyes. The mixture of confusing emotions come crashing at me like a hundred-foot-tall tsunami wave, sending my body into a state of shock. "Do you want to see photos of my son?" I say the first thing that comes to mind. My voice is barely a whisper. Part of me still doesn't want to share but deep inside I know that not talking about my boy isn't fair. How am I going to remember him if he's only in my head?

"I'd love to," Justice says, walking over to the breakfast nook table. He pulls up a stool and sits next to me.

With my shaking hand, I exit online banking and open my River folder, thousands and thousands of short moments of my son's life.

"He loved to pose," I explain as we flip through the images, Justice studying each one carefully in silence.

"Your little man knows how to work the camera." Present tense.

"Yeah...We took a lot of pictures. I have some prints too." *The prints Owen didn't want in our house.* I draw a deep breath, trying my best not to burst into tears. "He was diagnosed right after his birth...so..." The air in my lungs disappears. "I wanted as many as possible. I knew he wasn't going to make it, but he wanted to live so badly. He fought so hard." The tremor in my body becomes violent, but I can't make it stop. Then the words just keep pouring out. "When I got pregnant, I was so confused. It was an accident. Owen freaked out. But after I held him for the first time, it was like...everything changed in a heartbeat. He was so tiny and he was crying, and all I wanted for him was just to know that I was there and I was going to take care of him. I had all this love I planned on giving him until the day I die, and now he's gone and I have no one to give this love to and it's suffocating me."

Without warning, the air is so thick and heavy that I can't get it into my lungs. The room starts spinning, the pictures become too much. I let out a stifled sob and press the iPad against my chest. Maybe if I hug it hard enough, I could feel my little boy hugging me back. Just for a second. I would give anything to feel his tiny body and to hear the sound of his soft heartbeat.

"Shit. I'm sorry," Justice murmurs, wrapping his arms around me, his hand sliding to the back of my neck as he scoots toward me.

"Please...don't," I whisper. "If you try to kiss me right now, I'll hate you for the rest of eternity."

"That's not what I was gonna do, silly." He pulls me closer and cups my cheeks, gray eyes never leaving mine. "You're fucking beautiful and your husband is a piece of shit for screwing you over and for not wanting to be there for you. One day you'll have a person deserving of all that love you have to give. Just hang in there for a bit longer. Okay, Hazel?"

I nod silently and rest my head on his chest, letting the tears spill until there's no more left.

14 JUSTICE

THE MOMENT HAZEL asks me if I want to see the photos of her son is like a U-turn on a one-way street during rush hour. People like me are not supposed to feel the things I've been feeling for her these past two hours. If I could spend the rest of my week in her kitchen, just talking, I would. For a second there, I even forgot that I had to cut short the cartoons binge with my own son to help her with her car. The saddest thing is, I know as soon as I walk out the door, that bottle of wine we've been nursing is going to get empty real fast, and I, for some reason, don't want that to happen.

"I'm sorry about...yelling at you earlier." She leans against the kitchen counter, smoothes both palms over her jeans, and grabs her glass.

"That's okay. Not everyone can tolerate my fans."

"They are pretty crazy." Her eyes are half closed, lips red from the wine.

"Well, look at me." I spin on the bar stool, my knees brushing the table in the process.

She places her right hand over her mouth to conceal a smile and shakes her head.

"Hey, at least I'm still entertaining."

"That you are." She clears her throat.

"That's right. I have my moments."

The silence that follows seems to go on forever. She takes a small sip of her wine, puts the glass back on the counter, and defensively crosses both arms on her chest, which makes me wonder why she's standing all the way on the opposite side of the kitchen now. Maybe her body is fighting it just like mine. I almost want to ask her, but the better man in me decides against it.

Not the time and place, Justice. The woman cried senselessly for thirty fucking minutes and all you can think of is sex?

Only, I can't help it.

Sometimes I feel like a universal trash can, just taking it all in, sorting, recycling, turning most of it into my dark, ugly, twisted, and dirty art. Might be a little bit warped but still quite an accurate representation of what we, our generation, have become.

Right now, I'm recycling Hazel's emotions. I feel sad, hurt, and hopeless. Because that's what she feels. She doesn't need to tell me that. I can see it in her eyes.

What else do I see?

Desire. It's hidden under many layers of gloom and misery, but I know it's there. She trembled in my arms like a butterfly when I kissed her.

"So." I stop fidgeting on the stool and freeze to face her. The few feet of space separating us seem like an unnecessary element, but there's not much that can be done about it unless she changes her mind and sits back down where I desperately want her—next to me. "How long is this friend of yours gone for?"

"They'll be back at the end of February."

"And you can stay here until then?"

She nods. "I'm supposed to use this time to figure out what to do next." Her eyes divert to somewhere in the distance, past me, past the room, into mysterious nothing. "And that's when you come and ruin my peace and quiet." The words slice right through me. "And I hate you for dragging me into your mess."

"I'm sorry. I know you don't really like me..." Then comes the dickhead speech. "Well, parts of me."

She gives me a quick glance. "You just can't stop, can you?"

"Yeah, bad habit."

"Is it?" she purrs after a long pause, bringing the glass to her mouth again, this time her amber eyes peering right into mine. "Or maybe it's an act. Just like when you're on stage and you get to wear that mask. You're not really you. You're what others want you to be, Justice."

Her words drifting from across the kitchen cause a lump to form in my throat. She's damn good under the influence of alcohol. So good at reading some things that it scares me.

"Does it bother you?" I ask, shifting on my stool. "The makeup? Is it too creepy? Don't tell me you're a Nickelback kinda girl."

"Not really," she says. "And no, I'm not a Nickelback kinda girl. But I don't buy your concept band story. There's more to it, Justice." She takes a deep breath and carefully sets the empty glass back on the counter. Her third, if my memory is correct. "You're hiding your true self."

I'm slowly digesting everything that just came from her. The light shade of pink in her cheeks and the darkness consuming the golden spots in her pupils are a sure indication of the heavy buzz hitting her head right now. I'm almost certain that she's chosen that counter to lean on because she'd be falling into my arms if she were sitting any closer.

"What's your secret, Mr. Cross?"

"There's no secret." I shake my head. The way she just said my last name sounded both sweet and sexy.

"I showed you my son's photos," she whispers. "I let you use me and my name..." Her voice is so low that I barely hear it, but I can read her lips just fine.

"Is this one of those drunken confessions where we share things about each other no one else will ever know?"

"You think you're this big bad wolf, Justice, with all the attitude and crowds of pink-haired girls fawning after you and all that oral sex talk in your songs...and everywhere else. But you're not... Right now, you're sitting in my kitchen and you're just a pup, because deep inside, you're a human being and you're a parent. I want to know what made this human being create an alter ego that separates him from who he really is."

No one has ever called me a pup before. That's a first. "I have a wild imagination."

She shakes her head, a faint smile breaking on her wine-colored lips. "I liked the way you held my hand back at the station. Even my husband hasn't held my hand like that in a very long time."

My breath catches in my throat. I almost wish she wasn't saying this while she's buzzed. Sober Hazel would never admit she liked me holding her hand. Sober Hazel would slap me senseless for trying to bring up anything that revolves around physical closeness.

"What else did you like?" I ask carefully, trying to refrain from plugging "babe" into that question; my mind is recreating the images of us kissing in this very cabin a few days ago.

"Your turn to confess, Justice." She smiles again.

"I just can't win with you." My mouth is suddenly dry and my tongue is stiff.

"I think I deserve a little bit more than just what's in the tabloids."

"Fair enough. You ever heard of a band called The Gates of Hale?" I ask warily, running my fingers against the smooth surface of the table.

"Elijah Hale? Who hasn't? My parents love that band. They kept on spinning their tunes all through my toddler years."

"Right. Elijah is my uncle."

Hazel's mouth forms a perfectly shaped "O" as she lets out a soft gasp. Not quite the reaction I expected. Most people would jump and dance around like silly and then ask to get an autograph. But then again, this woman didn't even flinch at meeting me.

"Really?" she finally asks, tilting her head. "That's...hmm...interesting."

"You find that interesting?"

"How come it's not mentioned anywhere?"

"I don't want it to be common knowledge." I give her a one-shoulder shrug.

"Why?"

"Because it's fucking hard to be his nephew, especially when he doesn't approve of anything I do."

"How come?"

"He just doesn't like what I do. He thinks I'm an amateur and the theatrics are just that—theatrics." My voice sounds foreign. I can hear it bouncing off the walls and the tiles of the tiny kitchen like millions of ricocheting bullets. It's been a long time since I stopped giving a fuck about my uncle's condemnation, but this conversation happening right now is making me rethink everything.

Suddenly I'm sixteen again. Chance, Zander, and I are jamming in my father's garage. Mostly covers of my uncle's band, some Metallica, some Guns N' Roses, even some Boston stuff. We have three original songs—lyrics by me, riffs and bass lines are all on Chance since we haven't found an actual bass player yet. Everyone is hyped and nervous because this is the day Elijah Hale himself is visiting my parents while in town off tour, and he agreed to check us out.

When he finally walks into the garage in the middle of our rendition of Marilyn Manson's *Tainted Love*, my heart almost stops. I've been following The Gates of Hale for years. I can't believe that this five-foot-ten skinny dude with bangs who's wearing a funny hat and a handful of golden chains around his neck is my uncle who sells out arenas. And here he is, gracing our little jam session with his royal presence. He drops into the beanbag in the corner and gives us an encouraging nod. We finish the cover and decide to play one of the songs he wrote. Two minutes. Two fucking minutes is all we get. Wincing, he gets up and leaves without saying a word.

Later that night, when I hear him telling my dad how unoriginal my music is, I want to run to the nearest bridge and dive into the deep waters because all I ever wanted is to be like him. So much for a fucking role model.

"I think you've done a pretty good job." Hazel's voice is soft and sweet like cotton candy. "Some of the imagery you use in your videos or on stage comes off creepy because some people don't understand that art can take any form, even if it's not a form that's appealing to everyone. And I don't think you need to validate your success by putting religious symbols on your body for the audience to believe in you and your show."

"Do you find it disturbing?"

"No. Yes. Maybe." Her hands travel back to the kitchen counter. "God, religion, all that nonsense and I are not on good terms, if you know what I mean." Her eyes glisten in the last of the sunlight peeking into the room through the small window above the sink.

"It's who I am now, Hazel. I'm the show."

I created this monster in the heat of the moment when I was mad at my jerk of an uncle for telling me to do better. Nonetheless, in a very strange way, it pushed me to the edge. However, now I'm swaying on this edge, not sure whether I want to let go and fall or keep holding on to this stupid empire I've built.

But the strangest thing of all is that it appears so unimportant right now. Because today, for a brief moment, Hazel made none of it matter. How? I don't know. She just did.

"Don't you get tired of it, Justice?" Her eyes lock on mine, waiting for an answer that never comes.

I finish up my drink in silence. Sometimes normal seems like an interesting alternative. "Have you ever seen the Trans-Siberian Orchestra?"

"Huh?"

"If you don't have any plans tomorrow night, I'd love for you to join me."

"Orchestra?"

"Well, not exactly orchestra. It's a rock opera. They'll be playing their Christmas album. Dom got me the tickets a while back because I wanted to take Aiden, but he's been cranky with all this back and forth. He didn't sound too excited when I brought it up."

"Isn't he a little young to go to a rock opera?"

"He was one when he saw his first show."

"Really?"

"Only the material appropriate for kids." I laugh.

"I don't want to impose on your time with your son."

"You're not. The show is in Sacramento. It's a bit of a drive and he's exhausted from traveling. My mother is taking him to the Lego store tomorrow. So you're not imposing."

"Christmas music?" She licks her lips, looking up at the ceiling. "What happened to the insensitive jerk I met the other week?" A muffled laugh escapes her mouth as she stares at the tiny square patterns above her head.

"You know what, Hazel? Fuck you. You called me a pup ten minutes ago. You need to make up your mind whether you want a Chihuahua or a German Shepherd."

"Are those the only options?" Her eyes search mine. The blood in my veins starts boiling at the sight of the golden flecks peering at me from under those lashes. I'm too tired to fight the urge to get up and pull her into my arms. My fingers desperately want to play with her new, improved hair.

"We'll have to leave early. I'll pick you up at two," I say, getting to my feet.

"Two?" she mumbles, and I give her a slight nod as I head toward the door.

"Yes, two. I'll see you tomorrow, Hazel."

Part of me wants to get a hug at least, but I know that touching her right now is not a good idea. Feeling for her, in general, is not a good idea, but I can't help it. She makes me want to be normal, to be myself.

15 HAZEL

After wrapping up an awkward phone conversation with my mother, I pour myself a second cup of coffee and try to rationalize everything that's been happening to my family since my name became the joke of the year. Apparently, all my relatives, no matter how distant, are being stalked by the paparazzi day and night. Dad called the police twice because the reporters ignored the newly installed "No Trespassing" signs on the front lawn and had enough guts to ring the doorbell.

My iPad is in front of me on the table in the breakfast nook, and Justice Cross, the performer, is staring at me from the frozen screen of the paused YouTube video. A thin coat of white paint smoothed over his clean-shaven face accentuates his elegant features. The neat strokes disappear under a studded choke collar that's wrapped around his neck. The thick black eyeliner really brings out the color of his eyes. He looks deliciously dangerous with his hair slicked back and his mouth curved into a wicked smile. Men wearing makeup never appealed to me, but I find this version of Justice Cross very intriguing.

After a few minutes of staring at the slightly blurred image of the man who was comforting me in this very kitchen yesterday, I hit the play button and let the music fill the air. Justice reminds me of a panther. Gracious, quick, effortless. He either knows how to strategically position himself in front of the cameras at the right moment to get the best angle possible or he doesn't have a bad angle at all.

The fact that a twenty-thousand-capacity arena complies with the sing-along demands of a man who's picking me up in less than three hours makes me nervous all of a sudden.

I draw a deep, shaky breath and release my hold, scared that the coffee mug might slip from my trembling hand. The song comes to an end and the storm of applause and the camera panning over the raging audience make me feel even less relevant. Why would someone like Justice Cross take me to see a Christmas rock opera? Does he have no one else to go with?

Am I still on his sex list with an empty box next to my name that has to get checked one way or another?

I take my eyes off the screen and carefully study my plain, polish-free nails.

"Hey, Chicago! How the fuck are you doing?" His voice is deep, with a sexy hint of a rasp. Thousands of cheers cast into one deafening roar that emanates satisfaction. For both the band and the audience.

Gazing back at the screen, I catch a glimpse of the crowd right before the camera pans to the stage again, now showing Justice in all of his glory—leather pants and boots with a tight black sleeveless top accentuating his shoulders. The impressive six feet of masculinity towers over that vintage silver dynamic microphone with beads of sweat glistening in the electric blue light dripping down his temple. The crowd starts screaming and the camera pans back to them when the intro to "The Temple of Love" fills the room.

God, have mercy, I think to myself as I follow the lyrics. A close-up of his lips caressing the microphone makes me dizzy because that's exactly how they came crashing down on mine a few days ago— patiently, gradually, until it was the right time to attack.

Cold sweat breaks under the thin layer of my t-shirt, the cotton unpleasantly sticking to my back. No YouTube video ever made me this wet. Including between my legs.

"Fuck." I slide from the stool and circle the kitchen. After almost seven years of sharing a bed with a man, I'm pretty sure I know the difference between being excited about a new pair of shoes and being turned on by someone. And I think right now, the person staring at me from the screen of my iPad is turning me on.

My body is probably just reacting this way because it needs a release. Right?

"Okay, Justice. I'm sure everyone already knows about your tongue technique," I spout in answer to the partial line of lyrics my mind manages to register before I pause the video.

First things first: shower.

The phone goes off when I'm leaving the kitchen. Part of me doesn't want to take the call because this is most likely some tabloid weasel or the hair salon and I don't have the money yet. Or it could be Owen or my parents...or Justice. I stop in my tracks, turn around, and rush to the breakfast nook to grab the phone.

"Hey, honey," my mother's slightly worried voice greets me. "I just wanted to let you know Dad transferred you some money." She pauses. Our conversation earlier wasn't the most pleasant, mainly because she kept on asking about Justice. I'm surprised the incident with the police didn't rattle my father enough for him to refuse to help me financially.

"Thanks, Mom." I clear my throat. "I'll pay you back."

You better start working on your resume, Hazel. So far, you've done nothing but look over the job postings on Craigslist.

"It's okay. Don't worry about it," my mother says. "You don't have to come back right now. The jobs will still be here in February. Dad and I will help you out until your divorce is sorted. Besides, why is Owen rushing you so much? Did you read everything carefully? I mean, you've been together for a long time. Is there some sort of alimony included? There should be, at least until you get back on your feet."

"Mom, come on. Don't start." But she's already planted the seed. Owen could have at least warned me about the credit cards.

"Don't sign anything before Dad goes over it, or better yet, Uncle Roger."

"Uncle Roger is a criminal defense attorney."

"That's okay. It's better he looks at it than no one. You gave this man the best years of your life, and if he's going to just leave you without a penny or some sort of financial support, that wouldn't be fair."

"Mom, I'm getting half," I say meekly, but my argument isn't very convincing. There's not much to that half really. Our mortgage payments and medical bills were eating up all our earnings. A couple of thousand dollars maybe and a Prius. It won't even cover two months of rent if I were to get a place of my own. But asking Owen for the alimony seems low.

The doorbell interrupts our conversation.

A stranger with a clipboard beams at me once I pull the door open just enough to be able to see who's trying to disturb my already rocky morning.

"Hi, Hazel Alexander?"

"Yes," I mumble, the phone is still pressed to my ear, and my mother is patiently waiting.

"Just need your signature here and here." He hands me the clipboard, gesturing at my Prius parked in the driveway. "I'm with Billy's Auto Repair."

"Oh, gosh, sorry... Just a second. Mom?" I say into the phone, "I'll talk to you later."

Once we say our goodbyes, I swing the door wide open and grab the paperwork. The wind instantly finds its way under the folds of my oversized t-shirt. "What was wrong with it?" I ask in a shaky voice after scribbling my name on the paper near the checkmarks in exchange for my car keys.

"We replaced the battery and the mass airflow sensor."

"Replaced? But this car is barely two years old."

"It happens, ma'am. Sometimes the hybrid batteries fail prematurely." The man shrugs, scratching his forehead as if my question is a mathematical problem of a post-grad school level.

"H-how much do I owe you?" I swallow hard as my body trembles.

"It's been taken care of."

"By whom?"

"It says right here." He points at the clipboard. "Dominic Fiery."

"Thanks." I glance at the paperwork again in disbelief.

"Well, have a good one, ma'am. You better get inside. It's cold out here."

I slam the door shut as soon as the man gets off the porch and then

I head for the shower. New battery and an airflow sensor replacement can't be cheap, right?

After I wash off the sweat caused by the earlier physical reaction to the YouTube video of my escort for tonight, I rummage through some of the cabinets in Rayna's bathroom and retrieve a couple of bottles of nail polish.

It's not a date, Hazel. It's a friendly gesture. Yesterday you were upset, and he just wants to do something nice.

Nice, my ass. This guy doesn't know the definition of nice.

Not true. He's been behaving these past few days.

I'm halfway through painting my nails baby pink when the text message alert comes in.

Owen: I'll be leaving for Tahoe tomorrow morning to pick up the divorce papers. Can you have them signed by then? Thanks.

I stare at the phone for a few long moments, chewing on my bottom lip, then dial his number.

His greeting is short. "Yes?"

"Really? That's all you have to say? You could have told me about the cards at least."

"I'm sure your new boyfriend can cover your expenses."

"He is not my boyfriend," I retort.

"I don't care what he is, Hazel. I'm sick and tired of paparazzi stalking me. Let's just please get this over with."

He hangs up without waiting for my response.

After a few minutes of sitting in silence thinking about my crappy life and failure at college and motherhood, I start crying. Tears spill down my cheeks like a waterfall. The new nails and the new hair don't make sense anymore. Nothing does really. The vortex of eternal darkness and pain is back to claim my poor, restless soul and all I know is that I'm tired. Tired of pretending that life goes on when it doesn't. Not for me.

In the middle of my meltdown comes another message alert. My first thought is Owen, but after wiping the moisture from my eyes, I realize I'm wrong.

Justice: I'm leaving my place in a few.

Oh, God. I lost track of time.

Hazel: Almost ready.

The truth is I don't even want to go anymore. Sacramento is two hours away, which means I'll have to spend at least double that time in one car with Justice Cross.

A shiny limo pulls into my driveway at ten after two. The text message from Justice comes right after I slip into a pair of knee-length suede boots. Even the extra two inches of height and my new styled-to-perfection golden locks are not enough to boost my confidence. I'm pretty much a homeless college dropout. Why does Justice want me to go with him?

I hop down the porch and head for the wide-open back door of the vehicle. The driver gives me an encouraging nod when I stop in my tracks and cautiously peer inside. I'm not sure what exactly to expect. A stripper pole and a couple of half-naked chained-up girls? Or maybe Dominic and May. But there's no one inside except Justice. Thank God, he's wearing a simple black V-neck sweater and a pair of faded jeans. No spikes on the boots. Phew. Nothing as crazy as I saw him sporting earlier during my YouTube stalking session.

"What's all this?" I ask, sliding into the seat across from him. The door shuts behind me as soon as I settle.

"I'm not fucking driving to Sacramento myself." His eyes linger on mine for a few seconds then drop down to my breasts. I knew I shouldn't have worn this top, damn it. It's the only nice dressy blouse I have that might be appropriate for the opera, but of course, Justice will twist it into something lurid.

"Black lace is definitely you." He smirks, finally taking his eyes off my cleavage.

"I'm not going anywhere if you keep staring at me like that," I say firmly, pressing my knees together to stop them from quivering.

"Sorry." He runs his hand through his hair pushing some of the strands back. "You look very nice."

"Thanks. You look nice too." I swallow hard in an attempt to get rid of the huge lump that just magically formed in my throat.

The limo starts moving.

"You really didn't need to go out of your way," I croak, studying the posh interior. When my eyes register a mini bar to the right, I suddenly feel thirsty. My mouth is so dry that my tongue sticks to the roof of it. "We could have taken my Prius. Thank you, by the way. You didn't need to pay for the new battery either."

Who am I kidding? I'm broke as far as I know, because my husband, who's demanding me to sign the divorce papers, cut me off, and I had to beg my parents to loan me the money to cover the salon invoice. Pathetic really. I should be happy Justice took care of the auto repair, but that's not the case. Him paying for things makes me feel like...a hooker.

"We're not taking your Prius anywhere, babe." He laughs softly, brushing off my thanks as if it doesn't matter.

"We can handle it, right?" I breathe out, my pink nails digging into the fabric of my jeans.

His eyebrow shoots up in question while his eyes continue to peruse my modest outfit.

"Me and you, trapped in here for two hours," I explain.

"You make it sound like I'm the last person on earth you want to be around."

"N-no." I shake my head, still grasping my legs. *You just make me feel weird things I don't want to feel, and I don't know how to make it stop.*

Justice leans forward, his voice going down an octave or two. "Then why are you calling a scenic ride in one car with me a trap?"

Because I'm a woman who hasn't had sex in a very long time, and you've been trying to get into my pants since the moment we met. Right now, you're being all nice and charming, but I don't know how I'll keep it together if you try to hold my hand or kiss me again. And I'm pretty sure you will because we're in the back of a limo with the divider up.

But that's not what I say. "It just came out. I don't mind being in a limo with you...as long as you don't start making your sexual jokes. Just keep your part of the deal, okay?"

"I only want you to have a good time and relax a little. You need it." He pulls back, his gray eyes never leaving mine.

This is going to be a long, torturous night, I think to myself, studying the swirls of ink on his wrists as he rolls up the sleeves of his sweater and scoots toward the mini bar. I shouldn't have watched those YouTube videos. Now I can't get that stupid choke collar out of my head. Is he one of those kinky guys in bed? My cheeks start burning at the mere idea.

"Do you mind if I have some wine?" My heart is doing the type of crazy flips that a gymnastics team could probably only dream about.

"Promise me you won't pass out during the show." He smiles.

"No, just one glass," I say meekly. *Because this trip is a bad idea, after all.*

16 JUSTICE

"Okay, here's the thing," I whisper in her ear as we head for the entrance to the right of the stage. The security guard Dom requested is two steps behind, just in case someone spots me in the crowd. I have no desire to be discovered tonight like I was during the shopping center rescue trip. "The show is three hours long. The first part is the Christmas material. Then there's a break. If you don't feel like you want to stay for the second part, we can leave right after," I explain as we walk into the auditorium. The lights are already off, a carefully calculated move on my part because I don't want anyone to start pointing fingers as we get escorted to our booth next to the soundboard.

"Have you seen it before?" Hazel asks, clinging to me as we duck into the passage dividing the sections of the auditorium.

"Yes. Once. A while back actually."

"This is so not like you." She giggles into the sleeve of my sweater, wrapping her arms around mine even tighter. She's buzzed from the wine she had on the way here.

"Why not?" I ask in a hushed voice, following the venue attendant.

Little does she know about the kind of music I'm capable of creating. I wrote a whole bunch of sappy poems the other night after my family wrapped up Thanksgiving dinner. I was proud of my breakthrough because I'd been struggling with the lyrics.

"You sing about...oral sex," she whispers.

"Prince did too. Doesn't mean I can't enjoy a violin or a trumpet. You do know I play piano, right?"

"You do?" she gasps.

"Just say it. You didn't even pay attention to that part when you were snooping around my Wikipedia page." I snort, leaning into her. Most people miss the fact that the early music education of rock singer Justice Cross was classic-based. My lips involuntarily touch the top of Hazel's head as I pull her closer when we swerve into the narrow walkway between the rows. Her soft coconut and vanilla scent fills my nostrils. Shit. She smells divine, and I bet she tastes even better.

As soon as the venue attendant makes sure we're all settled in our booth, a waitress shows up. I politely decline the offer of alcohol and order water before Hazel takes charge and requests more wine. I let her have two glasses on the way because she was beyond nervous. Also, because when she's buzzed, she gets a little loose—less tense, less stressed, happier. I like watching her smile.

Dark elements, like the ones she's fighting right now, have always intrigued me. I find it gruesomely fascinating. I want to know what drives people to the edge and pushes them to jump or what makes them change their minds and press the restart button. Hazel needs the latter right now more than anyone I've ever met. She's already beautiful with all that darkness surrounding her like a cloak, but she can be so much fucking more and I want to be the one to witness her rise from the ashes.

The stage finally goes live. Dozens of blue laser beams slice through the dark auditorium, sending thousands of people into a state of visual shock. After doing what I do for over twelve years, the theatrics isn't something I care about. I've seen it all. I'm part of my own show, the mastermind and the executor behind The Deviant idea. Right now, I just want to enjoy the music and stare at the girl sitting next to me, watch her expression going from confused to stunned, hold her hand, wait for an occasional smile or a nod. Normal, that's what I crave. Badly.

"What do you think?" I finally whisper in her ear after the first two songs are over and the narrator is about to take the stage.

"It's different." She turns to face me, our hands locked on the armrest dividing the seats. It seems as if this has become the standard of sorts—me touching her in the most innocent way, despite all the ideas my filthy mind keeps manufacturing. Very high school because I don't need to hold a woman's hand to fuck her, but I feel the need to do so with Hazel. I feel the need to do many things with her and for her, both in a pure way *and* a dirty one.

"You like it so far?" I ask, waiting for validation. She hasn't said much since the beginning of the show. "We can leave if you're not enjoying it."

"Are you kidding me?" She shakes her head. "I love it." Amber eyes stare into mine.

Fire. That's what they remind me of. Scorching, relentless, unforgettable, burning a hole in my chest like a fucking torch. My fingers instinctively squeeze her hand as if she might disappear. But she doesn't. Not even when the performance resumes. She's still here, looking at me like I'm the only person in the theater and we're sitting in an empty arena with nothing but twirling lights and a stage full of marionettes. The streaks of gold and blue dancing in Hazel's hair make her look like an angel one minute and the devil the next.

I turn in my seat and lean forward, bringing my face closer to hers. The violins singing somewhere in the back of my head is the best soundtrack I could ever imagine. *This time it's going to be a real fucking kiss*, I think to myself, flicking my tongue over her smooth lower lip as the distance between us vanishes. She's still, breathless, and seems almost terrified at first.

Part of me expects a slap, but deep inside I know she wants a taste of me too. There's no point in fighting it because we're meant to happen, sooner or later. I can feel the damn fire burning everything that stands in the way to the ground, including this fucking concert.

I brush my lips against hers gently, again and again, trying to get a reaction.

"Justice," she mumbles into my mouth. She speaks quieter than a whisper, but somehow still above the music. I can't even hear anything anymore once her lush lips finally touch mine. My body reacts instantly, tingling with anticipation. I either have to do something about the hard-on she just gave me here or leave in the next ten minutes to avoid being caught on camera jerking off in the middle of the fucking violin solo.

I slide my hands to the back of her neck, part her lips with my tongue, and snatch a real wet, hungry kiss. The one I've been wanting since the beginning.

She pulls back just a little. Her eyes, now dark and heavy, drink me in.

"I want to get out of here," I murmur, bringing my lips to her cheek that's splashed with a myriad of dancing laser lights.

Don't hold your breath, Justice. Remember what happened last time you tried to offer sex as a solution.

After a few long moments, she nods. "Okay."

I grab her hand and off we go into the empty, dimly-lit walkway between the sections, without an escort. My heart's beating wildly in my chest. Wilder than it did when we won our first Grammy. The song ends when we're halfway through the auditorium and the lights turn on for a few brief moments, but definitely not long enough for the raging crowd to spot *hashtag Jazel* on the main floor heading toward the side stage exit hand in hand. I can't help but silently laugh at the stupid Twitter ship name as we duck into the narrow corridor packed with equipment.

The security at the back entrance gives us a polite nod and holds the door.

"Did she find her parents?" Hazel's voice catches me off guard when we stroll into the brightly lit VIP parking lot.

"Who?" I ask, my hand still grasping hers, my heart pounding. Women like Hazel— simple, middle class, non-famous—have never been of interest to me. Yet right now, I really want her to see the real me, beyond the performer, beyond the mask.

"The child in the performance. Does the story have a happy

ending?" A gust of wind tousles her golden locks as she steps back, her eyes studying me carefully.

"Yes." I nod, and my fingers squeeze her hand harder. "It's a happy ending story."

She tilts her head and gives me one of those intense tortured looks, gold threads sliding across her right cheek, the first hint of tears glimmering in the corners of her eyes. No, no, no! Is she going to cry over a Christmas tale about a fictional child? My stupid conscience is kicking in after hibernating for about a decade. I'm not going to fuck her if she's this miserable. That's not how I wanted it to happen.

The limo pulls up a second later and I help Hazel inside. This time we're sitting next to each other, my hand possessively resting on her knee. *Fuck being proper, Justice. Fuck it.*

The better man in me still thinks he needs a few moments to calm down, but my animalistic nature always wins. Right now is no exception. I run my fingers up her thigh and move over to close that inch of space separating us.

Hazel sinks deeper into the leather; her body seems so small compared to mine. The reflection of the arena lights dancing across the tinted windows of the limo slowly disappear into the dark as the car takes us farther and farther from the city. The silence goes on for a little while because neither of us has enough guts to start talking about what happened earlier in the theater. Doesn't change the fact that my cock is hard and I want to fuck her senseless. Instead, my thumb keeps brushing the surface of her jeans.

"I don't know how to do this." Her quiet voice finally interrupts the humming of the engine. "I've been married for seven years. The second half of that marriage was very...uneventful."

Uneventful as in no sex? This fact for some reason turns me on. I wonder if she's ever been with anyone but that loser, but my ego insists I shouldn't be bothered by that douche. We can't erase our pasts. Everyone is tainted in one way or another, but it doesn't mean the new memories will be soiled too. Nothing up until right now matters. "That's okay," I rasp out, looking into her eyes. "I'm a good teacher. I can show you how it's done."

She gulps, blinking rapidly. Her cheeks are the perfect shade of pink.

"Can we go slow?" she asks.

"We can go however you want, babe." My voice becomes a ragged whisper as I lean forward and plant a kiss on her lips, tentative at first, turning demanding and deep a few seconds later.

She tastes amazing. The perfect combination of sweet and fresh. Her tongue, unsure and submissive, finally starts following mine.

"Come here," I mumble into her mouth and, grasping her thighs, gently pull her onto my lap. Our bodies match perfectly as she straddles me, our faces a breath apart, our clothes a tangled mess.

Her small hands slide to the back of my neck, caressing my skin first, then she dips her fingers in my hair and ruffles it. "I always wanted to do that," she confesses.

"Is there anything else you'd like to do?" My hands explore the curves of her body, inch by inch. Her skin is smooth like velvet, her hair is soft, and she smells heavenly, like vanilla and coconut. I must have died and ended up in paradise, because she looks like an angel with a golden halo...and I'm about to make that angel come.

"Maybe," she murmurs, leaning into me. Her lips slowly and carefully brush against my cheek.

"Care to show me?" I husk out, my throat is suddenly closing up as I tug on the thin material of her top and roll it up to be able to see her creamy white skin. The sight of my fingers wrapped around her thin waist makes my cock ache. The fact that she's now shyly grinding against it doesn't help. I already know that a fucking hurricane is about to rage through the back of the limo.

"This is so wrong, Justice." She pulls back a little, her eyes searching mine while I get busy with the zipper of her jeans.

"Why?" I ask, cradling the back of her head, my other hand still fighting to get under her shirt.

"Because you and I don't belong together." She skims her fingers through my hair again, this time giving it a little tug. We both know the words coming out of her mouth right now are just a pathetic excuse.

"Tonight can you let go, Hazel?" I whisper, pulling her back down.

"I don't know how."

"I'll show you." I slide my tongue into her cleavage and slowly draw it up her neck, thinking of how I'd want to do that to every part of her body when we're both naked. "Or...I can make you."

Her head falls back and she lets out a faint gasp, the most erotic sound I've ever heard. Breezy and sensual and at the same time hot and sizzling like an inferno, sucking me deeper into the sinful world of desire and lust. I'm dead certain I'm going to hell. I knew that all along, but having this woman squeeze her thighs around me right now and breathe heavily into my mouth is like a little piece of my personal heaven. Those carnal sounds she's making are begging to be turned into a fucking song.

"Make me?" she whispers, arching her back.

"Yes, I can make you do a lot of things." I bury my head into the crook of her neck. "Just say the word. Tell me what you like, baby."

She slowly rocks against my body, creating the most thrilling sensation my cock ever experienced.

I push aside some of her hair and sink my teeth into her supple skin, nibbling and teasing, while her fingers are inspecting every inch of my body under my sweater.

My left hand is trembling as I slip it between her legs, tugging the lace of her black panties. Her jeans are fucking tight, but oh God! She's so wet and ready that I don't bother taking them off.

"I want to make you come, babe." I wrap my other hand around her frame and hold her still.

The amber in those half-closed eyes peering at me turns pitch-black as I thrust two fingers into her. She moans in delight, tossing her head back.

Here is this little theory of mine. Women are like candies—some sour, some too sugary, some even tasteless. But Hazel's a perfect combination of everything I love. She's the premium sifted marshmallow, covered by a thin layer of rich, silky milk chocolate—just the right amount of sweetness on the outside and flawlessly soft and creamy on the inside.

"I'm sorry I broke my promise," I whisper into her mouth, pumping my fingers, faster and faster. I can't go slow with her when she moves her hips like she's been born to fuck my hand. "Come for me, baby. I want you to come for me."

"Justice," she groans out, arching her back and grinding against my hand. The fact that my wrist is caught up in the folds of her panties and the jeans are restricting my hand's movements seems irrelevant at the moment. I can't take my eyes off her face, her flushed cheeks, her hair bouncing against her shoulders concealed by the black lace of the top. She's perfect in that sexual frenzy, visceral, like a wild animal who's been in captivity for a very long time. There's nothing more I want to give her right now but the sweet release she's been wanting all this time.

"Come on, baby." I slide my hand up her back, my fingers start squeezing the base of her neck as she violently pulls on my hair. "You feel fucking amazing, baby."

"Don't stop...Justice...don't stop." Her tongue darts out of her mouth and she wets her lips, then crashes them against mine, all while rocking against my fingers.

"I'm not stopping until you come, baby," I say, breaking the kiss for a second to catch my breath. "Ride it, baby. Come on."

"I want you to come with me, Justice," she mumbles, going for my belt buckle, her hands working the zipper. It's all so fucking uncomfortable because we're sitting in the back of the limo, her on top of me, her jeans messing with my ability to be more efficient. There's plenty of room, but I'm too busy finger-fucking her to even think straight, let alone change positions. No woman ever made me this excited. *Maybe because you mostly hook up with self-proclaimed vixens and spoiled brats.* This is different. This is as raw as it gets. A real woman with real tits, real everything, dripping wet not because you're some fucking rockstar but because she wants you for *you.*

"That's right, baby," I whisper as she wraps her fingers around my cock. Something tells me it won't take more than a couple of minutes because I've been on the edge for days. "This is perfect...you're perfect. I don't think I'm going to last long. You have no idea...what you're doing to me."

"Am I?" She lets out a faint moan, her hands gliding up and down, in sync with my fingers pumping her wildly.

I can feel her walls tightening around me. Her head falls back, eyes shut, mouth wide open, she comes really hard, loud, almost primal. My fingers are still inside of her, wet and exhausted, but I don't want to pull out just yet. The sight of her glowing face sends me over the edge. Combined with the warmth of her body and the flawless work of her hands, it's all I need to come a few seconds later. The perfect release.

"Oh my God." Her body is still trembling. She's like a slow-burn rock ballad with a mellow beginning, a haunting chorus, a touching guitar solo, and an epic climax.

Her thighs are slowly relaxing as I finally pull my hand out and bring it to my mouth, dragging my tongue against my wet forefinger. "I've wanted to taste you since that first kiss, baby. You're just as sweet as I thought you'd be."

"You *are* crazy, aren't you?" she purrs, her body finally sinking down.

"Crazy for you. Yes." My heart is doing double time. I don't want to let her go. I like the way she feels when she's like this—on top of me with her panties wet and her cheeks flushed.

"Why?" She brushes her fingers over my cheek.

I ignore her question. "Let's go to my place."

"Justice. I—" Suddenly, she looks lost. "What about your son?"

"He's at Crystal Bay with my family. We'll go to my cabin. Say yes." At this point, I'm begging.

"I can't. We shouldn't."

"Why not?" Panic is crashing into me like a hurricane.

"Please? Take me back to my place," she whispers, fixing her jeans.

"Did I do something wrong, baby?" I pull her closer, grazing my cheek against hers. This shit is not fucking happening. I need her. Now, tomorrow, day after tomorrow...next month...next year.

"No, no. You made me feel really good. I just...I need to think about it." She isn't making any sense.

"What's there to think about, Hazel?" My mouth turns dry and my stomach is churning.

"Nothing...I'm sorry." She slides to the side and grabs some tissues from the mini bar to wipe herself off.

"What are you sorry about? What's wrong?" I ask, ignoring the fact that my cock and my jeans are covered in my own cum.

"We shouldn't have done it," she says in an unsteady voice, looking away.

"Why not, Hazel?" I cry out. "We're both adults, obviously attracted to each other."

"I don't think we should talk about it right now. In the middle of the night."

"Fine," I grumble under my breath. Part of me wants an immediate answer, but mostly I understand that maybe giving her some time to come to terms with the idea of us is the best course of action, at least at this point. "Can you hand me some tissues at least?"

"Yeah," she says, her eyes avoiding mine.

We spend the rest of the drive mainly in silence. Uneventful, just like the second half of her marriage.

17 HAZEL

My heart's still racing when the limo finally swerves into the driveway of Rayna's cabin. I feel naughty yet excited, my insides still throbbing from his skillful touch. I just had one of the wildest orgasms in my life without having actual intercourse. Part of me wonders what Justice would be like in bed rather than in the back of a limo, what his stunning body would feel like on mine. But the other part of me, the predominant one who's devastated and guilty, is going crazy thinking about my little boy lying in the cold ground while his mama is getting her freak on. If I could crawl into his little casket and lie there next to him, I would.

"Hazel?" Justice rasps out once the limo comes to a stop.

"Please, don't," I whisper, heading for the door.

"Wait." There's a hint of vulnerability in his voice. "Don't I get a fucking explanation at least?"

"I'm not sure that what I have to say is what you want to hear." I swing the door open, and a cold gust of air crashes into me the instant I exit the limo. My legs are a quivering mess, probably the aftereffects of our make-out session, not the wind.

He follows me out into the chilly November night, and the heat of his body envelops my back as he closes the distance between us. His presence is both disturbing and pleasant, and I can't make up my mind whether I want him to hold me tighter or if it's best to push him away before the idea of us lures me into the madness I've been trying to avoid all along.

"I'm just...I don't think I'm ready for this," I choke out as he wraps his muscular arms around me and presses his chin to the back of my head.

"Just fucking talk to me, Hazel." His low, raspy voice makes me want to ask him to come inside and take me to bed, but then I try to snap out of it.

"What do you want from me, Justice?" My eyes stare at the front door of the cabin.

"What do you think I want?" he croons, sliding his left hand up my neck. His fingers skim through my hair and push some of the strands aside while his firm lips travel across my burning cheek.

"I don't know. But whatever it is, it's not for me." I finally muster some of my willpower to speak up. "I'm not into the whole booty call and fuck buddy concept." My voice is trembling just like the rest of me. His lips caressing my temple and his strong body pressed against my back are making it hard for me to concentrate, but I had to say it. He and I belong to two very different worlds.

"Don't fucking friendzone me in the middle of the driveway," he mutters in my ear.

"I'm not."

"You just called me your fuck buddy."

"No, Justice. That's not what I called you." I sigh in frustration because he's not listening to me.

"But is that what you think I'm looking for?" he husks out, his right arm possessively hugging me. "Because that's not what I want us to be."

"I don't know how *us* is going to work." The idea of there being an *us* is giving me anxiety.

He plants a series of butterfly kisses on my cheek. "How can you say that? You and I are fucking amazing together, babe."

I know I should be running for the door, but I'm afraid I'll fall if he lets me go. So I just stand there, confused and scared, with my back pressed against his rock-hard chest while his hungry lips slowly assault my neck. "How are we amazing?"

"You know. You felt it too back there, baby." He sucks on my earlobe gently, his breath burning me to the core. "I could fuck you like no one ever has. I could make you come in ways you've never imagined. I could satisfy all your dark fantasies. I could make you fucking fly. All you have to do is let me."

Owen has never said anything this daring to me in bed, not that he was a master of dirty talk in general. We enjoyed sex, even attempted experimenting during the first year of our marriage, but I doubt anything I've done before can compare to what Justice is offering. *Dark fantasy* is a totally different realm for me. I don't even think I had one until he came into my life. He makes me question everything, including my sanity. After all, the man got me wet via a semi-decent non-porn-related YouTube concert video.

"Is this how you envision *us*?" I ask breathlessly. "Am I one of your dark fantasies?"

"What are you scared of, Hazel?"

"I'm not scared. I'm getting divorced. I'm a mess, Justice."

He drags the tip of his tongue up my neck, drawing me harder against his body.

I pull his arms off me and turn to face him. "Being involved with someone right now, especially someone like you, isn't what I need."

"Someone like me?" He tilts his head, his dilating pupils taking over the color in his eyes, turning them into two silvery rings.

"You're...high maintenance!" A cry of despair mixed with anger leaves my mouth. "You have reporters stalking you wherever you go, your wife is fighting you over your son, you have a larger-than-life show to keep up... This isn't going to work. I don't want occasional hookups with a guy who lives his life under a fucking microscope."

Deep down, I know he doesn't deserve this. Deflecting my failures to him is unfair.

"Occasional hookups?" He frowns, taking a step forward. "Is that what you think I'm looking for?"

"We both know you aren't capable of anything more, so why start, Justice?" My voice sounds foreign, loud and angry.

"Why do you always assume? Why do you compare me to some asshole who can't even renew your fucking AAA?"

"You wanted an explanation. Well, there you have it." I place my hand on his chest. "Please, don't make this any harder. I really need to be alone right now. I'm sorry."

"You have no idea what I'm capable of, baby." He leans into me, his voice both suggestive and serious. My hand that's on his chest doesn't provide much of a barrier when his eyes are scrutinizing me in a way I can't handle.

"Justice, it's late and I'm tired. Please don't make me say things I'm going to regret later."

The rhythmic beating of his heart under my palm is begging me not to do this, but I've already made up my mind.

"Okay." Justice takes a step back, his gray eyes never leaving mine. A hint of a frown tightening his forehead. "If you need time, fine. You can have it, but you felt it too. You can deny it all you want, but you and I have something."

"Good night," I say on an exhale and charge for the door before he seduces me into another round of sex in his limo.

The bright lights of the vehicle sneak in through the living room window for a few brief moments once I'm inside. Then the humming of the engine slowly fades, leaving me alone and in silence.

I sigh heavily and lean my back against the cold door, looking for some sort of support to keep me from collapsing to the floor. Stinging hot tears spill down my cheeks as I finally let the misery in and help-lessly sink to my knees. Why are things so complicated? Why do I feel so wrong for wanting to see Justice again? Why do I get to live and my little boy doesn't? Why is life so fucking unfair?

"Please come back to me, River," I whisper between my sobs. "Please come back to Mommy."

The sound of nothingness that crashes at me in response is terrifying, just like the hole in my chest that grows bigger and bigger with each passing minute. I know that soon I'll no longer have a heart, and I'm petri-fied yet thrilled at the idea of that fateful moment. Feeling every possible shade of pain is beyond exhausting. It's better feeling nothing at all.

The buzzing of the cell coming from inside my purse slowly pulls me out of my teary trance. Whoever this person may be, he or she picked the wrong fucking time for a phone conversation. My first instinct is to ignore the call, but when the persistent ringing doesn't stop, I finally give in.

"Oh my God, Hazel! Why haven't you been picking up?" Rayna's voice, full of panic, detonates in my ear the moment I hit the accept button. "I've been trying to get a hold of you all week. I even called your mom. The reporters are bombarding us with emails. Someone even looked up Clay's LinkedIn page. What the hell is going on?"

I attempt to pull myself together enough to produce a coherent sentence, but my voice comes out as a pathetic squeal. "I'm sorry."

"Are you crying, Hazel?"

"No," I lie.

"Come on, hon. What's going on? Talk to me."

"I'm sorry. It's just really not a good time right now, Rayna."

"Is this because of all the press? Are you really seeing Justice Cross?"

I inhale slowly, trying to get as much air into my lungs as possible. My chest hurts from all the crying, but I hope the oxygen will help clear my head.

"I don't really know what's going on, Rayna," I say honestly.

"What about all those photos of you two?"

"I met him at a bar," I explain. "I was drunk. It was just one of those spur-of-the-moment things."

"Did you sleep with Justice Cross?"

"Sorta." I clear my throat and run my fingers against the cold wooden surface of the floor of her cabin. Getting to my feet sounds like a good idea right now considering that my right leg is asleep, but I'm too drained to move.

"What's *sorta*? Did you or did you not?"

"Yes, we had sex." *Close enough. And it was literally less than two hours ago.*

"Wow." Long pause. "How was he?"

"Are you fucking kidding me?" I can't believe her!

"Sorry. I had to ask. He's famous. Wouldn't you want to know if you were me?" she says apologetically.

"What does it have to do with him being famous? Sex is sex, Rayna. It doesn't matter if you have it with a celebrity or with your husband or with the guy next door."

"It does when it's Justice Cross," she counters. "The guy writes songs about all kinds of kinky sex."

"Maybe because it sells?" I offer a better, more logical theory. My fingers are now moving clockwise, drawing a long string of invisible circles. "You know, there are a lot of people who write about suicide, serial killers, or other creepy shit. That doesn't mean they're into that. It's all part of the package, marketed to a certain group of people."

"Okay...I'm sorry. Don't get so defensive. So he was dull in bed. I get it. That's cool. All I'm saying is if you invite him over, make sure to change the sheets before we come back."

"Yeah, I'll just get you a new mattress and send him the bill."

We both burst into hysterical laughter, something I haven't done in ages, something that feels really good too.

"I like the sound of that," Rayna says when the initial hilarity of my comment and of the situation in general wears off. "I miss the old you."

"I don't know if she's ever coming back."

There's a long pause.

"But can she at least give it a try?" Rayna's voice softens.

"I'm not sure."

"Look, I know you think this is bullshit, but have you thought about checking out the support group I told you about?"

"I'm fine. Really," I brush her off. "Hey, it's late. I gotta get some rest."

After we say our goodbyes, I get to my feet and head straight into the bedroom. My clothes and hair still smell like Justice: like the ocean, with a hint of some expensive spicy cologne. The temptation is too much. I can't help but bury my face into the folds of my top before tossing it into the laundry basket. Everything that happened in the limo on the way back from Sacramento is starting to sink in, the way he touched me, the way he said my name, the way he whispered all those indecent things to me, the way his flawless, firm body felt against mine. It was all too fast and too dirty, but at the same time, I loved the thrill and the novelty of it.

My mind keeps wandering to the limo ride, even when I step into the shower. Part of me doesn't want to wash off the remainder of his scent. Justice Cross should be the last thing I'm thinking about. Unfortunately, that's not the case tonight.

I toss and turn for what seems like forever. At around three in the morning, I snatch a bottle of wine from the kitchen and curl up in my bed with my iPad. First I google Justice, then I google his son, then I end up hopping to some other celebrity news that makes very little sense to me because I'm buzzed. The wine always relaxes me. In a weird way, it's like dark magic. Things are still shit, but they seem so trivial when I'm drinking.

Then in a brief moment of empowerment, I find myself browsing through a list of colleges and clicking on applications. It's the stupid drunk teenage *I-slept-with-a-rockstar* mentality that makes me believe that if a man like Justice has chosen me, I must be something special. I don't remember whether I fill anything out. The wine finally does its job and I fall into the cozy darkness.

18 HAZEL

I BLINK a few times to bring the huge pink blob shoved at me into focus and look back at the delivery guy proudly sporting the baseball hat with the Postmates logo.

"Just need your signature, ma'am." A huge toothy grin flashes at me from behind the rose petals as he watches me scribbling my name on a piece of paper. "Have a good day, ma'am."

With a heavy sigh, I return the clipboard. The Postmates guy hands me the flowers and marches off to his car.

After pouring myself a freshly brewed cup, I finally feel brave enough to read the message that came with the flowers.

I'm sorry I was a little out of line last night. I couldn't help it. You were phenomenal. Take all the time you need.

Justice ✝ ✝ ✝

The butterflies in my stomach are going crazy because, apparently, despite being a mess, I'm also phenomenal. I don't know what kind of dance the winged creatures are doing in my belly, but it's making every part of me tremble and my heart sing. This egoistic, over-the-top-confident, and twisted-minded man has gotten under my skin like a splinter, and I'm afraid I won't be able to extract him without medical help if I keep accepting his advances, whether they're in the form of flowers or bold sexual offers.

After I put the card back, I drink the rest of my coffee, which makes me feel reborn.

Don't kid yourself. That's not the coffee, Hazel. That's last night's sex action in the back of the limo.

I get dressed, do my hair, then apply eyeliner and mascara and leave the cabin by noon.

Both Sidney and the girl with the purple hair greet me when I walk into the salon forty minutes later. A third girl, who wasn't here last time, is busy with a client.

"Hi." I approach the front desk, my hand fishing for my checkbook somewhere in the bottom of my purse. "I just wanted to pay for my hair. I'm sorry about the...bank issues the other day."

"It's okay, honey." Sidney waves his manicured hand at me as I place my checkbook on the counter and grab one of the shiny pens from the metallic stationery holder to my left.

The girl's stare makes me both nervous and irritated, and my fingers slip when I'm about to scribble my signature.

"Is there something wrong?" I snap, lifting my eyes from the counter.

"No." Purple hair shakes her head.

"The new color looks amazing in those pictures, honey." Sidney grins, giving me a light, friendly pat on the shoulder.

"What pictures?" My mouth slants as he shoves his phone toward me with photos up of me and Justice being cozy in this very parking lot two days ago.

"Don't worry. I'm not advertising it as my work, honey," he says quietly, taking the device away from in front of my face. "Unless you don't mind." His blue eyes are now blinking at me rapidly, reminding me of a puppy waiting for a treat.

"You gotta be kidding me," I grumble under my breath, finishing up with the check.

Two teenage girls with their cell phones up in the air who are waiting for me outside the salon make things even worse. The semi-decent mood I had earlier is no more. I sling my purse over my shoulder and make a beeline for the parking lot, ignoring the young paparazzi and everyone else in my way.

The moment I get to the Prius, the leftovers of my self-control go to shit. Hot tears have ruined my attempt at makeup and have left a noticeable wet stain on my sweater right under my chin by the time I finally leave the Plaza.

Then, to make matters worse, the first thing my eyes register as I pull up to the cabin is Owen's black Mercedes taking up most of the driveway. His face is one huge, angry frown from the moment his tall figure emerges from the vehicle, and I can't help but notice the dark shadows beneath his eyes, the pinched lines in his brow, and how dull and lifeless his dirty blond curls look.

"Where the hell have you been? I told you I was coming by to pick up the papers. You can't even answer your phone?" His sharp voice follows me as I shuffle my feet toward the front door, a plastic bag with a bottle of Pinot Grigio I picked up at the liquor store on the way back dangling against my hip. The thing about Owen that's always wowed me the most is that he doesn't beat around the bush. He's quick at getting his point across. Whether it's to get married or to get divorced.

"I was out," I say meekly. Last night's limo rendezvous turned me into a complete mess. I forgot all about the divorce papers.

"Out?" He stops in his tracks with his hands tucked in the pockets of his winter coat, his jaw clenched and his dark, angry eyes aimed at me. "I've been driving for seven fucking hours, Hazel, and you went out?" His voice goes up an octave.

"Please don't yell at me, Owen," I bark, looking up from my purse.

"You could have at least told me what time you were going to be home," he says, taking a deep breath in an attempt to keep his frustration under control, his hands never leaving his pockets.

"You could have told me what time you were coming," I deadpan, finally getting the lock.

"I texted you this morning when I left L.A." Owen starts fuming again as my hands push the front door open. If my memory serves me right, I don't think I even checked my phone today, nor did I take it with me to the Plaza.

In silence, we step inside. My mind is racing and my palms are sweaty because I'm not sure my *still husband* is happy to see the two gigantic flower arrangements sitting on the kitchen table. There's so much to say, but at the same time, it's not quite clear where to even start.

Owen strides through the living room, his eyes scanning the interior of the cabin. Both hands are on his hips as he assumes the about-to-attack business pose he always takes when he's ready to close the deal. I almost expect a sales pitch instead of the obvious questions about Justice and the divorce papers.

"Are those from your new boyfriend?" He gestures at the flowers.

"That's none of your business." I head over to the kitchen and set the bag with the wine on the counter. "Technically, you and I aren't even a couple." Rayna's words creep into my head. "I can see whoever I want." In reality, I know that denying the whole thing would be the best tactic, but how the hell can you deny something that's already turned into a fucking Twitter campaign with photos of Justice all over me flooding the front pages of every single entertainment website?

"*Technically*, we're still married," Owen snaps. "Do you even care what people are saying? Did you see what they wrote about our son?"

"Of course I care!" I spit, throwing my purse on the floor, the contents flying in all directions. Rage and despair take over my mind and body. Now, after two years of denial, he wants to talk about River?! "Do you think I enjoy this? Do you think I sit here and wait for the next fucking article to see what else people cook up so that I can send it to all my friends and family? Do you think I want this?" I'm shaking uncontrollably by the time my speech is finished. Part of me wants to crawl under the table and cry, another part wants a drink, and then there's this small fraction of me that realizes that neither of those things is going to make the pain go away. At least not for long.

Owen's eyes lock on mine, his teeth clamped together and nostrils flaring. "Can I have the papers?"

"I haven't signed them yet," I reply, absentmindedly going for the cabinet above the coffeemaker.

"I drove all the way from L.A. to get this over with. We both need to move on," he says firmly, his voice ricocheting against my eardrums. The lack of further questions about Justice makes me think harder. What if he met someone? What if he's ready to press the reset button, leaving me and the memories of our son behind?

I swing the cabinet door open and stare at dozens of little jars stuffed with salt, sugar, and other spices that are slowly turning into a colorless blur.

"I'm going to have a lawyer look at them first," I whimper as my hands nervously squeeze the edge of the kitchen counter.

"Are you serious? You could have told me that yesterday," Owen protests.

I pull the bottle of Pinot Grigio from the shopping bag and set it on the countertop. My tongue is suddenly rigid and dry, sticking to the roof of my mouth.

"You could have told me you were going to cut me off. I can't even fill up the gas tank in my car! You hid like a coward, ignoring my phone calls and my messages. All you had to do was tell me to get a job!"

"First of all, I didn't hide. I was at my brother's in Arizona. Second, I don't owe you an explanation. You're seeing a man whose net worth is sixty million dollars. I'm sure he can fill up your tank."

My mind refuses to believe the person who promised to be with me 'til death do us part is leaving me with nothing but a Prius without a roadside assistance plan and a useless bedroom set. Maybe it's time I finally listen to my mother's advice. "I gave you ten fucking years of my life," I urge out, fighting the tears. "I dropped out of college for you. To take care of you and our son."

The distressing sound of the doorbell cuts our conversation short. However, in a way I welcome the interruption, because I hate myself for not denying having a relationship with Justice. And I hate myself for not trying harder, for not paying attention, for not being there when I had to. I hate the person I've become.

Owen gestures to the door and then tucks his hands back in the pockets of his coat. His face is gloomy with a hint of irritation.

I silently cross the kitchen to the front door and open it a bit. My heart drops at the sight of the all-black X-Men baseball cap.

"What are you doing here?!" I whisper-shout. Justice's gray eyes catch my gaze as he slides his boot into the small crack, obviously not willing to go until he gets to say or do what he wants.

"Look, I'm sorry. I know I'm supposed to give you time to think, but I needed to see you. I'm flying back to L.A." His deep voice is warm and cozy.

"I don't have time for this, Justice. I'm busy." My heart is still jerking around at the bottom of my belly, but the sudden weakness in my limbs makes it impossible for me to simply slam the door in his face. And although sending him away right now would be the logical thing to do to avoid a confrontation with Owen, my mouth won't articulate the words. This tall, muscular man I was all over last night is like a magnet pulling me through the damn crack and straight into his arms because deep down inside, I know it'd make me feel so much better than what I'm feeling right now.

"Whose car is that?" Justice asks, pointing at the Mercedes. "Is your friend back early?" He brings his hand to my cheek, and when his knuckles gently brush against my skin, a whole field of goose bumps break out on my arms and back.

"It's not a good time," I whimper, drawing his hand away from my face as my mind registers the heavy footsteps approaching from behind. My head is still stuck between the frame and the door when Owen yanks it wide open.

"Is everything okay?" Justice asks, the surprise evident in his eyes as they leave mine for a brief second to study my ex, then move back to me in silent question.

"It's fine. We're just talking," I say, wondering if he heard us fighting.

Owen steps in. "We're in the middle of something." As always, he doesn't beat around the bush. "And you're a scumbag for turning our grief into some cheap publicity stunt!"

"Enough!" I cry out, turning to face him. "Leave River out of it! Where were you these past two years? Why are you bringing him up now?"

"Why don't you look at yourself, pal, before you start judging me," Justice spits out. "At least I didn't leave my ex-wife in the middle of nowhere with unpaid credits card bills."

"Right, you left yours with a fucking shiner the size of Texas!" Owen comes back.

Everything after that is a blur. I'm not sure who throws the first punch, but the next thing I know, they're tumbling across the living room and dropping loudly on the floor. Owen, of course, has the upper hand. He wasn't labeled the school's troublemaker for no reason. Fights were his specialty.

In an attempt to get him off Justice, I grab the collar of his coat and yank it up. "Stop it, Owen!"

He rises to his feet and staggers back. Justice is still in a horizontal position with his eyes closed and blood dripping down his left cheek.

"I don't want to see you right now, Owen." I gesture at the door.

"Fine!" He draws a deep, loud breath that transforms into a horrid, all-consuming buzz in my ears.

"I don't want to see you right now," I repeat mechanically, blinking back the tears as my eyes avoid looking at Justice.

"Fine... If that's what you want. I expected more of you, Hazel. I really did. But if you're ready to trade your son's memories for a rich piece of ass, good luck with that!"

"You don't even want to talk about our son anymore," I cry out hysterically as he heads for the door. "You never want to talk about him! You don't want any memories!"

"You know what, Hazel"—he spins to face me—"at least I'm trying to move on. Every fucking day, I get up and I go to work and I do shit. And you know why? For you. I did it for you. So you could grieve in comfort. And I didn't even get a fucking thank you for that. And I'm tired of living like this."

My teary eyes absently follow my former husband's figure

outside to his Mercedes, my heart still pounding and the room spinning. The dull pain shooting through my wrist is probably due to my thoughtless attempt to get Owen off Justice. But that's not what sparks the new wave of tears. It's the words Owen threw at me. They hurt more.

Hurrying to the door to shut it, I glance back at Justice, his motionless body still on the floor, his eyes staring at the ceiling.

"I'm fine," he chokes out, his gaze shifting to me. "Just give me a couple of minutes, okay?" He swallows hard, bringing his hand to his face to inspect it for injuries.

"It's not that bad," I explain, wiping the tears off my face with my hands.

Justice slowly sits up and rubs the back of his neck. I rush to the kitchen to grab paper towels for him to clean up. My boot gets caught on the strap of my purse, which was furiously thrown to the floor earlier during my moment of blind rage. I bend down to free myself from the leather tangled around the heel and notice a stack of prints scattered under the kitchen table along with my notebook and some lip gloss.

"Oh no, no, no... I'm sorry, River," I mutter when I realize they're my son's photos. The ones Owen made me take out of the frames. I sink to my knees and slide under the table.

"Hazel?" Justice calls out, and then his body is hovering over mine, his warmth enveloping me from behind before he descends to the floor to help me collect the rest of the photos.

"Thanks," I say, slipping the last of the prints into the stack in my right hand.

"Of course." He sits down and wipes the blood off his chin with the back of his hand while his eyes search mine.

"After River died, Owen asked me to put all the photos of our little boy away." I choke back more tears. "It's like he didn't want to remember that part of our lives. I've been with this man for almost ten years, and after everything we've been through, I don't even know who he is."

Justice scoots over and wraps his arms around me. His embrace is comforting, which is what I fear most because I don't want to get too attached to someone like him, but something tells me it's already too late.

"I don't know why the fuck you married the prick in the first place, babe," he husks into my ear.

"Young and stupid?"

"Seems like a valid excuse. Or maybe he used some black magic to cast a spell on you."

"You read too many fantasy books, Mr. Cross."

"Eh, Aiden is an evolving—what do they call it—Potterhead."

"Isn't he a little too young for those kinds of books?"

"He doesn't understand half the stuff I read, but it puts him to sleep faster than anything else."

"River likes...liked...*The Little Prince*."

"That's not a kids' book either."

"I know. Sometimes I read him Marvel stuff too." I feel the need to change the subject. "I'm sorry you got beat up by my ex-husband."

"Ahh...I guess I'm one of those lover-not-a-fighter clichés. I don't normally engage in activities requiring violence these days. Did all that in my twenties."

"I see."

"And I'm sorry too. I think you've got some blood in your hair." His hand cradles the back of my head as he pulls me closer, resting his chin on my shoulder.

"It's okay." I bury my face into his jacket and close my eyes, hugging the stack of River's photos to my chest. "I don't want to let go."

"Letting go doesn't mean letting go of his memories, Hazel. It means letting go of the pain. You get to keep the rest."

"You can't use your lyrics to comfort me, Justice."

"I'm not. But now that you mention it... I might turn this into lyrics." He chuckles, stroking my hair.

"Why are you here?" I rub my cheek against his shoulder.

"Zander was in a surfing accident. I texted you this morning. Aiden is staying with my parents. I didn't want to go without seeing you first."

"Zander? Your drummer?" My heart starts thrashing. I don't know whether it's because his friend is hurt or because he's here to say good-bye. I know I shouldn't care. We don't belong together. Whatever happened yesterday was a one-time thing. Spur of the moment. Justice Cross can relax and put a check in the box next to my name on his extensive sex list. The logical part of my brain tells me it's best to forget about the way this man makes me feel altogether, but my stupid heart doesn't want to let him go.

"Yeah." Justice sucks in the air through his teeth. "I don't know what the fuck happened. He's been surfing since he was thirteen."

"I'm sorry." I pull back to be able to see his face. "How long will you be gone?"

"I don't know." He runs his fingers across my cheek. "Hey, I'm only giving you the space you wanted." The corners of his lips curl up a little.

"I don't know how this is going to work, Justice." I hug the photos tighter to me. "Everyone leaves. I don't want you to be the one to leave next."

He doesn't respond for a while. His eyes analyze me in silence as his arms stay locked behind my back.

"If we end this right now, it'll be easier for everyone," I say quietly.

"I don't want it to end, Hazel." He brings his face to mine, his lips caressing the corner of my mouth. There's still blood on his chin, but I don't really care about any of that. "I'll be back soon. I promise."

I swallow, trying to ignore the volcano erupting in my stomach as he lands a soft, playful kiss on my lips before pulling me up from under the table. We stand still, our faces a breath apart, our bodies burning for each other.

"You're making me late for another flight." Justice chuckles, tracing his fingers along my jawline.

"I'm sorry." I push against his chest, not hard, but just enough to put some space between us to help me stop wanting him. "Go now."

He moves to the sink and cleans up his face with the wet paper towel while I get the contents of my purse off the kitchen floor.

I follow him out of the kitchen and on the way to the door, his hand brushes mine gently as he whispers into my ear, "I'm taking you to dinner when I come back, baby. And we're going to talk like two adults."

I'm still trembling from his touch when he walks out, but as soon as the door seals shut, Owen's words come crashing down on me like a hurricane. Part of me hates him for saying them out loud, but part of me knows he's right. I was selfish and unsupportive. And I don't want to be that person anymore.

19 JUSTICE

I LOATHE HOSPITALS.

They remind me of death.

They remind me of everything I despise about myself, of everything I should have done to save my best friend from getting in too deep but didn't. Like a coward, I watched him from the sidelines. I watched him crashing and burning and I didn't lift a fucking finger.

A familiar smoky voice interrupts my thoughts. "You look chipper."

I lift my eyes from the floor and blink a few times to make sure the woman in front of me isn't a hallucination.

Rachel was an emergency replacement during our *Tied Up* music video shoot a few years ago. The moment she showed up on set with her long legs, lavender hair, and an attitude like the devil, I knew I wanted to bang her. And I did. Three years later, after Aiden was born and after my wife and I had established that being faithful to each other wasn't something we should keep trying to do.

"What are you doing here?" I pull down the visor of my baseball cap. I ditched the sunglasses disguise a long time ago, especially in public places. They tend to attract more attention than not.

Rachel ignores my question. "What happened to your face?"

"Nothing." Discussing the consequences of squaring off with Hazel's ex is the last thing on my mind.

"Any news?"

"The doctor is with him right now. Bone fracture," I explain briefly. In a way, I'm still in denial myself. I desperately want to believe the loss of the sensory function due to nerve damage isn't the final diagnosis. Zander's already fucked-up wrist simply can't take any more of a beating. Not when we're about to go into the studio to record a new album. "They just did the CAT scan. Still waiting to hear the results."

"Are you okay?" Her green eyes catch my gaze as she shoves both hands into the pockets of her tight red leather jacket.

The one thing I always respected about Rachel was the no-drama policy. We fucked and went our separate ways until we fucked again. Perfect arrangement. Talking to her in public now feels awkward.

"What do you think?" I grit my teeth.

"Gosh...Justice... You don't have to be a dick." A smirk touches the side of her mouth. "I'm just asking. We work together. Remember?"

I draw a deep breath and close my eyes. Her chocolate perfume invading my senses starts choking me. "Sorry. A little on edge lately." The truth is, I don't like chocolate anymore. I think I'm allergic to it now. However, I seem to have developed a craving for vanilla and coconut.

"You mind?" She takes a step forward and points to the chair next to mine.

"Suit yourself," I mutter, stretching my legs in front of me.

Part of me doesn't want her around. It's hard enough to pretend she's nothing more than a crew member when we're on the road. Having her sitting this close to me right now makes me feel dirty. For the first time in my life. As if I'm cheating on Hazel. Because yesterday I asked her to consider being with me in more than just a sexual way, but here I am sitting two feet away from a woman I fucked six ways to Sunday. Funny, it never bothered me before. It does now.

"Thanks." Rachel relaxes in her chair.

Act normal, Justice.

"Cruz and Wendy just went to the cafeteria to get coffee. You want some? I'll text him," I say, fishing for my phone.

"Nah, I'm good." She shakes her head, poker face in place, lips tightly shut. "Is Angelo here?" She's a better actress than my wife.

"He's on his way." I clear my throat, thinking to myself that our band manager wouldn't be interrupting his vacation for something as small as a surfing fender-bender. "From Cancun."

We sit in silence, waiting for our bassist and his wife to come back with the coffee. I'm glad they made up. Cruz's whining while we were on the road was driving me nuts. Rachel is on the phone, texting away. So am I. The news about Zander's accident is already trending on Facebook and Twitter.

The waiting room soon starts turning into The Deviant's remote office. The band's publicist, Samantha, shows up ten minutes later, armed with an iPad and a laptop. Angelo rushes in next. Zander's friends from Laguna Beach arrive after that, along with his parents, who just flew in from Seattle. I feel like I'm at a press conference.

"Where's Tyler?" Angelo barks, throwing his hands in the air. The permanent frown he's developed while managing us deepens on his forehead. He always looks to be on the verge of a nervous breakdown. And the shorts he's wearing, which have bright red and blue flowers and oranges, are the most horrifying ones I've ever seen on a dude.

"MIA," Cruz says, sipping on his coffee.

His wife, Wendy, is sitting on his lap, her inked hand snaked around his neck, fingers toying with his long hair. They're one of those typical over-the-top-PDA rock 'n' roll couples. Wendy's pixie cut has gone through at least thirty different shades of every color that's ever existed since Cruz literally snatched her from under the drummer of the opening band we toured Europe with years back. He was the dark quiet swagger type with the looks that could kill and the hair all women were jealous of. Chance often liked to make fun of this notion. He used to say all Cruz's bass power was in his mane. Once, after a wild tour bus party, Chance, while on some hard shit, attempted to cut a chunk of Cruz's hair as part of an experiment. Both ended up in the ER with broken noses.

"Again?" Angelo's voice drags me back to the hospital waiting room. He rolls his eyes, then shifts his gaze at me. "Justice?"

"What? Why are you looking at me?" I shrug, knowing all too well why. It's not a secret Tyler and I don't always get along. Not because he's a crappy guitar player. He's amazing. Any band that could afford him would steal him in a heartbeat. The problem is that he fucking complains about everything. And he isn't Chance.

Besides, Tyler's presence isn't going to make Zander heal faster.

"Don't give me this 'why are you looking at me' crap!" Angelo barks. "You two either get over your differences or you're looking for a new manager."

His words sit in the air, heavy and dangerous. This isn't the first time he's threatened to leave, but it's the first time he's blown up in public. The funny thing is that I want to just give it to him. Tell him to fuck off. I need a change. I crave to work with someone who understands me without words, someone who feels the music the way I do. And Angelo isn't that person anymore. None of them are. We're just a bunch of guys in their mid-thirties pretending to be twenty, milking this dying passion project of ours until there's nothing left. And the truth is, everything we had that was good, we gave away. It's only a matter of time until the fans start noticing how pathetic we are.

The words are on the tip of my tongue, but I don't say them. Doing it right now in the hospital would be low.

Cruz stares at me for a minute, a pained expression on his face. I think part of him feels exactly the same way I do about the band. He seems happier when he's back home with his wife and kids. Content and relaxed.

Samantha grabs Angelo's arm and pulls him to the side. "Relax, okay?" I hear her say.

"*He's* clearly not having a good day," Rachel mumbles, resuming her texting spree.

"No shit." I fold my arms across my chest and lean back in my chair.

Angelo's always been a hothead. His anger and drive did take us to the very top, but I'm not sure it's what's going to keep us together. He means well, but lately, we haven't been seeing things eye to eye.

"Excuse me." The nurse breaks up our gathering. "Mr. Shaw is back from the CAT scan. He'd like to see his parents first."

We wait some more. Then the nurse returns when I'm in the middle of composing a text message to Hazel. I'm not sure what exactly to say. I just want to know if she's okay after the confrontation her ex and I had earlier today.

"You can see him now," the nurse announces to the group. Everyone except Angelo and Samantha follows her down the hall. We pour into Zander's room like a bunch of kids streaming into a venue when the doors finally open up.

He looks like shit, face bruised, arm in a cast.

"The wave got me good this time," he rasps.

"One day it's going to swallow you, bro." Cruz sits on the edge of the hospital bed. "You better watch out."

"Man, everyone needs a hobby." Zander attempts to be witty.

"Have you tried sewing?" Wendy jokes.

"Yeah. It's on my bucket list, honey." He tosses his head back and tries to smile.

"What did the doctor say?" I ask, pulling up a plastic chair.

"They haven't returned with my CAT scan results yet." His voice drops an octave. "They'll probably have to cut me open a couple more times."

I don't like the sound of that. We're due back in the studio in two months. Zander isn't the kind of a drummer who half-asses on a record. He gives it one hundred and fifty percent whether he's playing a show or riding a jet ski.

His love for extreme sports has been bothersome since he was hospitalized with the surfing injuries the first time. It wasn't serious—the doctors patched him up good, but we were off tour. A year later, he got carried away during a rehearsal and damaged some nerves in his left wrist. Didn't toss the drumstick far enough and it came back and hit him. We were in the middle of the press campaign for the new album, and the label panicked like a bunch of pussies, told us they were going to look for a replacement. Zander got fixed up before we went back on the road. Missed only two shows in South America, but that and the previous injuries did a number on his wrist.

"Man, you really need to slow down with this shit," I say, shaking my head. "You're not twenty-one."

"He's right," Cruz chimes in. "You're pressing your luck, brother."

Wendy and Rachel are whispering in the back of the room as we go on with the conversation. When the nurse comes in ten minutes later and kicks everyone out, I say my goodbyes and head back to the waiting area, where Samantha and Angelo are both on their laptops, typing away.

"Justice," Samantha calls, getting to her feet. She moves closer and pats my shoulder. "There's a crowd outside. You should take the back entrance." Her voice is stern. "Let me get someone to escort you out." She grabs her cell phone to make a call and pushes me in the direction of the hallway. "Where did you park?"

"I got an Uber," I explain while she's trying to arrange security.

"Okay. Southeast entrance is probably best," Samantha continues, phone still pressed to her ear. "Wait here." She squeezes my shoulder before walking off.

I pull down the visor on my cap and position myself in front of posters about arthritis, pretending to read while my head begins to throb. The old version of me would probably just go outside, sign some autographs, and get on with this day. But the current version wants desperately to break free from the gossip hell my life has become.

"Hey." Rachel's voice comes at me from behind. "You're leaving?"

"Yeah." I glance at her over my shoulder, ignoring the anxious murmurs from across the hallway. "Looks like there's a bunch of people outside."

"Ah... The life of a celebrity." She tucks the lavender strand of hair behind her ear and tips her chin in the direction of two teenage girls. They're very young with that starstruck, borderline crazed, look in their eyes, and I wonder how they managed to sneak into the hospital and how their parents would react to the fact that they're drooling over some dudes who are twice their age.

"I think you need to get out of here," Rachel says in a low voice, snaking her arm around mine as soon as the girls pull out their cell phones.

"No shit," I grumble under my breath, following her lead before we get caught on camera.

"Come on. I know a way out."

We rush to the elevators in silence. I peel her arm from mine as the whispers stalk us down the hall. My hand in my pocket is clutching my phone.

Rachel speaks first when we get in the elevator. "You look like shit."

"Try being married to Nikki." I sigh loudly.

"Trust me, I wouldn't want to be in your shoes." She laughs, fiddling with her bracelets.

"No, you wouldn't," I mutter, squeezing my phone.

"So…you and the teacher?"

I turn my head and stare at her like a paranoid asshole, trying to understand what game she's playing.

Rachel rolls her eyes. "Relax. Just making small talk. You two have been trending on Twitter all week."

"Are you stalking my Twitter?"

"No, daddy." She throws my bedroom nickname at me and shoves her manicured finger into my chest. "I don't need to stalk you. I'm on your fucking speed dial. Now tell me that's not true."

The elevator doors open and we walk out to the lot.

"This way." She looks around to make sure the coast is clear and gestures for me to follow her up a ramp.

We stop next to a staircase, and Rachel waves at a dark blue Lexus. "That's me. The exit is on the opposite side. You need a ride?"

"I'm good. I think I got it from here."

She tilts her head and looks at me long and hard. "You're different."

"What's that supposed to mean?"

"Miss Goldilocks got under your skin."

"What are you, my therapist now?" I chuckle, opening my Uber app. The faster I get out of here the better.

Rachel moves closer. "Aren't you curious how I know?" She digs inside her purse and pulls out a pack of cigarettes. Her voice turns to a whisper. "Because you don't want to fuck me anymore."

I want to wipe that smirk off her face. Instead, I go the drama-free route. "I'm in the middle of a nasty divorce."

"Right." A laugh bubbles up Rachel's throat. "You remember the Red Riding Hood marathon?"

"What is this? A trip down memory lane?" I try to shove the

disturbing images of our three-day sex marathon while Nikki was getting her tits done to the very back of my head before the guilt swallows me.

Rachel sticks one of those extra slim cigarettes in her mouth and flicks the lighter. "No, just an observation."

"Are you fucking Zander?" I ask, watching the clouds of smoke spilling from her mouth and nose. I don't know how else to rationalize her being here today. She isn't exactly a close friend.

"Do you care?" She smirks.

"Are you?" I repeat the question.

She takes another drag and hands me the cigarette. Her eyes lock on mine. "No."

The silence that follows seems to go on forever. Part of me is relieved she's not sleeping with my drummer. We never had any rules except for one—always use condoms. She could be fucking five other dudes for all I know. I never promised her any exclusivity either. I'm not sure what's going on between us anymore, but she's right about me not wanting to fuck her. The only woman that's been on my mind this past week is Hazel.

I reach out for the cigarette and slip it between my lips. The taste of nicotine on my tongue feels foreign. I don't smoke on a regular basis, but when I do, it's never when I'm on tour or recording.

"He came on to me a few times," Rachel says.

"Zander?" I take a long drag and wait for verification. My mind is starting to work overtime. Maybe this is good. Insurance in case she ever decides to play dirty, which I doubt she would, but part of me wants to be certain.

"Yep."

"You like him?" I hand her back the cigarette.

"What?" She snorts.

"It's a simple question. Yes or no?"

"Why do you care all of a sudden? You never asked me if I liked you."

"You and I had an arrangement. That's different."

"Is that so?"

"I told you from the start that I wasn't available for anything but sex."

"Is Zander available? Why does it matter to you?"

"He's my friend. I care about him. If you want to go out with him, it's your call. But he can't find out about our arrangement."

"You know better than anyone I can keep my mouth shut." She pauses for a second and offers me the cigarette. "I have some good stuff in my car. Want a hit before you go? You look like you could use some."

I stare down at my Uber app, then back at her. Sealing this deal right now would be perfect. "Yeah. Sure."

We load into her Lexus and Rachel rolls us two joints. We smoke in silence filled with questions hanging dangerously in the air. A few minutes later, the weed is starting to put me to sleep.

"Feel better?" Rachel asks, shifting in her seat to face me.

"Yes and no." I pull the baseball cap off my head and rest my palm on my forehead. "I'm not having a good week."

"Does she make it better?"

My mouth feels dry and I'm hungry, but one mention of Hazel stirs me up. "In a way, she does and in a way, she doesn't."

"You're not an easy man to be with."

"I know... Listen. You understand if you start something with Zander, you can't go on the road with us anymore, right?" My tongue starts sticking to the roof of my mouth.

Rachel draws a deep breath, her eyes stalking me. "Are you telling me this because you care about Zander or because you want to cover your ass?"

Time to show my cards. "Does it matter if you're compensated enough?"

"What kind of compensation are we talking about?"

"You tell me." I take one last drag and toss the rest of the joint into the ashtray. "I better go before TMZ gets here."

"Sure. Thanks for the company."

The effects of the weed wear off by the time I get to my Beverly Hills condo. It's almost midnight and I'm exhausted as fuck, but my mind is back to Formula One mode.

I toss my jacket on the sofa, make myself a drink, and head into the recording room. After I walk over to my Yamaha that I haven't touched in ages, I pull off the dust cover and brush my fingers against the keys, trying to get used to the way it feels. I haven't written a single song in over a year, and all the keyboard parts for the last two albums were done by Zander. Somewhere between the first Grammy and the birth of my son, I lost inspiration, but these past few days, I've been finding myself randomly jotting down song ideas. I even wrote some during my flight back.

I play a few simple chords to warm up first and then give my creation a try. It's still just a bunch of notes awkwardly pieced together, but the fact that I've written something after this long of a break makes me euphoric.

My fingertips start burning with the need to get the tune out once I switch to the harmony. Each stroke of a key is a reflection of a feeling I've been harboring since the last time I actually composed something worthy. Anger, frustration, rage, confusion, fear. They're all embedded into this new melody, floating within the walls of my recording room. And that's just a small fraction of what my heart is attempting to say right now.

An artist is like a sponge. He absorbs everything before merging it with his own, just like I've been drawing all this hurt and despair from Hazel, which in a way reminds me of my own pain.

I once heard someone say that no true masterpiece could ever be born from happiness and content. The art that really touches you to the core and makes you rethink the meaning of life is always created at the lowest point of the artist's existence. I never understood the notion until after Chance died. One minute he was there—a lopsided grin on his happy face, always two girls, always willing to pose for the photos with fans—and the next, he was out cold on the floor of the hotel room, foam in his mouth, eyes bloodshot, cheeks yellow, fingers frozen.

And just like that, he was gone.

Two months after he died, I locked myself up in my home studio and wrote a whole album worth of keyboard parts. None of those tunes ever saw the light of day. Which makes me wonder if this new direction in my music is just another creative glitch or something my heart should follow.

I play around with the keyboard for a little longer, finish my drink and head to bed. But as soon as my head hits the pillow, I change my mind about sleeping and call Hazel.

She doesn't pick up. After staring at the ceiling for a few minutes, I dial again.

"Justice?" Her voice, muddled and sleepy, fills my head.

"I'm sorry I woke you. I wanted to say goodnight."

"It's okay. How's Zander?"

"He'll live." I pause. "He'll probably need a couple of surgeries, though. He busted his bad wrist."

"I hope it's not too serious."

"It'll take a little time, but it's fixable. He just needs to pick non-life-threatening hobbies."

Hazel laughs softly into the phone. It's her not-a-care-in-the-world laughter and I wonder if she's been drinking.

"I'll be back in a couple of days," I say and wait for her reaction.

"Are you coming back bearing gifts?" There's a hint of playfulness in her voice this time. Definitely the wine talking.

"Maybe." I grin to myself. Right now, her gift is fucking hard and needs some attention. This is pure torture. "Want me to describe it to you?"

She sighs. "I know what you're doing, Justice. Quit it."

"Quit what?" I snap. "You started it."

"I did not."

"Yes, you did."

"Sex talk is not going to happen."

The problem is that my cock doesn't feel that way.

"Okay," I mutter, disappointed. The better man is ready to take the fall and do the deed alone, but the asshole decides to give it one last shot. "Is there something in particular about phone sex that turns you off, Hazel?"

"It's hard to have phone sex with someone you actually never had real sex with."

"That's not exactly true... We did have sex in the back of the limo the other day."

"Not the kind of sex I'm talking about."

Yes, she's definitely buzzed. "What kind of sex are you talking about then?"

"I told you this isn't going to happen."

"So the feeling isn't mutual?"

"Justice..."

"How about this. If you're uncomfortable having phone sex, can I just say what I wanted to say?"

"S-sure."

The silence that takes over the bedroom is terrifying. I'm debating whether I should put it all out there or say only what she needs to hear right now. Giving her a lie would be easy because she won't even remember it tomorrow morning. It's one of those things that makes you feel good when you hear it. Nothing more, nothing less. But I don't think I have the heart to tell the woman I want to fuck silly some fluffy crap when all I can think about is burying myself inside her. She deserves the dirty truth and that's what I'm going to give her.

"Just so you know, I'm about to break our deal." My voice becomes a ragged whisper. Her sensual breathing makes me want to get in a car and drive to Tahoe.

"Is what you're going to say worth breaking it?"

"I hope so."

"Let me hear it then."

"Okay..." *Here it goes. All or nothing.* I inhale deeply and close my eyes, trying to recreate that moment in the back of the limo when she was coming undone in my arms—the blazing mess of her hair, the elegance of her natural body, the incitement her lips urged. She was perfect. As if she was crafted for my carnal pleasures only. "You have no idea how much I want to be inside of you right now, Hazel. The way you felt that night in the car, warm and wet around my fingers, with your flawless hands and your silky skin—like fire burning right through my soul. I fucking loved the way your body trembled and the way you screamed before you were coming down back to earth. The sexiest fucking thing I've seen in my entire life. And I want to do it again and again, fuck you until you're a tired, sweaty mess, baby. Really fuck you. Fuck you hard. Fill you up until you can't take it anymore. And then, after we're done, I want to wrap my arms around you, hold you, and lull you to sleep so we can do it some more when you wake up."

When I open my eyes, the room is spinning. The sound of my own heartbeat drumming in my ears is deafening.

"This was very dirty and very poetic," she whispers into the phone after a few long moments of excruciating silence.

"I'll take it as a compliment."

"Goodnight, Justice."

"Goodnight, Hazel."

Next stop: bathroom. Because this hard-on isn't going to take care of itself.

20 HAZEL

Popping another aspirin, I wash it down with freshly brewed coffee.

Up until this moment, Justice has been romancing me with flowers. He even arranged a replacement of the ones he sent prior to his departure. And today, it's a medium-sized box, wrapped in a crisp dark brown paper with a single red rose taped to the top. Knowing the man and considering that I called his porno speech a couple of days ago poetic, this could be anything. I almost expect a dildo or a pair of handcuffs with some elaborate cross design.

My fingers anxiously tap-dance against the surface of the kitchen island as I sip on my coffee while staring at the package that was delivered twenty minutes ago, and I'm still a bit skeptical about its contents when I finish my first cup. My mind keeps replaying our sex conversation, the part about filling me up in particular. The whole thing was bizarre, but to say I didn't like what I heard would be a lie.

A text message alert catches me off guard. I stare down at my phone for a few seconds, contemplating whether I should respond or ignore it for now and wait to reply after taking a look at what's in the box.

Justice: Did you like the present?

Hazel: Haven't opened it yet.

Justice: Why not?

Hazel: The delivery guy woke me up. Still pissed. Don't want to project my bad mood onto your gift.

Justice: Aren't you in the same time zone? It's noon where I'm at.

Hazel: And where exactly would that be?

Justice: Just landed in Tahoe.

Hazel: Welcome back.

Justice: Back to the present. I want you to wear it tonight when I pick you up.

Hazel: Bossy much?

Wear? My imagination starts to run wild. Some kinky lingerie? Stockings and a garter belt? I've heard men like that. I never wore anything of the sort for Owen. Our sex was naked. Including some of our early experiments. But back to my current situation. Does this mean tonight is the night Justice Cross is planning to fuck my brains out? Until I'm a sweaty mess?

The text message notification chime rips through my dirty thoughts and makes me jump off the bar stool.

Justice: If that's what it takes to get you to agree to a date with a guy who you are already allegedly seeing.

Hazel: Based on the rumors cheap gossip-hungry magazines are spreading on the Internet.

Justice: Why do you always find a way to make me feel like an insensitive asshole when I'm trying to prove the opposite?

Hazel: Is that what you're doing right now? Trying to prove that you're not a jerk?

Justice: Right now I'm trying to ask you on a real date. No paparazzi. Just me and you. So I can get to know you better.

Hazel: CRINGE.

Justice: What did I say?

Hazel: GET TO KNOW ME BETTER? This is so last century. No one even uses this as a pickup line anymore.

Justice: Are you calling me old?

Hazel: No. Just unoriginal.

It takes a little while for him to finally respond to my last text.

Justice: That hurt.

Hazel: Sorry. That's not what I mean.
Justice: It's okay. You are forgiven. Under one condition.
Hazel: ????
Justice: Wear my present tonight. Please. I'll pick you up at 8.

I'd like to think that it's the guilt over calling him unoriginal that makes me agree, but deep down, I know it's not.

I spent the last few days doing a lot of thinking. I also worked on my resume and filled out a couple of online job applications. I did some grocery shopping and I went out for a run. It made me feel better about myself.

What's the worst that could happen? Justice and I are all over the internet

Hazel: Okay.

Justice: Have to go. Aiden and I have a lunch date. P.S. I hope I got the size right.

Better not be a garter belt, I think to myself, putting the phone aside.

My mind keeps wandering off to our little make-out session in the back of the limo once I get enough courage and start unwrapping the gift. I feel relieved and a little bit turned on when I realize that the black lace hidden under a layer of white tissue paper is a one-piece halter body suit. No stockings or other funny stuff. My hands shake as I carefully place it on the couch. After a few minutes of studying the intricate swirls of the delicate fabric, I stomp back to the kitchen and pour myself a glass of wine, although mixing it with the coffee might not be such a good idea.

I draw a deep, tremulous breath and take a few sips of my wine.

You're going to look terrible tonight if you keep on drinking. Droopy eyes, slurred speech, smelling like liquor, impaired motor functions. You might not even remember the sex.

"Crap." Gritting my teeth, I dump the rest of the alcohol into the sink.

My eyes dart to the lingerie lying on the couch, then to my feet that haven't seen a pedicure in forever.

I'm not going on a date with a rockstar looking like this.

Google, help me.

An hour later, I find myself occupying a pedicure chair in a spa down the street from the Plaza. Two Asian girls are prettying my feet and hands while my back is being subjected to a full shiatsu massage.

Mom, please forgive me for spending your money on this, but I'll pay you back. I promise.

By the time the makeover is complete, it's almost three. On the way out, I'm tempted to swing by the shopping center to check out some of the clothing stores, but the possibility of running into Justice's fans, who are now religiously stalking the Plaza, makes me change my mind. Plus, the lack of finances doesn't help either. So instead, I head back home to finish getting ready for tonight's date.

After going through my modest selection of clothes in the closet a few times, I decide that taking a bubble bath with some of Rayna's vanilla oil might be a good way to help with my anxiety. My mind is desperately trying to understand where exactly the lead singer of the decade's most controversial rock band fits into my complicated life. The obvious answer is nowhere, but somehow, we've reached this strange point in our so-called relationship where not at least giving it a try would be stupid. And what do I have to lose really? I've given ten years of my life to a person who promised to cherish me and to love me until the day I die, and all that's left of that is a stack of divorce papers and my shattered heart.

Once I'm finished with my bath, I try on Justice's present. Part of me hopes he didn't get the size right, but that's the part of me who's in denial, the part who's still convinced that letting the man with the religious symbols permanently embedded into his sinfully beautiful body finger-fuck her in the back of his limo was wrong. However, her evil twin, the part who enjoyed said wild adventure, is very excited, maybe even wondering if the present does come with some sexy accessories that will be revealed later on as the date progresses.

The way the soft, almost non-existent fabric clings to my breasts and waist as I spin in front of the mirror makes me feel feminine again. It's been a very long time since I've worn something this sexy. And oddly, it fits just right. What are the chances a man can get the size of a woman's body right going off one heavy make-out session?

Closing my eyes, I let my mind go back to the night of the limo ride and slowly run both hands down my sides. A dark part of me wants to recreate the burning-to-the-core sensation of his skillful touch.

Don't overthink it, Hazel. Or you'll end up driving yourself nuts and fuck up your makeup.

At ten past seven, when I'm finishing up my hair, the muffled sound of the doorbell announces the arrival of my date. My heart is doing summersaults in my chest as I rush to the front door. All the rules of seduction that women have crafted for centuries are being washed down the drain. It would be a smart strategy to have Justice locked out on the porch for another ten minutes, but who needs to make the man wait when you know the two of you will end up having sex anyway?

The first thing my eyes register the moment I swing the door open is a sly grin on his unshaven face. He hasn't used a razor since before he left for L.A. and I must admit that at first, the sight of the beard frightens me. It's not even the realization that my skin will eventually come in contact with his facial hair when we kiss, and I know we will, but instead, it's the change itself and the fact that he's been gone a few days and still thought about me during that time.

As soon as the initial shock over his appearance settles in, I analyze the rest of him. Black V-neck sweater, dark blue shirt underneath, a pair of faded jeans, boots. No accessories and, thank God, no baseball cap.

"Hey." He closes the distance between us, his gray eyes raking over my body.

"Hey." My hand is still on the doorknob when he places a kiss on my forehead, a gesture I didn't quite expect, at least not right now, not after he confessed to wanting to fuck me senseless. This man is a walking contradiction.

He pulls back a little and runs his palm over his cheek, then follows with a question. "You don't like it?"

"No. You look...nice. I'm just not used to seeing you this way."

"I only have the luxury of not shaving when I'm not touring." Justice chuckles. "I hope you don't mind." His hand slides up my shoulder and slowly brushes over the neckline of my beige sweater, gently pulling the fabric to the side. His forefinger slips under the lace strap of his present. "Looks like I guessed the size right."

His touch causes a fire between my legs. "Yes. You did."

Justice carefully puts my strap back in place and runs his right hand down my side, his long fingers giving it a light, playful squeeze.

"You have an amazing body, baby," he whispers in my ear. "I can't wait to see it."

"You already saw it." My brain is in total disagreement with my mouth making it sound like I don't want the same thing.

He pulls back, his eyes searching mine. "Not like the last time, baby. I want to see your body wrapped around mine while you're screaming my name."

I swallow hard and draw his hand away from my waist. "Let me just grab my things." To say that two years without sex turned me into an emotional mess says nothing for my current condition.

I find it somewhat strange yet liberating that Justice ends up driving his Jeep instead of getting a limo. Who knows what kind of trouble the private back seat and the freedom from operating a vehicle could have gotten us into.

"Ready?" he asks, starting the engine.

"I think so," I mutter under my breath as he brushes his hand over the fabric of my skinny jeans. My dirty mind is already picturing a repeat of the limo ride. Part of me isn't sure how he can accomplish this challenging task while driving; however, with everything between my legs already soaked, it probably won't be that hard.

I'm ashamed of my own thoughts when instead of moving his hand higher, he grabs my hand and laces our fingers together.

So much for kinky sex in the car, Hazel. You might think you're irresistible in this little lacy thing, but a man surely isn't going to risk his life to give you another orgasm.

Twenty minutes later when we pull down a block with warehouse-looking buildings, restaurants, and bars somewhere in the heart of the historic downtown, I still have no clue what his idea of a date is, but at this point, even if it's something as unoriginal as having dinner or watching a movie, I don't really care. The hand-holding alone feels like nothing short of heaven.

"Are you going to tell me what we're doing here?" I ask cautiously as Justice maneuvers his Jeep toward valet parking. The crowds swarming around the lot suddenly seem intimidating, threatening even. What are the chances some of these people will recognize us? What if the paparazzi are camped out here? They tend to show up every time Justice decides to make a public appearance. He's not even wearing his disguise today. I don't think I can take another crazy convention of The Deviant fans.

"What's wrong, babe?" he asks as the car comes to a stop.

"Where are we going?" I unfasten my seatbelt.

"It's a surprise."

I squeeze my eyes shut for a second and count to three. Let this be a fun night without the invasion of privacy that usually follows this man around.

Hand in hand we make a run for one of the entrances, leaving the Jeep in the care of the valet attendant. Worried about the possibility of being ambushed, I fail to assess my surroundings. My brain resumes working only when Justice slows down in front of a door with a *Private Event Only* sign.

Does this man ever read?

"Hold on." I yank the sleeve of his sweater, pointing at the printed sign as he grasps the handle. "It's closed, Justice."

He takes a step back, and his eyes jump from the sign to me, a sly grin on his lips. "That's us, babe."

"Us?" I gasp, looking up at the neon letters above my head. *Ice Castle.* Is he serious?

"Yes. I rented the place." He pulls me into his arms.

"You rented an ice skating rink?" I murmur into his neck. My heart starts to race again. This man is as insane as they come.

"I didn't want you to think I was unoriginal. What did you expect? A trip to a church and sex in the confessional?"

I can't hold back the laughter. The alternative does sound intriguing, but I doubt I'd feel comfortable enough to go through with the latter part.

"It can be arranged if you want to give it a shot, babe," Justice says suggestively, his hands running up and down my back.

"I'll think about it." *Probably not going to happen.*

"Come on. I don't want any more photos for those sick fuckers to make cash off you, babe." His lips caress the tip of my ear. Ironically, he's the one who set the whole photo op thing in motion.

Inside, an older man in a uniform greets us. After I try on a few different skates and find the right size, he gives us the basics on where the restrooms, the cafeteria, and the emergency exits are located and gets back to his check-in desk.

"What happened to the rest of the employees?" I ask as we make our way through the empty building, my eyes taking in all the Christmas décor adorning the walls. The soft instrumental music playing in the background is oddly comforting.

"We don't need anyone," Justice says. "It's a private event, remember?" He stops in his tracks in the middle of the lobby and wraps his arm around me, pulling me closer with one hand and grasping our skates in the other.

"You wanted me to wear your present while learning how to skate?" I stifle a giggle. "Is this a dress rehearsal for the Olympics? Do you have your tights?"

Justice brings his lips to mine and utters into my mouth, "The present is for after we're done skating, babe." The lingering scent of his cologne and the scruff on his chin brushing against my skin turns my legs into a wobbly mess. *A little bit of caveman in him feels nice.*

Shit, I don't think I can even walk right now, let alone get on the ice. Damn pheromones.

"For later?" I breathe out, digging my fingers into his muscular shoulders to avoid falling down.

"Yes." He pulls back a little. "But first we're having dinner."

"Dinner?" My lips are going into a state of withdrawal over the kiss that almost happened. Who would have thought Justice could be such a tease?

"Of course. I'd like to feed you before we get to the exercise part, babe." He chuckles, leading me to the cafeteria.

A skating rink employee rushes out from the back to take our order when we approach the counter.

"Their steak burgers are amazing," Justice whispers in my ear while

I'm studying the menu board. My heart is drumming in my chest, my body is buzzing. I feel sixteen again, alive and free.

After placing our order, we take the table overlooking the ice and wait. The red and green Christmas lights dancing across Justice's face remind me of the made-for-TV holiday movies Mom and I used to watch when I was little. In the end, the Prince Charming would always come to the rescue, kiss the girl, and they would ride off into happily ever after. But sadly, real life is nothing like that. For a long time, I thought Owen was my Prince Charming. Now, I don't know what to make of our marriage. As for the man shamelessly devouring me with his eyes right now, part of him is still an enigma. One minute he's an arrogant jerk, the next he's gentle and caring.

I'm too nervous to eat when our food finally comes out. The winged creatures in my stomach are making it really difficult to concentrate on anything besides the man sitting across the tiny cafeteria table from me. So after nibbling on the burger and a few fries, I state that I'm full, but apparently, I'm not convincing enough, especially since most of the food on my plate is still untouched.

"You hardly ate anything," Justice says, digging into his burger.

"I don't want gravity to bring me down when I put those things on." I nod toward our skates that are sitting on the bench in the corner.

Being the only two people in the whole building right now, not counting the other two employees, is both odd and flattering. This humble throwback to my teenage years when Christmas was still my favorite holiday makes me feel special. I can't believe a man like Justice would be brave enough to take a woman to an ice rink instead of playing it safe with a traditional trip to a luxury restaurant.

"I won't let it." He dips a fry into his puddle of ketchup and slowly brings it to my mouth, his gray eyes never leaving mine.

"You don't have to feed me. I'm a big girl," I say, my gaze darting to the black swirls of ink disappearing under the rolled-up sleeves of his sweater. I like that he has clean, untouched-by-a-needle, areas of skin on his wrists.

"Shhhh... It's a do-over. Wanna get it right this time," Justice whispers, brushing the fry against my trembling lips. His voice is deep and sensual, with a little bit of a rasp. The man has a special gift. He can turn anything, even a shoestring potato, into an object of erotic foreplay.

"Come on." He tilts his head, a suggestive smile gracing his face.

I obediently part my lips and let him slip the French fry into my mouth.

"See. No sweaters were harmed." Justice smiles, running his thumb over my lower lip.

I'm completely undone by his touch. Right now, skating seems like the equivalent of climbing Mount Everest and I'm not so sure I want to embarrass myself in front of this man by repeatedly landing on my ass due to my clumsy limbs.

"Is this a do-over of our first meeting?" I ask after a long pause.

"So you do remember?" He falls back into the chair, crossing both arms on his chest.

"I wasn't *that* drunk."

"You were passed out cold while my ex was screaming her guts out less than twenty feet away." He chuckles.

"Is this some sort of a trip down memory lane?" I ask, shifting in my chair.

"Yes. No. Maybe." Cryptic messages.

"Then what is it?"

"It's called getting to know you better." He leans forward, placing both elbows on the tabletop. "You still find it cringey?"

"A little. You never told me why you were at that bar."

"I was checking out my nephew's band."

"You have a nephew?" This comes to me as a bit of a surprise.

"Yeah. Jake. My sister's kid."

"You never mentioned a sister."

"Mom, Dad, older sister. They all live here in Crystal Bay. The bar belongs to my dad's friend."

"So"—I playfully kick his ankle with the tip of my boot—"you're not a foster child who grew up in rural Alabama and moved to L.A. at the age of sixteen hoping to conquer Hollywood? No living under a bridge?"

"Are you sure you aren't confusing me with someone else?" He laughs.

"No." A soft giggle escapes my mouth. "I'm kidding. I read that you grew up around here. It's not some top secret classified information like your relation to Elijah Hale. A little vague but still easily searchable on the net. There wasn't much about your family, though."

"I try to keep my family away from all the press nonsense," he explains. The tone of his voice is now serious. "No one needs to know who my parents or my siblings are. It saves them the headache of dealing with stupid people."

"Understandable."

"One innocent photo can turn your life into a nightmare." His eyes carefully study me, waiting for my reaction.

I swallow hard and push the plate and the utensils aside. "Yeah." Whatever little appetite I had is lost for good.

"I really am sorry, Hazel." There's sincerity in his voice. He means it.

"That's okay. We wouldn't be here right now..."

The silence that follows seems to go on for an eternity. The Christmas décor suddenly feels hollow and gloomy and reminds me that River isn't her to celebrate with me. No matter where I go or what I do, the memories will keep haunting me for the rest of my days. Every minute that passes by is a minute without my son.

"I come from a place I long to return to," Justice says quietly.

"Is this from one of your songs I haven't heard?"

"No, this is Dante Alighieri. The Divine Comedy." He smiles. "Sometimes you have to go through all nine gates of hell before getting to paradise, where you're destined to end up at, baby."

The air suddenly leaves the room and the walls start to close in on me when the realization that this *is* my final destination hits me. "What if there's no paradise?" I ask breathlessly.

"There is." His hand slides across the tabletop in the direction of mine. "You just have to go through hell first. No shortcuts."

"Are you there yet?"

"Not yet. I'm still stuck in inferno, traveling through the nine concentric circles of agony. I know paradise exists, and I know if I try really hard, I might get a glimpse of it before my days on this earth are over. I just can't seem to let go of all the old ways."

An insignificant part of me is confused and scared, but mostly I'm stunned by his confession. He's uncomplicated and at the same time complex, a paradox of a person with the real version lingering somewhere in between.

"Why can't you?" A light tremor takes over my body again.

"I'm trying." He grasps my hand, his thumb brushing the inside of my palm. "I have a hard time separating what's real and what's not anymore."

"Is this real? The date? Is this what you wanted to do or what you thought would be a good way to impress me?"

"Both." He smiles.

I'm flattered, but the words don't want to come out. Something tells me it's not my turn to speak yet, so I sit there enjoying the warmth of his touch, the closeness of his body, the intimacy, and the simplicity of it all as if this man isn't the same person who has hordes of teens chasing him day and night.

"I don't really talk to anyone about this." He clears his throat. "Not even my therapist. He always gives me the generic bullshit about forgiveness and acceptance when I try to explain how I feel, so I stopped bringing it up."

I nod silently.

"My childhood friend Chance and I started the band when we were teenagers. He was our lead guitarist. He OD'd in the middle of the tour right after we hit it big." Justice closes his eyes for a few seconds and inhales deeply. "We were this brand new killer band everyone was talking about, on the road for months and months, fucking nonstop. All the major festivals wanted us, and the label kept adding tour dates. It became overwhelming, physically and mentally. We wanted a fucking break, at least to recharge our batteries.

The problem is that when you're in a band, the suits are the ones calling the shots, especially when it's your first record deal. They're out to milk you dry. All the guys in the band were doing drugs, mostly coke, because they kept us going. Chance liked to experiment. He wrote sick riffs when he was high. It was good at first because we had so much fucking material, enough for more than two albums. His brain worked day and night.

We were on the road, fucking tired of bunk beds, planes, time zone changes, and we were playing shows, partying, fucking women, and writing music—always high. This one night, we were sitting in the hotel, tossing around some ideas, and Chance was on a roll. He co-wrote some of the lyrics, and we got stuck on the second verse, spent two hours trying to come up with a good line and suddenly it was going nowhere. He figured it'd be a good idea to give our creativity a boost."

The air escapes my lungs.

"He miscalculated though," Justice continues. "By the time the paramedics arrived, he was already a goner."

"I'm so sorry."

"The thing is, everyone, including me, knew he needed help. He used to shoot heroin before the shows, then it got to the point where he had to go backstage during the drum solo to get another fix because he couldn't last through a fucking ninety-minute set without baking and messing up his parts. One time he was so fucked up, we had to stick a fucking needle into his vein to make him fucking get up. And I just let it happen. Instead of telling him no, I said yes."

The air is heavy, thick, and hot, like liquid metal, burning right through my lungs as I take a deep breath in an attempt to calm down.

"Does it get any better?" My voice comes out in a form of a pathetic squeal. I want verbal validation that eventually, the pain over the death of someone you love dearly eases up, but his eyes tell me otherwise. "Do you ever stop thinking about it?"

"I can't do that. We grew up together, made music together. I'd be nowhere right now without him. He died right in front of me. It was like a fucking apocalypse in slow motion. Sometimes you block it out to make room for some other things, but sooner or later it comes back and hits you really hard. Harder than before because you keep holding it in. What I understand now is that the only way to stay sane is to embrace it instead of pretending like it never happened."

"I don't know how to embrace the death of my son."

"It'll come to you. One day you'll figure out how to concentrate on the good only, Hazel."

"When?"

Justice gets to his feet. "I don't want this date to be depressing. That's not why I brought you here." With one skillful motion of his arms, he pulls me off the chair and nods in the direction of the skates. "Let it go, baby, okay?" He brushes his lips against my temple. "Just because they aren't here doesn't mean they don't want us to live a little."

I pause for a moment and try to shake off my sad thoughts. "Do you know how to skate?" Part of me is wondering if maybe this man has some other hidden talents like breathing fire or flying a plane.

"I used to come here with my dad and sister. But it's been a very long time. I might not be as good as I was back in the day."

My worst fears are confirmed fifteen minutes later when I find myself desperately grasping the rail, my whole body unsteady from the lack of leverage and my legs not cooperating at all.

"Come on, let go!" Justice yells at me from afar, his tall figure lingering in my peripheral vision as I concentrate on trying to straighten up.

"Easy for you to say." He got on those skates like a pro and effortlessly flew across the rink in all of his grace, leaving me speechless and numb. Is there anything this man can't do?

"You're not going to fall, Hazel!" he urges. The quiet swooshing of his skates grating against the artificial ice approaches me from behind.

My stomach is in one huge knot when his fingers lock on my shoulder. He pulls me into his broad, muscular chest and whispers into my ear, "I've got you." His hot breath burns the back of my neck as he slides his hands down my sides to hold me in place while I'm doing my best not to take a nosedive onto the ice. Then, suddenly, my body is all too aware of the feeling of his belt buckle thrusting into my skin through my sweater and the delicate lace I'm wearing under my clothes. It feels foreign, too soft and too expensive. It belongs in the bedroom, not here.

"Please don't let go." A pitiful whine escapes my mouth as I release the rail, trying to ignore the tingling in my belly.

"I won't." His hair tickles my neck as he rubs his unshaven chin against my cheek, both arms possessively clasped around my waist. Some days, Justice Cross reminds me of a panther, dangerously slick and graceful, but other days, like today, he's a big fuzzy, sensitive cat looking for some human affection and comfort. The problem is, I'm not sure I can indulge his yearnings just yet, not in this half-frozen, half-quivering state of distress.

"Bend your knees, baby," he orders, sliding his hands up my stomach.

"What?" I gasp.

"You've got a really dirty mind." He laughs. "Just bend your knees or you'll fall."

I do as he says.

"Alright, hold on." He slowly spins me to face him. "Are you okay?"

I nod in response, watching the colored spotlights dance across the glossy white surface of the rink. The view is both breathtaking and distracting. I wonder if he requested the whole Christmas theme for tonight specifically or it was already set up for the general public.

"Come on." Justice grasps my hands and carefully pulls me toward the center.

Two seconds later my legs are already splitting apart. "I'm going to fall," I shriek nervously, hoping that digging my fingers into his flesh with all the strength I've got will prevent me from the embarrassing descent, but gravity wins.

"You're not." Justice stops in his tracks, but the rescue mission fails miserably when my knees buckle and I lose my balance, sending us both down. My ass is the first to connect with the surface.

"Fuck," I say on an exhale after the back of my head hits the ice next. For a second there, I may even see stars—it's hard to say with all Justice's weight crashing into me. What I do know is that this isn't exactly how I imagined his body would feel on top of mine. I expected the experience to be...softer. And less painful.

"Are you okay?" I can hear Justice mumble into my neck, his legs entwined with mine, the blades of his skates scratching the ice as he readjusts his position and props himself up on an elbow.

"I'll live." I close my eyes for a moment. The throbbing pain in the back of my head is distracting. "I just don't think I can take any more skating tonight."

"Sure. Do you want to get out of here?"

"Yes." I sniff, feeling guilty over ruining the remainder of the night.

By the time we get the Jeep back, the headache caused by the collision with the ice has turned into a dull sensation somewhere at the base of my skull. But it's nothing I can't handle. Not when my body is suddenly back to wanting Justice.

As soon as we're inside and buckled in, Justice grabs my hand and rests it on his thigh. "You feeling okay?"

"Yeah."

"We can swing by the pharmacy and get some Tylenol if you don't want to wait 'til we get to my place."

"I'm fine." I shake my head, smiling internally. *His place it is.*

"Are you sure?" He leans over the armrest, his breath tickling the side of my face as he says in a low, seductive voice, "I still plan on fucking you senseless, baby...unless you think your head trauma will be a problem."

"No, no problem." A quiet moan escapes my mouth the moment his firm lips slide across my cheek causing every inch of my trembling body to ignite at that instant.

"I just wanted to make sure, baby. Because it won't be pretty." Justice laughs a little, pulling back.

"Who said I'm expecting pretty sex?" I say under my breath.

"That's what I like to hear."

21 HAZEL

"You're positive you don't need Tylenol?" Justice says into my mouth, gently pushing my quivering body against the door as we stumble inside the cabin. He thoughtfully cradles the back of my head to prevent it from any further damage the vicious attack of his lips on mine is about to cause.

His tongue is an excellent combination of good and evil. Sweet and soft one minute, bitter and demanding the next.

"Fuck Tylenol." I run my hands up his shoulders and sink my fingers into his hair. It's sinful for a man to be this beautiful. He's not big, but he's rock solid in all the right places. Tall, lithe, and sizzling hot against my body.

"I'm going to ask one more time—are you sure, baby?" He breaks the kiss. "Because once we're in the bedroom, I'm not letting you leave until sunrise."

"Is that a threat?" I moan, my hands roaming around his back. Where are all these erotic sounds coming from? For a woman who's been off sex for quite some time, I sure have a wide array of reactions.

"It's a promise." He slowly drags his tongue down my neck, and his fingers entwine with mine. "Come on. Let me show you what you've been missing all this time, baby." He nods in the direction of the bedroom with a naughty grin on his wet lips.

The reflection of the water slipping in through the open blinds of the wall-to-wall window dances across his face as we walk through the living room. Dirty Hazel wants to rip his clothes off and ask him to fuck her in the middle of the dark hallway. Against the wall. With the stupid plaque hanging above her head. The full *Justice Cross, the rockstar* experience. But I'm curious what the real Justice is like. When he's stripped of his fame and fortune. Is that man any different?

We step into the bedroom and he shuts the door. His hands slide under my sweater again, stroking down my back, then gradually making it to my stomach. Our bodies move slowly to the quiet beat of the lapping water, following the lake's sublime rhythm.

"Let's get rid of this." Justice grabs the hem of my sweater and pulls it over my head.

He takes a second to drink me in, long fingers tracing a line above my collarbone and moving down until he cups my breasts. If not for the delicate fabric of the bodysuit giving me some semblance of a barrier, I'd probably be feeling faint.

"Is there something in particular you like?" He brushes his thumb against my left nipple, and the lace no longer helps . Every part of me burns from his touch, and my heart is beating its way out of my chest. There's a gasp stuck somewhere in the back of my throat. Justice steps back into the moonlight streaming through the glass of the vaulted ceiling, and his eyes meet mine. "You're fucking beautiful." His voice is a ragged whisper, and the expression on his face is one of a predator stalking his prey.

"Your turn." I reach out for his clothes, unsure where to begin.

"As you wish." He starts undressing. First the sweater, then the shirt, his dark, hooded eyes never leaving mine. The asshole enjoys torturing me by being extra slow. Button by button. The man is a natural-born entertainer.

Shit. I think I've lost my mind.

"Do you like what you see?" Justice asks, a wicked smile touching his lips.

"I've already seen it," I say teasingly.

He moves closer. "Not in action." A smirk tilts the corner of his mouth.

My eyes study his flawless chest and abs. He doesn't have a whole lot of tattoos, but the ones he does have are scattered all over his body, some small, some larger, with the patches of blank skin in between. His stomach and neck are barely touched with ink. The designs are sophisticated, moody, religious. He looks dark and hungry, almost demonic, with his tousled black hair splayed across his broad shoulders.

His arms tighten around me and he pulls me into a deep, sensual kiss that soon turns into a passionate assault, his tongue rough and skillful.

"Look what you did, babe," he groans, sucking on my bottom lip as his erection glides against my jeans. "This time I'm not letting you go anywhere until this is all taken care of."

"And I'm not leaving until you make good on your promise."

"Oh. I *will* keep my promise, baby." He brings his lips to my neck, and I let out a low moan when he sinks his teeth into my skin.

He pulls back a little and traces his index finger along my jawline. Then his other hand tugs on the waistband of my jeans, eyes seeking permission. Not that he needs it.

The wildfire between my legs messes with my motor skills during my attempt to undo his belt buckle. What did they say about sex and bicycles? Why am I just discovering that it's a lie right now, at the most inappropriate moment ever?

My hands start to shake when I drag down his zipper.

"Relax, baby." He cups my head and pulls me into another kiss. This time it's gentle and delicate, his lips barely touching mine.

Hazel, the grieving mother and soon-to-be ex-wife, miserable and ruined in her own solitude, isn't here right now. What's here is a woman who wants nothing but to satisfy her animalistic desires, a woman who hasn't felt anything in over two years.

"Let me get these for you." Justice descends to his knees and starts working on my boots. His hot breath fans against my skin, the heat penetrating the thin lace of the bodysuit. When he brings his head closer and places a soft kiss above my belly button, a wave of tingles spread through my insides and down to the aching spot between my legs. I let my fingers toy with his hair while he undresses me, then my jeans and boots join his shirt and sweater on the floor.

Once I'm wearing nothing but the bodysuit, he draws me closer and buries his face in the soft fabric, his cheek pressed to my stomach. He slides both hands across my thighs and cups my ass.

This is torture. Another second and I'm going to come undone with him still on his knees, examining my bare legs.

"Tell me what you want," he grinds out, his voice an elegant mix of dirty and tender. "Tell me how you want me to fuck you, baby."

A shiver runs down my spine. I didn't know there were options. What I do know is that the material between my thighs is soaking wet.

His warm hands smooth over my sides as he gets to his feet, the height of his body now towering over my own.

I reach out for him, and my lips brush his inked skin. I carefully study the designs, wondering what they could mean or if it hurt when he had them done. But when my eyes come across his son's name on his left pec, the floor underneath me starts to shift. The hole in my chest is suddenly bigger than ever.

I'm a bad mother. Why am I here when my baby is seven hours away, alone in the cold ground?

Guilt twists my insides and my body goes limp for a brief second.

"Don't stop," Justice says quietly, his fingers slipping under my lace straps, which he carefully removes from my shoulders, slowly dragging them down until my breasts are exposed.

"Fuck, baby." His thumbs stroke against my nipples while his firm lips dance along the length of my neck. He takes his time, his touch slow and calculated.

My fingers go for his jeans to finish what I started a few minutes ago. The cool leather of his studded belt feels rough against my skin.

"Justice," I purr. There's something exceptional, something distinctive about his name. It's surprising how much I love saying it out loud.

"Yes, baby?" he whispers against my skin. His tongue travels down my breasts, leaving no piece of my upper body untouched. He frees my arms from the confines of the bodysuit and traces his fingers across my ribs.

This man is ruining me slowly but surely.

My emotions are all over the place, and apparently, my judgment is fogged too, because the things I'm thinking about are unfamiliar and unnerving, dark even.

I draw a deep breath and finally let it out. "I want you to hurt me." My request comes out in the form of a squeal instead of the planned sexy rasp.

This doesn't intimidate him. Not even a bit. "You like that, huh?" Straightening up, he dips his hands into my hair and pulls it gently to angle my head up just enough for him to be able to look into my eyes. "Why didn't you tell me sooner?" A wicked smile plays across his lips. "I don't keep any of my toys in here."

For some reason, his confession doesn't surprise me. A man sporting a choke collar in front of an arena full of people is probably not into vanilla sex. If anything, it makes me want this even more. It makes me want the real Justice, not the one who's going to give a pathetic pity fuck.

"I've never done it before," I admit, staring back at him.

"Okay." He releases my hair. "Are you sure?"

"I'm sure."

"Look, if you've never done it before, baby"—he draws me against his body, stroking the small of my back—"we can start with something a little less...dangerous."

Adrenaline simmering in my veins crushes the leftovers of my common sense. I push against his chest. Hard.

"Come on, Justice! I don't need this boring compassionate sex! I haven't been with a man for over two years. I want you to fuck me like you mean it!" My heart is drumming so loudly that I can barely hear myself speak. "I want to see the real you!"

"This *is* the real me." His eyes dark and wide, zoning in on me.

I'm shaking like a leaf on a tree caught up in a thunderstorm. "Cut the bullshit." My voice pitches high.

Justice doesn't see my hand coming. Not until it smacks him across his unshaven cheek, producing an ominous echo. He grabs my wrists and pulls my body against his erection. Part of me expects an angrier response, but deep down I already know he's not as easy to crack as I thought.

"Come on, Justice." My trembling voice fills the room as I try for another slap. "I want you to fuck me like you mean it."

He intercepts my hand midair. "Be careful what you wish for."

Then we're a raging mess again—lips crashing, chests heaving, material ripping. It's scary and exciting at the same time, how much I enjoy the stormier parts of this make-out session, like when he grabs me a little rougher or when he pulls my hair harder.

"Please, Justice," I drone deliriously, grabbing ahold of his belt. The buckle is cold and solid between my fingers. "Will you make it hurt?"

"You're insane, baby," he tells me as I pull his jeans down to his knees and let them fall to the floor. He tosses them aside with his foot, his mouth returning to mine.

"I think you like insane." I put the belt around his neck. The crazy Hazel's trying to decide which Justice she likes—the crowd-pleaser or the bedroom version of him.

"What are you doing?" he asks, seizing my wrists.

God, this is beyond insane. I've never even had any interest in such things, yet right now I desperately want him to spank me, choke me, and drag me through my own nine circles of torment. "I'm showing you how I want you to make me feel."

I've gone crazy. The kind of crazy where there are no inhibitions. Drawing my tongue up his firm chest, I release the end of the belt, then slip my fingers into his hair, wrapping it around them. And the way his breath hitches when I sink my teeth into his flesh definitively means he's giving me the green light, so I jerk my hand, thinking to myself how happy I am that his hair is long.

He responds with a startled gasp. The most erotic gasp I ever heard from a man. Low, raspy, sensual. "Fuck, Hazel."

"Come on, Justice... What's it gonna be?" I let the belt go and slap his other cheek. Once, twice. Until his skin starts to turn red from my touch.

"You're playing with fire, baby," he growls, trapping me in his arms.

"What's it gonna be, Justice?"

"How do you want me to make you feel?" He rubs his cheek against mine, his stubble scratching me. The cold belt buckle stuck between our hot bodies.

"I want you to walk me through your inferno. I want you to show me." I make one last attempt to slap him because I can tell by the darkness in his eyes that he's close to flipping the switch.

"What's your safe word?" His lips near my ear, and his voice softens for a brief moment.

My scrambled mind refuses to cooperate. I'm trying to think of something but what comes out of my mouth is a slur.

"We need a safe word, baby, if you want me to show you those things you're asking about," he insists. "I need to know your limits."

"Stop," I say, panting, because that's the extent of my brain activity at the moment. Not very original.

Justice spins me around, his hands grabbing at the roots of my hair, violently jerking my head and the rest of my body in the direction of the bed, my scalp burning from the sudden assault.

"Is that all you've got?" I cry out as he pushes me onto the mattress, facedown. His heavy breathing pounds against my eardrums along with my own heartbeat.

"I've got a lot more." He leans into me, his voice gentle as if he's looking for reassurance that this is the way I've chosen to be fucked. There's no need, though. There's no turning back now, not when I'm one huge pile of adrenaline splayed on his massive bed with his flawless body above mine.

"Bring it on," I say rolling over to face the man.

He's a piece of art, like an antique sculpture. The epitome of male beauty drawn against the lingering moonlight seeping into the bedroom. And I want him to rip me apart, torture me into an orgasm.

"We're not going to need this." He slowly glides his hands up my thighs and under the lace, teasing my stomach a little before freeing me from the leftovers of the damaged bodysuit, pulling it down and over my legs that are dangling off the edge of the bed. Then he positions himself in front of me, spreading me with his knees. His eyes rake over my naked body, his chest rising and falling, his hands playing with the belt.

After a few long moments of silence, he nods toward the middle of the bed. "Scoot back."

I silently slide up the mattress, my insides trembling with anticipation.

"Sit up."

I do as he says.

"On your knees. Turn around."

My heart is beating so hard that I'm pretty sure Justice can hear it.

"Last chance, Hazel." His voice drifts at me from behind as I sit there with my knees buried in the mattress, staring at the headboard, naked and shivering, equally excited and terrified to play this game.

"I'm not buying it, Justice," I say firmly. "I didn't sign up for some cheap shit pretend version of you."

The mattress shifts under his weight as he descends on the bed, grabbing a handful of my hair again. "Is that what you want?" He pulls hard and fast.

"You can do better than that," I cry out. The physical pain is strangely refreshing.

"You want better?" he growls, biting my shoulder.

"I don't feel it, Justice...if you don't make it hurt." My voice is a lewd prayer, desperate and angry, a plea for what normal people shouldn't want.

"Fuck it," he groans, slapping my ass. Not hard, just a sample for now.

"Come on." I throw in a word of encouragement.

"You want more?"

"Yes."

"Okay, baby, bend over." He smacks that same burning spot he hit just a few seconds ago. This time with full force, causing me to jolt forward. A muffled gasp on the brink of sobbing leaves my mouth as he pulls my hair again, yanking me back up. For a second, there are black dots in front of my eyes, similar to the stars I witnessed earlier at the skating rink.

My voice turns hoarse from all the screaming. "I can't fucking feel you!"

"Don't tempt me, baby...don't fucking tempt me!" he says into my neck, pushing me back down, leather and metal sliding across my skin.

"Come on!" My mouth is dry, my stomach twisting into thousands of tight, throbbing knots.

I can feel him finally letting go as he draws a loud, deep breath, reminding me of an animal released from captivity, finally able to run free. The real Justice Cross. Wild and unrestrained. Just like me. He's right, after all. We're amazing together.

My fingers dig into the sheets the moment the belt smacks across my back, another half gasp, half sob ripples through my lungs. My body is buzzing from a mixture of the sensations.

"Don't let go," I whimper, feeling his grasp on my hair weakening. "Again!"

He hesitates for only a brief second. The next hit is a little harder. I can tell he's getting the hang of it because each slap is more methodic.

It leaves me breathless, crying, and asking for more. Part of me is scared to even know why. The pain is excruciating, invading each section of my body. Nothing like I've ever felt before.

"Get up!" Justice snarls. The slaps end. My back is on fire, spasms rocking my lower stomach.

"Come on. Keep going." I jerk as he attempts to wrap his arms around me and cup my breasts. "Come on."

"Baby...I need to fucking come. You made me wait all this fucking time." He pushes my hair aside and tightens the belt around my neck. "You have no fucking idea what you're doing to me. You have no fucking idea..." His whisper gets lost in my own moans as he slips his fingers between my legs, pushing into me just a little, his other hand pulling on the belt.

"If you're going to fuck me, Justice, you have to make it count," I choke out, fisting the sheet, my body quivering.

"I told you I'd fuck you until you're a sweaty mess, baby," he mumbles into my back, his second finger sliding into me. "I'm a man of my word."

My belly squeezes in response. The moment I push against his hand, looking for more action, he yanks the belt up. My lungs start constricting from the lack of air, tears welling up in the corners of my eyes, skin burning.

"My house, my rules. I'll tell you when you can come." He smacks my ass again.

I gasp. My vision blurs. My mind is trying to process the pain when the heat of his body suddenly disappears. I inhale sharply, letting the smell of sex, sweat, my vanilla and his spice fill up my aching lungs. The sounds of the bedside drawer sliding open and the rustle of the condom wrapper replace my screams. Seconds later, warm hands smooth over my thighs, thumbs rubbing into my skin. Intensifying his grip, he pulls me back up against his length to let me feel him, one hand between my legs spreading them wide, another one on the belt. I want to see his face, but the unknown is just as exciting.

"Last chance to opt for slow and easy, baby." He rubs against me, but I'm too far gone. "Last chance." He repeats in a honey-dripped voice.

"Get to business, Justice," I say on an exhale.

"You asked for it, baby. Don't say I didn't warn you."

He yanks the belt, angling me up to his liking and pushes into me with one fierce thrust.

"Oh my God." I clench my teeth, suddenly wanting to take my words back and switch them for the slow and easy option. It never occurred to me that after two years without sex, this would feel like the first time all over again, very painful and very uncomfortable despite all the fluids my body has been producing all day. The problem isn't the lubrication. It's the damn size. He's barely fitting in there.

"Fuck, Hazel." He pushes into me harder, his wet chest pressing against my aching back. "Baby, you're so tight." His labored breathing grows louder. Just like his thrusts as he keeps pounding into me, totally unaware that I wasn't ready. Soon, it all turns into one chaotic mix of screams, panting, skin smacking, and sweat dripping on the crumpled sheets.

I'm trembling from the strange combination of pain and pleasure. The man is fucking me into oblivion and my body doesn't know how to resist his size anymore. It hurts, but it's the kind of hurt I like.

"Do you want me to stop, baby?" he asks after another tortured cry leaves my mouth. "Do you want me to stop?" His lips brush against my ear, his hand readjusts his grip, and the belt snaps around my neck again, cutting the air off for a brief moment. I'm surprised he knows just the right time to let go. Makes me wonder how many times he's done this particular trick before.

"No." I shake my head, grasping his other hand as he wraps it around my waist, his body viciously slamming into mine. "I want you to fuck me harder, Justice."

All these strange, dirty things I'm asking him to do to me. I had no idea I'd like being manhandled this way.

He groans in response. Both hands on my hips, holding me in place as he thrusts harder and harder, causing my knees to slide across the sheets, burning my skin in the process.

I can't feel my own body anymore, just the bliss wrapped into a blanket of endless agony. My screams mix with his; my leg muscles start to cramp up.

"Are you close, baby?" Justice rasps into my hair. "Are you?"

"Yes...yes...yes… Just don't stop." This is the last plea that escapes my mouth before I combust. I come undone in his arms with his chin pressing into the back of my head as he kisses my hair. His own release comes just a moment later. Loud, sweaty, violent, yet sweet.

Unable to stay still, I tumble forward, facedown, trying to catch my breath as his hands slip between my neck and the sheets to take off the belt while he remains inside me. My skin stings a little from the friction of the rough leather, but I don't care. I suppose it's safe to assume I'll have tons of marks tomorrow morning, but right now I just want him to hold me tight like he promised.

"You're fucking amazing, baby," Justice mumbles in my ear, finally pulling out. He stands up to get rid of the condom first, then drops on the bed and rolls over onto his side to face me. His wet hair tickles my skin as he brings his head closer to place a gentle kiss on my cheek. The animal who just broke me down is gone; he's a fuzzy cat again, soft and cuddly, like a gigantic toy.

"Thanks." My voice is barely there because my throat is dry as sandpaper, and my pulse is racing.

"Let me get some water," he says when his breathing is back to normal.

Unable to speak, I nod silently, watching him as he leaves the bedroom. The aftershocks of my orgasm are still rocking my body, light tingles running across my skin—some of them pleasant and some with a bit of pain. I'm slowly coming to terms with the fact that Nikki Deville's husband just fucked me in the way I never imagined I'd want to be fucked.

Justice is back in a couple of minutes with two bottles of water.

"I'm sorry if I was a little bit out of control." He strokes my hair, pushing some of it away to get a better view of my face that's half buried in the damp sheets. My peripheral vision catches the corners of his lips curling into a smile as he wraps his arms around me and pulls me to him.

"I liked it. I wanted it. I wanted to see the real you."

"The real me isn't always pretty, Hazel."

"It doesn't matter. No one is. We can be unpretty together, Justice, doing unpretty things."

"Hmmm...I like that. Why don't you get some rest now, okay? We've got more unpretty things to go over, baby."

22 JUSTICE

MY MIND IS STILL LINGERING SOMEWHERE between post-sex delirium and physical exhaustion when the distant sounds of running water draw me back to reality. I snap my eyes open and stare at the mess of crumpled sheets. A distorted rectangle of light streaming across the floor from the narrow crack of the half-open bathroom door grabs my attention as I shift on the mattress.

My cock is sensitive, legs and arms sore, head spinning from the sudden overload of sensations. The despicably dirty images of Hazel screaming my name and begging for more while I rammed into her from behind are sending cold shivers down my sticky back. God, she was so fucking tight and wet inside, almost brand new, never fucked that way before. I could tell by the way her body reacted. A wild animal, quivering beneath me, savagely crying and clawing through two years of pain.

I roll onto my back and stare at myriads of stars up above.

Fuck. This woman is something. I never thought she'd have this kinky side to her. But then again, the quiet ones are always like expensive, daring gifts; they're elegant on the outside, yet you never know how scandalous they may be once you unwrap them.

The air in the bedroom smells of Hazel—vanilla, coconut, and sex.

An odd combination of innocent and dirty. My cock twitches at the idea of fucking her a million other ways, the things I could do to her...the things I could make her feel.

A muffled sob that echoes through the walls of the bedroom starts tearing my sex fantasies apart. For a while after that, it's just water splashing before there's another sob and then more. I lie there motionless, barely breathing, listening to the agonizing weeping that drifts from the shower. Part of me doesn't want to believe what I'm hearing, but the voice blending with the water that's thumping against the tiles is Hazel's.

Swinging my legs over the edge of the bed, I sit up and wait a little longer. My chest constricts each time another sob ripples through the air. All sorts of ideas are burrowing their way into my head now, the one about me miscalculating my strength being the scariest one. She said she wanted it; she never asked me to stop. What the fuck do I do now?

My eyes register the mess of clothes on the floor— jeans, sweaters, boots, socks, and the ripped-to-shreds lingerie I gave her. This bedroom hasn't seen sex of that sort ever.

I get up from the bed and walk over to the bathroom. The frosted glass of the shower stall that's filled with thick clouds of steam reveals only a vague silhouette of Hazel's body. Slumped shoulders shaking violently, head hanging low, loud sobs echoing off the walls. The heavy air makes it fucking hard to move, let alone breathe.

"Hazel?" I slide open the shower door. My eyes widen at the sight of her back, red streaks splayed across pale, silky skin. Any broken skin is mostly thin scratches, but there's one tiny cut under her left shoulder blade. The first signs of bruises are already showing on her thighs.

"Hazel?" I step into the shower, my throat closing in, my heart slowly descending into my stomach. The hot temperature of the water pouring down on us from the showerhead only settles in after I process the sordid results of our sexual exploits.

"Hazel?" My voice is trembling.

She doesn't react.

Part of me wants to hug her, but I'm too fucking scared to touch her. I don't know where or how anymore. "Baby?" I reach out for her shoulder and move forward, just enough to feel the natural heat of her body, but with an inch of space remaining between us.

My fingers stroke over the wet strands of her hair and I carefully push them to the side to scan the ragged red marks encircling her neck.

"If you need to go to the hospital..." Panic rattles inside me. I know fucking better not to say shit like this after dominating someone the way I dominated her, but she's in tears.

She shakes her head and rests her forehead against the wet tiles of the stall, water dripping down her small body. Funny thing, but it's the first time I've gotten to see her up close in this much light. *Really see her*. Because everything that happened earlier in the bedroom was in the dark, not just the lights-off kinda dark but the obscure out-of-body dark where your mind isn't present, only your senses, where your whole essence is in its own bubble of seething pleasure.

"Please talk to me, Hazel," I beg, my lips reaching out for her ear, my other hand carefully running down her side and then her stomach.

"He never cried," she mumbles after a few agonizing moments of silence. "He was so used to being sick and being surrounded by doctors and machines and endless blood tests. He was just a little boy who thought that it was okay for people to stick needles into his body..." Her voice is shaking, almost impossible to hear through the wall of water.

"I'm sorry." I brush my lips over her temple. My chest presses against her back when she shifts, causing me to withdraw. I don't want to hurt her, and I'm not sure how sore she is.

"Did you know that ninety-eight percent of children with leukemia go into remission after the treatment starts?" she asks, placing her right hand on a tile for support.

"No." I swallow hard, unsure if she can even hear me.

"Why does my baby fall under the two percent category?" The eerie whisper drifts through the shower stall. "Why?"

"What can I do, Hazel? What do you want me to do?"

"I just want to know why," she whimpers. "I want to know why my child is a statistic."

I'm at loss here because I've never had a woman I just fucked crying in my shower over her kid. I never even had a woman crying after sex with me. Period. There's this scary voice deep inside me, maybe my conscience, that keeps feeding me with the chilling idea that she's not really crying because she's missing her little boy, but instead, because she's physically hurt and now that the high of the mix of pleasure and pain is gone, agony is the only feeling that's left and she regrets what happened.

"Hey, he isn't a statistic." I smooth both hands up her stomach, pressing my lips to the back of her head in a low voice that I hope is somewhat soothing. I fucking hate seeing her broken down and miserable like this. "Baby, he isn't a statistic, okay? I'm so sorry he's not here."

"It's not fair, Justice. It's not fair some people who kill and rape get to live...and my baby doesn't." She sobs. "He never hurt anyone."

"I know...I know. If I could change that, I would, Hazel. I would." I'm fighting the urge to hug her when her body starts collapsing to the shower floor. In a panic, I pull her into me, both arms locked around her small frame while she shudders violently, tears mixed with the water running down her cheeks. Her porcelain skin, wet and silky, is sizzling hot against mine, even the coconut scent is still there when I nuzzle her hair. She's dangerously intoxicating in her sadness. It makes me want to hold her this tight forever, until there's no more pain left.

"I'm sorry, baby...I'm sorry," I whisper, not sure these are the words I should be saying. "I'm sorry."

She responds with a strained sob, finally snapping out of her delirium and grasping my arms for support. For a while, we just stand there, in a shower stall full of steam, scorching water beating against the glass and tile, with her battered back pressed into my chest and her nails digging into my wrists, holding on for dear life.

"Talk to me, Hazel," I plead, brushing my lips over her temple. "Talk to me." The fact that I can't see her face right now is killing me.

"Sometimes I feel so fucking useless." She presses the back of her head to my cheek. "I'm a failure as a mother because I couldn't do anything to stop my son from dying."

"That's not true. You're an amazing mother." There's a grammatical error somewhere in my sentence since technically she *was* a mother, but I can't make myself say it out loud. The slideshow I saw on her iPad a couple of weeks ago, the life of that little boy is here and now.

"I don't know what my purpose is anymore. I don't know where to go from here and what to do...because the only person who really needed me isn't around."

"Don't fucking say that. *I* need you...*I* do. You don't have to go anywhere, Hazel. Stay here with me and we'll figure it out. I promise." The egoistic asshole in me is suddenly scared that she may not feel the same way about what just transpired in the bedroom, that maybe for her, it was just a one-time thing.

"Why do you want to be with me, Justice? I'm a mess." Her body relaxes into mine.

"What do you mean *why*?" My heart starts thrashing. It's a valid question really. The problem is that I don't know the answer. Or maybe I do, but I'm too scared to dig deeper and find something that shouldn't be found because it goes against my beliefs. "I just do. I like it when you're around. It makes me question things...about me."

She doesn't respond right away; her fingertips keep drawing circles over my inked arms as we continue to stand under the stream of hot water until the better man in me reminds me that I spanked the hell out of this woman—among other things—just a couple of hours ago and she's probably in need of medical attention whether she wants it or not.

"I'm sorry if I hurt you." I release my hold and draw back a little to inspect the marks.

"It's fine." She turns to face me, her amber eyes bloodshot from all the crying. "I wanted it."

"Look." I cradle the back of her head and whisper, "This isn't how it's done, baby."

The truth is, she got to me. *She really did.* There are some parts of me I don't want to share with anyone, not unless I pretend it's an act. The stage gives me that freedom. But tonight I snapped because she kept on channeling that other person, the dark fuck who's hiding behind the makeup, who no longer knows what's real and what's not. And because Hazel wanted to meet him, I gave that to her.

"Come on." I shut off the water and help her out of the shower. "Let me take a look."

We dry off and then she's silent and still while I treat the scratches on her back with alcohol. Makes me think about her son and wonder whether he took after his mom, both so accustomed to pain.

Once I'm finished, we return to bed and snuggle under the sheets. And for some reason, it feels natural. Our bodies fit together perfectly.

"Justice?" she mumbles into my chest.

"Mmmm?" I smooth my hand up her bare shoulder, relishing in the intoxicating softness of her skin.

"What did you mean when you said this isn't how it's done?"

"It means I don't want you to seek him out anymore."

"Who?"

"The other guy."

"Why not?" There's genuine curiosity in her voice. She doesn't ask me which other guy I'm talking about either. She knows.

"Because I don't know if I want to be that person anymore."

"If this is a part of who you are, why hide it?"

"I'm not. I just don't want him to take over my less dark part—you know, the father and the better man that I'm trying to be—even though I think I'm failing miserably." I laugh a little at myself and pull her closer, trying my best not to touch her back.

"You're not failing. Not at all."

"Thanks. You have more faith in me than I do."

She grasps my left hand, the one with the magic word inked into it. Her fingers tiptoe across my wrist, then thread with mine and lock them together.

After a few moments of silence, I mutter into her hair, "Why did your husband ask you to put all the photos of your son away after his —" My mouth won't open to say the word "death" so I just let it hang there.

"I think everyone copes with the death of a loved one differently. I think that's how he coped. Maybe it was too painful for him, but it was equally painful for me to be living with him under one roof and pretend like we never had a child together. I don't blame him for not wanting to be with me. I think most of it is my fault actually. He isn't a bad guy for not wanting to look at the pictures of our dead son day after day. I think he found the strength to move on and I didn't. And that's why we're no longer together."

"I'm glad you're not with him. I want you for myself."

"Justice." Her voice is quivering. "I don't want my son to just disappear into nothing as if he never existed."

"It's not going to happen." I place a kiss on top of her head, my eyes staring at the silvery stream of moonlight peeking into the room through the skylight.

"River spent so much time at the hospital and never complained. Everyone was so nice and helpful. But sometimes I just couldn't take it. I'd go to the restroom and cry. Their sad looks gave it away. He wasn't going to make it. And I hated myself for being so useless. I tried to get involved with the hospital after he died, but it was too much. I just don't understand why this disease is still taking lives."

Her body starts trembling against mine.

I'm lost for a moment because I'm not sure what to say to that. Cancer doesn't give its victims an option to decline. "I'm sorry," I say in a low voice after a long pause. I know I keep telling her that, but I'm at a loss for anything else.

"Remember you once asked me if I had any hobbies?" Her voice sounds different all of a sudden. It's lively and sweet.

"I take it it's not skating?"

A soft smile touches her lips. "I suck at skating."

"No shit."

"I used to paint with watercolors. In school. My parents were convinced I was going to be the second van Gogh."

"You were that good, huh?"

She nods, her eyes twinkling.

"How come you never showed me any of your artwork then?"

"I haven't painted anything in years." Her hand slides to the back of my neck and her fingers start toying with my hair. "This one time, my parents signed me up for a community art show. I didn't really think it was a big deal at first. Our works were hung up at the local coffee shop. My mom even bought a frame for it. I didn't really care about winning a free breakfast. I just wanted people to see my painting. Some other girl won the competition, but later that night when all the parents were taking down everyone's artwork, the owner of the coffee shop asked me if my painting was for sale. He offered me a hundred dollars for it."

"Wow, you must have been really good." I laugh softly, running my hand up her shoulder. "Or the dude was a perv."

She stifles a giggle. "No. He kept the painting at the coffee shop. They hung it above one of the booths across from the entrance. You can see it right away when you walk in."

"What's in that painting?"

"It's a field of red tulips. My mom told me his late wife loved tulips and he bought the painting because it reminded him of her. She'd passed away a few years earlier from a heart attack."

I hold my breath, not sure what to say. There are thousands of words spinning in my head, but not a single one seems like the right one.

Hazel closes her eyes and says quietly, "Sometimes I think death has been following me all my life."

"Don't." My thumb brushes over her lower lip.

We lie there in silence until she finally starts dozing off. For the first time since I met her, she looks peaceful. Like a child.

When the early morning rays of light start peeking into the bedroom, I give up my fight with insomnia, slip into a pair of jeans, and head into my small music space in the basement.

After warming up with a couple of harmonies on the keyboard, I get to my feet and pace around the room. Everything with Hazel is different now. Not because we fucked, but because she's willing to accept the darker side of me, because it doesn't scare her, and because she doesn't ask for anything in return. Unlike my soon-to-be ex-wife.

Fired up, I go back upstairs to grab my phone and call Dom.

"What's going on?" he groans. "Just don't tell me another Nikki disaster."

"Nah, forget about Nikki. Can you to do some research for me?"

"What kind of research?"

"I want to know which hospital Hazel took her son to for treatments."

"Can't you just ask her?"

"No."

"Alright. I'll find out. Are you okay? Is everything okay?" His voice full of concern.

Funny thing, but I don't even remember when the line really blurred, when exactly Dominic turned from manager to personal assistant, nanny, and private investigator. And the list goes on.

"Yeah. I'm fine. Just a lot going on."

"Okay. Later."

After ending the phone call, I stare at the digital clock for a while, thinking that it's time for breakfast, but I have nothing but coffee here, which is probably not enough, not after the kind of sex we had last night. The better man in me feels responsible to feed the woman who's in his bedroom right now, but the spoiled asshole isn't quite sure going out is a good idea. The fear of paparazzi getting photos of me and Hazel with her neck looking like a BDSM playfield wins.

I dial Dom's number again.

"What now?" he growls.

"Can you handle having some breakfast delivered for me?"

"Sure. What are you in the mood for?"

"Something nice. For two. And flowers."

"I see." He clears his throat. "I'll get right on it."

"Thanks." I end the call and go back to the basement to work on my music.

23 HAZEL

I BLINK a few times to bring the blurred image of the nightstand lamp into focus. I'm hurting everywhere, especially between my legs. My stomach spasms at the memories of last night's sex encounter and everything after, including my shower meltdown and my confession about my teenage hobby. Emotions start choking me on the inside. Fear. Confusion. Embarrassment. Lust. Crashing down on me all at once.

I draw a deep breath and slowly roll over onto my back. My skin stings when it comes in contact with the satin sheets. Shifting my gaze to the skylight, I stare at a pear-shaped fluffy cloud floating above my head. My chest stiffens because I can't seem to remember how many days it's been since River left me. All I can think of is Justice. His hands and his body everywhere. Touching me in a way no one has ever touched me before.

Is this a part of that letting go he told me about? Or is this just me forgetting my little boy?

Swallowing hard and feeling distressed, I sit up and look around the bedroom, trying to come to terms with the fact that I lost my count. My head is hurting and my mouth is dry. I'm not sure if this is how it's supposed to feel after a night of rough sex. I've never done it before.

Sliding from the bed, I carefully wrap myself up in the sheet. It smells of sex, sweat, and Justice—spicy with a hint of ocean breeze. My body trembles at the mere thought of him being inside me last night. Heat starts flooding my cheeks and my knees buckle. I have to lean against the nightstand for a few seconds.

Once I'm in the bathroom, I position myself in front of the mirror and stare at my reflection. Suddenly, all my insecurities start crawling back into my head. Too thin, too short, too pale. Deep down I know I shouldn't worry about the way my body looks. Justice made it clear how much he loved it. Genetics did wonders after I had River. I lost all my pregnancy weight in less than two months.

I spin to inspect my back, and my hands start shaking at the sight of red streaks on my skin.

You asked for it, Hazel, remember?

When my mind settles, I turn the faucet on and splash some cold water on my face. The sound of the door shutting followed by familiar footsteps out in the bedroom catches me in the middle of the improvised finger-tooth-brushing process. I spit the paste into the sink and yank the sheet up to hide my exposed breasts right before Justice makes an appearance.

He strolls into the bathroom, his eyes searching mine in the mirror. "Hey." He approaches me from behind. The sight of this man wearing nothing but a pair of jeans makes me giddy. My stomach squeezes in response as he smooths his hands up my shoulders, his fingers getting lost in the mess of my hair.

"Hi." I fist the sheet pressed to my chest, suddenly all too aware of those shadows beneath my eyes and the red marks on my neck. Okay, the last one was my own doing. I literally had to beat it out of him.

"Did you sleep okay?" He moves closer, leaving just a tiny bit of space between my back and him, the lingering heat of his flawless body already working its magic.

"Yeah." My mind is going a thousand miles a second because we need to talk, but my tongue refuses to move. Instead, I just stand there like a statue, wrapped in the sheet, knees buckling, heart thrashing.

Justice brushes the tip of his nose against my ear. "There's breakfast."

His voice is low and sexy, those bedroom eyes scrutinizing my reflection in the mirror. The outline of his broad, inked shoulders hovering over mine makes me look thinner and smaller than I already am.

"I'm sorry things got a little out of control last night." He lightly sweeps his knuckles over the traces of red on my neck.

"Will you please stop saying you're sorry?" I ask, slowly easing back against him.

"I didn't mean for it to get that rough," he says into my hair, his hands toying with the folds of the sheet.

"I wanted it rough." The truth is, *I wanted to hurt*.

"Don't ask me to do that again, please." The hot breath hitting the back of my head is causing a whole new wave of tingles to blast through me.

"I'm not scared of who you are."

"I know you're not." His fingers tug on the fabric wrapped around me. "But I *am*."

The sheet slides to the floor and all my eyes register before I fall into him is the reflection of my naked body pressed into his chest. He runs his hands up my stomach to cup my breasts and buries his head into the crook of my battered neck. The reversed reflection of the black letters, so bold against the skin of his fingers wrapped around me, sends me over the edge, and a soft moan escapes my mouth when his nearness starts luring me into another sexual oblivion. My thighs tighten as he gently pulls me against his erection, his firm lips continuing their slow assault on my neck.

"If you don't stop me right now, we're never going to make it out of this bedroom," he purrs into my hair, brushing his thumbs over my nipples. "And I need you to eat, baby."

"I don't want to stop you." I close my eyes and drown in him completely.

"I know...me neither...but we can't have you hungry and dehydrated." He's breathing heavily as he pulls back a little, both hands lingering on my breasts. "You're fucking beautiful."

I bite back a smile and with my eyes staying closed, I rub my head against his unshaven chin. The soreness between my legs is now on fire.

"Let me get you a t-shirt," he says, withdrawing. My body instantly misses his heat. I'm still in a sexual trance when Justice comes back with one of his t-shirts, and I pull it over my head and follow him into the kitchen.

"I wasn't sure what you like," he says against my neck as I peruse the breakfast buffet in front of me.

"Are you feeding an army?" I ask, dumping some sugar into my coffee.

He presses his chest to my back, trapping me with his body against the kitchen counter. "Didn't want to take a risk."

"Bacon, really?" I smile to myself, inspecting one of the many plates.

"What's wrong with bacon?"

"Nothing. It's tons of fat and calories."

"You need calories, baby." His hands run down my sides, enclosing my waist. "Because we're going to work out a lot."

I take a small bite of a blueberry danish and wash it down with coffee. My mind has wandered off to some post-sex-euphoria realm where the pain and the worry don't exist.

"Are you going to eat or are you going to keep trying to fuck me while I'm having breakfast?" I pinch off a piece of the pastry and send it into his mouth over my shoulder. This man is going to be my ruin. He even had flowers delivered along with the food.

"Do you really have to ask?" His lips make their way down my neck again, causing a whole trail of goose bumps all over my arms and back.

My body trembles from the sexual tension between us. I'm scared I'm going to drop the coffee as his fingers gently run up and down the fabric of the t-shirt while he grinds his groin against my ass.

"Hazel?" The slight rasp in his voice makes every part of me tingle with delight.

"Hmm?" I grip my coffee cup harder.

"I have to leave in a bit."

Aiden. Of course. I forgot about his son. I forgot he has to go back to his family. To his life.

"Yeah." I set the coffee on the counter before my hands betray me.

"You can stay here if you want. Spend the night. We can do something tomorrow."

I feel shitty for making him split his time between me and his little boy. Especially in the middle of the battle against his ex. The parent in me wants him to leave and never come back, but the woman who went to heaven last night needs him more than air.

"I don't want to take away the time that belongs to your son, Justice."

"You're not, baby. He's used to me being gone. I can make this work."

I spin around to face him. My heart beats like a drum. "What are we?"

A small frown appears between his brows. "What do you want us to be?" He catches my gaze.

"I don't know." My throat starts closing as my eyes register his son's name flashing at me from his chest.

"We're—what do they call it?" A faint smile touches his lips as he brings his face closer to mine. "Hashtag Jazel?"

"We are?" I gulp. "You said it was an ugly ship name."

"I know, but this definitely isn't one of those friends-with-benefits arrangements either." He kisses the corner of my mouth. "Not with you." The lingering scent of the blueberry danish on his lips reminds me of my mother's baking. Reminds me of what having a home used to feel like.

"Besides, the whole world already thinks we're an item." He smirks. "I just need a little time to get my divorce finalized."

I nod silently. His words are turning me into a wet mess again. My hands make their way up his chest, touching the patches of ink adorning his skin. It scares me how I can't get enough of this man.

Justice reaches for my coffee cup and moves it and the danish to the side, then with one smooth motion, he lifts me up and plops me down onto the counter.

"What are you doing?" I cry out, grasping his shoulders for support.

"Having breakfast." He slides his right hand up my thigh and under the hem of the t-shirt. His eyes are dark, greedy, and full of lust.

"Is this the kind of breakfast you were talking about all along?" My voice comes out as a moan as he forces himself between my legs, his tongue tracing along my jawline. The things he's doing to my body are unbelievable.

"That and I'm also making it up to you for last night," Justice growls into my stomach, descending to his knees. "I loved watching you come." He grasps my ass with both hands and kisses my inner thigh, then pulls me forward a little—just enough for him to position his head between my legs. "I want to make you fly, baby."

I feel exposed with him seeing me without my panties in broad daylight, but my insides are craving his touch.

He's about to eat me out on a kitchen counter. Oh my God.

"Please." I sink my fingers in his hair as he rolls up the t-shirt for better access.

"Just relax for me, baby." He presses his lips into me.

The kitchen walls start shifting when he brushes the tip of his tongue against my clit. My body lurches and my hands instinctively pull on his hair, looking for some leverage because the counter seems to have disappeared. I can hear my own moans echoing somewhere in the back of my head and my own heartbeat thrashing in my ears. My insides are on the verge of exploding, my eyes closed, my stomach bottoming out. This is so different from last night's sex. Gentle and sweet, each stroke of his tongue pushing me further into a world of endless euphoria. His mouth ravishing my most intimate parts in a way I've never dreamt of is making me hot and dizzy.

"Oh my God, Justice," I cry out, arching my back as he pushes his tongue deeper into me.

My body tightens, my legs cramp, and my breath catches in my throat, along with a scream. I pull his hair harder and squeeze my eyes shut, giving in to the final part of the race for nirvana, which crashes into me like a fierce ocean wave.

I'm still panting when he pulls back a little and brings his wet lips to my stomach, leaving a small trail of kisses above my belly button, his arms draped around my shaking frame.

We're both silent for a few minutes as my mind slowly descends back to planet Earth.

"You taste amazing," Justice moans into my mouth after getting to his feet.

I pull down the t-shirt and let him help me off the counter. My legs are weak and my head is spinning. Whether it's due to lack of food, the orgasm he just gave me, or a combination of the two, I'm wobbling enough to have to grasp his shoulders for support.

"Finish your breakfast now." He smiles, grabbing a new danish from the package he pushed aside earlier to make more room for our bit of action. "You need to eat, babe."

I don't know where exactly the man gets this caring streak. He's like a Rubik's Cube—hard to read at first with all the colors mixed up, but easy once solved. Each side represents a different trait of his personality—affectionate, smart, talented, and sometimes dirty.

"I wanted to show you something." He strokes my hair as I put another piece of pastry in my mouth. His touch is soothing, almost magical. It makes the pain go away.

"Really? What?"

"Come on." Grabbing my hand, he pulls me away from the kitchen counter and walks me through the hallway. We stop in front of the last door on the right, across from the laundry room, where we had our first fight.

"Be careful. It's a little steep. Old house," Justice explains, pushing the door open.

"I didn't know there was a basement," I say as we descend down the narrow staircase, my eyes widening at the sight of all things music here, my heart beginning to race. This is his personal space, where he probably created some of those dirty songs. Intriguing.

"I don't use it often. I'm in Tahoe maybe once or twice a year when I need a break from being famous." He laughs. "That's when we usually don't write anything. I just call it a standby emergency demo room in case some ideas come to me when I'm off. There's no live room here," he explains, walking me over to the keyboard set up in the middle.

"What's a live room?" I ask, watching him fiddle with some buttons. Everything looks so foreign, expensive, and complicated.

"A live room is where the band performs. Then you have a control room. Sometimes, depending on what you're recording, there will be both a control and a mixing room. That's where you have all your monitors, your mixing boards. Where your audio engineer turns your pile of ideas into the magic you hear on a CD." A soft laugh escapes his mouth.

My mind slowly transports into a state of bewilderment as Justice starts going into details. Suddenly he's not an oversexualized sadist who likes to wear a choke collar on stage and slap a woman's ass while in bed, but a geek whose knowledge of music terminology blows me away. Add in the fact that he's spilling all this information on me while shirtless in front of the keyboard. I'm not so sure I'm even awake at this point, and if this is a dream, I don't want it to end.

"What?" His voice pulls me back to reality.

"Sorry?" I shake my head.

"You're staring." A slight smile dashes across his lips.

"I'm sorry." Blood rushes to my cheeks.

"Don't be." He wraps his arms around my waist and pulls me gently against his body. "Stare all you want. The more the better, actually."

"So is this what you wanted me to see? The place where you write your dirty songs?" I place my hands on his bare chest and absorb the warmth. The rhythmic beating of his heart under my palm is calming, the kind of distraction I need right now.

"Well, most of the dirty stuff isn't born here actually." He releases me from his hold to give his full attention to the instrument. His hand hovers over the keyboard for a few moments.

"You're a lefty?" I ask, watching him try out a basic tune.

"Nothing wrong with that." He shrugs, glancing at me, a hint of a smirk on his lips.

I bite back a smile. My mind takes me back to my high school years. I was determined to become the best watercolor artist in the world. I never picked up a brush after River's death. I guess the artist in me died along with my son.

I shake off the unsettling feeling and turn my attention to Justice. The way his fingers effortlessly dance from one key to another makes my skin prickle. His body tenses, eyes darker with each stroke. He's not in this room right now but somewhere in the other realm, the realm of music. I've never seen anything created in such a beautifully intimate manner.

The melody is simple yet full of anguish, with darker undertones that make my heart race and my stomach flip as it progresses. I'm almost on the edge when he withdraws his hands and looks at me.

"What do you think?"

"It's very sad," I confess.

"I haven't written anything in a very long time. Zander's been composing all the keyboard parts for the past few years."

"You used to write keyboard parts too?"

"Yeah. All the early albums. I played them too. I don't anymore. This is the first instrumental piece I've done since before Aiden was born."

The air in the room disappears. My head starts to spin. *I'm falling so hard and I don't want to hurt any more than I already do.* "And the keyboardist in your live videos?"

"We just hire out for the tour. We've had the same guy for a couple of years now."

Justice takes a step forward, drapes his arm around my body, and gently pulls me against him. "I think it might be your fault. You multiply everything dark and everything decent in me by a thousand...and I don't know if that's bad or good, Hazel. I just know that I like it. I like it a lot and I want to write music."

I bite the inside of my cheek and blink at him a few times.

"I had the right words." His eyes lock on mine. "I just didn't have the right person. I'm far from perfect. My life is very complicated, but I want you to be a part of it."

"I don't want to be just a name on your list of sex accomplishments."

"You're not." He brushes his nose against my cheek. "We're exclusive, baby. I haven't been with anyone since I met you and I have no interest in doing so."

Whatever those right words he said to the wrong person were, the ones he's saying to me right now are more than enough.

"Look what you're doing to me." He pulls me against his chest to expose his secret—the frantic, almost violent pounding of his heart.

"You're doing the same to me," I say quietly, locking my hands on the back of his neck.

"Okay, then we're even." His soft laughter that fills up the room as he kisses me is the sweetest thing I've heard in over two years.

24 JUSTICE

ON SOME DAYS, I feel like the best father a-three-year-old can wish for because I can buy Aiden anything he wants. But on days like today, I have no clue what I'm doing. The truth is, my parents probably know my own son better than I do. Which makes me think of Hazel. Makes me understand why she refused the compensation. Money can't buy the life of a child back.

"Are you sure you're not hungry, buddy?" I call out from the front of my Jeep. My eyes catch Aiden's reflection in the rearview mirror as he shakes his head. He's clutching his Elmo, legs dangling from his seat, eyes on the road.

"Are you sure? Because once I get on the freeway, we're not stopping anywhere until we get home."

He shakes his head again and slumps into his seat. The duck-feeding excursion we'd planned for days turned into a muddy disaster the moment we got out of the car. The rain came out of nowhere, scaring away everyone in the park.

"You know"—I tighten my fingers around the steering wheel—"we need to get you a new seat soon."

"A big boy seat?" Aiden perks up, the corners of his lips curl up a little.

"Yeah, a big boy seat." I nod. "You're growing too fast, buddy."

"Why aren't you an s-man today?" He puts the Elmo aside and pushes the loose strands of hair off his face.

Once Nikki and I tried to get him to agree to a short haircut. He cried all the way to the salon. Part of me was proud of my son for not wanting to fit the societal standards, but part of me knew he was going to get teased for being different one way or another. Some kids at the daycare made fun of him a few times because of his long hair. Nikki gave the administration hell for not addressing the bullying problem. And to this day, I'm not sure if she was doing it for the press or because she truly felt that no child should ever be harassed for the way he looks or acts.

Side effects of marrying an actress.

"You mean X-man, right?" I articulate every word so he understands the difference between *X* and *S* because I don't want my son to tell other people his dad is an ass-man. Well, maybe I am, but he doesn't need to know that.

"S-man!" Aiden shouts from his seat, grinning at the mirror.

"Say *X*, buddy. Not *S*," I correct him.

"S-man!" His sparkling laughter fills the car.

"Don't say *S*, say *X*, Aiden."

He tosses his head back and giggles. "S-man."

"You're doing it on purpose." I glance at the reflection of my dark green baseball cap in the rearview mirror. I don't know why he's so attached to that X-Men cap that I can't find anywhere.

When we finally get back to my parents' house, it's almost three. My sister and my mother are out back, redecorating the den. They didn't like the way Dad put up the Christmas lights.

Corrine catches up with us in the hallway. "You two are home early."

"It wained." Aiden lifts his tiny foot off the floor to demonstrate the dirt sticking to his boots.

"Why don't you go wash up, huh?" I ask, kneeling down to help him with his jacket.

"I got it, Dad," he says with a serious expression on his face and charges down the hall, screaming, "I'm getting a big seat!"

I straighten up and take off my coat. My head feel like it's going to explode from entertaining my son since six this morning. I adore him to death, but at the same time, I don't think I'd make it without the help of my parents and my sister.

Corrine shakes her head and gives me a shoulder squeeze. "You look exhausted."

"I'm sure you know why. You have one of your own." I chuckle, giving her a light punch. "They are like Energizer Bunnies, aren't they?"

"Pretty much, and the battery never runs down." She laughs. "I'm just glad mine is nineteen and can tie his own shoelaces."

We walk over to Aiden's room to make sure he isn't playing Pirates of the Caribbean with his footwear in the tub. As instructed, he's changing into his home clothes, dirty boots on the bathroom floor under the sink.

"You want something to eat, sport?" Corrine inquires, helping him with his socks. "Grandma made some rice pudding."

Anything Grandma makes, Aiden eats. No need to ask him twice. I don't possess the magic Gladys does. I struggle with him and the food at times.

Twenty minutes later, Aiden is out cold in his room. This is when I finally get the time to sort through my messages and voicemails. First, I call my lawyer back to get an update on the divorce and custody. I'd hate for the little guy to have to go back to Malibu while I'm here. I wanted him to stay with my family until after Christmas. Getting Nikki to agree to this arrangement would probably take an army of lawyers or a couple of dirty tricks, like threatening to publicize her latest trip to rehab. But I need for it to happen. Because once I start working on the new album, I won't be able to dedicate this much time to him. Even though the label has already pushed back the dates. Zander's first surgery is scheduled for next week. The good news is that the recovery prognosis is great. The bad news that is it's going to take up to four months and there's been talk of hiring a different drummer for the studio sessions.

Next, I call Samantha to see if there are any updates on Zander's replacement.

I'm on edge when I get off the phone with her. The suits at the label don't want to wait more than three months and if Zander's not going to get back on track by April, we'll be forced to play along.

I get up from the chair and walk over to the window that looks out at the mountaintops that are covered by thick layers of snow. Then my eyes dart to the large fountain in the middle of the yard. My grandparents bought this villa when properties here were dirt cheap. I loved growing up in a place without the exhaust fumes and insane traffic. I want Aiden to know what it's like to breathe fresh air and to be able to go outside without people shoving their cell phone and cameras at him. Because that madness is what's waiting for him in L.A.

I close my eyes and listen to the sound of my childhood home. The light chatter of my mother and my sister in the den, the chirping of the birds outside my window, the floor creaking under the weight of my body as I cross the room.

After taking a shower and changing into more date-appropriate clothes, I go to Aiden's room and kiss him goodbye. He's still sleeping, his hair a mess. He probably won't care that I'm not around when he wakes up. This is his normal. Part of me doesn't want to leave, but part of me wants to see Hazel badly.

"I'll be back tomorrow," I say, peeking into the den. Gladys lifts her eyes from the box of ornaments and gives me a long evaluating stare. "I'm going to the cabin."

"You mean you're going to see that woman?" My mother tilts her head.

Corrine straightens up and sets a string of Christmas lights aside. They've been doing this nonsense all day. I'm convinced they rip it apart every two hours and begin again just to keep themselves busy. It took me five minutes to hang up the lights in Aiden's room back in my condo.

I ignore the question. "Call me only if there's an emergency."

"Are you going to bring her over or do we have to read the tabloids to be in the loop with what's going on between you two?" Gladys croaks. "What do they call you? Jazel?"

"Mom, really?"

"What? You're the hottest couple of the month." Corrine smirks.

"I'll ask her," I mutter under my breath.

"Yeah. I'm dying to meet her, Justice." My sister dips her hand in the box with the snowflake confetti and tosses some at me.

"Very funny." I jump to the side, looking for something to get her with, but all the non-fragile items are out of my reach.

"Get out of here before Mom makes you help us." Corrine chuckles.

"Later." I spin around and hurry to the door before they get crazy with their interrogation.

As soon as I'm in my Jeep, I call Hazel. "Are you hungry?" I ask, starting the car.

"A little."

I can hear her smile on the line. She sounds different when she's excited about something. Lately, her voice has this unique ring to it, peaceful and almost content, but it's nearly impossible to catch unless you listen carefully. The first time I ever heard it was when I took her skating and then again when she told me about her painting.

"I'll pick you up in…let's say"—my eyes scan the dark rain clouds gathering on the horizon—"an hour."

"Ummm…I actually cooked something today." She pauses, waiting for my reaction.

The only two women who ever cooked for me are my mother and my older sister. "What did you make?"

"I don't know how to cook oysters, so I baked chicken."

I laugh into the phone. "Trust me, oysters are the last thing on my mind. I eat nothing but oatmeal and broccoli when I'm with my son. It's an integral part of my fatherly duties since he won't eat anything healthy unless I set an example. Chicken sounds delicious."

"If you don't like my cooking, we can always go out." Her voice is hesitant.

"We're definitely not going out. And can you do me a favor and wear something sexy, baby? If you have a pair of stockings and a cute apron…" I say suggestively, my imagination going wild. My cock is hard at the thought of all the dirty things I want to do to her tonight. All night. Until the morning. Until we're both a mess.

"I'll see what I have, rockstar."

The rain breaks when I'm halfway to Tahoe, but by the time I get to Hazel's, it's pouring again and my hands hurt from fighting the steering wheel. The roads here are shit during fall and winter. I pull up to the cabin and scan the surroundings before getting out of the car. Then my paranoia over being followed by paparazzi makes me hit the gas and pull up closer to the cabin. Not that it matters. Hazel and I are a couple. But I don't want gossip-hungry reporters or obsessed fans stalking her place.

After making sure the coast is clear, I shut off the engine and rush to the porch, my boots thudding against the wet sidewalk. My clothes are soaking wet by the time Hazel opens the door.

"I'm sorry. No flowers today." I wrap my arms around her frame and gently push her inside as my lips capture hers.

"Justice," she mumbles between our kisses, running her hands over the wet sleeves of my jacket. "Close the door, please."

"Right." I push it shut with my boot and continue my slow assault on her mouth, ignoring the candlelight and the dinner for two.

"Sorry, I don't have anything sexy," she says quietly, pulling me to the table.

Before we take our seats, I cradle the back of her head and inhale her slowly. She's fucking delicious, like a piece of red velvet cake. Classy and exquisite. Even in her plain white shirt and skinny jeans. I'm almost scared to touch her because I know if I do, things may get out of control before we even get to the dinner part. But at the same time, I'm scared she'll disappear if I let go.

"We'll have to fix that, baby. I'll take you shopping sometime this week," I whisper in her ear as my dirty mind pictures her body wrapped in black lace while screaming my name.

Once we sit down to eat, silence takes over the cabin for a few minutes. Hazel shuffles her food around with her fork, and her eyes keep darting to the bottle of wine sitting in the middle of the table, but she doesn't dare touch it.

"I talked to my friend today," she says.

"Which one?"

"Rayna. The one who owns this cabin." She sinks her front teeth into her bottom lip and waits for my reaction.

"Okay." I send another piece of chicken into my mouth and set my utensils aside. "What about?"

"Her husband, Clay, is one of the partners in a property management company. They're looking for another receptionist and Rayna said she'd ask Clay to give me the job."

I'm speechless for a few moments because the concept of dating a woman who answers a phone for a living is something entirely new to me. "Is this what you want to do?"

"It's a great opportunity." Hazel squeezes out a smile. "Besides, I have to start somewhere. I'm on my own now."

"You're not on your own."

"That's not what I mean. I need to start thinking long-term. What am I going to do when you're gone? Sit and wallow over your photos with your teenage fans that have been twisted by the tabloids and your ex's PR team? I also can't live off my parents' money anymore."

"You can stay at my condo."

"It's not that, Justice." She sets the fork aside, and the desperate look in her eyes suffocates me. "One semester in college, nine months of pregnancy, and taking care of a sick child for four years pretty much sum up my resume." Her voice cracks. "Not everyone gets to write songs about sex for a living."

"I'm sorry." I inhale sharply. "If that's what you want."

"No. It's not. I know nothing about property management or phone etiquette…and I hate dealing with people with all my heart, but I have to do it. For my son, for my family, for myself."

She rests both hands on the table and stares at me, long and hard. The glow the candlelight gives her porcelain skin makes me want to reach out to touch her cheek to make sure she's real.

"Hey, this may sound like it's coming a little out of the nowhere." My voice goes low. "I'd love for you to come with me to Crystal Bay for Christmas."

She bites her lower lip and blinks a few times. "Justice." She looks calm on the outside, but there's a storm in her eyes. "We only met a couple of weeks ago."

"What the fuck does that matter?" I move the plate aside and reach for her hand.

"It's just...what are your parents going to think? You're still married."

"My mom has seen me drunk, high, and in a hospital bed after I OD'd. She even bailed me out once. Introducing her to a woman I'm dating is nothing compared to that long list of my asshole-of-the-decade accomplishments."

I conveniently hold back the fact that Gladys even caught me having sex with an older chick in our guest house when I was seventeen.

"It's just..." Her shoulders slump. "I don't want to rush into anything. What if they don't like me? What if they think I'm trying to get my hands on your money? I don't want this—what we have right now—to be any different...not yet." She drops her gaze to the floor.

"It's all over the news anyway. Me and you. What's the point of hiding out if they know I'm seeing you?" I squeeze her fingers.

"It's not just that."

"Then what is it?"

"Eventually, you'll have to go back to your other life and I'll have to go back to mine."

"Yeah. So what are you scared of, Hazel?"

"Everything," she whispers, lacing her fingers with mine. "Your fans, paparazzi."

She's right. She has to share me with a whole lot of other people. I'm a performer, a father, an ex-husband, a lover. I'm the show that has to go on no matter what. I'm doomed to carry the weight of my own empire until the day I die.

"I don't have another life, baby—I just have a very complicated one. But we can make it work."

Right now, the table between us is like the Grand Canyon. She's just a few inches away but it feels like hundreds of miles. I need to have her body against mine, to tell her all these things my mouth is threatening to spill, but the food, dishes, and candles sitting in front of me are distracting.

"Dance with me?" I ask, getting up from the chair and holding my hand out to her.

She takes it, saying, "I'm a little rusty. I haven't danced in years." A blush colors her cheeks as we walk over to the middle of the dark living room, fingers entwined. The reflection of the candle flames jumping across the walls have given the room a magical look.

"I won't hold it against you, baby." I gently pull her to me.

She wraps one arm around my waist and places the other around my neck, her delicate fingers sinking into my hair, her nails leaving a trail of shivers down my spine. "What's this?" She pulls a tiny snowflake from my hair.

"Oh, that. I can explain." I chuckle softly, dipping my nose into the golden mess on her head. "My sister and my mother tried to rope me into decorating the house, but I escaped."

She clings to me, her feet bumping into mine as we clumsily shuffle in a small circle around the living room. I brush my lips against hers. She tastes amazing, just like the first time we kissed. Sweet and fresh. My tongue slowly slides into her mouth, seeking more, and she responds instantly, easing into me, her body trembling.

"I want you to meet my son. Come over for Christmas," I say, stroking her shoulder.

She doesn't respond but I can feel her heart beating like a hummingbird's wings.

"Shouldn't we have some music?" she finally says.

"You forgot what I do for a living?"

"Well, bring it on, rockstar," she coos into my chest.

"Just don't laugh. It's still a work in progress," I warn her.

"I won't."

"Promise?"

"Promise."

"Okay." I clear my throat and bring my lips to her ear, my fingers lost in the thickness of her hair. My voice is a little rough at first, more an embarrassing whisper. But the way she holds her breath as I keep humming the tune I've been working on all week makes me want to sing to her until the day I die.

25 HAZEL

I WAKE up to the distant sluicing of water, my face buried in the blanket, my body buzzing with desire. Last night was weird. Justice and I danced and talked until we couldn't keep our eyes open anymore. By the time we made it to the bedroom, he was so tired that the moment his head hit the pillow, he passed out. We both slept in our clothes.

I slowly draw the blanket away from my face and glance over at the wide-open door of the bathroom, my eyes taking in the sight of Justice's silhouette beyond the frosted glass of the shower door, clouds of steam turning his ink into dark splotches. The fact that I'm actually seeing this man is gradually starting to sink in.

I reluctantly look away from the shower and scramble for my phone to check the time. The dark, lifeless screen reminds me that I've been purposely avoiding the damn thing because of the reporters. The thought of changing my number has crossed my mind at least twice since the madness started.

I roll over to the opposite side of the bed and grab Justice's iPhone. When I press the home button, I'm overwhelmed by a long string of notifications flashing at me from the screen. I blink a few times to bring the tiny text and the digital clock into focus. Deep down, the woman in me who promised to trust him knows that reading those text previews is wrong, but my fears suddenly come crashing back at the sight of all these messages and I can't resist.

Angelo: The label wants to set up a meeting. Need you back in L.A. next week.

Gary Schmidt: How does next Wednesday work for you?

May: Justice, I REALLY need you to go over the options I emailed you last night.

Cruz: Give me a call, bro

Rachel: Found this in my car.

I narrow my eyes at the photo preview of an X-Men baseball cap attached to the message and re-read the text. My hand starts shaking and my index finger slips across the screen, sending the trail of notifications back to the beginning of the thread.

I've never been the type of woman who checked her husband's phone bills or emails. I trusted Owen completely. Not even once in ten years of us being together did I attempt to invade his privacy, but Owen isn't Justice. He doesn't have hordes of teenage fans stalking him day and night.

So, he saw someone while he was in L.A. He got into her car. What's the big deal, Hazel?

I feel dirty for snooping around. Tossing the phone on the night-stand, I swing my legs over the edge of the bed and absently stare at the floor. What are the chances I'm being played and all this is just another publicity stunt? What if everyone who is behind the PR charade, including Justice, is laughing at me right now? What if this is some new sick reality TV show?

The light thumping of footsteps fills the air. Lifting my head, I lock my gaze on Justice.

"Good morning," he says, crossing the room wearing nothing but a towel wrapped around his hips. The droplets of water sliding down his inked chest and his perfectly toned abs make him look like he just walked off a magazine cover.

"Good morning," I reply meekly.

He bends down and wraps his fingers around my ankle, his gray eyes sealed on mine, muscles flexing under the inked skin on his arms as he runs his hand up to my knee.

"I waited for you in the shower, baby."

"Oh."

"I have to leave soon."

I hate myself for looking at his phone. The stupid text message from Rachel ruined my morning. All I can think about now is his cap and his other life, beyond these walls.

"Who's Rachel?" I ask quietly.

His hands freeze on my thighs for a brief moment. "She doesn't matter, baby." He moves closer and plants a kiss on my cheek.

"Did you see her when you were in L.A.?"

He pulls back a little, his shoulders slumping. "Are you spying on me now?"

"No, Justice, but when a woman texts you a photo of something you left in her car, it makes me think things." I draw his hands away from my body and slide from the bed.

"You're checking my phone?" He doesn't look mad. Disappointed? Yes.

I circle around the room. Part of me regrets asking about Rachel. "I'm not checking your phone. Don't twist my words. I saw the message by accident." My voice is unsteady.

Justice gets to his feet. "She's nobody. She doesn't matter."

"Are you fucking her?" I blurt out, folding my arms on my chest.

"What?" His mouth twitches. "Rachel's our makeup artist. She was at the hospital when I went to see Zander. We talked. What on earth gave you the idea I fucked her?"

I feel stupid for making a scene, but my inner rebel is still raging. "Then why didn't you say so?"

"I like it when you're jealous." He moves closer.

"I'm not jealous," I retort, biting my lip.

He wraps his arms around my waist and tugs me against his wet body. "Yes, you are."

His gaze lingers on my breasts as he gently pushes the fabric of the shirt off my shoulder.

"No, I'm not."

"You can deny it all you want, baby, but you are. And I fucking love it." Justice buries his head into the crook of my neck. His firm lips caress my skin, sending tingles down to my belly. Then he sinks his teeth in, his other arm cradling my head. The man is a master of seduction.

"Fuck you." I push against him.

"Say that again." He locks his arms around me, not allowing me to escape, and my knees betray me when the tip of his tongue glides across my cheek.

"Fuck you," I whisper through clenched teeth and make an attempt to free myself from his grip.

"That's right, baby," he growls into my ear. "Fuck me."

The adrenaline is making me crazy. "Sometimes you're so conceited, Justice." I move my hand to the back of his neck.

"And sometimes you're so fucking stubborn," he comes back.

I weave my fingers into his hair and pull hard.

He lets out a startled gasp. "You like to play rough, huh?"

The truth is, I don't know. I just want to feel. And it feels best when it hurts. *When it hurts with him.* I spin in his arms, determined to escape, but he hauls me back and I slam into him. His hands on my hips and his fingers digging into the fabric of my jeans, the growing bulge under the towel is now pressed into my ass.

"See what you made me do, baby?" He brushes my hair away from my neck and nips at my skin, then bites into it, deeper and harder.

I gasp, my eyes drifting closed while his hand works my zipper and his other one slides into my jeans. He pulls me into him tighter and his scruffy cheek scratches the side of my face as the tip of his finger reaches the sensitive bud under my panties.

"Is this what you want, Hazel?" he husks into my ear, stroking my clit.

The adrenaline rushing through me is too much. I can't put the things I feel or should be saying into words right now. My body is a quivering mess.

"Is this what you want, baby?" Justice repeats as his lips travel down my neck, sucking and teasing, his tongue dancing along the path. He yanks my jeans down to give himself some room to work and a loud moan escapes my mouth when he quickly slips two fingers inside me, his other hand wrapping around my waist and squeezing hard.

"I love how fucking ready you are for me, baby," he growls, grinding his erection against the lace of the panties I'm still wearing.

I move my hips to meet the wild thrusts of his rough fingers, my back bumping against his chest while he works me higher and higher.

"I want the other guy, Justice," I choke out, lifting my arms to lace them around his neck for leverage. "I want the other guy." The sleeves of my shirt start absorbing the water that's dripping from his hair.

"You know I don't like it when you call him out," he whispers raggedly, his fingers pumping into me, faster and faster.

"Right now, I don't give a fuck that you don't like it." I manage to get a full sentence out somewhere between my moans. "I want the other guy." My demand is met with another, much harder thrust causing my back to arch and my toes to curl. My arms fall down to my sides, wet fabric and damp hair clinging to me as the tingling in my body turns into a massive shockwave.

I'm on the edge when Justice withdraws his fingers and wraps both arms around me, whispering in my ear, "I warned you, baby."

Pulling the towel off, he spins me around and shoves me toward the bed. His glistening body hovers above mine as I fall onto the blanket. He yanks my jeans off, tosses them to the floor, and lowers himself on top of me, his hips pressing in, taunting me. The friction of his flesh against the lace of my panties creates a new, exhilarating sensation deep in my core.

"I'm going to fuck you"—he brings his face to mine—"really hard, baby." A wicked smile touches his lips. "But first I'm going to watch you fuck yourself."

He smashes his mouth against mine, tongue sliding in. I sink my fingers into his hair, pulling him against me, wanting to feel his body dominating mine. My legs wrap around his waist, my nails scraping over the inked skin on his back, digging in as a punishment for the stupid message from the makeup girl.

His hand seeks out mine. He brings it to his mouth and licks my index finger. Dark brooding eyes never leave me as droplets of water drip from his hair into my cleavage.

"I want to watch you come, baby," he breathes out, taking both my index and my middle finger into his mouth, his tongue swirling around them as he starts sucking.

I'm trembling with anticipation and fear. I've never done this in front of a man before, not even Owen. Sure, I've gotten myself off a few times in the past. I'm human, after all. But having Justice watch is different. More intimate.

He brushes his knuckles against my cheek before pulling back, his eyes raking down my body as I put my hand between my legs and press my wet fingers against the bundle of nerves, my other hand dragging my panties to the side.

"You're fucking beautiful, baby." He smooths his palm over my thigh, his touch distracting me from the task.

"Don't stop, baby." His voice drifts from above as he gets comfortable.

Closing my eyes, I concentrate on the sensitive spot between my legs, and in just a few moments, I'm headed for euphoria, my body tense, my muscles cramping. The moans escaping Justice's mouth turn me on even more, and when my eyes flutter open, they lock on his, dark and hungry. A hint of a smile flashes across his slightly parted lips. The man is a fucking orgasm in the flesh. Just the sight of his body alone makes my insides giddy and wet.

"Come for me, baby," he whispers, digging his fingers into my thigh, his other hand wrapped around his length.

I'm both burning up and shivering, and the thought of Justice enjoying the show drives me higher. Not sure when exactly I got this daring about sex, but I stop for a second and bring my hand to his mouth, silently asking him to wet my fingers again, then I slip them between my legs, pulling the lace of my panties aside again for him to be able to watch.

"That's right, baby." His eyes widen as I give in to the pleasure. "Let me see you fuck yourself."

My heart is racing, my thighs constrict, and the desperate need for release is starting to take over my body and mind. The sound of his voice as he keeps whispering the dirtiest things is pushing me further and further into the deranged madness. I can feel my own walls tightening around my fingers as I thrust them deeper and deeper.

"Say my name, baby," he orders.

"Justice," I mumble deliriously, my eyes screwed shut, my lungs out of breath.

"Louder, Hazel. Louder," he demands.

"Justice!" I cry out, my fingers pumping faster. My panties slip from my hand. I'm too far gone to worry about them right now.

"Tell me what you want, Hazel."

A loud gasp escapes my mouth as I start coming undone.

"Tell me, Hazel!"

"Fuck...Justice...I want you to fuck me until it hurts." My mind shatters, letting the massive spasm rock my body.

He grips my thighs and drags me across the bed. His body, lithe and slick with water, covers mine, our faces a breath apart. His hand cups my cheek and he stares at me long and hard as if he's trying to read my mind. "Tell me what you really want, Hazel," he requests, his voice different. Serious.

"I want you to make it hurt," I whisper, trembling in his arms.

"No." His mouth is near my ear. "Tell me what you *really* want."

There's a moment of deafening silence that's filled with painful desire. The word that escapes my mouth is otherworldly and ominous. "Salvation."

He pushes a stray hair off my forehead and pins my hands above my head. "If this is what you want from me, then I shall give it to you, baby. Under one condition."

"What condition?"

"Will you sin with me first?"

"Are these your lyrics you're using to talk dirty to me?" I bite back a giggle.

"Not right now, but they can be, depending on what I'm doing. And right now, I'm doing you and it has nothing to do with my lyrics." He smirks, striking his cheek over mine. "You didn't answer my question."

"You know the answer to that."

"I want to hear you say it."

"Yes, I'll sin with you."

He rubs his length against my panties and uses his hand to work around the wet lace. When the fabric is out of the way, he drives into me without warning, fast and hard, stretching me to the very limit. My body shivers from the overload of sensations and my insides melt around him. There are no more boundaries between us, no more separation.

When his strokes start pushing me across the bed, I wrap my arms around his neck and pull him closer, needing to feel him against me badly.

Then his groans grow louder as he plunges into me with all his strength. It hurts so good that I want more.

"Harder, Justice." A staggered gasp escapes my throat. I'm on my way to heaven as my legs tighten around his hips. "I need you to fuck me harder." Another delirious request for pleasure on the verge of pain.

"Like this?" he growls, pounding into me.

"Harder, Justice," I moan, my hand encouragingly slapping across his sweaty cheek.

"Like this?" His thrusts are relentless and calculated, just the right amount of pain sifted into an endless ripple of pleasure.

"Yes...yes...yes," I moan, winded, sinking my teeth into his shoulder, my fingers digging into his slippery back as his breathing becomes uneven and fast.

"Let me feel you come, baby." A frantic whisper leaves his mouth.

My body starts shaking in ecstasy. I'm on the edge of the cliff, waiting for him to push me further, every ounce of energy ready to carry me into the bliss of rapture. For a moment, everything disappears, then it explodes into a million sparkling pieces, leaving me completely drained, shattered, and dizzy. My eyes are still squeezed shut and my muscles are tense with the remnants of mad desire when I feel the warm fluid spilling across my stomach, his helpless body pinning me down. The hard sweat-drenched chest covers mine like a hot wet blanket.

The silence that follows next is filled with only the sounds of our erratic breathing, the aftereffects of my orgasm running through my body in shockwaves.

The comedown is agonizing.

"Justice," I mumble after a long pause, my eyes staring at the ceiling as I try to figure out what's missing. *The view of the stars above my head.*

"Shhh." He rolls to his side and presses two fingers against my lips.

"We didn't use a condom." My voice is quivering as I turn my head to face him.

"You have nothing to worry about, baby." His smoky gaze catches mine. "I promise you."

I swallow hard, my heart jolting. My stupid rage got the best of me. The text message from Rachel with all the accompanying questions flashes through my head like a siren in the middle of the night. Can one woman be enough for someone like Justice? Sure, fast, angry sex is great, but it's never better than an STD. "It's not that...it's...I don't know who you've been with before me."

He buries his head in my hair. "I'm sorry, baby. I'll make sure we're more careful next time. Trust me. When I say you have nothing to worry about, that means I'm good. I'd never do that to you."

His honey-like voice makes my heart race even faster. My logic turns off when this man is around. Part of me wants to believe him, the other part wants to slap him silly for getting carried away.

"See what you're doing to me? I can't fucking think straight when you're around." He scoots over to the nightstand to check his phone. His other hand is still gently rubbing my shoulder. "Now, I need to take another shower. Care to join?"

I bite back a timid smile, blood rushing to my cheeks. "Was your plan all along to get me to shower with you?"

He rolls back to me and places a light kiss on my forehead as a mischievous smirk tilts the corner of his mouth. "Don't move, baby. I'll get you a towel."

"I told Rayna you're buying her a new mattress if we have sex in her cabin."

"I can buy her a new cabin if she lets me keep you forever." His soft laugh fills the room as he heads for the bathroom to grab a clean towel.

Does he really mean it? Forever is such a strong word.

I close my eyes and try to remember how many days it's been since River's passing, but the number doesn't come to me. And I don't know whether it makes me sad or happy.

Once we're done showering, I make us some breakfast and we spend the rest of the morning cuddling on the sofa in the living room and talking nonsense, mostly me picking Justice's brain about touring and him picking mine about the painting I sold to the coffee shop owner when I was a teen.

The strange need to be around people grips me right after he leaves. I hate sharing him, but at the same time, I'm glad we have some time apart because being with him this much is so intense that it scares the hell out of me. All of a sudden, I want to do the things I did before River's death. Cooking, cleaning, dancing, painting with watercolor.

I don't really remember the drive to the mall. What I do remember, very clearly, is standing in front of the store with the painting supplies, staring at the display, trying to understand why I stopped creating art in the first place. I loved it so much. After a few minutes of studying the merchandise, I saunter inside and look for a sales person.

The adrenaline rush from getting my hands on a new set of brushes and a watercolor kit is incredible. It's like finally seeing a spark of light in a dark tunnel. For a second there, I even forget how much I miss Justice.

Ignoring occasional stares of other shoppers, I hurry back to the parking lot, bags with supplies in both hands, stupid grin on my face. As soon as the trunk of my Prius enters my line of vision, the air leaves my lungs. I come to a grinding halt in the middle of the aisle, my fingers choking the shopping bag handles. There's a car to my right, waiting for me to move, but my legs won't listen. The fresh spray paint job decorating my bumper is making me sick.

It could have been anything. Loser, whore, cheater. Why out of all words did they have to choose this one?

DRUNK.

26 HAZEL

I'VE GONE MAD.

I created a Twitter account.

To spy on Justice's fans, specifically the ones who have been stalking me here in Tahoe.

There's also a small fraction of me that's sometimes terrified that he might be cheating. The doubt planted by the stupid photo from Rachel a few weeks ago has been eating at me ever since. In my gut, I know he isn't. But his frequent trips to L.A. rattle me from time to time. Especially after the graffiti incident.

"Are you going to stare at your phone until next year?" Justice asks, his eyes never leaving the snowy road. Last night he finally shaved his beard off. I was starting to appreciate his caveman look because he was becoming less and less recognizable when in public. We actually managed to go out to dinner a few times without his crazed fans attacking us in the parking lot or asking for photos inside the restaurant.

"This is very entertaining." I wave my phone at him. Reading his fans' tweets has really made me question the sanity of today's society. "I had no idea you actually had someone sucking you while recording vocals for 'The Temple of Love.'"

"Baby, fans love spicy stories." He chuckles. "They also make up half the rumors you read online. It doesn't mean I fuck every single female who looks my way. Besides, crazy shit like this always helps with the sales. Did you know 'The Temple of Love' hit number five on Billboard a week after the gossip started?"

I love it that Justice has no filter. It saves us a whole lot of drama. At times, he comes off as a conceited asshole, which he is, but he also has another side to him, which most fans probably don't know about. Deep down he's a softie.

"Okay. But why would someone want to donate their breasts for you to cry on?" I spout, showing him another disturbing tweet I came across a few minutes ago.

Justice slides his hand to the back of my head and rubs his thumb into the base of my neck. "Because they want to help?"

"Oh God." I laugh out loud. "I don't know if I'm ever going to get used to this."

"Do you want to be on my next record, baby?" he asks in a suggestive tone. "Because I'd love to have you scream my name while I'm laying down a vocal track."

His fingers continue the slow assault on my neck. It feels good. Everything he does feels good. Even when he starts snoring after a round of sex or when he says ridiculous stuff like right now.

"You're sick." I slap him on the shoulder, burying my head into the sleeve of his winter coat.

"And you're jealous."

"Am not."

"Sure you are." He snakes his arm around me and places a soft kiss on my head.

"Watch the road, rockstar," I whisper into the fabric.

"Yes ma'am."

The snow is coming down so hard that the winding mountain road starts disappearing under the blanket of white flakes as we approach Crystal Bay.

The last few weeks have been strange. Not in a bad or a good way. Just strange. Different maybe. I didn't want to tell Justice about the graffiti at first, but couldn't get the paint removed on my own, so he saw what had been done to my car. The next day TMZ had a field day with his "if-you-have-something-to-say-to-the-woman-I'm-seeing-say-it-directly-to-my-face" social media rant.

After things calmed down a bit, I started painting. A lot. My attempts have been pathetic, but it's made me feel really good about myself. Especially with Justice being back in L.A. We've spoken on the phone every night, and some of those conversations have turned R-rated. I never did anything of that sort with Owen. The truth is, lately I haven't been thinking much about my marriage. My ex still integrates into my life, mainly through his lawyer, but he's no longer the center of my universe. He's just a person I used to love, a person who no longer matters to me, a person who no longer makes me feel anything but bitterness.

My heart jumps up to my throat when the car starts descending down the hill toward the gates of the huge Spanish-style villa.

"What if they don't like me?" I ask, holding my breath. Only, it's not his parents I'm worried about. I'm scared of meeting his son. I'm scared he won't want me near his dad because I'm not his mom, because I'm a stranger.

"They will," Justice reassures me, his hand grasps mine and he gives it a light squeeze.

Easy for him to say. His family is used to his escapades. Mine, however, is still in shock over my decision to spend Christmas with the Hales. Well, my dad didn't say a word, but my mom asked me to tell Elijah Hale that she's a big fan when I accidentally revealed the fact about Justice being Elijah's nephew. Though I highly doubt Elijah will be there.

When we pull up to the property, Justice punches the code into the little pad to the left of the entrance and the massive, snow-covered gate rolls to the side to let us in. The view of the huge Christmas tree set up in the front yard takes my breath away.

As soon as the car comes to a stop, I want to turn around and run back to Rayna's cabin. My body is dead frozen and my mind is racing like an express train. I'm about to meet the parents of the man who's done so many unspeakable and very dirty things to me.

"Are you okay?" Justice inquires.

I nod silently, staring at the front deck with the dome-shaped windows. I can see people moving behind the glass, more Christmas lights and décor, faint music drifting out from the inside. My fears of not fitting in come crashing at me all at once. I don't know how to behave around rich people, and judging by the size of the property, this family is definitely wealthy. No wonder Justice doesn't take no for an answer. He was probably spoiled rotten as a child.

A tall female figure emerges from the front entrance as I carefully check for the carrot cake sitting at my feet. Took me over six hours and four attempts to get it to look like the picture I was using as a reference. Apparently, baking isn't like sex or riding a bicycle. Once you stop practicing, you forget. I can't even remember the last time I baked anything before yesterday. Must have been years back when River was still alive.

The woman waves at us from the deck. "Hey, you two!"

Justice handles the cake while I retrieve the large package we both picked out for Aiden. "This is my sister, Corrine," Justice explains as we walk through the courtyard.

Their resemblance is striking. She has the same facial features but softer, the same black hair, the same eyes—deep and all-consuming but with a hint of aqua. She wears her jeans just as well as Justice does, showing all her curves in the right places. Must run in the family. She doesn't look a day older then thirty-three or thirty-four, even though I know her son is already nineteen.

"Did you two take a detour through Alaska?" Corrine shouts at us when we hop up on the deck.

"You could say that." Justice chuckles. "It sure feels like Alaska." He hands her the cake and tousles his hair in an attempt to shake off the snowflakes. "Hazel made a dessert."

"Thank you. You didn't have to do anything," Corrine says, peeking into the bag. "Looks yummy. Aiden will probably devour it in one sitting." She smiles a dazzling, toothy smile. The toothpaste commercial kind. Expensive and flawless.

I stiffen at the mention of Justice's son and press the gift box to my stomach.

"Relax," he whispers in my ear as we follow his sister inside. His hand is on the small of my back, his hot breath tickling the side of my cheek. "My family can't wait to meet you."

I smile at him meekly, trying to ignore the tremor in my body. There are people everywhere who are dressed to impress, an odd combination of high fashion and wild rock 'n' roll. Silk, leather, satin, denim. And the jewelry. Tons of it. Flashy and bright. So bright I'm having a hard time separating the necklaces, bracelets, and earrings from the actual Christmas décor. This exclusive fashion show makes me feel irrelevant. Even in my new lace off-the-shoulder flare dress Justice bought me the other day specifically for tonight.

"Ah, look who's here!" A female voice drifts at us from the depths of the house as an older woman in a maroon dress emerges from the crowd. She gives Justice a peck on the cheek and turns to me. When our eyes meet, I feel a light tingle in my chest. I don't need an introduction to know who she is. The way she looks at Justice is the way I used to look at River.

"Hi. You must be Hazel." Her voice, raspy and deep, reminds me of her son. She's refined, dressed to kill, oozing money and power. One of those women who's like a fine wine—only getting better with age.

"Hi." I draw my trembling hand away from the gift box and extend it for a shake, but the woman scoops me into a hug before I get a chance to blink. Aiden's present is smashed between our bodies for a brief second.

"I'm Gladys," she says, releasing her grasp.

"Hazel brought a cake, Mom," Corrine states.

"I helped," Justice chimes in.

"You're a bad liar, honey." Gladys smirks at her son. "You can't even do your own laundry."

"I'll take the cake to the kitchen," Corrine says, waving at Justice. "Want to help me?"

"I'll go find Aiden." He gives me a shoulder squeeze and disappears among the guests, leaving me one-on-one with his mother.

"Let me show you where you can leave your things." She smiles, her eyes still taking me in when we duck into the crowd and she walks me through the living room full of people.

The house is gorgeous, with wood floors, a vintage fireplace, and floor-to-ceiling dome-shaped windows look out at the mountain range. Elegant but homey. The artwork decorating the walls is mostly photographs or paintings of famous musicians. Jimmy Hendrix, Eddie Van Halen, Prince, Keith Richards. There are a few concert photos of Elijah Hale and a few of Justice.

I stop in front of one where he's lying on top of a black grand piano, microphone glued to his mouth, eyes closed. I can tell this photo is old because he looks very young and very thin. Before Nikki.

"You have a beautiful house," I say, studying the shot.

Gladys runs her fingers across the canvas. "This was taken eleven years ago. When Chance was alive. They were a wild bunch back then." A sad smile touches her lips as she spins to face me. "Justice stopped playing the piano altogether after Chance died."

Her confession shocks me a bit. *He didn't tell her he's been writing new music.*

"Justice told me Aiden likes Marvel action figures." I drop my gaze to the package in my hands. "My son liked them too."

Gladys nods. Her neat, thin eyebrows pull together. "I'm sorry about your little boy. I can't imagine how hard this must be. No child should ever leave this world before his parents."

My fingers squeeze the gift box harder. "River would have been six this Christmas."

We move to one of the rooms where I deposit my coat and finger brush my hair, and back in the living room, I get introduced to Justice's father. He's tall and fit, with a charming smile, a charisma to die for, and tons of gray hair, which doesn't make him look any less impressive.

My anxiety takes over my mind completely. I really want to grab a glass of champagne from one of the trays, but the hurtful word spray-painted on the bumper of my car a few weeks ago is like a blaring siren in my head. Every time I think about a drink, it crashes into me like a ton of bricks.

"Aiden likes to play hide-and-seek when we have guests over," Gladys explains, resting her hand on my shoulder and leading me through the crowd. We pass a state-of-the-art kitchen and the dining room and enter another, quieter part of the house.

My heart pounds like a sledgehammer as we approach one of the bedrooms. Gladys peeks inside through the small crack, then takes a few steps back and smiles at me. "I'll be in the living room."

I slowly push the door open and drink in the picture of Justice sitting on the floor with his legs crossed. Aiden is right next to him, tossing around his Legos. He's wearing a pair of dark blue jeans and a matching hoodie. A bright red Iron Man cape and a pair of tiny Nikes complete his outfit.

"Hey," I whisper, looking at Justice. My arms are wrapped around the gift box—I can't seem to let go of it. As if it means letting my son go too.

Justice looks up at me from the pile of Legos. "Hey." A soft smile touches his lips. He strokes Aiden's hair and coos at him. "Buddy, I wanted you to meet a friend of mine. Her name is Hazel. She brought you something."

A friend of mine... How do you tell a three-year-old kid you don't love his mom anymore? How do you make him like someone you like?

I descend to the floor next to Justice and set the box in front of the boy. "Hi, Aiden. Your dad told me you like superheroes." My voice sounds foreign. My heart is now running a marathon in my chest.

"I don't know why, of all days, he chose to be shy today." Justice chuckles, brushing the long, dark strands off his son's face.

Aiden scrunches up his nose and reaches out for his present.

"You want me to help you open it?" I ask.

He shakes his head and fiddles with the shiny paper. When he finally manages to rip a good portion of it off, his eyes widen.

"I told you he liked superheroes." Justice touches my shoulder. I've never seen him this content. Perhaps just a glimpse when he's with me, but not like right now—stripped of all his labels, fame, and money.

"I can see that." I nod at the cape.

"That's Corrine's doing." Justice laughs softly, then turns to his son and says, "What do you say, buddy?"

Aiden's too busy demolishing the rest of the box.

"Come on, sport. You say thank you when someone gives you a present, right?" Justice tries again.

"It's okay." I rest my hand on his knee. "He's probably just tired. You have so many guests over."

"Oh, this is nothing. He's been to at least three dozen red carpets. He knows what's up."

"It's really okay." Kids are complicated. Sometimes they like to be the center of attention and sometimes they don't. River had really good days when he was convinced he'd become an astronaut and he had the days when he didn't want to see anyone.

Aiden finally lifts his face from the set and looks at us. His big eyes, blue and bottomless like the ocean, are sizing me up. He grabs one of the action figures from the box, hops up, and charges for the door, his red cape hovering behind him as he crosses the room.

There's a painful burn in my stomach that spreads to my lungs, leaving no room for oxygen. I suddenly feel dizzy. The box with the rest of the action figures turns into a shapeless blur.

He didn't like my present. He didn't like me here.

"Hazel?" Justice calls out, moving closer. "You okay?"

"Yes." I blink through the mist in my eyes. "Just a little over- whelmed. Can you show me the bathroom? I need a minute." *I need a drink.*

He gets to his feet and helps me off the floor. "Of course." His eyes search mine as he draws me closer. I like the calm his embrace brings, but I don't want him seeing me cry.

Once I'm in the bathroom, I let the tears out. My chest heaves uncontrollably. My mouth is dry. My head throbs. My cheeks burn. I lean against the door and stare at my reflection in the mirror above the sink. This new and improved version of Hazel looks sexy and confi- dent, but inside, she's still sad and broken. Because she hasn't really moved on.

A knock on the door interrupts my pity party. "Hazel?" Justice calls out. "Are you okay?"

"Yes. Just a second." I grab a handful of tissues and get rid of the traces of tears beneath my eyes.

You're fine. You're here because his family wants you here. Don't panic just because his son didn't want to talk to you.

Drawing in a deep breath, I turn around and pull the door open.

Justice is waiting for me in the hallway and Aiden's hiding behind his leg, his ocean blue eyes studying me carefully.

"He's a little cranky today," Justice explains, brushing his son's hair. "But he's sorry he ran off, and he has something for you too."

"Oh." That's all I say, watching the boy kick the floor with his tiny sneaker. He shuffles his feet in my direction. Once he's near me, he pulls his hand from behind his back and hands me a small cupcake, yellow with pink icing on top. He's staring at me just like his dad, long and hard, as if his life depends on it.

The moment I accept the cupcake, Aiden takes off.

"I promise he liked your present, and he's not normally like that," Justice explains, moving closer. He cups my cheeks and brushes his lips against mine. "I think he's just getting tired of constantly going back and forth between here and L.A."

"Okay." I bring the cupcake to my mouth and take a small bite.

"You better share, baby," he growls, going for the cake with his mouth. Then his hand slides down my side and he slaps my ass gently.

"Dessert before dinner, Mr. Cross?" I scold him playfully.

"Yes, I've been a very bad boy and I'd like to get punished." He traces his fingers up and down my back. My legs start shaking from all the teasing.

"Oh…you'll get what you deserve."

"Seriously?" Corrine's voice catches us off guard as she emerges at the other end of the hallway, hands on her hips, eyebrows cocked so high on her forehead, you'd think she didn't have any. "You two need to stop making out like high schoolers. Come on; dinner's ready."

Time seems to come to a standstill at the table. The food is amazing, but my appetite seems to have left me. Thirty minutes later, my plate remains half full and my hand is reaching for a bottle of wine, but Justice's warm palm covers mine and he gives me a pained look before I get to it. He doesn't want me to drink. At least not tonight, not while I'm under the same roof with his son. And I do manage to last through dinner, but after dessert, my anxiety starts turning me into a neurotic mess. I sneak out onto the deck and join Corrine and her modest wine party.

The taste of vanilla and dark cherry tingles against my tongue as I take another sip of Cabernet Sauvignon. There's a dash of guilt some-where deep inside me, but I overlook it since my sober self can't seem to get it together. My sober self is awkward and clumsy and feels out of place. All these people I've never met in my life are looking at me, smiling, whispering. Some are bold enough to strike up a conversation, but most aren't sure where to go after the initial obligatory how-are-yous.

"Your father was in a band when he was younger?" I ask Corrine.

"Small local band. They never pursued it seriously. Only Elijah," she explains.

"How come?"

"Not everyone has the guts to entertain twenty thousand people night after night."

"Makes sense." I nod as I continue sipping on my wine. It's bitter-sweet, just like me. "Do you mind me asking why your family doesn't exchange gifts on Christmas?"

There a long moment before Corrine finally gives me the answer. "Our mother asks everyone to donate the money we'd normally spend on presents to a non-profit she helps. This is something our parents decided to do after Chance passed. We do it for Aiden, though." She doesn't elaborate more. Instead, she changes the subject. "Hey, do you want to spend the night here and come with us tomorrow? We're taking Aiden skating after lunch."

Her invitation leaves me speechless. Staying over wasn't in my plans. "I didn't bring anything with me."

"Don't worry about it. I'm sure we have everything you need. The room next to mine has its own bathroom."

My chest stiffens. I feel like I'm in high school and this is my first sleepover. Except I'm staying at a boy's house and for some reason, I'm expecting his parents to be okay with us sharing a room.

Corrine clears her throat. "Sometimes Aiden sleeps with Justice…"

"I understand."

Our conversation goes on for what seems like forever until I'm sleepy from the wine and my eyes hurt from staring at the dark moun-tains as if they hold an answer to all my questions. Which, of course, is silly because they don't. But looking at them somehow brings me peace. Or maybe it's just the house. Maybe it's being able to take a peek into the world that gave me Justice, his family.

By midnight, the guests are gone, and Aiden is fast asleep in his room. Gladys is still putting the finishing touches to cleaning her kitchen when Corrine takes me to her room to pick up a few things I need to get ready for bed. Then she shows me to the bedroom next door. The moment my head hits the pillow, my phone buzzes on the nightstand.

"Mom?"

"Hey, honey. Did I wake you up?"

"No."

"How did it go?" she inquires. The question about Elijah Hale never leaves her mouth.

"It went...fine, I guess." The floor-to-ceiling window on the opposite side of the room offers a breathtaking view of the mountaintops sprinkled with snow that glimmers in the moonlight. "Is everything okay?"

"Yes, honey. I just wanted to make sure you aren't regretting spending Christmas away from us. You've only known this man for a few weeks. I'm afraid you're jumping from one relationship to another so fast—"

"Mom." I cut her off. "Please don't. I had a good day and I'm not in the mood for one of your lectures." Besides, from a practical standpoint, my ex and I haven't been in a relationship for over two years. A man and a woman living under the same room doesn't always mean they are a couple. Most of the time, it felt more like we were roommates.

"You remember you have an appointment with Mr. Wilmer on the third?" my mother prods.

"Yes, I do." How can I not? This is my last chance to get Owen to pay alimony. His lawyer insists that I don't deserve any, but according to my mother, Mr. Wilmer is the best in the business. For the upper middle class that is. Lawyers like Gary Schmidt are probably way out of the league of my parents' budget.

A thumping noise outside in the hallway interrupts my conversation. When I draw the phone away from my ear and wait, the door creaks open and a tall male figure slips into the dark room. The moment he steps into the moonlight, I know it's Justice. His hair's a mess and he's wearing a pair of yellow pajama pants with pictures of pizza slices, but I'd recognize him in a heartbeat, even in a Batman suit if it came down to it.

"Mom. I'll talk to you tomorrow," I whisper into the phone and hang up.

"I just wanted to say goodnight." Without waiting for my permission, Justice slides under the blanket and wraps his arms around me. His head rests on the massive pillow next to mine, and his lips touch the tip of my ear.

"What are your parents going to say?" I stifle a giggle when he tries to kiss me.

"My parents are very well aware that we fuck, baby." He runs his hand down my side. "The only reason you're sleeping in a separate room tonight is because Aiden's here and I don't want him to ask me weird questions if he finds you in my bed."

"You always use the dirtiest words." I sink my hands into his hair and pull gently.

His eyes drift closed and he tosses his head back. "Don't tempt me." His voice is barely above a whisper. He's sexy even without trying, as if it's programmed into his DNA. Even in these awful pajama pants. Even when he's playing Legos with his son or trying to steal my cupcake.

I'm not sure if he can see me blushing, but I'm positive he can feel me trembling against his body.

"I'm sorry… It was just one glass." The truth is, I don't remember how many. I was more than simply buzzed. It may have been two or three.

"I'm not mad. I just want you to stop looking for answers in the wrong places before it's too late." Justice pushes the stray hair away from my face and cups my cheek. "Thank you."

"For what?"

"For being here."

I don't respond. I don't know what to say.

"What's the name of the coffee shop you sold your painting to?"

"Why? You're not going to try and stalk my teenage doodles, are you?"

"Maybe. If I'm ever in the area."

"I doubt you hang out in Encino."

"I'm not going to stalk. I promise."

"I don't remember. It's in the little shopping center on the corner of Ventura and Balboa. Next to the nail salon... Well, I don't know if the nail salon is still there actually."

Silence takes over the room for a while as we lie in each other's arms.

"I've never done anything like this in my life," Justice says quietly, cradling the back of my head. "I walked into you like walking into a fire, knowing I was going to burn, but I fucking did it anyway because it felt right then, and it still feels right now. I let you see the sides of me I never let anyone else see."

I'm an emotional mess. I feel like shit for drinking tonight and for doubting him even for a second. "Justice—"

He covers my mouth with his hand and brings his lips to my cheek, his body hovering over mine. "Goodnight, baby. My bed will miss you tonight."

My heart is beating like a drum when he places a soft kiss on my forehead, detaches himself from me, and leaves the room.

27 HAZEL

I LIFT my eyes from the coffee mug and rest both hands on the tabletop. Breakfast has never been my favorite meal of the day...at least not until today. I'm convinced it's the house and not just the people who live here.

"Are you sure you don't want to go skating, buddy?" Justice pulls Aiden onto his lap. "We've been talking about it for weeks. Remember?"

The boy shakes his head and shoves his finger into the piece of cake sitting on a plate in front of him.

"I told Hazel we'd take her," Justice continues, brushing his son's hair off his face. "She doesn't know how to skate either."

I bite back a smile at the memory of our skating date, the moment I landed on my ass in particular.

Corrine sets her coffee on the table and scoops out some of Aiden's cake with a spoon.

"No." The boy clutches the plate with both hands and jerks it aside.

"You don't want to share with Corrine?" Justice coos.

Aiden shakes his head again. His eyes are fixated on the dessert, his face sour. I wonder if this is because of me or if it's just a bad mood.

I watch their exchange silently. The mix of emotions building up in my chest is so intense that I'm afraid if I open my mouth, they'll come out in the form of a scream. The way Justice hovers over Aiden reminds me of Owen and River. They were inseparable at first, but as our little boy grew older, his separation from his dad grew too. I don't know whether Owen gave up on him at some point or he just didn't want to get in too deep because he knew we'd lose River soon. All I know is that it hurt like hell.

"He's been like this all morning." Corrine's shoulders slump in defeat when Aiden slides from his dad's lap and rushes out of the kitchen.

The muffled sound of his delicate footsteps roars in my ears. I wrap my hands around my coffee mug and stare at Justice.

He tosses his head back and exhales loudly. "He did *not* get his mood swings from me."

"You think?" Corrine scoffs, grabbing the plate with Aiden's cake.

"I'm pretty sure." Justice shifts his gaze to me. "Tell her, baby."

"Oh." I swallow hard. "He's definitely his father's son."

"See." Corrine waves her spoon in front of her brother's face. The smile of a winner touches her lips.

A few minutes later, the drumming of Aiden's sneakers booms through the house before he breezes into the kitchen like a tiny tornado, circling around the table, toys clutched in both hands. After several loops, he stops next to my chair and puts one of the action figures from the box set I gave him yesterday in my lap.

"Thanks," I mumble, looking at him and then at Justice.

"He wants you to play with him," Corrine explains, sending another piece of cake into her mouth.

"Okay." I study the mini Hulk.

Aiden extends his hand and shows me another figure. "I'm I-won man."

"Iron Man," Justice corrects. "It's *R*, not *W*, buddy."

"He's three," I mouth at him.

"Dad is an s-man." Aiden smiles, pointing at his father.

First I think that my hearing plays a trick on me. "What?"

"S-man." Aiden's grin is bigger than this whole house.

"That is a bad word, sport," Corrine cries out.

Now I'm certain the kid just called his dad an ass, which is probably not far from the truth.

"He means X-man," Justice explains.

"Oh." I cover my mouth with my hand to hide the smile because something tells me my boyfriend might not like this nickname.

Aiden laughs and pulls on the hem of the winter dress I'm wearing, the only dress in Corrine's wardrobe that actually fits me and is appropriate for a casual breakfast with Justice and his family.

"Let's play," Aiden says, blinking at me rapidly. His voice echoes through the house as he disappears down the hallway.

"Come on." Justice slides from his chair and takes me to his son's room.

Once inside, I feel fear and panic crawling under my skin. I'm not sure what to say or what to do because Aiden isn't my child, but in this moment, I wish he was. So bad that it hurts.

"You Hulk." The boy points at the green monster figure still clutched in my hand.

"Okay." I nod, descending to the floor.

"I'm I-won man." He sets his toy on the small plastic table and makes a whooshing sound.

I do the same.

"We fight."

"Okay."

"Do you like super he-woes?" Aiden asks, tilting his head.

"Yes. Very much."

"Me too."

For a while, the two of us play with the action figures. When Aiden loses interest, he tosses them aside and drags one of the plastic boxes into the center of the room to show me the rest of his toys. My heart jumps to my throat the moment he pulls out a red furry Elmo. River had the same one in a blue ABC sweater.

"I know how to dwaw," Aiden says, getting to his feet. He runs across the room to grab his coloring book and his crayons from one of the shelves.

"Oh wow," I whisper as I watch him doodling random shapes in random colors all over the pages. "You're really good at that, aren't you?"

He nods his little head and hands me a bright red crayon. "You want to dwaw with me?"

"Sure."

We keep *dwawing*, trying out different colors, adding some details of our own to the pictures on the pages. I'm so thrilled to be interacting with Aiden that I don't even notice the outside world; therefore, the voices in the hallway don't really reach me until he tosses the crayons aside and hops to his feet.

"Mom!" His face lights up.

Two seconds later, the door of his room flies open and a pair of icy blue eyes meet mine.

Nikki.

I'm still on the floor, sitting in a pile of toys and holding a crayon while Elmo grins at me like nothing's happened. A small part of me hopes this is a dream and I'm about to wake up. Only, Nikki Deville is as real as it gets. Here, in Crystal Bay. On Christmas Day. Why? Justice told me she'd be picking up Aiden after the holidays.

"Hi." Nikki fake-smiles at me, lifting her son off the floor. She rests his head on her shoulder and whispers in his hair, "I missed you, my sunshine. Are you excited to go home with Mommy?"

The woman is money, power, and beauty. Everything that I'm not yet now, I have to compete with.

"Yes." Aiden jerks his head and wraps both arms around her neck, his tiny fingers sinking into her perfect platinum blonde hair.

I swallow hard and avert my gaze. My insides are screaming, but my body is frozen.

"Why don't you go say goodbye to your grandma and grandpa, sweetie." Nikki smooches her son before putting him down.

Justice emerges in the doorway a second later. He kisses the top of his son's head and whispers, "Mommy and Daddy are going to talk. Go play with Grandma and Corrine, okay?"

The oxygen leaves the room along with Aiden. I drop the crayon and try to hold back the tears. The wallpaper designs turn into a blurry mess. Justice brushes past Nikki and helps me off the floor.

"Really?" Her lips twitch in annoyance. Sadly, this doesn't make her any less gorgeous. At some point, every woman on the planet has probably wanted to be Nikki Deville for at least a day. I have to confess, even me. Once. After I saw her on the big screen for the first time. She was phenomenal.

"You're supposed to pick him up tomorrow," Justice growls, placing his hand on my shoulder. I don't know if this is his way of protecting me from his ex, or just a reflex, but the gesture makes me feel powerless. "You could have at least called ahead."

"I'm flying to New York in five days," Nikki counters. "I'd like to spend some time with my son."

"It's not my problem that you all of a sudden have to fly to New York. We had an agreement."

"I'll be gone for a week. You can have him then." Her smile doesn't reach her eyes.

"We had an agreement, Nikki," Justice repeats.

"I'm his mother and you're still legally my husband." She throws one last ice-cold stare at me and leaves the room, adding, "I don't have to call you when I want to see my son."

The silence that follows next is deafening. The air in the room is heavy and stifling.

"I'm sorry." Justice pulls me into his arms.

"Maybe you shouldn't have fought the restraining order after all," I mumble into his chest. I hate the fact that my body won't stop shaking, even with him holding me tight. It's like a part of Nikki is still here, laughing at us.

"Are you okay?" Justice runs his hand down my back, his fingertips heating my skin through the fabric of Corrine's dress.

"Yeah." I nod. Only, I'm far from okay. I'm about to have another meltdown and I really don't want anyone, especially his ex, to see it. I pull back, rubbing my watery eyes. "Just give me a few minutes."

I rush to the bathroom. Once inside, I press my sweaty back against the door and try to breathe. I'm not sure whether the reason behind my panic attack is seeing Nikki with Aiden or simply the shock factor of her being here, but it hurts like hell. It hurts so much that I want to drown all this pain and misery.

When the Deville hurricane that just raged through the house starts dying down, I step out into the hallway and listen to the voices in the living room. Corrine and Nikki are arguing, and I almost convince myself to make an appearance, but the wall of artwork I'm facing holds me hostage. It's not a secret that this family doesn't like Nikki, but part of me is still unsure whether taking a stand right now is a good idea. Hesitant, I stop in the middle of the hallway, my eyes studying the photo of young Justice. The provocative and aggressive in its capture imagery seizes all my attention. I don't hear or see anyone until Nikki's voice jolts me back to reality.

"He's a great lay, isn't he?"

I turn my head to face her and try not to panic. She's standing too close. Too close for me not to notice how flawless her skin is, how perfectly blue her eyes are. And it makes me want to disappear.

"You and Justice are separated." My voice is small, as if I'm trying to convince myself it's okay to sleep with the man whose wife is less than two feet away from me right now. Guilt is a shitty feeling.

"I'm going to be very clear." Nikki's piercing gaze locks on mine. "I'm very sorry about your son, but I don't want you to play house with mine. You can fuck my husband however you like, but if I see you anywhere near Aiden again, I promise you, Justice will start spending more time in court than on stage. Do you understand?"

There's an angry roar in my head. It's so loud I can't hear the words coming out of my mouth. "You're an alcoholic. You'll never be able to get full custody."

Nikki smiles, showing me a perfect set of milk white teeth. "At least I'm an alcoholic who does something about it. You're just an alcoholic." Her voice turns into an ugly whisper. "I will ruin you if I see you near my son again."

I swallow hard and clench my fists. There's a scream stuck in my lungs, but it just stays there.

"Don't cross me, Hazel," she says, heading for the door to Aiden's room.

Still shaken up and unable to move, I listen to her pack his things. My mind is trying to recover, but all I can think of is having a drink.

28 JUSTICE

I GRIP the steering wheel of my Jeep harder and turn on the high beams. The snow falls in slow motion. My chest stiffens at the sight of the feathery flakes being systematically destroyed by my windshield wipers. Just another reminder of how fragile everything in this world is.

The trees that shimmer in the moonlight on both sides of the road look like gigantic crystals. I hardly remember a Christmas this beautiful. Maybe when I was a kid. When things were simple. When I could still appreciate the exquisiteness of nature. How ironic, there's nothing simple about my life right now. Having a shitload of money doesn't make it easier. It makes it harder.

"Hazel?" I call out, my eyes never leaving the dark, snowy road.

She doesn't respond.

"Listen..." I lift my right hand from the wheel in an attempt to stroke her hair, but the approaching turn makes me change my mind. The words are stuck in my throat until we finally pull up to her friend's cabin. She unbuckles her belt, slides from her seat, and rushes to the front door. I shut off the engine and follow her inside.

"Look, Hazel...I'm sorry I put you on the spot." My voice is rough from all the earlier arguing with Nikki.

She takes off her coat and tosses it on the couch.

"What the fuck is this? Some kind of silent treatment?" I growl, shoving my freezing hands into the pockets of my winter jacket. She looks like a lost lamb, but her eyes are the opposite. They're burning right through me like a wildfire.

She sighs heavily, her shoulders falling. "I hate the fact that she can just come in and rain on our parade whenever she wants."

"This is temporary," I say, moving closer.

"I know." She breezes past me into the kitchen, her lingering coconut scent embracing me for a brief moment. The words I was going to spit out earlier but held back for some unknown reason are starting to choke me from the inside. I have all these feelings for her, but I don't exactly know what she needs to hear right now since she's sweet one minute and sour the next. So instead of saying anything, I stare at her new watercolor set and the unfinished painting on the kitchen table.

Hazel pulls out a brand new bottle of wine from one of the cabinets and retrieves the corkscrew from the drawer. I've never really addressed her drinking before. I tried to control the amount of alcohol she drinks in one sitting, but never the drinking itself. Now, watching her fight the corkscrew makes me wonder whether she really has a problem and whether I should be doing something about it.

"So what? You're just going to get drunk and check out?" I test the waters.

"Really, Justice?" She peers at me through her thick lashes, her gaze a mixture of sultry and innocent. As if she's not sure which part of herself she wants to embrace—the devil or the celestial being.

I walk over to her and try to grab the bottle, but she clutches it with both hands, like a kid whose toy is being confiscated.

"Hazel. Fucking stop," I say into her hair, pressing my chest to her back.

She hugs the wine tighter. "It's not fair." Her voice is low and angry.

"What's not fair?" She tenses as I run my hands up and down her shoulders. "What's not fair, baby?"

"Life." She sniffs, her body relaxing into mine.

"So what then?" I move some of her hair aside and kiss her neck gently. "Are you going to let my crazy ex drive you into a drunken hysteria?"

She doesn't respond.

"You're going to let her do that to us?" I keep pushing the subject, pinning Hazel to the counter. She doesn't resist when my hand reaches out for the bottle. As soon as the wine is out of the way, I wrap both arms around her body and draw my tongue across her cheek. My jacket is restricting my movements, but I don't care. She feels steaming hot against me. Like my own personal sunshine. The curve of her small, round ass teases my cock in the best way possible when she shifts under my weight.

"Do you know what I want, baby?" I ask, running my fingers over her ribs.

"I think I have a pretty good idea." She shivers under my touch, tossing her head back. Her shallow breathing turns into soft moans when my hands slide down to her thighs and I squeeze them. Not hard but hard enough for her to know I don't plan on being nice tonight. She's never asked me to be gentle, not even once since our first night of kink, but like the better man I'm supposed to be. I've given her a little bit of everything. I've shown her all the options, all the sides of me she should know about. Nice, dirty, angry, and tender.

"I'm going to fuck you like this," I growl, yanking her skirt up. "Wearing this dress...and these boots. I'm going to fuck you really hard, baby."

She starts grinding against my erection, taunting me even more. Her voice is barely above a whisper. "I'd like that, Justice...very much."

"Say it, baby." I love hearing her talking dirty.

"I'd like for you to fuck me very hard," she purrs, splaying her hands out on the kitchen counter.

"Say it again, baby." I want to ram my cock into her. I want to make her scream my name.

"Fuck me, Justice," she begs. The sound of her voice sends shivers down my spine. My body is buzzing with the anticipation, and the thought of dominating her puts me over the edge. I'm hard as rock. So fucking hard that if I don't do something about it in the next couple of seconds, I feel like I'll explode. I wrestle off my jacket and throw it on the floor. Lowering my zipper, I growl in her ear, "Bend over, baby."

She obeys. She always does. She loves this game just as much as I do.

Yanking down my jeans and my boxers with one hand, I pull down her panties with my other. She tosses her head back, and seeing the streams of gold cascading down her shoulders gives me goose bumps. I never thought I had a thing for hair. Not until I saw her in that bar.

Every part of me aches with desire. I thrust into her hard and fast without a warning. She gasps, her body tenses, resisting at first. She's tight, warm, and wet. Perfect around my cock. Grabbing her hips, I slowly pull out and pump into her again. Harder and faster.

"Oh God!" she cries out, clawing at the marble counter, meeting each thrust of my hips with a loud moan. "More."

I slide my hand up her back and fist her hair. "Tell me you want me to fuck you harder, baby."

"Yes."

"I can't hear you, baby," I tease, pulling her hair. I know how she likes her pleasure. Mixed with pain.

She shudders, tightening around my cock. "Yes...Justice... Fuck me harder...please!"

"Like this?" I growl, pumping into her wildly.

She whimpers in response. Her cries make me want to torture her all night, torture her until she can't take it anymore, until she melts in my arms.

I let go off her hair and smooth both hands over her perfect ass. She gasps when I spank her, the sexy catch in her breath echoing through the room.

"How do you want it, baby?" I pull her away from the counter and kiss the back of her neck.

"I want to see your face when you punish me," she whispers.

Part of me is still scared of her always craving the pain, but I can't tell her no.

I pull out of her slowly and spin her around. Her cheeks are flushed, eyes blazing like fire, lips parted. She lifts her chin, wraps her arms around my neck and pulls my mouth to hers. The kiss is savage. It tastes like anger, frustration, and...blood.

"Justice—" Her hands slide down to my chest and she draws back a little. "Make me feel...please."

She doesn't need to ask twice. As a matter of fact, she doesn't need to ask at all. I can read it in her eyes. The desperation, the lust, the desire to move on. I lift her off the floor and set her on the counter. She wraps her legs around me and tugs on my shirt. Our bodies are in perfect sync when I pump into her again. Her eyes flutter, she digs her nails into my shoulders and slides to the edge of the counter to meet my thrusts.

"You wanted to see my face, Hazel?" I sink my hand in her hair and wrap it around my wrist so that she can't move.

The sounds of groans and skin smacking mixed with the clanking of the dishes inside the cabinets fill the house. I'm burning up and my heart is racing. My body can't get enough. I rock against her harder and faster, holding her still with my other hand, our lips barely touching. She cries into my mouth softly, her nails leaving marks on my skin, the heels of her boots drumming against my ass.

"Can you feel it, baby?" I cradle the back of her head, her silky hair still tangled around my fingers. She nods, her desperate eyes never leaving me. Her forehead hits mine when I ram into her really hard. She arches her back and lets out a loud scream as her hand slaps against my shoulder. Then she spasms around my cock, thrashing wildly. A cue for me to pull out. The better man in me is cursing up a storm for not remembering about a fucking condom, but the truth is, I'm a goner. I was the moment she walked into The Black Lagoon. She makes me forget everything, even my own name. With her, I'm someone else.

My body explodes seconds after hers. We're both sweaty, covered in cum. Her fingers clench the folds of my shirt, and she moans into my chest as her orgasm fades. She looks so angelic after we fuck.

"I'm sorry," she murmurs against the wet fabric of my shirt, her hot breath leaving trails of goose bumps on my skin.

"For what?" I brush her hair off her face.

"For being a shitty Christmas date?" She lets out a faint laugh.

"Mmm..." I kiss the top of her head. "I don't think I'd consider this date a failure. I did bang you."

"Is that what it was? You banging me?"

"I thought you liked when I talked dirty to you?"

She doesn't respond.

"Hey." I draw her face away from my chest and whisper in her ear. "It's not just sex, Hazel. You know that, right? It's never been about sex." My heart is in my throat. The words I'm looking for aren't exactly the ones I said, but I don't know how else to explain my feelings to her. Or maybe I do. I'm simply scared to dig deeper.

She nods. "I know."

"I don't bring just anyone over for Christmas to my parents' place... Only people who matter to me."

She gulps under my gaze. Her eyes are full of fear. "So I matter?"

"Yes, you fucking matter, baby."

I don't know why the fuck she needs to ask this. Maybe she needs the reassurance because of her ex or maybe she likes to hear me voicing how much I actually care about her.

The muffled buzzing by my feet drags me back to reality. I hate when my cell phone goes off at moments like this. When I'm with her.

"Fuck." I look down at the mess we made. "You have paper towels nearby?"

Hazel throws her arm back to the counter behind her. "Voila." She shoves a handful of napkins at me. A wild smile touches her lips. "We don't ever tell anyone about this. Rayna would kill me. Your sister would kill you too."

"How did my sister get involved?" I snort, grabbing the napkins.

"It's her dress."

Uh-oh. "You're right. My sister doesn't need to know about me coming all over her dress."

After cleaning up the mess and getting my jeans back in place, I pick up my coat and search the pockets for my phone.

"Wanna take a shower with me?" Hazel inquires, smoothing the dress over her thighs on the way to the bedroom.

"Do you really have to ask me that?" I chuckle, following her.

She doesn't say anything, just laughs softly.

Once we're in the bedroom, I toss my phone on the nightstand and undress. She disappears into the bathroom. The sound of the running water and her heels clicking against the tiled floors starts giving me ideas. With her it's never enough.

When I walk in, she's still wearing the goddamn dress and boots. Her hair's damp from the thick clouds steaming the bathroom, a few loose strands sticking to her pink cheeks.

"Can you help?" She smiles at me shyly, turning her back to me.

I move closer and run my hands down her sides. Slowly.

"Ummm, the zipper is right here." She slides her fingers to the base of her neck.

"I know." I kiss the top of her head, thinking that this is how I want the rest of my life to be. With her. Having sex in the most inappropriate places, taking showers together, seeing my parents once in a while, playing superheroes with my son. Even making fun of her painting attempts. I want it so bad that it hurts.

By the time we finally make it to bed, it's past midnight. I'm tired. Her warm naked body feels divine against mine, and she smells like coconut and vanilla, the sweetest combination ever. The moment my head hits the pillow, I'm gone.

I'm not sure what time it is when the rattling of my phone wakes me up. It roars on the nightstand like a mini bomb. I snap my eyes open and I sit up. Nikki's name flashing at me from the screen makes me want to throw the damn thing into the toilet and flush it, but the irritation turns into panic when I realize that she never calls me this late anymore unless it's an emergency.

My heart spasms from her hysteric screaming. "Where the fuck have you been, Justice? I've been calling you since we landed. I need you to come over. Right now."

"To L.A.?" I whisper, looking down at Hazel. Terror crawls up my skin.

"Yes."

"Why?" I toss the blanket aside and slide to the edge of the bed.

"I took Aiden to the ER. He got sick on the plane." She's half sobbing now. I can't understand the rest of what she says because I'm slowly losing my mind. The only words I hear are *Aiden* and *hospital*.

"Which hospital?"

"Cedars-Sinai."

"Okay. I'll be there."

After ending the call, I dial Dom.

"It's late, Justice. And it's still goddamn Christmas." He yawns into the phone.

"Can you get me on the first available flight to L.A.?" I ask, rubbing the back of my neck. The fear building in me is paralyzing.

"Of course." His voice is full of concern now. "Is everything okay?"

"Aiden's in the hospital. I don't know anything yet. Just get on it, okay?"

I toss the phone on the bed and cover my face with my hands. For a few moments, it's just me and the darkness. I'm bouncing from one black hole to another.

Reality rushes back in when a soft whisper fills the room. "Justice?"

I draw my hands away from my face and stare at the wall.

"Justice?" Her voice cracks. She grips my shoulder and scoots closer. Her body is warm and inviting, but the fear remains. Bigger than ever.

"Hey, baby," I rasp, grabbing her hand. "I have to leave. I'm sorry."

Stroking my hair, she clings to my back. I can feel her heart thundering in her chest, but she's quiet. We sit like this until Dom calls back with the flight information. A small fraction of me doesn't want to leave, because she's here. But my son isn't and right now, he's the one who needs me the most.

29 HAZEL

I WAKE up to the distressing sound of the doorbell.

My head starts spinning when I try to sit up. I blink a few times to bring the surroundings into focus. The first rays of light glistening on the horizon peek into the room through the slits of the half-closed blinds. My fingers come in contact with the bottle of wine while scrambling for my phone on the nightstand. Last night's memories crash at me all at once.

I tried to finish the painting I started before Christmas, but gave up around four in the morning. The brush didn't want to listen. The anxiety and the strange feeling of inevitable doom finally got to me after a long fight. Justice would have hated me for opening that bottle of wine, but I couldn't take the torture. I couldn't just sit and wait for his call. Not when we're hundreds of miles apart.

Still half asleep, I slip into a robe and rush out of the bedroom, a sick part of me hoping to see Justice, but I know it's impossible because he's in L.A. with his son. Whoever woke me up is already gone by the time I make it to the front door. I rub at my eyes and carefully pick up the package. Nothing but my name scribbled on it. No return address, no shipping label. After looking around the front yard to make sure this isn't some paparazzi joke, I walk back inside and inspect the package one more time. It's probably just another present from Justice.

Holding that thought, I run to the bedroom and check my phone. My heart sinks when I realize he hasn't texted me since he left for L.A. The cabin still smells like him. He's everywhere. In the bathroom, in the shower, in my bed. His deep, gentle voice is humming in the back of my head as I rip the package open. This must be some kind of a mix-up. There's a bottle of champagne and a stack of phone bills inside the box that aren't mine, but when my eyes jump to the top of the page, my stomach churns. The papers rustle in my hand when it starts to tremble.

Drawing a deep breath, I go through the pages one by one. My already failing heart stops each time my eyes come across a blue high-lighted phone number that keeps popping up on almost every page. Eventually, I have to lean against the dresser for support because I feel sick to my stomach. The last text message exchange Justice had with the owner of the number is very recent.

There's a roar in my head when I finally get to my phone and dial the mysterious number. It's the sound of me breaking. I don't remember anything but the fire burning through my chest until the line clicks and the female voice on the other end drags me back to reality.

"This is Rachel." Her voice is expressive and smoky.

Rachel as in the band's makeup artist Rachel?

My heart is doing double time and I can't stop shaking. "I'm sorry." A pathetic whimper escapes my mouth. "Wrong number." I hit the end call button and toss the phone on the dresser, unsure of what to think. Was he sleeping with her or was all this work-related? What are the chances I'm overreacting?

The frustration simmering in my veins grows wild when my eyes zero in on the champagne. I grab the bottle and throw it against the wall, putting every ounce of strength I've got left in me behind it as a scream, an ugly cry of defeat, leaves my lungs. My torn-apart heart is pounding so hard, my chest hurts. My head is spinning and my mind refuses to accept the consequences of my tantrum until I'm quaking from raging anger surging through me like hot, deadly lava. The room's a mess; there's glass and champagne everywhere. Oddly, it's the best and possibly the most artistic representation of what my life has become. Shards and shards of a once beautifully packaged product.

After examining the chaotic results of my outburst, I stomp into the kitchen, retrieve a new bottle of wine from one of the cabinets, and drink myself silly on the couch in the living room with my phone on my lap and the phone bills on the coffee table. My hands are itching to call Justice, but I don't want to bug him while he's with his son, and I don't know if I truly want to talk to him anyway. I feel lost, angry, but most of all guilty for making him split his time between me and Aiden, for spending my parents' money, for not being strong enough to fight for my sanity. The truth is, I'm too miserable to stand up to my fears.

The muffled buzzing wakes me up in the middle of the night. I rip my eyes open and absently stare into the darkness, my hands fishing for my phone among the pillows. The call is from Justice, but I just let it ring. Part of me wants to hear his voice badly, but the other part of me, perhaps the rational one, is re-evaluating our relationship. The fans, the paparazzi, Rachel. What if there are other women? What if he becomes tired of me? There are so many questions and no answers.

The silence in the cabin is terrifying and I hate it with all my heart because my life should've been filled with the sound of my son's laughter. But instead, I hear the desperate howls of my soul, pleading with someone up above to either give me my sanity and my boy back or put me out of my misery once and for all.

The phone rings again. This time I pick up.

"Baby," Justice mumbles, his voice tired. "I'm so sorry I didn't call earlier. It's been one hell of a day. Did I wake you up?"

I keep holding my breath while he's talking, hoping this helps me get rid of the tremor in my body, but it doesn't.

"Hey," he calls out. "Everything okay?"

"H-how's Aiden?" I ask, staring at nothing in particular.

"He's still in intensive care. The doctor said it's some kind of infection. They brought down his fever a bit, but that's it for now. We're just waiting."

"Is...she there?"

Pause. "She went home a few hours ago. She's coming back in the morning."

I want to ask about the phone bills, but my tongue doesn't move. *It's not the right time, Hazel. Not when his son is in the hospital.*

"Try not to panic, okay?" I give him the same advice I was given by my son's doctors so many times. Letting a child see his parents' fear is the worst. "He'll be fine."

"Sorry, baby, I've got to go. I'll call you tomorrow." He ends the call abruptly, leaving me with the strange aftertaste of all the questions I never asked.

For a while, I just sit in silence, thinking about everything that's happened to me since my move to Tahoe and about the possibilities ahead of me. Justice and me together no longer seem like a good idea. Getting a job and a place of my own should be on my list of priorities. Finalizing my divorce too.

Sleep comes at sunrise. I pass out again. On the couch. Exhausted and miserable. I dream about the paintings and about my son, about a white picket fence and about my husband coming back home from work. Only, I can't see the man's face. Part of me is convinced it's Owen, but I already know that Owen and I are never going to get back together.

I wake up around lunch, and my body hurts from being in an uncomfortable position for so long. The battery on my phone is about to die. After locating the charger and taking a shower, I get back to the kitchen to make some breakfast. My eyes keep diverting to the stack of papers on the coffee table as I butter my bagel, but a sudden buzzing of my ringtone causes me to drop the knife on the counter. I rush through the living room to answer the call, convinced it's Justice, but my hopes are dashed the moment I see Rayna's name flashing across the screen.

"Hey, hon." She doesn't sound like herself.

"Hey."

"I didn't want to text you—" She stops mid-sentence. Her voice is a gravely whisper.

"What's going on?" A cold shiver zips down my spine.

"You haven't seen it, have you?"

"What are you talking about?"

"Nikki's TMZ interview?"

"What interview?"

"I'm sorry, Haz—"

I hang up before Rayna finishes her speech. There's a mad fire raging through me. I'm not quite sure how to describe all these feelings taking over my mind as I search for my iPad.

The screenshot of the interview is all over my Facebook and Twitter newsfeeds. Drawing a deep, shaky breath, I click on the video and watch Nikki Deville stride through the paparazzi-packed hospital parking lot, two security guards escorting her to her vehicle.

Someone starts shoving a microphone at her as she approaches a black Escalade. "How's Aiden, Nikki? Is he doing better? What are the doctor's saying?"

You gotta be fucking kidding me? She just walked out of the hospital, still wearing the same clothes she had on when she came to get her son from Tahoe.

I can feel the hairs on my neck standing up as another reporter joins the interrogation. "Nikki, is Justice here with you? Are you two still on for the divorce?"

Part of me hopes Rayna was confused when she called and there's nothing to this video—just the footage of Nikki, but I'm wrong. She stops in her tracks and faces the camera, her icy blue eyes staring at me from the screen of my iPad.

"Justice and I do not bring our son into our disagreements," she blurts out.

Liar!

The voices of other reporters behind the camera are starting to turn into a jumbled mess accompanied by the rapid clicking of the flashes.

"What about the domestic abuse allegations? Any of this true?"

"Nikki, are you going to fight for full custody?"

"Hey, Nikki. Over here. What do you think about Hazel?"

Oh God! I know I need to stop watching this, but I can't. I'm frozen stock-still with my eyes glued to the screen and my stomach churning, fear crawling over my skin.

Nikki straightens, a hint of a smile touches her lips. "I'm very sorry for her loss. I hope she gets the help she needs to move on. Alcoholism and depression go hand in hand. I'm not just saying it. I've lived it. Getting out of that slump is impossible without professional help. I hope you get better, Hazel."

My heart jumps up to my throat as I watch people shoving more cameras at Nikki. She doesn't shy away from putting on a show, even with her son in the hospital.

"How about you, Nikki? Are you doing better?"

"I'm doing great. Hazel should consider a treatment program if she wants to keep seeing my ex-husband. He's a recovering addict after all."

I look up from the iPad and stare at the dark water lapping beyond the glass of the floor-to-ceiling window. Rage starts choking me from the inside. There's something suspicious about this interview. It reeks of fraud.

I close the video player and type my name into the Google search bar. The images that pop up on the page one by one are mostly of Justice and me, and the ones where he isn't present are some blurry cell phone photos featuring my shopping habits. There's a couple where I'm at the grocery store in the middle of an aisle with wines and spirits, which both scares and infuriates me. The headline is nauseating.

Justice Cross Has a Type: The Rock Singer Loves the Ladies Who Love Cocktails.

A long string of comments below the photo is a discussion of my drinking habits and how unlucky Justice is for getting involved with another alcoholic.

I scroll down to the very bottom of the comment section and stare at the recommended articles. There's screenshot of our neighbor Lloyd standing in front of his house with a microphone in his face and a screaming headline beneath the thumbnails of the video.

Who Is the Woman Dating Justice Cross? The Neighbor Reveals the Shocking Truth.

30 JUSTICE

A RECOVERING ADDICT. The newest lie about me to come out of Nikki's mouth.

Naturally, the press and the fanboys have been eating this nonsense up like candy, spinning and twisting the stupid TMZ footage for more angles.

Fuck my life. And fuck Nikki.

The driver turns up the classic Boston tune up front. The catchy guitar riff is a great distraction considering the gloomy thoughts that have been haunting me since the moment I boarded the plane. The peaceful arrangement with Nikki isn't happening. This is the last New Year's she's spending with Aiden on her terms. As soon as I'm back in L.A. I'm speeding up the sole-custody proceedings.

The snow slowly zigzagging onto the ground has turned Tahoe into a quaint-looking town. Quiet and charming. Like an old black and white movie with a happy ending. A town where my own personal amber-eyed piece of heaven is waiting for me.

My heart starts racing when the car finally pulls up to the cabin. A small part of me is still wired and angry, but I know that if I don't let all the Nikki shit go at least for tonight, it'll ruin my time with Hazel. This past week was a nightmare with Aiden in the hospital, tabloids talking crap, and everyone, especially May and Dom and the label, breathing down my neck.

I swing the door of the vehicle open, grab the roses, and step into a wall of dancing snowflakes. The air that fills up my lungs is crisp and pure and I want to keep inhaling it until I pass out.

The sight of Hazel's standing on the porch makes me smile. She's wearing an oversized t-shirt and a pair of long blue socks, and the wind tousles her hair when she reaches the steps. My dirty mind can't help but imagine her naked on top of me in those socks. The ideas I get when I'm with her have no limit.

"You're going to freeze, baby," I tell her, hopping up the stairs. "Get inside." My mouth covers hers as we step into the house.

"Are these for me?" she asks, pulling back. Her gaze shifts to the flowers.

"How did you know?" I smirk and give her the roses, trying to steal another kiss in the process. My body is aching with need. I want her here and now and I want her bad.

"Just an educated guess." She laughs softly, heading for the kitchen to get a vase.

"You've been busy." My eyes register a couple of new paintings on the table as I scan the room for alcohol or anything hinting at her drinking while I was gone.

Paranoid much, Justice?

"Yes. I've been working on my feathering," she babbles, going through the cabinets.

"Feathering, huh?" I chuckle looking at the screen of her iPad. The browser's open and there's an email from admissions in her inbox. "Does this feathering include me and you in the bedroom?"

"It's a watercolor technique." She snorts out a laugh and turns the faucet to fill the vase with water.

"So what does this feathering entail?" My eyes dart from the iPad to the piece of paper with purple blobs, then back to the iPad. "You didn't tell me you applied to college."

"Oh." Hazel spins to face me, vase still in her hands. "I didn't really. It was just one of those weird nights. What am I going to lose by filling out a college application, right?" She changes the subject. "I actually spoke to someone at Clay's office. My job orientation is next week."

I let the subject of college go. "Okay." Work means she'll be back in L.A. and I won't have to divide my time. The only reason I gave Aiden two days with Nikki is because I felt fucking guilty about leaving Hazel alone on New Year's Eve. "That's great. Are you still sure about that?"

"What? Answering phones for a living?" She puts the roses into the vase, folds her arms on her chest, and leans against the kitchen counter. "I'm pretty sure my painting attempts aren't going to sell for much."

I love it when she gets feisty.

"You can do whatever you want, baby." I move closer and wrap my arms around her. "Anything your heart desires." My tongue starts teasing the tip of her ear.

She squirms a little and tosses her head back, her eyes drifting closed as her skin sizzles against mine. I want to take her right here on this kitchen counter and fuck her just as hard as the night I left for L.A. And then, instead of the lullabies, I want to sing her some of my dirty songs.

"Did you miss me?" I draw her in the direction of the kiss. "Did you?"

She sinks her hands in my hair and moans softly as our bodies drink each other's heat.

"Come on, say it." I fumble with the buttons of her shirt, longing for verbal validation. She seemed somewhat distant the few times we spoke on the phone while I was in L.A.

"I did. A lot." Her voice begins to shake. "I've been thinking a lot too, Justice."

"What about?" I keep holding her in my arms like my life depends on it, but part of me is already fearing the worst.

After a few moments of silence, she frees herself from my grip, her eyes never leaving me. "About us." She's as white as a ghost.

"What's there to think about?" My pulse starts to spike.

"We need a break, Justice... I need a break. I'm sorry. I didn't want to do this over the phone."

My asshole ego is screaming like a banshee. I flew from L.A. to spend New Year's with her for this? I left my son with my ex just to get dumped by the woman I met at a bar two months ago? But that's just the tip of the iceberg of how crappy I'm feeling right now.

"What?" My heart is about to jump out of my chest. "Is this because of the circus in the press? You know this is going to blow over in a week or two, right?" Only I don't quite believe that myself. Nikki really overstepped her boundaries when she publicly called Hazel an alcoholic, causing another tabloid shitstorm. And knowing my ex, this is going to get worse. The best way to handle the situation is to ignore it.

"No," Hazel retorts, shaking her head. "I hate that you have to choose what holidays to spend with me and what holidays to spend with your son. It's not supposed to be like this."

"If Nikki has something to do with this—"

"No," she interrupts me, "but I do have a problem and I can't do anything about it with you around."

"What do you mean?" Cold sweat trickles down my back as I follow her through the house, my heart drumming, my pulse pounding against my ears. Confusion, fear, and rage rattle me. "What the fuck do you mean, Hazel?"

She spins to face me when we're in the bedroom, her amber eyes boring into me like they want to set me on fire. "You're consuming me. You're like a black hole, Justice. Your fans and reporters are stalking me day and night. Taking my photos. Posting them online. Making up stories. Nikki's fans are calling me names. Some kids went to my parents' house yesterday demanding to see me. And I just keep waiting for the other shoe to drop. This life isn't for me. Not the right-now me."

"I'm sorry." I take a step forward to close the distance between us. "Why didn't you tell me earlier?"

"What for? So you could ask your publicist to send out another press release where you ask teenage girls obsessed with the man who sings soft porno to back off? I don't think this will work and I don't want to add more problems to your pile. Besides"—she looks away—"not when your son is in the hospital."

"Look, he's better and I'm here." I reach out for her to pull her into my arms. We're dangerously close to each other and I'm drowning in the scent and the warmth of her body. "I'm going to handle Nikki. This is temporary."

"It's not just her." Hazel places both palms on my chest in an attempt to push me away when I try to hug her.

"Don't fucking do this right now, baby."

"You told me Rachel was just a makeup artist." She grabs a stack of papers from the dresser and hands them to me. "Is she?"

I stare at the papers, dumbfounded, my mind trying to make sense of the numbers until I finally realize what they are—my phone bills with Rachel's number strategically highlighted with a blue marker. The one Nikki always uses for learning her lines. I know her habits better than anyone. "Where did you get these?"

"Delivered to my doorstep." Hazel rolls her eyes. "I don't know if I can do this with you gone all the time."

"But I'm not gone right now."

"But you will be."

"For fuck's sake." I toss the papers on the floor. "This was before I met you. You know that. It was just a fuck."

"There are two years' worth of messages from two in the morning. That's a whole lot of fucking!" She throws both hands in the air.

The wounded asshole in me takes over. "I'm not a saint, baby. But I'm sure you noticed. Heavenly creatures don't fuck like I do." I'm pissed at her for not giving me the benefit of the doubt. But I'm also terrified that she's serious about the break. I just got here and it already feels like she's a thousand miles away.

The silence gripping the room drives me nuts. I grab her arm and pull her against me. She tries to resist, but her body says otherwise. This is the rough and angry version of us, lusting and hurting.

"I'm not looking for a saint," she says quietly, sinking her nails into my skin. "I need to be able to trust you."

"I'm sorry I wasn't honest," I whisper in her ear, snaking my arms around her waist. My pulse is skyrocketing, my blood rushing through my veins like liquid metal. I'm hard as a rock against her softness. "Let me make it up to you." My lips travel across her cheek. Slipping my fingers under her shirt, I kiss the corner of her mouth.

She shudders under my touch. "Sex isn't going to help us solve the problem."

"The only problem we have is me always wanting to fuck you silly."

She breaks the kiss and slams both hands into my chest. "No, Justice. We're not going to survive this relationship if all we do is just fuck and ignore the fact that we're still married to other people."

"Nikki isn't going to be a problem much longer."

"It's not just Nikki." The despair in her voice makes my skin crawl. "Didn't you hear anything I said? I need to get better. I need to get help and I need to figure out what to do with the rest of my life. And I can't do that with half the planet gossiping about me and my family."

"Am I a part of that plan?"

"It's the only way I can be with you."

The room starts spinning. "I don't want to take any breaks." I have this strange need to keep touching her, as if I don't, she'll forget what it feels like to be with me. I smooth my palms over her shoulders and up her neck to cup her cheeks.

"I know. But can't you see?" A sad smile touches her lips. "We're doomed, Justice. I'm a mess and your life is just too complicated right now." She presses her body to mine and whispers into my chest, "I want you to finalize your divorce and I want you to finish the album. Then I want you to go on tour, sell out arenas, make your fans happy." Her tears burn like acid as she cries into my shirt. "While you're doing all these things, I want you to think of me, and when you get back, I want you to tell me if you still feel the same about us." She clings to me harder, her hands in my hair, her lips on my cheek.

"This is a long fucking break, Hazel. I fucking need you right now, baby." *I need you in my corner badly while I'm fighting my ex, the record label, and everything else that comes my way.* I'm shaking and I'm not sure how to gain control over my emotions. She's pure and inviting against me like a slice of heaven and she makes me feel so many new things. "I love you."

Hazel looks up at me like she's in shock, tears still streaming down her face. The room starts vibrating from the strange mix of want and desperation, and it fucking kills me that she doesn't say it back. A small part of me submits, but my body and heart refuse to accept her conditions. I slide my hands to the back of her neck and draw her closer, my mouth capturing hers. Then we're a panting mess again, ripping each other's clothes off and fighting for air. There are no words, just angry and loud sex. I do everything she asks of me, fuck her until she's unconscious, until my name is the only thing she remembers.

I leave the next morning without waking her up.

31 HAZEL

Day nineteen. Without Justice.

New year. New life.

At least I'd like to think so.

I stare at the computer screen and try to make some sense of the new spreadsheet that's been thrown at me, but the numbers are giving me a headache. Moments like this make me regret dropping out of college. Women raising kids get their degrees every day. I could be running an art gallery or designing clothes for a living right now. Instead, I'm sitting in a cubicle and watching customer service tutorials for fifteen dollars an hour. Oh well. Not every mother attending college has to take care of a child who's going through endless rounds of chemo.

It's been a week since I started at Pacific Paradise Properties. Ironic, but the company's name doesn't quite capture the atmosphere inside the office. If anything, working here feels like working in hell. The never-ending buzzing of the phones, printers, and fax machines is pure torture. A tiny fraction of me is excited because this is my first real job and I'm supposedly moving on, but mostly I'm just miserable. The business attire I have to wear and the professional demeanor I have to maintain are driving me insane. The best part of my day is always the drive home when I'm alone in my car, secretly listening to The Deviant's music.

"How are you doing, Hazel?" Stacy, the girl who I'm supposed to shadow today, calls out from her seat. I'm surprised she has the time to chat with me. Her phone has been ringing all day like it's possessed. And that's on a Friday. How is she still smiling? Her cubicle reminds me of a fireplace mantel with dozens of family photos and other memorabilia on the walls. She's bubbly and young and she wears a pencil skirt like a pro.

"I'm fine. Thank you." I nod from my spot, ignoring the urge to get up and leave. I make an attempt to smile too even though I don't feel like it.

"Let me know if you need any help." She bats her heavy-with-mascara lashes at me and reaches out for the blinking red button on the keypad to take the next call. "Pacific Paradise Properties. This is Stacy speaking. How can I assist you today?"

I spin in my chair and get back to battling the numbers on the spreadsheet. My imagination takes me to a parallel universe where Justice and I are together and his photos are decorating my workspace. Not the barely recognizable, V-neck sweater-clad caveman Justice. The choke collar, makeup, and boots-with-studs Justice. I wonder—how would proper Stacy react to my gallery?

Paranoia creeps its way into my mind when another receptionist from the cubicle across the room waves at me. Everyone here is fairly nice. There's coffee and pastries for breakfast, crackers for lunch, and a lot of pretentious thank-yous all throughout the day. I'm surprised no one has asked me about Justice yet, but I'm almost certain the lack of questions is Clay's doing. He probably instructed the employees not to discuss this topic, even though Justice and I are still the main gossip in town. We didn't really break it off officially. Everything said on New Year's Eve was between us only. No press release followed, no Instagram posts, no tweets. Justice wants for the world to keep assuming we're together, despite the fact he and I haven't spoken since that night.

The rest of the day is just as dull as the whole week has been. I sit in my chair and study the spreadsheets and the diagrams. At five o'clock sharp, I'm out of the office. My feet hurt from wearing an uncomfortable pair of new shoes for nearly nine hours, but I don't care. I pretty much run through the parking lot, terrified of the reporters. On my first day at the office, a bunch of people with cameras were waiting for me by the elevators after I got off work. I had to ask building security to help me get to my car. Apparently, separating myself from Justice didn't do me any good. Part of me even regrets the decision.

The need to hear his voice is stronger with each passing day. My mind tries to play the rational woman card, but my heart longs for him more and more. The "out of sight, out of mind" method doesn't seem to work when it comes to Justice. He's everywhere. On the news. On the billboards. On the radio. I know I need to stop listening to his music, but I can't. His scent, a mixture of spice and ocean breeze, is still on my skin. His minty taste is still on my tongue. He's like a shadow, following me everywhere.

I hop into my Prius and argue with myself for a few minutes. When it becomes evident the pros are outweighing the cons, I open my brand-new private Instagram account and check his latest post. It's a short, shaky video of him behind the keyboard. He's playing the same tune he played for me back in Tahoe after our first night together. I watch the recording at least seven times, smiling at the caption below.

Step aside, James Cameron. Aiden finally cracked the mystery of cell phone videos. P.S. Working on some new music. Can't wait for you to hear it #TheDeviant2018

✝ ✝ ✝

Warmth floods my chest and spreads to the rest of my body. I stalk his feed for another ten minutes and head to the storage building to pick up some of my things.

Confusion and fear brew inside me while I sit in my car in front of the unit for what seems like forever. My life has become a bunch of boxes packed with things I may never need or use again. A handful of mementos, reminders of what it used to feel like before River's death.

Shoving both hands into the pockets of the new blazer my mother bought me specifically for my job, I walk into the tiny space and scan the area. My heart thumps like a caged hummingbird. It wants to break free, to escape this dull, dusty place. After a few long moments of silence, I reach for the switch and turn on the light.

This is where I stashed most of my stuff before leaving for Tahoe, including some of my old clothes I didn't really have the need to wear after my baby's death—a few expensive dresses and nicer shoes. Shuffling through the boxes one by one, I carefully inspect the contents and set aside a few outfits that seem appropriate for the office. Part of me still can't believe these used to be my clothes. Feels like another life, another person.

My hands won't stop trembling as I pack the bag. When finished, I scan the unit one last time and head for the door, but my eyes catch sight of a small box with River's name on it tucked under a table. We donated most of his clothes and toys after he died. I hardly remember keeping anything, because Owen didn't want me to. This must have been my mother's doing.

Setting the bag aside, I kneel down in front of the table and pull out the box. The anticipation of holding something that belonged to my baby creates a strange buzz in my head. Painful memories start slipping into my mind. How do you tell a four-year-old he's going to die? How do you even explain what death is to a child whose life barely started? How do you keep a smile on your face day after day, year after year, just to make him feel loved and happy?

I brush the dust off the top before removing it and look inside. Elmo's red fuzzy mug is gawking at me from the depths of the box. It's the same one Aiden has, only in a blue ABC sweater, pants, and sneakers. I pull the toy out and press its tummy to see if it still talks. The low squeal that fills up the storage unit indicates that Elmo probably needs new batteries.

Just like my life.

After a few minutes of absently staring at the furry figure, I bury my face in it and inhale sharply. The smell of dust and bubblegum shampoo seeps into my lungs, reminding me of the after-shower scent of my son's body. Tears spill down my cheeks as the memories crash into me all at once. Four years of chemo. Four years of hope and torment.

What if my choices could have been better? What if we didn't kiss him or hug him enough?

I cry for what seems like forever, 'till a stranger's voice fills the space.

"You okay, miss? You need any help?"

I bite back a sob and glance at the door. There's an older man in a construction uniform standing outside the unit. A strained *sorry* escapes my lips. I put down the toy and wipe the moisture from my itching face.

"You sure you don't need any help?" the man asks again.

"No, thanks." I shake my head and attempt to smile.

"I'm down in 325 if you change your mind."

"Thank you."

When the stranger is gone, I get to my feet, lock up the unit, and head home. Facing my parents suddenly horrifies me. The other day, after finding a bottle of wine in my closet, my mother begged me to see someone. She slipped a bunch of Alcoholics Anonymous brochures into my purse the next morning. They fell out of the side pocket when I was buying my lunch at the Mediterranean place across the street from our office, humiliating me even more than the tabloid headlines.

The dread of being subjected to the silent treatment from my father and a pestering speech from my mother makes me pull up to a grocery store halfway home. Justice's fans have been bringing flowers to River's grave like clockwork. Last weekend someone ignored the *No Trespassing* sign and instead of leaving the gifts near the lawn, left a basket with fresh lilies on our doorstep. It came with a poem for my son, a poem written by a complete stranger. And even though I could appreciate the sentiment, the constant donations consisting of plush toys and mini trucks has opened up the old wounds.

Having Elmo sitting on the passenger seat next to my purse reminds me of how much I miss my son and how much it hurts knowing I'll never get to hear him laugh. When the pain becomes unbearable, I get out of my car, walk into the store, and buy myself a wine cooler variety six-pack. They don't taste as good as real wine, but they're sweet and bubbly and they're twist-offs.

Elmo keeps grinning at me as I get back behind the wheel. Part of me knows it's just a toy, but part of me doesn't want it to watch me drink. I feel guilty. Like a failure. The approved college application, the new job, and the upgraded wardrobe don't make much sense at the moment. Nothing does.

There's a tremor in my hand when I reach out for the volume control to turn up the radio. The song playing is off The Deviant's first album. A mixture of sexy, bold, and very raw.

I listen to it with the six-pack still on my lap and my hands inside my purse, thinking about Justice, about his New Year's Eve confession, about our last night together, and about his little blue-eyed boy. The alimony ordeal makes me feel dirty and cheap. Trying to get money out of one man while thinking about another isn't who I thought I'd become. Yet here I am.

I also think about the stupid YouTube video where our neighbor Lloyd calls Owen and me a dysfunctional couple. There was no shocking truth, just a bunch of ramblings. His fifteen minutes of fame that stirred up a whole lot of people who had no life. The comment section had me both crying and laughing. It hurt for a while and then it stopped, because deep down, I knew I wasn't the woman people made me out to be. Neither do I want to be right now. That's why drinking myself into oblivion suddenly seems like a very cowardly way out. It also makes me a liar. I promised Justice the break would be my attempt to get better. Instead, if I don't get hold of myself, I'm likely to become another DUI case.

After hiding the coolers in the trunk, I skim through some of the embarrassing brochures from my mother and pick one with a local address, which happens to be just a few streets down. A quiet corner lot with plenty of trees, flowers, and soft yellow beams illuminating from the pole lights.

I park my Prius in one of the guest spots and check the brochure again to make sure this is the right address.

There's a huge knot forming in the pit of my stomach. My mother could have sent me to a clinic but no, instead she chose to send me to a place, correction—an institution I've been secretly despising for over two years. A church.

My eyes sweep over the sign that's peeking out from behind the long jacaranda branches. I stare at the letters long and hard, my heart racing.

HE HEALS THE BROKEN HEARTED
PSALM 147:3

The emotions clog my throat, and for a second, I can't seem to get any air into my lungs. On impulse, I scramble for my phone and shoot off a text to Justice. There's this sick part of me that craves him every second of every day.

Hazel: Hey

After ten minutes of pointless waiting, the desire to just drive off almost wins, but the nagging voice inside my head tells me not to give up. Not yet, anyway.

The meeting room with a dozen chairs arranged into a tight circle is in the very back of the building. It's spacious, filled with light chatter, the aroma of freshly made cheap coffee and hazelnut creamer.

I slowly drink in the small crowd and shuffle my feet toward an empty corner, unsure of what to do next. A blocky middle-aged man disengages from the group of people gathered near the long table with cups and utensils. He approaches me carefully, and his smile is warm but guarded at first, as if he's trying not to overwhelm me with the sudden friendliness.

"Hi. I'm Derek. First time here?"

I nervously fist my purse. "Yes."

His smile grows wider, deepening a net of wrinkles around his eyes. "Take any seat you like."

"Do you mind if I just listen today?"

"Of course." He nods, pointing at the table. "Why don't you grab some coffee before we begin?"

"Sure." I follow Derek into the crowd, my heart drumming in my chest. The fear of being recognized overwhelms me so much that I forget about the text message I sent Justice earlier until the moment I get out of the meeting and find no response.

32 JUSTICE

My fingers wrapped around the plastic handles of the oversized bag feel clammy and stiff. I've done plenty of charities in the past, but this is different. This is the same hospital where Hazel's son died, and I can almost taste the desperation filling the cold sterile air.

"Thank you for meeting us on a Saturday, Doctor," Dom says as our procession strolls through the oncology department.

The echo of my footsteps ricocheting off the bare walls makes my head hurt. The stout smell of illness mixed with the scent of the sanitizer scratches my lungs like a hacksaw each time I take a breath.

"The art of saving lives has no days off, Mr. Fiery," the doctor responds. He's a small man in his fifties with a head full of gray hair holding a clipboard. "Someone is diagnosed with blood cancer every three minutes."

The words make my skin crawl. While part of me is terrified to see what this disease does to a child, like the sick fuck I am, I crave the knowledge. I want to understand how it feels, how *she* feels.

"Mr. Cross is very interested in the family sponsorship program," Dom says on my behalf, his voice distant.

I haven't said much because there's been a battle in my head since the moment I discovered a text message from Hazel when I woke up. It somehow slipped through the cracks yesterday when I got out of my studio and didn't check my phone before going to bed. Part of me had already given up hope that I'd ever hear from her after twenty days of complete silence.

The short three-letter word uncovered a whole new palette of feelings in me.

Dr. Morton smiles at us politely, but it's not a toothy smile like I get at restaurants or from people trying to kiss my ass. It's a lips-shut smile, professional and honest. "Of course." His sharp dark brown eyes size me up as he gestures toward the hallway. "Let me have you meet some of the children. They love guests."

Of course they do. Just maybe not the guy who writes disturbing softcore porn songs.

For the first time in my life, I'm ashamed of my own perverted vision of art. I realize that my music might not be the kind of music I'd want my son to listen to when he's twelve. Of course, he's seen me live before, but from backstage with his ear protection on and people censoring the show, he only gets to see a fraction of who I really am. Those aren't the moments I'm most proud of. It's the rare lullaby times, soft and intimate, without the instruments and the band backing me up, when it's just the two of us that I cherish. I wish I had more of those peaceful father-and-son nights.

Fright trickles down my spine when we stop in front of the room at the end of the hallway. Fragments of the doctor's speech, the number of deaths caused by blood cancer every year specifically, are now permanently imprinted into my brain.

After a faint knock on the door, we enter a room and are greeted by the strained smile of a woman I've never seen in my life, which makes me feel like an intruder, a stranger, prying into the tragedy of another family.

"Mary. How are you?" Dr. Morton extends his hand for a shake. The dark shadows beneath those tired eyes and the slumped shoulders remind me of Hazel when I first met her. No matter how much a parent tries to hide the despair, it still seeps through like poisonous gas. Invisible, but no less destructive.

Dr. Morton introduces us to the mother one by one. A sad smile touches her lips, but she isn't who we're visiting today. It's her little boy sitting on the hospital bed, surrounded by tubes and monitors.

My heart shrinks at the sight of the frail body, the pale face, and the bruising on his small arms. In reality, I'm panicking, wanting to leave. But Hazel's words about keeping it positive in front of a sick child push the fears away.

"Hey, Connor. How are you feeling today?" Dr. Morton walks over to the opposite side of the bed to check one of the monitors.

"Okay." The kid nods energetically, his big, curious eyes shift to the bag I'm holding.

"We have some guests today, buddy. You think you can spare a minute?"

His bald head bobs in agreement. "Sure."

"Hey, man," I say, pulling out a chair and settling next to the bed. "I'm Justice."

"Is that your real name?" Connor asks, blinking at me. His thin fingers fidget with the folds of the hospital blanket.

"Yep. My parents tried to be creative." A soft chuckle leaves my mouth. Sometimes I wonder if Mom and Dad were high when they were picking a name.

"Are you a rockstar?" Connor's lips spread across his face into a huge grin. The kid is definitely sharp. Even though the term "rockstar" makes me cringe on the inside. It's very eighties and very cheesy. And definitely not who I aspire to be.

"How did you know?" I lean forward and place the bag on the floor.

"You have a lot of tattoos." He scrunches up his little nose. "Did they hurt?"

"A little at first. Not so much after." At this point in my life, pain is secondary, just a sting. Makes me wonder if Connor thinks needles are normal.

"How old are you?" he asks, his eyes diverting back to the bag full of toys.

"Pretty old," I say, smiling at him. My heart is drumming inside my chest as if it's Zander practicing.

"I'm seven."

"You're a big guy. I'm almost five times that."

"Oh, wow." The kid stares at me for a few moments. "That's a lot. Are you married?"

"Sweetie," his mother interrupts our banter. "Remember what I told you about the questions we can and can't ask?"

"That's alright," I tell her and turn my attention back to Connor. "Wanna see what I got?"

He nods again, his big, inquisitive eyes never leaving mine. As if he's trying to read me, trying to understand why the room is full of strangers and why some dude he's never met before is interested in talking to a seven-year-old boy with leukemia.

I move the chair closer and set the bag on the edge of the bed. Silently, Connor sinks his hands into the pile of toys and starts digging. Carefully and slowly, inspecting each one.

After a few long moments of plowing through the bag, he looks up from the gifts and asks, "Can I have more than one?"

His mother gives him a light brush on the shoulder. "Sweetie, you'll have to share these with the other kids."

"It's okay. You can have as many as you like," I say encouragingly and signal for Dom to hand me one of the iPads we bought specifically for the visit.

"Wow! Thanks!" Connor beams. His twinkling eyes remind me of Christmas lights when he gets his tiny hands on the package. The fact that a kid fighting for his life needs so little to smile makes my heart both bleed and sing, makes me feel powerful and at the same time lost and weak.

Once we say our goodbyes and walk out into the hallway, the pain in my chest becomes overwhelming. I can't seem to get enough oxygen into my lungs because each breath is a fucking struggle, as if an invisible hand is squeezing my insides. A wave of dizziness and nausea crashes over me out of nowhere.

"I need a minute," I whisper to Dom, fighting for air. "Where's the restroom?"

"End of the hall to your left." The doctor's voice echoing off the walls of my skull makes my head ache.

"Thanks." My tongue feels thick in my mouth; my back's covered in cold sweat. All I can think of right now is puking.

By the time my feet get me to the restroom, my heart is an over-heated engine brutally jerking around my rib cage, my legs and my arms are quivering, stomach churning. A paralyzing fear crawls up my skin as I prop myself against the sink and turn on the faucet. This is different from my early occasional cases of stage fright. This is a new feeling of hopelessness like I've never experienced before.

Death is inevitable. In the end, we all have the same fate. But we also have the opportunity to make a difference, make this glimmer of time that we call life count. The question is whether I've been using what's been allotted to me wisely. Five times seven equals a whole lot of shit no one will care about after I die.

Sucking in a labored breath through my teeth, I splash some water on my face and shut my eyes. This is why Hazel likes to be alone so much. Because the darkness is comforting and safe. Because nothing can shatter her if she has no one left. Only, I don't want to accept that. I don't want to waste my life on angry, rude, and heartless people like my ex-wife or the money-grabbing suits from the label who think they can decide what direction my art should be taking this year.

After a few long moments of dreadful cold silence except for the sound of water running from the faucet, I fish for my phone and respond to Hazel's "hey" text with "hey yourself." My eyes zero in on the screen for some time, waiting for an answer, but it never comes. The knock on the door brings me back to reality.

"Justice?" Dom's voice drifts from the hallway.

"Yeah?" I call out, shutting off the water.

"You alright? You've been in there for almost ten minutes. You need anything?"

Good question. *Am* I alright?

I grab a stack of paper towels from the dispenser, wipe my face, and head for the door to unlock it. Dom quietly slips inside and props himself against the stall.

"You want me to get a nurse?" he asks.

"Nah, man." I shake my head, tossing the wet paper towels into the trash can.

"You're not fine. You're green."

"Probably ate something bad."

"Right." He folds both arms on his chest and gives me a few more seconds.

"Don't fucking look at me like that." My attempt to put on an asshole mask fails.

"You wanna tell me what's going on?"

"Shit." My insides seize up at the memory of the seven-year-old boy digging through the bag of toys. What if that were Aiden? Just the thought of my son being that sick makes me shake. His infection scare was bad enough. I didn't sleep for three days straight after he got admitted to the ER. "I won't scrap any of the new songs I've written," I blurt out.

"Come again?"

"I don't care if the label doesn't like the new direction."

"Man, are you seriously worried about what Angelo said the other day? The dude is a walking mood disorder."

"I fucking am." Our manager somehow got a hold of the demo I sent to Cruz and his reaction was less than encouraging. He called my lyrics depressing. The kind of music our fans don't want or need to hear. "This is the best stuff I've written since Chance died. If Angelo or the label don't like it, they can suck my ass."

He also insisted I let our touring keyboardist, Kace, handle all the piano parts, like he's been doing it for the past three years.

The truth is, the new material sounds nothing like The Deviant music. It's lacking the key component of all our songs—the eroticism—but it does have a better message. I'm proud of what I've written and I don't care that Zander thinks I'm becoming soft and that Cruz wants me to "sex up" the lyrics.

When we walk out of the hospital two hours later, my head is still spinning from meeting so many children and their parents today. Once in the car, I switch my attention to the phone while Dom is debriefing the driver on where to go next. There's a text from Hazel with a photo of a new painting. It's a flower with baby-pink petals and a dark green stem on a blue background. Her art has gotten much better. The intensity of the details and the amount of work she's been putting in her creations amaze me.

Justice: Nice.

Hazel: Thanks.

Justice: How are you?

Hazel: I'm fine. I'm staying with my parents. The job sucks.

Justice: Sorry.

Hazel: I saw your Instagram.

Warmth flutters in my chest and stomach.

Justice: Are you stalking me?

Hazel: Not at all. When are you going into the studio?

Justice: We have to push the dates. Maybe April. Zander's hand is messed up bad. We might need to get a different drummer to record the single.

Hazel: Oh no! I hope he gets better.

Justice: Aiden is obsessed with cell-phone videos now.

Hazel: I imagine. He is pretty good for a three-year-old too. Better than some teenagers. Did you teach him to hold the phone horizontally too?

Justice: Yes.

Hazel: Send me some more?

Justice: Sure. Send me some of your art too, Picasso?

Hazel: It's van Gogh, not Picasso.

Justice: What's the difference?

Hazel: Have you seen Picasso's art? You're Picasso. I'm van Gogh.

Justice: Point taken and art lesson very much appreciated. P.S. Do you want to have dinner with me?

There's a long pause. I'm almost convinced I fucked up, but she responds a few minutes later.

Hazel: I do, but that would be cheating. We are taking a break. Remember?

Justice: Yes, but it's just dinner. No strings attached.

Hazel: I'm sorry. I'm not ready just yet.

Justice: I understand.

Hazel: Go make some art, Picasso. Bye.

I grin at my phone like a fool, a wave of bliss engulfing me. For the first time in three weeks, I feel calm. I don't know what made her change her mind and text me, but I'm fucking glad she did. I feel that despite this break, despite the label push-back on my new music, despite Zander delaying the album recording, and despite Nikki's attempts to gain sole custody of our son, everything will work itself out. It has to. Every bone in my body senses the change.

I'm fucking Picasso.

That's what she said.

33 JUSTICE

Funny, but I knew very little about Hazel when we were screwing each other back in Tahoe. Now that she isn't around, I seem to know a lot more. The things I probably shouldn't even bother with because it was her other life, her life before me.

"Justice?" Cruz calls across the room.

We're at his home studio, trying to toss some ideas around to spice up my demo of "Amber". Not that the song needs any spicing up. If it had been up to me, I would've left it bare. Just the keys and the vocals, but we're a fucking band. Or at least we're trying to stay one.

It's just the three of us now since Tyler is in North Dakota. Road tripping. That's his idea of good times. I used to laugh at his disappearing acts when we were off tour, but I get him these days more than anyone. The pressure the band has been under since Chance's death is agonizing, but for some reason, I'm only now starting to feel it. *Really feel it.* We're still expected to do better, to be more original, but the truth is, we probably can't because the only lick of originality we had got buried along with our friend. We're just picking up the pieces.

I try to ignore the dread that's been eating at me since last night and focus back on the studio session right around the time the song comes to an end.

"You with us, man?" Zander raises an eyebrow, spinning in his chair. He looks out of place with his cast, but he insisted on coming down.

"Yeah." I stare at my phone sitting near the mixing board and try to figure out how to tell him that turning this song into another rock-it-til-you-drop-it festival anthem isn't what I have in mind. Too bad there's no nice way of saying his ideas sucks and mine don't.

"We've done this before," I finally come out with it. "We keep on replicating the same sound, like we've been doing for over a decade."

"That same sound sells our records and fills up the stadiums," Zander counters. He isn't wrong, but I don't want to do the same thing over and over. Neither would Chance have wanted that. He'd be packed with all sorts of innovative ideas.

"For how much longer?" I ask him, checking my phone. Hazel and I have been in a nonstop text message relationship since the day of my first hospital visit. A little over a month now. She's mostly been sending me snapshots of her watercolor works. Some in progress and some finished. I asked her out to dinner again on Valentine's Day, but she refused.

"For as long as we can, man." Zander shrugs, the fingers on his good hand tapping against the chair arm. "It's the money-making formula. Why risk it? People like what we do. People pay a lot of money to see us live."

"I think we need to explore new sound," I say as my eyes sweep over to the phone again. The lack of response from Hazel is driving me nuts. The text I sent her last night is still unread, which isn't like her. At least the new crazy-texter version of her who enjoys exchanging snippets of our art and photos of our meals. The whole nine yards.

What if she's drinking again?

"You want to be one of those fools who loses half the fan base by exploring new sound? Be my guest. Just don't use the band moniker." Zander gives me a blank stare.

"You need to step back," I say quietly, but my heart is racing. I know it took him a whole week to finish programming. He can't use his fucked hand at all, but the beat isn't what I had in mind. Not even close. "The drums are way too fast for this song."

"Just cuz you touched a fucking keyboard for the first time in over six years doesn't mean it's going to sell an album."

Zander's words sting like a motherfucker, and I want to give him a pass because he's fucked up on his pain meds, but the money talk drives me to the very edge. "Can you stop thinking about how much dough you can make at least for a fucking second?" I get to my feet and grab my lifeless phone.

"Everyone needs to relax," Cruz interjects from his spot. "Why are we stuck on this one song? Can we move on?"

"Because Mr. Douchebag here thinks he's pissing platinum tracks," Zander barks, lifting his bad hand in the air.

"We keep doing the same shit over and over and over again! I'm fucking sick and tired of singing 'The Temple of Love.' There's more to us than what we are right now if we let it happen," I say on the way out.

"Where are you going?" Cruz yells.

"To explore new sound under a different moniker," I rattle off, slamming the door shut behind me.

The weight of my own words and everything that just transpired in the studio hits me once I'm in my Lexus, driving down the hill with my phone clattering in the cup holder and my hands choking the steering wheel so hard, my bones are about to crack.

I don't know what came over me or why exactly I blew up, but sitting there and trying to rearrange parts of the songs we've already written to disguise them and pass them off as something new felt like cheating. Cheating ourselves and cheating our fans.

I send another desperate text to Hazel when I'm sitting at a red light, undecided about where to go next with my music.

Justice: Hey. I haven't heard from you since yesterday. I just wanted to make sure you're okay. Talk to me.

Whether it's the dead screen of my phone or just the strange desire to somehow be closer to her without imposing, I find myself driving around the part of the Valley I've never been to before, the white-picket-fence world with its quaint cottages and American flags out on display. I wonder whether some of these nine-to-fivers listen to The Deviant music or prefer something more civilized. The kind of stuff they could play in front of their elderly parents and their kids. The kind of stuff that doesn't have tease-me please-me lyrics. I wonder if any of these housewives, daughters, and sisters have to hide out from the hordes of gossip-chasing paparazzi and creepy strangers who leave random things on their doorsteps. I even wonder what it would be like living in one of these houses and coming home every night to a hot meal instead of hauling my bags from one hotel room to another night after night, year after year.

I wonder because I never had that and I don't know how it feels. My life is an endless string of tour dates, interviews, public appearances, workout sessions, and long studio hours. Aiden is basically filling the holes in my busy schedule.

There's tightness in my chest when I pull the Lexus into the cemetery parking area, and my stomach lurches the moment I get out. There are rows and rows of lost lives and grieving families spread out in front of me for as far as the can eye can see. Thousands of tombstones. Dull, uniform, compact. Unexciting.

Distant sounds of the city traffic fade as I make my way across the green lawn, nervously looking for River's grave. Ironically, it's impossible to miss because of all the flowers. A whole sea of them. Roses, lilies, sunflowers, peonies. The colors stand out so much that it hurts the eye.

I shove my hands into the pockets of my jacket and stare down at the floral mountain, emotions choking me from the inside. For a second, I truly believe they're going to come out in the form of a scream, but then they just twist me up until the pain is everywhere. Mind, body, soul.

It's already dark out and I'm still sitting in my car in the cemetery parking lot when my phone chimes. Hazel's name flashing at me from the screen causes my heart to flip, and I almost drop the damn thing while typing up a response because my hands are shaking so badly.

Hazel: Hey, Picasso. Sorry. Late night at the AA meeting yesterday.

I'm filled with pride. She's been going to those religiously since last month and they seem to be helping.

Justice: Got ya. You just had me worried for a second.

Hazel: Why?

Shame and regret fill my gut, but I'm too scared to tell her the truth, the truth that I subconsciously always expect her to fail.

Justice: Because I'm always wondering where you are and what you're doing and I can't fucking stand this separation. I want you near.

There. I said it. It only took me a little bit less than two months to tell her how I really feel about this stupid break.

Hazel: We are still married to other people.

Justice: My divorce hearing is in two weeks.

Hazel: What about Aiden?

Justice: She wants sole custody.

Hazel: Do you think she'll get it?

Good question. Nikki and I are far from being parental role models.

Justice: No, but her lawyers are good. I don't think I'll get sole custody either.

Hazel: I dropped the alimony. I don't want anything from him anymore.

Justice: You don't need fucking alimony from a guy who stiffed you forty bucks for AAA. You've got me.

Hazel: Stop trying to seduce me into a straying from my path of independence.

Justice: That's what I do.

Hazel: Also you need to take it easy on the flowers. Valentine's Day is over.

She turned down my dinner invitation then, but that doesn't prevent me from trying it again now.

Justice: Sorry. I will make sure they deliver only twice a week.

Hazel: My dad says your obsession with me is not healthy.

Justice: He is not wrong. P.S. I'm leaving for Crystal Bay in a few days to spend some time with Aiden. I want to see you. Please. On your terms.

Hazel: Maybe after your divorce hearing.

My heart starts dancing in my chest. It's a victory. Small but still. A "maybe" from her is better than "I'm not ready."

Justice: Okay, van Gogh. Don't try to wiggle your way out of it then when I'm back.

Hazel: Okay, Picasso.

I get all giddy at the sight of the kiss emoji. I don't know what it is about her, but the fact that she makes this stupid teenage crap seem like it's the most exciting thing ever has me believing we're going to work out. One way or another.

34 HAZEL

Eighty-three. The number of days passed since the last time I saw Justice.

Seventy-five. The number of days passed since the last time I had a drink.

Nine hundred and twelve. This is the number I hate the most. It's the number of days passed since my son's heart stopped beating.

One thing I figured out recently is that there's no way around numbers. However, there's a way to live with them. Peacefully. There's a way for the uniform and the imaginative to co-exist. Just like all these new feelings have been co-existing within me since the moment I met Justice.

"Would you like some more water?" The waitress stops by my table for the third time. Her eyes lock on mine and I wonder if she's one of those girls who reads TMZ or listens to The Deviant's music.

Justice and Nikki's divorce has been all over the tabloids ever since the details of the preliminary hearing were leaked to the press a few weeks ago. There's a new shocking headline almost every day. There's name-calling and dirty secrets, things I never knew could stir up this much outrage. Reporters have dug into everything. His DUI, his overdose, his rehab trip, his so-called infidelity. I promised myself not to read any of it, but the dirt just keeps seeping into my life from every corner. The stalking of my parents' house and my office has resumed too. Even the camouflaged "leave-us-the-fuck-alone" press release from camp Justice didn't do me any good. It did enrage Nikki and her team, however.

It's made our lives miserable. And in a way, it's made this break pointless.

"You know, I'm just going to order," I tell the waitress, glancing at my phone one last time. "My friend should be here any second."

I'm not sure whether I'm nervous because I haven't seen Rayna in so long or because of the lack of text messages from Justice. The divorce proceedings and the press campaign in support of the new album and the upcoming tour dates kept him busy all week. We barely spoke, which on some nights made me want to drink myself into a stupor. Once, I almost gave in, but common sense shone through while I was conducting the search for the key that opens the secret liquor cabinet in my dad's study.

As promised, Justice asked me to dinner again after the preliminary hearing. Refusing the offer seemed like a smart move at that moment, mainly because if he and I were to be seen in a public place, it would simply cause more grief to my parents and extended family. Now, I'm not so sure. Watching him struggle through court proceedings makes me feel like a coward.

Rayna shows up right after I place my order. She's a bubble of laughter and cheer. Always in her element. A ray of sunshine, making her way through the sea of dining room tables.

"You look gorgeous. Oh my gosh. Your hair—I love it!" She reaches for a cheek kiss and a hug first, then drops into her chair and stares across the table at me for a while, her expensive perfume filling the air around me.

"Is there something on my face?" I ask, feeling uneasy under her gaze.

"No. You're just so different. I can't believe I haven't seen you in over four months." She dodges all the extra formalities and fists the menu. "Lunch is on me, by the way."

"I have a job," I protest. The salary is next to nothing compared to what Rayna and her husband make, but paying for my own meals with my own money makes me feel good about myself.

"You get it next time." She draws in a deep breath and leans across the table. "I have news." Her eyes, bright and sparkly, search mine.

"You're moving to Europe for good?" I throw out my first guess, even though I know they'd never do that because of Clay's business. Getting him to take time off was like getting a mountain to come to Mohammed.

She shakes her head.

I squirm in my chair, my chest tightens. News is never good. Not in the universe I live in. "Don't keep me in the dark. It's nothing bad, is it?"

"No." Her voice turns to a whisper. She pauses for a few seconds to give me some time to get ready. "I'm pregnant! Twelve weeks."

Suddenly, there's no air in the room. The walls start closing in on me. I know I should be happy for Rayna. She'll make a great mom. But a mix of jealousy and dread rattles my insides. Why now? Why her? Whoever's upstairs handling things sure has a sick sense of humor.

"Wow." That's all I can muster up after a few long moments of silence.

"I want you to be the godmother, please." Rayna's hand slides across the table and grabs mine. "That would mean so much to me."

I reach out for my glass of water and take a sip. Is she doing this out of pity or is she really going to let a recovering alcoholic raise her child if something happens to her?

"This is just so unexpected," I confess, trying to summon all my strength and not fall apart right in front of her. *I really need a drink.*

"If you want to take a few days to think about it, it's fine." She finally lets my hand go. "But there's no one else I'd want to ask. There's no one else I *can* ask."

Somehow, I do believe her. Her family is all about career and money, not taking care of a child.

"Thank you…really. It's just—" There are no right words to describe what I'm feeling. It's a strange blend of hurt and delight, sad and happy.

"Of course. You're my best friend. Besides, that might make Justice

Cross my baby's godfather." She bats her eyes at me, and there's playfulness in her voice. "You're still together, right?"

Although I can appreciate Rayna's attempt to turn the comment into a joke, I need more time to process the news. I had no idea my reaction to her having a baby would open up the black hole inside me. "It's complicated."

"You said you two were talking."

"Yes. Almost every day. It's weird, but I think the distance is good for us. At least right now. At least until we're both divorced."

"That bitch isn't going to let him off easily, huh?"

Rayna's words hang in the air like a huge mushroom cloud. Toxic, impossible to ignore.

"I don't want my family to be brought into the middle of it." My chest spasms from the whirlwind of Thanksgiving memories. Seeing my son's name in the tabloids was horrifying. Justice is going through a similar turmoil right now. Sure, he's used to it. That's been his life ever since he chose to be the pleaser of the masses, the self-proclaimed freak show. But seeing photos of Aiden slapped on the front page of every gossip-hungry website is unsettling.

"What about your divorce?" Rayna raises her eyebrow at me.

"It's done. Just waiting for the paperwork in the mail."

"Good." She nods. "As soon as your rockstar boyfriend gets rid of his ex, you two better stop hiding."

I cringe at the rockstar commentary. Somehow, this is no longer the word that pops up in my head at the mention of Justice. "We're not hiding. It's just not a good time for us to be seeing each other. She's already making his life miserable because of the custody issue."

"You know what, Hazel?" Rayna hisses, bringing her body forward. "Fucking stop and listen to me. All your life you've been doing things for others—your parents, Owen, River. I don't know if you even realize, but right now you're doing the same thing for him, trying to make his life easier. But he doesn't need it. What he needs is you by his side to get through this shit with his ex. Keeping your distance isn't the answer here."

I blink at her rapidly, trying to understand whether the hormones are causing this fury or she's seriously wanting me to be with Justice.

"But hey, at least hashtag Jazel is still trending on Twitter." She laughs out to release some of the tension between us.

I roll my eyes but forgive her anyway because Nikki doesn't even get a fucking hashtag.

We refrain from discussing Justice further when the waitress comes back to take Rayna's order. Obviously, everyone in L.A. is ready to sell their soul to the devil for a juicy piece of information or just a bunch of speculative ramblings. Kinda like Lloyd, whom I've been secretly hating ever since his infamous interview about my drinking habits. Instead, Rayna and I spend the rest of the lunch catching up on other things.

I feel content and happy leaving the restaurant, but the news about her pregnancy is starting to have a strange effect on me by the time I get home.

Masking my dread with a smile in front of my parents, I rush to my room and bury myself in my homework. Or least, I try to. Today is one of those nothing-makes-sense-anymore days and the homework doesn't cooperate.

It's twenty past six when I pull up to the church parking lot. Typically, I attend AA meetings on Wednesdays and Fridays, and I dedicate Saturdays to errands and homework, but the news about the baby and the developing feeling of guilt over not being there for Justice stir something up in me.

I don't know the people gathered here today. I sit in the very back and listen to their stories, hoping no one recognizes me, even though having no opinion on outside issues is one of the traditions. Deep down, I know I'm safe here; my name won't be dragged into the conversation. But paranoia has become an unremitting part of me and on the days like today, I feel like letting it all go and crawling back into my hole of despair would be easier.

Most of these people are moving on with their lives, and I'm not. Or at least I don't feel like I am. I'm still where I was eighty-three days ago. Wrecked, lonely, and confused. Hiding from the world. The only difference is that now I have a job I despise, college assignments to get through each week, and I don't drink, which doesn't erase the fact that I want to. Every second of every day.

I drop my gaze to the Twelve Step Program brochure lying on my lap. A woman gave it to me when I came in because she was under the impression this was my first time. My mind takes an inaudible inventory of all the steps, trying to understand what exactly I'm doing wrong. Why is my spiritual awakening not happening like it is for the rest of these folks? Am I not deserving one?

It's almost eleven when my Prius comes to a halt near the mailbox that belongs to Lloyd. I sit in my car, chewing on my bottom lip. My eyes stare at the rain porch of the house across the street. The house that used to be mine.

There's a huge real estate sign out on the front lawn, the grass is trimmed, the fence is freshly painted. The place looks lonely, despite the living room windows beaming light.

After a few more minutes of pointless fidgeting, I shut off the engine, get out of my car and walk over to the porch. The heaviness in my chest doesn't let me think this through. Part of me wants to turn around and run before I'm face-to-face with my ex-husband, but the desperate need to tell him how I feel keeps me going.

The sound of the doorbell coming from the inside causes my heart to jolt. A mix of memories washes over me when Owen swings the door open. We're both still and silent for a moment, and a line on his forehead deepens, but his gaze never falters.

"Hey… Sorry." I tuck my hand into the back pocket of my jeans and take in the living room full of boxes. "You have a second?"

Owen clears his throat and reluctantly moves to the side to let me in, a pained expression etched into his solid features. "Sure. Is everything okay?"

"Yeah." I step into the house, my heart racing and my hands sweating. "I just wanted to—"

I don't get to finish the sentence because a woman materializes on the other side of the room. She is ridiculously young, probably close to twenty, tall, tan, and somewhat stunning, even wearing a black and red plaid shirt and a pair of jeans. Her face isn't stained with despair like mine.

"I'm sorry," I choke out, feeling even more awkward. *In my own house.* "I didn't know you had company."

"It's no big deal. We're just packing," Owen explains. "This is Mariela. We work together."

Our greeting exchange is dry and quick. After that, the two of us excuse ourselves and move to the kitchen to let Mariela keep filling boxes. The air in the room is hot and heavy and I'm already having second thoughts about this.

Owen goes first. "You doing okay?" He thrusts his hands into the pockets of his khakis.

"Yeah." I run my palm over the cold surface of the kitchen table as if touching the things that used to be mine is going to give me the strength to speak my mind. Instead, my mouth produces a question it shouldn't. "You and Mariela are seeing each other?"

Owen nods. "We are."

"She seems nice." That's a lie. I spent less than a minute with her in one room. She could be a mean bitch, but if that makes my ex-husband happy, so be it.

"She's great." He pauses, his eyes assessing me. "What are you doing here, Hazel?"

"I just"—my heart constricts—"wanted to say I'm sorry."

Silence fills the kitchen like a poisonous gas. I'm not sure what to expect from him at this point.

Owen draws his right hand from his pocket and rubs the back of his neck. "You don't need to apologize. It's done. We can both move on now. Go date your famous boyfriend and I'll be figuring out things on my end." There's no repulsion in his voice. Just a touch of bitterness and maybe sadness.

"It's not about the divorce." I take a deep, shaky breath and let the words flow. "I wasn't there for you after River died. I didn't realize it then, but I realize it now. I made your life miserable and you didn't deserve that." A throbbing pain shoots through my chest. "I was selfish. And I'm sorry for that."

Owen blinks at me rapidly, and the wrinkle on his forehead relaxes. "It just wasn't meant to be, Hazel." His voice is calm and reassuring. "I'm not mad. If there's someone or something else that makes you happy, you should take the chance."

My heart skips a bit. "I hope you and Mariela work out."

"She's very understanding."

"I'm glad."

We stare at each other for a while, neither one of us knows what else to say, but this time, the silence is different. Peaceful. Like a warm California night. Full of hopes, dreams, and our own secret desires.

I call Justice from my car. My emotions are all over the place, my mind a combination of scrambled and clear.

"I just wanted to hear your voice." I cut right to the chase. The formalities seem so unnecessary. Redundant and pointless at this point in our warped relationship.

"Wow." His voice, gentle and familiar, fills my car as I adjust the Bluetooth volume. "Are you okay? Is everything okay?"

"I'm fine. I just haven't heard from you today."

"Sorry. It's been a hell of a day. Aiden is staying with me until the next hearing."

"Oh, okay. I'll let you go then."

"No, don't." The rasp in his voice sends tingles down my spine. "It's almost midnight. He's asleep."

"Is it on Monday?"

"The hearing? Yes."

"I'm sorry, Justice."

"For what?"

"For not being there."

"You know how you can make it up to me?" he asks.

"How?" My hands start shaking and I have to squeeze the steering wheel really hard not to lose control of the car.

"Have dinner with me. We can't keep doing this. Speed-texts and late-night calls aren't going to solve anything, baby. After Nashville I'm only here for a few days, and then I'm back on the road until the end of the year."

The little voice in my head tells me to say yes, but there's a part of me that's still scared of all the press attention.

"I just want a little bit more time with my son," I whisper.

Justice doesn't respond. The horrible silence goes on for what seems like forever.

"I'll talk to you tomorrow, Hazel." His voice sounds withdrawn and tired.

"I'll think about it," I say quietly, my heart beating out of my chest.

"Goodnight, Hazel."

"Goodnight."

By the time I get home, the dinner idea doesn't seem as dreadful as it did a week ago.

35 HAZEL

My love life takes a back seat on Monday afternoon when I get a hysterical phone call from my mother. Uncle Roger has had a heart attack and is in the hospital. The family matters distract me from all things Justice—the hearing, the impending departure. The dinner plans. We don't really get to talk until Wednesday night, our conversation short and scattered.

It's ten past seven on Thursday when he shows up at my parents' house unannounced. I'm rushing through the class assignment that's due in the morning when the knock on my door comes. "Hazel, honey?"

"I'm studying, Mom," I yell, not moving my eyes from the laptop screen, even though the text is just a blur. Uncle Roger scared the hell out of everyone. Seeing him in the hospital hooked up to the machines brought back some unpleasant memories.

"You have a visitor, honey."

My heart begins to race. I straighten up in my chair and pinch the bridge of my nose, my mind trying to identify all the people who could be wanting to see me. The list is pitifully short unless the reporters are included. "I'll be right out."

"Okay. I'll have him wait in the den. Dad is watching TV."

A sudden wave of envy washes over me. That was supposed to be my life. Quiet family nights with homemade dinners and cheesy movies. Instead, I'm living with my parents while they enjoy their retirement.

After giving myself a quick once-over in the mirror and fixing my hair, I exit the room. My mother is in the kitchen, the best spot to spy on us through the mosaic window in the wall separating the main house from the den. She's still wired up after spending the last three days in the hospital. My father simply ignores everything. I wouldn't expect any other reaction really. Long gone are the days when my parents tried to advise me on dating and such.

My eyes drink in Justice slowly as I step into the den. He looks different, hair longer, face thinner, a hint of stubble shadowing his jaw. My gaze shifts to his broad chest, then roams over his body, scanning the patches of ink on his wrists.

My chest tightens, my body starts buzzing. "What are you doing here?" I lock my hands behind my back to prevent them from accidentally touching him. Exhausted or not, he hasn't lost any of his magnetism.

"I'm leaving for Nashville in a few days." He moves closer. "I just wanted to see you since you keep turning down dinner."

"I'm not turning it down. Things have been a little crazy." That's the truth. I have been thinking about his offer. A lot.

"Is your uncle okay?"

"He's better." I try to sound calm, but my heart is flatlining and my knees are shaking. I was the one who wanted Justice gone and now that it's real, it makes me reconsider everything. We don't make much sense apart anymore. I find myself wanting to drink even more now that he's not around and it becomes harder and harder with each passing day.

"Good. If there's anything I can do—" His voice trails off, eyes still locked on mine. Burning me to the core.

"Thanks," I reply meekly, looking over my shoulder to make sure my mother has enough decency not to openly stare at us.

"If you don't have any time right now, we can do it when I get back from Nashville."

"You and me in a public place is a bad idea, especially right now. With all the chaos around you."

He holds my gaze. His eyes, stormy and bottomless, are scrutinizing me. "I don't care about the press, but I can't protect you from this mess if you don't let me."

Panic trickles down to my stomach in a form of a painful spasm. I'm no longer sure I can be this close to him and pretend like we're nothing. My tongue feels thick and useless in my mouth, but I gather the leftovers of my self-control and speak. "How long will you be gone?"

The question is stupid because he's told me before, but I'm so nervous I can't remember anything. So much for taking a break. He still has the same effect on me that he did when we met. The man is all-consuming. He owns my mind, my soul, my heart, my everything.

Justice thrusts both hands in the pockets of his jeans, perhaps for the same reason I keep holding mine behind my back. We're desperately wanting to touch each other. "Four weeks."

"Are you recording with the different drummer?" The pieces of the conversations we've been having this past month are finally starting to come back to me. The label forced the band to hire a backup in case Zander wasn't ready to record. They have a new single scheduled for a worldwide release in May. They have a different set list, a different stage setup. His life isn't just a series of court appearances. It's also sleepless nights and business meetings.

"Doctors cleared Zander last week," Justice explains.

"Don't tell me The Deviant's next album is country?" I bite my bottom lip and wait for his reaction to my joke.

A soft smile tilts up the corner of his mouth. "Nah. We're just working with a different producer. Need a change of scenery."

"I see." I drop my gaze to the floor, unsure what else to say. The combination of texting and distance has turned me into an awkward creature who has no idea how to talk to a man in person. Even if this man has been all over me, inside and out. Literally.

Justice clears his throat and steps closer, erasing whatever distance is still left between us. "It doesn't have to be you and me, baby." His voice turns to a whisper. "It can be *us* against the world."

The air leaves the room when he slips his fingers in between mine. Effortlessly, as if he's been practicing this move since the moment we parted ways almost four months ago.

"I know—" My voice betrays me. I start tripping over my own words and thoughts. "Ever since my name became attached to yours, it's been so difficult. Sometimes I can't breathe. I just want a moment of peace, a moment with my son's memories before I let go."

"You know what I've come to realize? I think I was wrong when I told you to learn how to let go that night at the skating rink. You don't have to if you don't want to."

"I need to because I don't want to make the same mistake I made with Owen."

"I'm not him, Hazel." There's a hint of frustration in his voice. "Sometimes holding on to something or someone you really love isn't bad. I think this love you have for your son is who you are, Hazel." Justice brings his face to mine, his breath, hot and minty, fans against my cheek. "I have a confession to make."

A mix of horror and admiration spreads through my chest as he tells me about his hospital visit. The air in the den is thick and heavy and there's a whole lot of silence after he's done talking. I don't know whether I want to slap him or hug him. He did something unbelievably questionable behind my back. He snooped around my son's life. Part of me hates him simply for not asking me, but part of me appreciates him for not making a spectacle out of it.

"Why didn't you tell me any of this?" I say quietly.

"I wasn't sure how to. I needed to see it with my own eyes to understand. There are so many other kids just like him. Other families. He can do so much good, baby."

The idea gives me anxiety. "I don't want my son's name to be on some banner."

"It's not like that." He squeezes my hand. "The world is shit, baby. There will always be people who will twist things, people who will go out of their way to make you feel bad, people who will hate you for not being up to their standards. Jealousy is a cruel and ugly thing, but there are good people too. People who deserve more." His other hand reaches for my cheek. "People like you." He looks at me long and hard.

"This is how we celebrate his life. This is the support other families need when no one else but your son can give it."

I'm confused, undone, and infuriated. There's a scream stuck somewhere in my lungs. His words sting and burn all my wounds while his touch heals them. "He isn't just my son, Justice." My voice cracks, so does my heart. "Owen is his father and he won't want River's name to be on some campaign."

"It's not a campaign, baby. It's a sponsorship program. This isn't for press. This is for people who aren't as fortunate. It's how your little boy gets to help others. Just think about it. That's all I ask."

I still from his closeness. Thousands of thoughts race through my head. Him holding my hand in a very non-sexual way makes me dizzy and restless. I don't even know who he is anymore, but he is definitely not the man I met five months ago.

"You don't have to make a decision right this second or even this year. The offer stands indefinitely."

"You come here and tell me all these things right before you leave?" I throw at him, fighting the sudden tears.

His hand slides to the back of my neck. The heat of his body consumes me like a supernova. I'm Alice, tumbling down the rabbit hole, on the way to the unknown. Suddenly, the things that complicated everything when I broke it off seem very unimportant.

His mouth is dangerously close to mine. His lips are inviting. His touch is slow and deliberate, calculated even. Impossible to ignore.

"You don't get to do this," I whimper, resisting the kiss, but my body has already given up. Every part of me burns with desire. My cheeks feel so hot, my mother could probably cook eggs on them right now.

Justice sucks in a loud breath through his teeth and grabs a fistful of my hair at the back of my head, pulling me into him. He kisses me wildly until I'm dizzy, his lips now firm and demanding, and I love the surge of adrenaline that rushes through me.

"Justice, stop," I moan, pushing him back gently. "This is my parents' house. My mom is probably stalking us from the kitchen."

He releases his hold and whispers against my cheek, "I'm telling you all these things in your parents' house and not out in your front yard because I mean it—I'm not plotting some anti-Nikki PR campaign that involves you and your son. And give me one reason why I should hide my feelings from your family or the rest of the world?"

I don't say anything because my motives don't make sense anymore. Break or no break, paparazzi will still chase me. Nikki will still drag him to court. The sun will still rise and set. The question is, with or without him.

He takes a step back, his eyes, dark and puzzling, study me for some time. His words sit in the air, heavy.

"What do you want me to say, Justice?" I ask in a low voice.

"That you feel the same for me as I feel for you. That I'm not just some fool."

"You're not a fool. You're just...you were too complicated for me back when we met."

"Am I still?" He cocks a brow.

"I don't know." I shake my head. And that's the honest truth. There's no middle ground with him. He comes with chaos. "Maybe we can have the dinner when you get back."

He walks over to me and places a soft kiss on my forehead. "I'll text you from Nashville."

I'm trembling like a leaf when Justice exits the den, taking the leftovers of oxygen and my self-control with him. All I can think of is raiding my dad's liquor cabinet, but instead, I lock myself up in my room and start painting.

36 JUSTICE

THE DEAFENING ROAR of the audience stalks me backstage like a creepy shadow while my feet thump down the narrow staircase. The show's still going. There are three more songs in the setlist. "Amber" is up next.

Dozens of hands plunge at me all at once as if I'm walking through a crowd of zombies. Waters and towels dancing in front of my face. Peeling off my in-ear monitor, I grab one of the bottles and down it in three gulps.

The organized mayhem surrounding me is nauseating. My throat burns and my chest aches. There's sweat everywhere, on my back, arms, legs, hair. I can feel it eating at my skin like acid. My body, wrapped into multiple layers of leather, spandex, and cotton is still sore despite this being our fifth night. I'm not sure whether I should blame it on my nearing thirty-five or the lack of discipline this time around. I half-assed my pre-tour gym regimen because of the custody ordeal. Nikki's stunt at the last hearing almost cost me my rightful time with Aiden. Because of this shitstorm in the press Hazel chose to postpone our dinner. Being physically ready for the road wasn't something I desired to concentrate on. Not with my life turned upside down.

Dom's face swims into focus first. He gives me a pat on the back and directs me toward the small area reserved for the changeover.

"Honey, you have to sit down." Colby, the band's new makeup artist, waves his hands at me. "You're too tall." He rolls his eyes and points at the tall chair. "It's a shame you're straight. Where do they make Goliaths like you?"

I like him. He reminds me of a younger version of myself. No filter and totally in touch with his sexuality. He's got great aura and he's got a boyfriend, which pretty much eliminates the possibility of another disastrous secret affair with a makeup artist.

Zander was pissed when Rachel pulled out of the gig. For a second there, I thought she wasn't going to play along, but she kept her word.

Someone points a bright light at me and Colby runs the makeup remover wipe from my temple down to my neck, his nose screwed up in concentration. The cool air stings my skin. I feel like layers and layers of dead weight are leaving me.

"Can we get his collar off, honey?" He snaps his fingers and one of the wardrobe girls does as he says.

There's racket outside in the arena. Audience is going nuts for Zander. He's about to do his famous ten-minute drum solo while I get ready to do the unspeakable, go back out mask-off. Nervous doesn't even start to describe the complete palette of my feelings.

"Are you okay?" Colby asks, tossing the wipe into the trash can someone just placed next to my chair.

I nod and close my eyes for a second. The sick fuck in me who just sang a dozen songs about fucking needs to take a back seat for the next one. Easy to say. Not that easy to do. Not with all this noise around me and in my head.

We rehearsed "Amber" until our ears bled. I know every chord like I know every hair on my son's head, but the dread is still there, twisting my gut. The adrenaline rush I always experience while performing is turning into a mix of stage fright and paranoia, something I thought I overcame at the beginning of my career. Today, exposing myself like this feels like the first time all over again.

"Five minutes, Justice," Samantha yells from above. She flew in this morning specifically for the live debut of "Amber". The single itself got its first airplay eight hours ago, but I have been deliberately avoiding the internet to make sure the initial reaction of the fans doesn't mess with my mojo tonight. Another Elijah Hale effect isn't happening. Not with the music I wrote for Hazel.

Colby starts working on my other side.

"Can you fix his eyeliner?" Samantha requests.

"Where?"

"He looks like he just woke up." Her voice pitches.

"He told me to remove everything," Colby says, sounding very annoyed.

"Take it easy, Sam, okay?" Dom steps in. Just like me, he isn't having her domineering character.

My Zen is interrupted. "What the fuck is going on?" I snap my eyes open and stare at them as they face off right in front of me. Un-fucking-believable.

Samantha's eyebrows pull together. She shakes her head and gives my makeup artist a frustrated look. "He needs eyeliner at the very least."

"Give me the mirror," I growl, extending my hand. Another roar blasts through the arena. Tonight is a full house. The crowd is wild. The band has been sounding pretty tight despite all the tension "Amber" caused. The label and the PR folks did a good job with the pre-tour campaign. I haven't seen this many sold-out shows since the *Need* tour.

"I don't like it," Samantha says, her finger is pointed at my face. "I don't know why we even agreed to this, Justice. This isn't what the fans want. Not in the middle of the setlist."

I'm unsure whether she is talking to me or to the wall, but her words stir me up. I fought for the new stage setup and for including "Amber" into the encore sequence tooth and nail. Listening to the ramblings of a woman who knows nothing about the art of song-writing and the pressure of performing live isn't how I envisioned my last seconds before baring myself in front of twenty thousand people.

I glance at my reflection once I get my hands on the mirror. "This is fine."

"Put on some eyeliner, Colby," Samantha insists.

The brush doesn't make it past my nose. I jump off the chair, slapping his hand away from my face in the process. There's a blur in my eyes and a roar in my head. Deep down I know it's not my makeup artist's fault that the suits still think of me as their puppet, but the other guy lurking inside me, the spoiled asshole, is furious.

My heart is beating its way out of my chest.

"See what you did." Colby's voice, distant and hurt, reaches me from behind. "Don't you know, better than anyone, he doesn't like to be bossed around?"

Dozens of blinking eyes follow me. Some full of surprise, some horror.

"Justice, come on, let's get this finished," Samantha calls out ignoring Colby's bold remark and Dom's warning. Her hand is in the air, but she doesn't dare touch me. Touching me right now is *really* not a good idea.

"We do it my way." I look at her, blood pounding behind my ears. "If you don't like it, I'm out."

The crowd in the arena explodes, the screams of the fans and the violent pounding of the drums swallow my words but I know Samantha heard me. So did the rest of my road crew.

"Fine." She folds her arms on her chest. "Do what you want. But if all the sold-out tickets are going to resurface on StubHub tomorrow, that won't be my fault."

"Let's get this going, guys," Dom insists. He tries to keep his distance when Samantha is near since they aren't seeing eye to eye and once their disagreement turned into an obnoxious fight, but essentially, he still hovers. He's doing it right now too.

I'm back to my chair, eyes closed, fingers wrapped around the arms. I do what I always do when I'm on edge. Check out. Imagine I'm in a dark quiet room. Alone. Thinking about happy things. Sadly, there aren't as many as some people believe. It's Aiden's face, his eyes big, hair messy. I hear his giggling and mispronouncing letters until Zander's voice booms through my head. He cracks one of his jokes. The audience rages for a good minute.

Colby runs a brush through my hair and pats my cheeks. "Fabulous. Go get them, tiger."

I put the in-ear monitor back in and check the receiver pack, attached to my belt. A mix of dread and hope dribbles down my chest when Tyler's silhouette shows up at the top of the stairs. Cruz is right behind him. The clapping out in the arena goes on for another minute. Zander is collecting his share of well-deserved fan love.

As soon as he is done bowing, the auditorium goes dark. The road crew only has a few minutes for the changeover.

Zander hops down the stairs, stretching his wrists. We barely made eye contact earlier onstage. We don't make one right now either. He's in his own little world. The people in his entourage are swarming around him like bees.

"'Amber' fucking rocks," Dom whispers against my cheek, squeezing my shoulder. "They're going to love it. Don't let that twat tell you otherwise."

The twat is obviously Samantha.

The air backstage is heavy and thick despite state-of-the-art ventilation at the venue. The mandatory group hug feels cold and unnatural. We stopped cheering each other on after Chance died. It's more of a reflex now. Kinda like closing your eyes when you sneeze. You don't really want to but you can't do it otherwise.

The tips of my fingers tingle with anticipation as I go up the stairs. Taking the stage first feels strange. It's always been Cruz, Tyler, Zander, and then me. Always in that order. Tonight, it's the opposite. Tonight, Kace isn't going to back me up on the keys either.

My eyes sweep over the black grand piano set up in the middle. She is a beauty. Sophisticated. Crystal clear. Warm. The distant chatter of the crowd grows louder when I step into the blue spotlight. There's white sparkling fog everywhere. It's seeping in from all four corners. The gasp of the audience turns into a roar. Thousands of voices all cast into one full of shock. Maybe enthusiasm. Maybe even disappointment.

Shaking off the dread, I walk over to the piano and wave at the endless stretch of dark in front of me. My stomach flips and my hands start to shake because it's time for an explanation.

The crowd is silent, waiting patiently.

Clearing my throat, I descend on the bench and fiddle with the microphone. Up until now, I didn't have the need to combine my good with my bad. Justice Cross, the performer, was always bad. Justice Cross, the father, was always good. There were some gray areas in between but for the most part I found a way to separate them if needed. Tonight, I have to make the two people trapped inside me work together.

"You might be wondering, right?" I say into the microphone and stare at the blind spot where the audience is supposed to be. I'm almost glad I actually can't see their faces.

They respond with another roar.

Joke. The fans love it. "Now you know how I look. I'm not that pretty."

Laughter. Then there's a female *You're a god, Justice!* shriek. Typical for The Deviant shows.

"We have a special treat for you tonight." I pause for a second to take a breath. There's a battle in my head. Saying "we," when in reality the song is my baby, seems far-fetched. I have to remind myself this isn't my solo show and I'm in a band with three other guys and have to honor our agreement. "Some of you probably already heard our new single 'Amber.' It came out today."

More cheers come from the crowd. Good.

"We're very fortunate to do what we do for a living. All thanks to you guys." I close my eyes and go on despite the clapping. "We're fucking lucky to be able to afford this mind-blowing state-of-the-art production and you're lucky you get to be here tonight, you get to share this moment with us." My voice trembles. "Sadly, there are some people who aren't as lucky. They are struggling to pay bills, to put food on their tables, to be able to get the medical help they need." The words are starting to fail me. My thoughts are a fucking mess.

The arena is silent and still. I could hear it holding its breath. Every single person.

My heart is racing and my fingers are burning with need. "This song is dedicated to those who aren't as lucky as we are, those who aren't here." Part of me wonders if the crowd understand what "here" really means, but I don't want to bore people with philosophical ramblings. It's not why they come to The Deviant shows. They want to get entertained. "This is a little different. Thank you."

The first stroke is shy. Clumsy even. My hands don't feel like my own, my voice is unsure and shaky. It takes me a few seconds to finally find my sound. It comes to me in the form of a whisper. Subtle and fluid. The emotions are starting to clog my throat by the time I get to the chorus.

Tyler's guitar joins at the end of the second verse. When the full band steps in during the bridge, I'm already crushed into millions of pieces. Broken apart for the people to see what's inside. There's something extraordinary, something pure and glorious about singing without the mask. It's the human connection. The freedom of being myself. The infinite bliss of finally letting everyone see me for who I am.

The last two songs are a blur. Their lyrics are carved into my consciousness like an ancient saying into a stone. It's an autopilot mode with the brain off and the body on, each movement so well-rehearsed you don't need to think about it.

When the lights finally illuminate the arena, thousands of cell phones are thrust at me. The electrifying buzz seething beneath my skin is something new, something I haven't felt before.

The warmth spreading through my chest alternates with the unfamiliar heaviness as my feet carry me down the stairs, away from the maddening screams of the fans and into the post-show backstage chaos.

Dom tosses me a towel and a water.

I switch off the transmitter and take out the monitor, my mind and my vision foggy. The standard back-patting and hands-shaking routine with the band and the crew feels forced. My body craves a shower and a minute alone. Thank fucking God, Dom pulls me from the selfie-hungry crowd of guests and ushers me to my dressing room before I start saying shit others aren't supposed to hear.

A quarter to midnight, when I've already cleaned up and changed in to a pair of jeans and a t-shirt, comes a knock on the door. Zander saunters in without an invitation.

"You going to avoid us all 'til the end of the tour?" he asks with a straight face, handing me his phone.

"Not in the mood," I growl, glancing at his Twitter feed. He's always been a social media junkie. Posting his own shit everywhere unlike myself. But then again, outside the band, Zander Shaw is just a loaded OC surfer dude with a heart of gold and too much ambition. He doesn't need to worry about his image. People love him.

The silence taking over the dressing room is unsettling. This is the first time I'm lost for words in Zander's presence. Two reasons. The Gates of Hale's retweet of the live performance of "Amber" and the fact that I'm not sure what he and I are anymore.

He slides the phone into the back pocket of his jeans. "If you don't want to do this, you can just tell me." His eyes are intense. "No one is stopping you from writing the songs you want, man. Just don't fucking shit on the band and the idea that belongs to all of us. Me, Cruz, Tyler…Chance."

The memories hit me hard. We're young and ridiculously stupid again. Brainstorming in my father's basement. One idea is crazier than the other. All we know is we want to be rocking until we're dead. Ironic. Chance's line. He lived his dream. Me? I don't know whose dream I'm living, but it doesn't feel like mine. It feels more like a nightmare.

"What do you want me to say?" I choke out.

"I want you to fucking admit the fact that your heart isn't into it anymore."

He is wrong. My heart wants nothing more but to keep doing what I've been doing all my life. Just differently.

"We've got fifty-six more shows to play. That's the job."

"Fine. If you don't want to talk about it now, we'll talk about it when the ticket sales drop."

As soon as he leaves the dressing room, I look for my phone and call Hazel.

37 HAZEL

I'm on my lunch break, hiding inside the bathroom stall with my headphones on and my heart pounding like a sledgehammer. I'm equally excited and terrified to hear the single. The internet has been buzzing about new music from The Deviant for a while now, feeding my curiosity even more.

"Amber" premiered worldwide about an hour ago while I was trying to explain the payment deadlines to the manager of one of the properties Pacific Paradise took over last month.

Taking a deep breath, I open the iTunes app on my phone and type the band's name into the search bar to pull up the song. My back is pressed to the cold wall of the stall and my silk shirt is starting to stick to my skin.

I hesitate before pressing the play button. Not because of the possibility of disappointment but because of the possibility of getting overly emotional. Anything that has to do with Justice always challenges me mentally. Not something I want while at an office full of people who are still waiting for something dramatic to happen, because one of their receptionists is allegedly having an affair with an internationally acclaimed rock singer.

The song's intro vaguely reminds me of the piano piece Justice played for me in Tahoe after our first night together. His voice, deep, sensual, and unusually raw, comes in next. One intricate layer follows another, turning the song into a mind-blowing arrangement of sounds and lyrics that leave me speechless when it finally ends.

I can't stop thinking about Justice's hospital visit confession. Part of me still hates him a little for offering something as daring as having my son's name on his cancer research sponsorship program fund without discussing it with me from the beginning, but part of me wants my little boy to live on somehow.

The urge to call Justice is overwhelming. My finger is on the call button when there's a knock on the door.

The rest of the day is just as exciting as a day in a cubicle can possibly be. I get held up with a few last-minute tasks and by the time everything's done, it's almost six thirty.

I run late to my AA meeting but sit through the second half of it like a trooper, listening to everyone's stories about making amends to the ones they hurt and sifting through my own inventory of people I've yet to confront.

Sadly, the miserable part of me entertains the idea of going to a bar right after the meeting. The only reason I don't end up throwing away my nearing five months of sobriety is because I can't wait to see a live performance of "Amber." I literally race home.

My phone goes off in my pocket when I'm on the porch.

"Have you seen it yet?" Rayna's voice fills my head as I unlock the front door. She's been following all things Justice very closely since I told her I'd have dinner with him.

"No, I just got out of the meeting," I explain, rushing to my room, purse dangling against my hip.

My parents are in the living room, barely paying attention to me. It almost reminds me my quiet days before Owen. Mom and Dad were convinced I was on the right path and didn't need any supervision.

"Call me after you watch it," Rayna says. "We'll need to discuss, hon."

"Okay, but don't spoil it. Bye." I shut the door behind me, toss my jacket on the floor, and turn on my laptop, anxiety and anticipation twisting me up inside.

I could have looked at the video on my phone back in the parking lot after I got out of the AA meeting, but it felt weird doing it on church grounds. Watching twenty thousand people all crammed into the tiny screen of an iPhone cheering a man who's into spanking and choking me in bed and atop of other unfit-for-sex pieces of furniture just didn't seem right. Even though "Amber" isn't that kind of song.

"Amber" is a spark of magic in the eternity of musical darkness.

I open YouTube and type *the deviant amber live* into the search bar.

The uploads popping up on the screen are all raking in thousands of comments and views. I scroll through the first ten, my eyes slowly studying the screenshots. There's one with a close-up of the stage and Justice on the piano. *Without his makeup.*

The video is a little shaky and out of focus at times, but I don't really notice any of that. My eyes are glued to the screen of my laptop where Justice is. He's stunning with his hands flying above the keys and his eyes intensely thoughtful.

My chest expands from all the emotions. By the end of the song, I'm a mess. Second time today, but now even messier. I scroll down to the comment section below the video. He told me dozens of times not to read anything on the internet about us or the band, but I can't help it.

ttonya this is so beautiful i have no words
marko34 this is different
arialovejustice HOLY SHIT!!!! NO MASK?
OffTheHuk89 What is going on even? Is he not wearing his makeup?
DeviantJunkie Bro should just ditch the makeup
DarthVaderRulez This is not Devisnt msc what happed / is the new albu m all going to be like this????? Sombd tell me its not true! cum back to da dark side
Connie Sloan I love this band. I love Justice. He is the best singer ever. So talented.
Mari Rodriguez Wow, speechless.
Jenny666 Very emotional. Did he write this for his son?
Deviant4EVER Not for his son. For his girlfriend's son.
LOLA Ohmygod! This is so insanely beautiful.

Jenny666 I didn't know he had a girlfriend.

Deviant4EVER   http://www.tmz.com/2017/11/24/justice-cross-and-his-girlfriend-caught-making-out-in-the-mall-parking-lot/

JusticeCrossIsMyPapi Wait! What? I thought they split. Justice my hubbi!!! XOXOXO

crazycrazyxxx Repeat button raped

KingCody Wow, Justice, my man. Vocals on point!

GeorgieS He wouldn't be divorcing his wife if they split, would he?

silvia89 What does his divorce have to do with his current girlfriend? Makes no sense. Nikki is a bitch. She set him up.

QUEENNIKKILOVE How the fuck you know she set him? You're her assistant, bitch? He beat on her and cheat on her all this time. Nikki is single mom now. For all single mom's out there. Say no to domestic violence! ENOUGH IS ENOUGH!

crossmyheartjustice Shut the fuck up, you pussy-sucking crackwhore! Justice never did anything to her. She admitted she fell and withdrew the charges.

emmalovesmusic Where can I get me a man like Justice?

Nairi Khaleed This song is life. Very deep and very emotional.

Jojo96 I'm crying.

aria janet I have a three-year-old and a five-year-old. So sad his girlfriend lost her baby. It breaks my heart just thinking about it. Justice is an amazing artist. I wish them happiness and love, and babies.

QUEENNIKKILOVE BITCH TRYING TO TAKE NIKKI'S SON. GO BACK 2 YOUR HOLE YOU CAME FROM. AIDEN OFF LIMITS!!!! HE ONLY HAS ONE MOM. QUEEN NIKKI!!!

Sonny Hwang Justice has a girlfriend? Didn't they break up like last year?

inthetempleoflove Best band ever. Love the new direction. Can't wait for the new album. sending you love from Albuquerque.

F4ckU Band sounds like shit. Fucking sell out.

DeviantForLife Shut up you moron. Band sounds tight. If you don't like the new single, don't listen.

QUEENNIKKILOVE QUEEN NIKKI 4EVER!

DinoMino ohhhhh shit trolls rolling in like it's free lunch at the local church

With my body shaking from the sight of the ugly, ignorant comments, I fish for my phone, still not sure whether to call him or Rayna.

It goes off in my hand like a little grenade before I make up my mind, and I press the accept button and bring it to my ear. My tongue still numb and unresponsive to the pleas of my brain, all that comes out of my mouth is a muddled "hey."

"Hey." Justice's voice on the line is rough and low after the show.

Pause.

"Hazel?" he calls out.

My scrambled mind desperately fights the impending flood, but the tears win.

"Baby, are you crying?"

I place my palm over my mouth so that he can't hear me sobbing and shake my head, at first not quite realizing he can't see me. He's over two thousand miles away doing what he loves while I'm stuck in this tiny hell of a room that day after day keeps reminding me of everything I once had and lost.

"Hazel? Did something happen? Are you okay?"

I bite into my lower lip and wait for the tremor in my body to stop.

"You need to talk to me, baby. Otherwise I'm getting on a plane and flying back to L.A."

"No, no. Don't," I whimper, wiping my cheeks with the back of my hand.

"What happened?"

Dumping my really chaotic thoughts on him over the phone isn't a good idea, yet I still do. "I just...miss you," I say quietly, staring at the laptop screen. "I miss you like crazy."

There's a soft chuckle on the line. "You're crying because you miss me?"

"Yes." It's a partial lie, though.

"I thought you wanted a break?"

I get up from my chair and walk over to the window, my eyes sweeping over the barbeque grill outside that my father bought recently. "I did, but you make it so difficult for me to forget you."

"Is that what you're trying to do? Forget me? Is that why you wanted the distance?" There's panic in his voice.

"No. I just wanted for the insanity to stop." Out of sight, out of tabloids route. Apparently, it didn't work.

There's another long pause. We're listening to each other's breathing.

Justice is the one to break the silence. "Do you want me to stop? I'll stop touring if that's what you want."

God, no. I'd never want him to give up what he loves. Not for me. Asking him to choose would be selfish. Music is who he is. "You don't have to alter your life to be with me," I say, leaning against the wall for support. My tongue is finally taking charge. "I love you the way you are. With all your flaws, your dirty mouth, your nutty fans, even your obsessive-compulsive disorder."

A laugh bubbles up his throat. "Let me guess, that's what your father calls my flower deliveries? Obsessive-compulsive disorder?"

"Yes. My mom loves them, though."

"Say it again," he says quietly.

"Yes."

"Not that. The other thing you said."

"Obsessive-compulsive disorder?"

"Before that, baby. I want to hear it again."

"Oh…" A faint gasp leaves my mouth. "The I-love-you thing. Is that the one you're talking about?"

"That's right."

"I love you."

He doesn't say anything back.

"We're so screwed up, Justice," I whisper, staring into the ceiling.

"We're not."

"I'm telling you that I love you for the first time over the phone. That's screwed up."

"I needed to hear it. Right now is perfect." His voice on the line is shaky.

"Just come back to me."

"I never left, baby."

It's almost one in the morning and my phone is about to go dead when we finally end the conversation, both exhausted yet somehow thrilled.

I sit at my desk for a while, eyeing the dark screen of my laptop, processing everything that just transpired between Justice and me. Are we a couple again? Are we going public with this? What's going to happen to Nikki and Aiden? What's going to happen to my parents and Rayna?

What do those three words mean really?

My hands are itching for a paintbrush and my muse is longing for some music. Yes, it's very weird to pay two dollars for the song written by the man you're sort of in a relationship with, but that saves me a whole lot of repeat button clicks.

After making sure "Amber" is ready to go, I spin in my chair a few times, clear my desk, and get my painting supplies organized. The first blob is bright pink, a color I don't favor at all. The color my life probably lacks the most. The color I'm going to force into my existence whether my heart wants it or not.

The next blob is bright orange. Then purple. Then red.

The music humming in the back of my head is starting to give me insane ideas. I paint and I paint until my eyes start to close, until the first rays of light begin to creep into my room.

38 JUSTICE

W E   S I T in a small booth at the very back of the restaurant, holding hands and staring at each other like two lovestruck teenagers on the brink of their first relationship. A massive floor-to-ceiling rimless fish tank with aqua-colored LED lights separates us from the chaos of the main dining area.

We're silent while the waiter fills up our glasses with sparkling water and lights the candles on our table.

A fraction of me still doesn't believe this is real. *She is real.* Sitting in front of me, colorful and exquisite, just like the flowers in her paintings. The same woman who used "obsessive-compulsive disorder" and "I love you" in one sentence.

I'm nervous beyond comprehension. I'm also terrified there might be a crowd gathering outside. The oddest thing is that Hazel doesn't seem to care. She didn't even reject me when I asked her out for dinner in a public place when part of me expected an excuse or an invitation to do it somewhere where no one could see us.

"I've never had to wait this long to get a woman to agree to dinner with me," I confess once we're alone.

"I like to play hard to get." The corners of her cherry-red lips perk up.

The reflection of the candlelight in the sparkling water dances along the length of her golden hair. Her makeup and the dress she's wearing are elegant and sophisticated, and her smile brightens the room. Simply put, she's stunning. I've never seen this side of her, not when we were in Tahoe, not even when she came over to my parents' house for Christmas. Thinking back, I don't know if I ever knew the real Hazel, the woman whose life wasn't marred by her son's cancer.

"You look great," I say, and I mean every word. It's not an empty compliment just to try to get her to sleep with me. Sex would definitely be a bonus, but it's not something I'm going to pursue tonight. What I'm wondering is whether she's going to say it again or we're going to leave it for next time when we're alone, when the threat of the possible paparazzi ambush isn't as real as tonight.

There's a contentment in her eyes that wasn't there the last time we spoke in person. A little bit of fire too.

"So do you." Her cheeks pink as if she just read my mind, the dirty corners of it. "I like the new hair."

"That was my line." I laugh as her small fingers reach for the strands falling over my chest. I haven't really trimmed it much like I usually do when I'm on the road. It's probably grown a good four inches since January.

"I'm thinking of cutting it short," I say. The brilliant idea of altering my looks came to me a couple of weeks ago.

Hazel shakes her head. There's a hint of panic in her eyes. "Don't."

Her reaction makes me laugh. "Why not?"

"I like you like this." She wraps a strand of my hair around her index finger and tugs on it.

"What else do you like?"

She blinks at me a few times, her other hand, warm and delicate, tensing in mine. "Can we not rush back into this?"

My heart slams into my ribs. Bliss, confidence, and admiration are stirring somewhere deep inside me. "We can do this however you like." I bring her hand to my mouth and kiss her knuckles. I fucking miss the feel of her skin on my lips. I miss watching her eat. I miss listening to her talk.

When the waiter comes back to take our orders, we're still holding hands, menus forgotten. Why waste time eating if I can use every second of my spare time staring at her? I only have two days with Aiden and one day to meet with my lawyers before the band flies to Europe. My schedule is like a conveyor belt. Nothing in my life ever stops.

I understand why Hazel doesn't want to be a part of the constant movement, but the asshole in me isn't backing down.

I draw the envelope out of my pocket and slide it over to her.

She tilts her head in question, eyes blazing in the flickering candle-light. Looking at her is like looking at a firestorm. Mesmerizingly dangerous.

"The next run is fourteen weeks," I say, holding her gaze. "I'm only going to be back for three days and gone for another two months."

She lets the information sink in, then fiddles with the envelope. Her hand trembles a little when she finally reads the ticket. "London?" She looks up at me from under her lashes.

"It's my birthday. I want you to be there. We're playing two shows at the O2 Arena that weekend and then we have three days off after."

The somber look on her face tells me she's struggling with the answer.

"How about sightseeing?" A desperate plea escapes my mouth. "Say yes."

"I'll have to miss work." She takes a deep breath. "That's also the weekend of Rayna's baby shower and I'm the godmother. If I fly in on Thursday, I'd have to leave on Saturday morning."

"I'll ask Dom to get you on a different flight. Just come."

Hazel slips the ticket back inside the envelope and smoothes both palms over the white paper. Her gaze drops to the tabletop, a small frown line materializing between her brows. There's a moment of deaf-ening silence between us.

"Okay, but I can't miss the baby shower," she finally says, a hint of a smile gracing her lips.

Funny, six months ago she was the one who drunk-slept through Thanksgiving. Now she has all these places to be at and she's devoted to every event and meeting.

We barely touch our food. The dinner consists of mostly hand-holding, talking, and looking through my cell phone collection of Aiden's photos. The sex-deprived asshole lurking somewhere in the depths of my dark mind is secretly praying for her to reconsider the decision to take things slow, but it's just wishful thinking really.

It's almost ten when I finally ask for the check. The walkway to the lobby is dark, empty, and not long enough. Slowing my pace, I pull Hazel closer and wrap my arm around her waist. Each step sends me closer to my strange world of never-ending routine and organized chaos. The world I don't want to go back to right now. *Or ever?*

The intimacy and the simplicity of tonight's—dare I say it?—date makes me want to drop everything and run away. Preferably with Hazel. To some place exotic that's not on the map.

Is this what it's like for other people, those with blue- and white-collar jobs?

"Thanks." She spins on her heels to face me when we're halfway to the exit. "I'm glad we did this."

"Me too." I wait. Wait like a puppy waiting for a treat. I wait for her to say those words out loud again, but she doesn't. Her eyes do, just not her lips.

The glass doors facing the buzzing-with-traffic street at the end of the walkway are like my own rendition of the gates of hell, a thought that triggers something in me. I'm still not sure how to feel about my uncle suddenly praising my music on his band's social media. We haven't spoken in almost seventeen years. Why bother now?

He tried calling only once right after Chance died. I never returned the gesture, neither did I talk to him at the funeral.

"Hey." I reach out for Hazel's face and cup her pink cheek. My inner gentleman is battling with my cock's wish to ask her to come to my place right now, but the rational and mature Justice who's supposed to pick up his four-year-old son from his ex at eight in the morning takes charge. "You know what I've been thinking about lately?"

"What?" She looks up at me, her lips slightly parted, inviting me in.

"Sometimes I wonder what it would be like for us if we were just a couple of normal people with office jobs."

"We're never going to be normal, Justice." She stares at me intensely. "I don't think I want to be anyway."

My heart is racing into overdrive when my hand slips to the back of her neck. Her soft hair coils around my fingers like a piece of expensive silk, and my mouth finds hers, barely touching it. I hear her breathing me in as we both still in the dark walkway, bodies and lips ready to crash together. This moment—the sweet and tender fraction of a second right before the actual kiss where her every scent is mixed with mine—I want to take a photo of it, then carve myself open and stash it inside so this exhilarating feeling will never leave me.

We kiss madly until we're both dizzy, our tongues dancing a wild tango, without paying any attention to the other patrons or the restaurant personnel. Let them fucking watch us. Let them take pictures.

When Hazel pulls back to catch her breath, my head is spinning like a carousel. Her eyes meet mine. Her cherry-flavored lipstick is gone.

"You're fucking paradise, baby," I say, placing my thumb on her bottom lip that's swollen from all the kissing. She doesn't respond. Her tongue sweeps over the tip of my finger, a cue for me to back off before things start heading into R-rated territory and we're on the fucking six o'clock news.

We walk out from the lobby into the warm California night, hand in hand, both slightly terrified of a possible ambush. But all we get is a few turned heads as I escort her to the Uber.

She presses her warm mouth to my cheek and whispers before getting into the car, "I'll see you in London, Picasso."

"See you in London, van Gogh."

39 HAZEL

I USED to get really bad anxiety attacks when River was still alive. It felt like the world was on the verge of a catastrophe and no one but me knew. The same feeling of doom grips me the moment I step off the plane. The serious faces of the authorities trailing through the terminal of Heathrow Airport along with their dogs have me panicking.

I step away from the human traffic and set my carry-on on a bench to check my phone. As soon as the airplane mode is off, countless messages start flooding the screen. Most of them are from my mother and Rayna. There's also one from Dominic and six from Justice. The text from my father is always an indication of something bigger, not necessarily better. Something on a more global scale. This time he isn't wrong either. The news gets to me before I even reach the baggage claim area.

The police caught someone trying to sneak explosives into a bus station in Westminster. Three hours ago while I was on the plane.

That explains the dogs.

My parents hated the idea of me flying to London. My mother kept on asking why I couldn't wait for the band to come back to the States and why I had to leave the country three days before Rayna's baby shower. My father decided to stick to the silent treatment method he's been practicing with me all his life. Only Rayna was genuinely excited. She even offered her help in case I needed to gift wrap myself for Justice before boarding the plane. We had a good laugh.

"Hazel?" A familiar voice rips from the crowd as soon as I get to the carousel. "Over here!"

I spin on my heels and see Dominic waving at me from afar, my bag already at his feet. He looks tired and thin, much like Justice in his recent press photos.

Customs takes forever. We spend a good hour getting out of the swarming-with-the-police airport. My body is tired and wants a hot shower. My heart is the opposite—alert and wants Justice. We haven't been texting each other as much lately, mainly because of my finals and the time difference. Instead, we've talked on the phone whenever we could.

"You have dinner reservations at Alain Ducasse at eight," Dominic says as we exit the terminal. He shows me to the black limo waiting for us at the pick-up zone. "Justice is at rehearsal. I'll have the car pick you up from the hotel and he'll meet you at the restaurant."

The traffic on the way to the hotel is bad, probably worse than in L.A. I spend most of the drive staring out the window while Dominic spends his time on the phone arguing and making arrangements. The skies that are heavy with rain remind me of my ominous Tahoe days. I hated the woman I was back then.

We arrive at the hotel around seven and use the back entrance to take the elevator up to the top floor where Dominic shows me to my room. As soon as he's gone, I jump in the shower, my mind reeling.

Meeting Justice in a pair of jeans and a t-shirt would be absurd right now. The dress I've chosen cost me a small fortune, but it's unlike anything I've worn before—a delicate satin twist-front knee-length piece. Its smooth fabric clings to me like a second skin.

At the restaurant, I'm escorted to a private room and offered several appetizers and a variety of non-alcoholic drinks while I wait. I can't help but wonder how much Justice is paying for all this extravagance, even though the money is definitely not an issue for him. The silverware and the plates are so refined and so shiny that I'm almost scared to touch them for fear that I'll leave a fingerprint.

My heart all but beats out of my chest when Justice rushes in twenty minutes later. He pulls me into a semi-awkward hug in front of the waiter, the rich earthy smell of his leather jacket flooding my nose, and his lips on my temple feel warm and rich. His presence is all-consuming, overriding all my emotions so that I almost forget how tired I am.

"I wasn't sure you'd be up for dinner." He sits across from me and pulls off his baseball cap, his eyes on me wide and wandering.

"I slept on the plane."

"I can't fucking believe you're here," his whispers, reaching for my hand.

"It's your birthday. I said I'd come." My pulse leaps when he tightens his grip. There's a strange desire to never let him go simmering beneath my skin. The feel of our fingers locked together is just so…right.

We eat slowly, staring at each other. It's become our thing. With him, words aren't necessary.

Halfway through the dinner, I pick up my portfolio hidden behind my chair and retrieve his birthday present.

Justice sets his utensils aside, and his eyebrow slides up his fore-head in question.

"I can't afford to send you fresh flowers every week," I say in a shaky voice. "But I can paint."

"You painted for me?" There's an expression of surprise on his face.

I nod, handing him the present. My heart trips in my chest.

He runs his large palm over the dark brown parchment paper and gives me a thoughtful look. His eyes are still just as intense as they were the night I met him, even with the dark circles beneath them and the weight loss. Being on the road is wearing him out.

"Hanging it above your bed isn't mandatory," I laugh a little. "It's also closet friendly."

"I'm not putting your painting in the closet, baby." He rips off the paper and stares at the canvas for a few moments. His lips tightly shut, his face concentrating, a small frown deepening above the bridge of his nose.

His voice is abnormally small. "Thank you." He looks up from the painting. "It's beautiful."

There's a mean voice somewhere in the back of my head. It belongs to the old Hazel that Justice Cross picked up in the bar—a pathetic excuse of a woman. She wants to make an appearance. "You don't have to put it up if you don't—"

His mouth covers mine before I finish the sentence. The kiss is unexpected and raw. It almost knocks the life out of me and at least a fork and a knife off the table. Maybe a glass of water too, but neither do I care nor do I hear anything except the sound of my own heart singing.

"I love it, baby. I do," Justice husks against my cheek before returning to his seat, his gaze trained on me, his eyes big and intense. "I wanted to take you someplace cool," he says, his fingers brushing over the frame of my painting. "But we can skip it if you're tired. The traffic might be bad."

I shake my head. Two nights in London with one already committed to the band's show. No way I'm passing up the opportunity to see the things I may not ever get a chance to see. "I'm game if you are."

"All right. Let's get out of here then." He puts his baseball cap on.

Ten minutes later, we're seated in the back of the limo with a sea of umbrellas on the sidewalk and other vehicles surging around us. The city is buzzing with electrifying energy, despite the weather.

"It's not far," Justice whispers, his lips close to my cheek but not touching. Deep down I expect him to start playing around with my skirt. The old version of him would probably be halfway to my panties right now, but he's unusually still, his warm hand grasping mine.

The limo comes to a halt and we sit in one spot for about a minute or two. I stare at the light drizzle beating against the tinted glass of the car and the colorful neon lights shining behind the misty air.

"You wanna make a run for it?" Justice asks readjusting his cap and pulling down the visor over his forehead in an attempt to make himself less recognizable.

"Where are we going?" I reach out for his hair and tuck some of the strays behind his ears.

"Over there." He points at the tiny flickering lights and the tinted glass pods up in the air.

"You're taking me to a Farris wheel?" Flutters spread through my chest and stomach. I haven't been on one in ages. Not since before River was born.

"Not just any Farris wheel." Justice adjusts the collar of my coat. "Come on. You'll see." He scoots toward the door, instructs the driver where and when to pick us up and jumps into the foggy London night. His hand reaches out to me as I step out of the car and we make a beeline to the crowded sidewalk.

My heart beats like a drum as we rush over to the entrance before someone spots Justice. Once inside the VIP section, my mind finally calms down a bit. I've accepted the fact that people will be approaching us when we're in public, but there's still this need to have one more night of privacy with him before all hell breaks loose.

"You're crazy," I whisper while we're being ushered in the direction of the pods that are sitting above the ground. My eyes can't keep up with all the lights and colors. Only after the glass door of the capsule slides shut, cutting off the outside noise, do I finally come back to my senses.

"Since you're only here for two days, I had to come up with a good plan to show you all of London in one night," Justice murmurs against my cheek, pressing his chest to my back.

The pod starts moving, causing my legs to buckle.

"I don't know if this was such a good idea," I whimper feeling light-headed as the ground beneath us starts disappearing in the mist. "I think I might be afraid of heights." Not exactly true. Roller coasters were my guilty pleasure once. The view of the city in front of me, with all its bright moving spots, glimmering streaks, and the curling River Thames, is breathtaking. Foreign but at the same time familiar.

Justice nuzzles my hair. "I've got you." His arms encircle my shaking body.

Silence that fills the pod as we slowly crawl up to the sky is bizarre. Otherworldly. The sounds of the city dissipate into the darkness underneath the shifting floor of the capsule, leaving us one-on-one with sparkling London.

Only when we get to the very top, and the other pods are no longer blocking the view, does my confidence returns to me. Spinning on my heels to face Justice, I draw him closer and press my lips to his. The kiss is never-ending. It's gentle, barely there at first, turning into wild and wicked by the time we start to descend. I don't remember much but the feel of Justice's mouth on mine as we head back to the hotel after the ride is over.

The limo drops us off at the back entrance. Justice draws the portfolio to his chest when we load into the elevator, his eyes zeroed in on me as if he's trying to read my thoughts. I'm too dazed to think about anything but the kiss, possibly the longest one in my entire life.

"Am I always this colorful?" he asks once the doors close.

I shake my head and lean against the wall of the cab. My toes are starting to hurt and my body is finally demanding a horizontal position. Sleeping on an airplane will never beat sleeping on a bed no matter how comfortable the first-class seats are.

"Lately, yes." I nod, fisting my purse.

Justice is quiet for the remainder of the ride, his face soft yet slightly withdrawn, his messy hair hanging loose over his shoulders. We walk over to my room, hand in hand. As soon as we're inside, he sets the portfolio and my purse on the table and leads me toward the middle of the suite. His arm slips under my coat and curls around my waist, his eyes holding me hostage.

"May I have this dance, my lady?"

"Only if you provide the soundtrack." I move closer and press my lips to his stubbly cheek, breathing him in, savoring every moment of this blissful calm.

Our feet shuffle in shy circles, Justice humming an unfamiliar song against my ear. There's something in his voice that wasn't there when he sang to me the first time. Something new, something raw, something very intimate. We dance until the room is hot, our bodies gradually traveling in the direction of the bedroom.

"Is this slow enough for you, van Gogh?" he whispers against my skin when we're in the doorway, his breath burning me to the core.

"You didn't have to try this hard with the dinner," I say, dipping my fingers into his hair. "You know I don't care about the three-hundred-dollar steak, right? That's not why I flew across the Atlantic."

"You only get the best when you're with me, baby." He pulls me into the bedroom and shuts the door.

The darkness in the suite is both comforting and unnerving. After six months of text-messaging and talking on the phone, I'm not sure what he's like anymore, what being with him is like anymore. He's changed a lot. In a way, it scares me.

"I don't need the best. I just need you," I whisper.

Justice backs me up against the wall facing the floor-to-ceiling window. His silhouette drawn against the city lights that flicker in the drizzle dominates my line of vision. The air in the room starts vibrating when his mouth presses to my cheek. His lips dance their way down to my neck while his hands roam around the fabric of my dress. He brings his palm down and under my skirt and runs it up my thigh.

My body takes every last drop of the warmth he's offering, and there's a playful smile toying around his lips when his mouth returns to mine. My heart hums in my chest, my breathing quickens, then I grab a fistful of his hair and yank it at the roots. Not hard, but enough to get him going. The truth is, I don't know if I want him to hurt me tonight. Feeling more than what I'm feeling right now terrifies me.

"I fucking missed you," Justice whispers, running both hands up my sides. His raspy voice shreds me to pieces. "Do you know how many days it's been since the last time I was inside you? His palm slides across my ribs and around my waist. "Two hundred days, baby. Two hundred days since I unraveled you. Two hundred days since I kissed you like this." He presses his body to mine and kisses me on the lips again, but this time his tongue is a mind-blowing blend of ice and fire.

I'm speechless and broken apart by his confession. My legs are a quivering mess, and so is my heart.

He silently helps me out of my coat, picks me up, and carries me to the bed, his firm body sizzling hot against mine. I'm shaking when he lays me back against a pillow as his eyes drink me in from above.

"Do you like what you see?" I ask quietly. Part of me almost expects my own famous *I've-already-seen-it* comeback.

"I do." He nods, taking off his jacket. His t-shirt is the next to go. Then I take off my shoes.

My heart stops for a brief second when his hand pushes the dress off my shoulders. The familiarity of his touch when his palm cups the lace of my sheer red bra pulses through me like an electric shock. He inhales me slowly, warm, skillful lips tracing along my collarbone.

There's something divine about the graceful movements of his body as he slides down on the bed and his mouth finds my toes. He works his way up excruciatingly slowly, his teeth lightly grazing my skin as his hand strokes my inner thigh. Then the tip of his tongue explores me inch by inch.

"Do you like that, baby?" he moans against my leg. "Do you like it when I worship your body like this?"

I'm at a loss for words. I love him dirty, rough, and painful. But I also love this gentle side of him, the side I've conveniently ignored all this time because I didn't think I deserved any of his kindness.

"Do you?" he asks again, peeling off my soaked panties.

"Yes." I nod, staring at the white ceiling. "I do." My head is spinning so much I have to close my eyes.

His lips reach between my legs and he flicks his tongue against my clit. A moan escapes the back of my throat and I fist his hair, wiggling on the sheets. His mouth is soft and wet and pure bliss, taunting with the promise of a sleepless night. He works me fast and high, undoing me until my body can't take it anymore.

My eyes are misty and my cheeks are wet as I scream and fight for air, emotions jamming my chest.

"Hey, hey, hey." I can taste myself as Justice kisses the corner of my mouth. His thumb brushes my bottom lip. "It's okay, baby."

There's a lump in my throat and I can't seem to catch my breath. I throw my arms around his neck and bury my face into his hair in an attempt to hide my sob, but the stupid tears have a mind of their own. They spill anyway, and two seconds later I find myself crying like a baby. I've only fallen apart after sex once, and that was when I lost my virginity to Owen, because it hurt like hell. I'm not sure why I'm crying now. Not because I'm unhappy. I'm anything but.

Justice strokes my hair. "If you're this emotional when I go down on you, baby, I'm afraid to take it any further. I don't exactly remember CPR."

"I just need a minute," I mumble through the fog in my brain, drawing him closer and kissing him silly.

This new level of intimacy between us, without the pain, startles me.

"Say it, baby," he rasps against my mouth, his body tensing. There's despair in his voice. He pulls back a little, his eye searching for mine. "Say it, Hazel."

Heat floods my chest and my stomach. I'm on the edge of a cliff again, staring into the abyss full of the familiar and the unknown. The insignificant parts of my brain are still fighting it, but my heart is ready to jump. "I'm in love with you," I say quietly, fisting his hair. "All the versions of you. Dark. Light. And everything in between."

The silence that takes over the room seems to go on forever. The air between us crackles with electricity. His heart beating like a drum in his chest shadows the wild pounding of my own when he kisses me on my lips, easing me into the madness that comes next. His tongue explores my mouth viciously, his shaking hands struggling with the folds of my dress.

I don't remember the exact moment we lose our clothes. I'm too possessed by his flaming touch and his seductive whispers.

His fingers reach out for the aching spot between my legs. "Do you want me dirty tonight?" he asks, brushing his thumb over my clit, teasing. His voice is like velvet. Rich, warm, and addictive.

A surge of searing pleasure rushes through me. "I want all your colors," I moan, arching my back. Black for savage. White for gentle. Purple for naughty. Red for delicious.

His mouth comes back up sliding over mine, his hair falling over my cheeks soft like a feather.

He drives into me carefully, letting me get used to the way he feels because my body attempts to resist his size. His gaze, sultry and paralyzing, holds mine hostage as I moan quietly and claw at his neck.

"I want you to look at me, baby"—his palm cups my cheek—"when we're making love." His mouth swallows my gasp. His body starts rocking against mine slowly, filling me with steady strokes. "I love you, Hazel. I love you, baby. You're my fucking paradise." His voice trembles, his lips capturing mine.

"I love you too," I mumble, draping my arms around his damp-with-sweat neck. "I love you so much…you have no idea." The words escaping me—some dirty and some tender—turn into a long string of feverish confessions. They keep us up until we're both a mess. A breathless, dirty, and beautiful mess.

40 JUSTICE

THE RHYTHMIC BEATING of the rain against the window wakes me up at around eight. My throat is sore and my muscles ache the way they shouldn't before a show.

I sit up in bed, my eyes sweeping over Hazel's body. She's curled up on her side, clutching the sheet. Her hair is splayed across a white pillow like a golden halo, her face serene.

Last night was fucking magic. We fucked—correction—made love until goddamn sunrise.

I slide from the bed and search the pockets of my jacket to check my phone for today's itinerary. Zander and I have an interview with BBC at one thirty. Soundcheck is at three, then another interview. Meet and greet is at six. Dinner at seven. Makeup at eight. The show isn't until nine thirty. The set is about eighty minutes long. Done around eleven. Another hour to get back to the hotel. All I've got with Hazel is midnight to four in the morning before we have to leave for the airport.

The sudden need to hear her voice slams into me like an express train. The morning is still ours. We could go out for breakfast. Just the two of us.

"Hey." I kiss her cheek.

"Mmmm?" She rolls onto her back, her eyes flutter open. She stares at me somberly.

"How are you feeling?" I rub her shoulder.

"Besides being sore because you rode me all night?" A smirk tilts the corner of her mouth. "Like I've been run over by a truck."

"You're just jet-lagged," I explain. Part of me feels guilty for waking her up this early.

"What time is it?" She covers her mouth with her palm and yawns.

"Eight."

"Another hour, huh?" She snakes her arm around my neck and yanks me down. "Then you can do whatever you want with me."

My cock hardens against her softness. I want to bury myself in her, get lost in her warmth. Over and over again. But I also want her rested for tonight's show. I didn't fly her across the ocean for a night of fucking. "Why don't I hit the gym while you're catching up on your sleep?" I whisper in her ear.

"Sounds like a plan." She nods, pressing her lips to my cheek. "Happy birthday, Picasso."

Thirty-five. I'm officially entering the middle-aged category. The thought gives me chills. "I'll be back soon, baby."

Her body relaxes on the sheets, eyes hooded as she watches me leaving the bedroom.

I walk over to the table, open the portfolio, and take out the painting Hazel gave me last night. My eyes study the intricate details. The colors are so bright, they nearly blind me. Each stroke is neat and calculated, a piece of art in its own right. There's no doubt she worked on this for a while. I just had no idea she saw me like that—with all my scars and secrets out in the open, with all my blues, and pinks, and reds, and blacks.

The image is still crisp in my mind when I get out of the shower and head to my room to get a sweatshirt. My chest swells with pride as I step into the elevator, despite the voice of doubt that's crept its way into my head.

This is so fucking stupid, Justice. What part of let's not rush into it didn't you get? You're going to scare her off.

I dial Dom before my fears make me change my mind. "Can you

arrange breakfast for two and some flowers to Hazel's room by ten thirty?"

"Sure. Remember you and Zander have an interview at one."

"Just send me the address. I'll be there." I hit the lobby button and press my back against the shiny wall of the elevator cab.

"Listen, Justice." Dom clears his throat. "I think it's safer if we all go together considering the city is on high alert." His tone is clipped.

My chest stiffens as I pull the hood of my sweatshirt over my head. "What time are we leaving?"

"Noon."

I let out a sigh of disappointment and rub my stubbly cheek.

The elevator doors slide open and I hurry out into the lobby. Seeing the small crowd of teens in The Deviant shirts gathered near the front entrance double doors makes me turn around. Normally I wouldn't mind a group this small, but today I don't want to waste my time signing autographs. Besides, knowing how crazy British fans are about the band, there's a good chance this session could turn into another TMZ story.

Once I'm in the back seat of my ride, I pull up Google Maps on my phone and search for the nearest Cartier store, which is thirty minutes away and doesn't open until 9:30.

Fuck.

For some reason, the sound of rain beating against the roof of the car gives me anxiety. My inked fingers tap out a wicked dance on my thigh as I stare into the wall of mist ahead of us on the road. By the time we finally pull into the empty shopping center, I'm dizzy and hot. Partially because what I'm about to do is probably the most impulsive thing I've done in my entire life, but the thought of Hazel going back to her life in L.A. without some kind of a declaration of how I feel for her has me freaking out like a teenager before a first date.

"Sir?" the driver calls out from the front seat. His accent is thick and posh.

"Wait here," I say firmly, shoving a hundred-dollar bill at him and exiting the vehicle.

I bang on the door of the jewelry store at nine twenty sharp. There are a couple of sales associates already setting up for the day. I see their silhouettes moving around through the thick tinted glass of the front entrance. I bang harder until one of them walks over to me, his eyes narrow slits as he gives me a perplexed look.

I slap my black Amex against the wet glass so he can read my name. The man studies my card for a few seconds before unlocking the door.

"We're not open for another ten minutes, sir." He shows me to a chair in front of a display filled with pendants. His younger colleague is gawking at me with his mouth agape. Maybe it's because he recognizes me or because I lack manners. Who gives a fuck?

I ignore the invitation to sit down and get right to business. My voice is razor-sharp. "You're open for me. That is, if you want the commission." My heart is drumming in my chest as I walk over to one of the displays and absently scan its content. "I'm looking for something classy." My voice trails off.

"May I ask what piece of jewelry?" the man who let me in inquires from his spot.

I turn around to face him and read his name tag. "Pete?"

"At your service." He smiles at me meekly and fingers the collar of his ironed-to-perfection white shirt.

"I'm looking for a ring, Pete," I say, handing him my credit card. "And I'd appreciate it if you didn't open the store for the public until I'm done."

He blinks rapidly and tugs on his tie. "I can't do that, sir."

"Yes, you can, unless you want a crowd of teenagers in freaky makeup storming in here and stealing shit."

He nods slowly, his eyes glaring at my ink.

"Let's get going, fellas." I clap my hands. "I've got a show to get ready for."

I leave the store at quarter to ten with a platinum 1895 Solitaire ring in my pocket.

Once back at the hotel, I head over to Cruz's room, but after banging on his door for five minutes, I get no result.

"Yo!" Zander's voice, coming from the bank of the elevators, reaches me when I'm about to go back to Hazel's room. "Tyler and the homeboy went out for breakfast. You good?"

My eyes zero in on the brace he's wearing. It's the second time over the course of this week, which worries me. "Yeah."

"You sleep at all?" He grins, moving in my direction. "Cuz you look like you've finally been fucked properly."

I flip him off and squeeze my hand around the velvet box still in my pocket.

"Is she here?" Zander asks, fumbling with his keycard.

We've been trying to mend things lately. The tour isn't nearly halfway through. Artistic differences or not, keeping it civil within the band is important to me. Especially after the disagreement we had.

I ignore his question. "You busy?" Anxiety rattles my insides. I'm slowly coming to terms with the fact that I bought Hazel a sixty-thousand-dollar gift. Nikki's full set cost me half of what I just paid. But then again, I was high and didn't put much thought into that purchase. It was more of a the-brighter-the-bling-the-bigger-the-headlines situation. Right now, things are very different. It's not me buying Hazel a chunk of precious stone to claim her as mine. It's me getting her something timeless and elegant to complement her fire and beauty.

"Nah, what's going on?" Zander gestures for me to follow him to his room. Part of me is still not sure whether asking him for advice, or even telling him about my intentions, is wise. It's not like he is an expert. He's never even had a steady girlfriend, let alone someone he'd buy a sixty-thousand-dollar ring for.

His suite is a mess. Music roaring from the speakers and drumsticks, clothes, water, and snacks everywhere. I'm always puzzled by how quickly he turns hotel rooms into man caves.

"You alright?" He shuts the door and rakes his brace-free hand through his blond hair. "Where's your lady? Am I ever going to meet her or what?"

"You should get this looked at, man." I point at his fucked-up hand. Not a very subtle stalling technique.

"Ah, it's no big deal," he says matter-of-factly and changes the topic back to Hazel. "Is she even real or what?" He's expressed his concern over her being imaginary several times since we got on the road.

I suck in a deep breath through my teeth. My palm is on fire when I pull out the Cartier box from the pocket of my sweatshirt. I need to tell someone. Not because I need validation, but because there's a storm brewing inside me, and I'm afraid if I don't, I'll just end up screaming about it from the roof of the hotel.

Zander's jaw drops to the floor. "What the hell are you doing, dude?" He rolls his eyes.

"Fuck," I mutter, pushing my wet hair away from my forehead. My emotions are all over the place. The music pounding against my eardrums is making my head spin, nausea swirls in my stomach. "I don't know, man." And that's the honest truth.

"Let me see." Zander snatches the box from me to inspect the contents. He fiddles with the ring for a few minutes, staring at it intensely, and completes his examination with a loud whistle.

"What do you think?" I ask as a light tremor starts taking over my entire body.

"I didn't know you two were this serious. You're sure you don't want to enjoy your freedom for at least a couple of months? You just got fucking divorced. And who knows when this custody crap is going to be over."

"The custody crap is never going to be over," I snap. "Unless Nikki fucks up. And I don't want to sit around and wait for her to do that."

"When are you going to give it to her?"

I take the ring back. "Tonight."

"You're sure?"

"Yeah."

"You're a fucking dog." Zander punches me on the shoulder. "The least you can do is introduce her to me."

Panic crawls underneath my skin at the sound of the familiar—way too familiar—female voice. "Babe, did you see my—"

My head snaps in the direction of the bathroom. Rachel is at the door, naked, eyes lasering in on the Cartier box. She drops the deep whiskey tone and sends me a fake smile from across the suite. "Oh, hey, Justice. Didn't know you were here."

"A warning would have been nice," I growl at no one in particular, hiding the ring in my pocket.

"Come on, put some fucking clothes on, babe," Zander yells as I charge for the door, my eyes wanting to un-see everything they just witnessed.

Sure, Rachel expressed her interest. I had a feeling something was going on between those two, but I didn't know it was this massive. By all means, they can fuck, date, and do the red carpets together all they want. I just wish someone would have told me she was going to be here this weekend.

41 HAZEL

She eyes me with curiosity from across the lounge, curling her long lavender strand around her index finger. I smile back, calmly, wondering if she's aware her history with Justice is no secret to me. My chest stiffens a little when our gazes meet, but I don't falter.

She isn't the one he loved all last night until sunrise.

Our introduction earlier was brief. She showed up in the lounge with a group of men, dazzling like a diamond, her chocolate fragrance plaguing the air around me. The moment she said her name, I knew she was *the* Rachel. I recognized her voice. We didn't get to talk much. Someone grabbed me right after the greetings exchange.

"Have you met Wendy?" Dominic's voice snaps me back to reality. He pulls me in the direction of a small woman with a bright purple pixie cut. She's sipping on something vaguely resembling a margarita, which causes my stomach to churn from the dread of being face-to-face with an actual drink.

I draw a deep breath and remind myself I've been sober for over six months and I'm about to become a godmother to a little guy named Rocco.

Wendy is sweet and bubbly and almost distracting enough, despite her margarita, when Dominic leaves me for a few minutes. He's been on edge ever since we arrived to the venue. Even the smile on his face can't mask his anxiety.

It's almost quarter to eight. The band was supposed to be done with the meet and greet a while back, but the road closures and the checkpoints around the city pushed back the schedule. The arena feels like a zoo, packed with police officers, dogs, bouncers, press, VIP guests, and the raging crew.

The lounge starts to empty out when Dominic returns.

"They just finished the interviews," he explains, moving his eyes up from the screen of his iPad. "Let me show you to the dressing room."

We make our way through the backstage maze. Dominic is two steps ahead of me, visibly distraught. My milk chocolate brown midi dress seems out of place in this kingdom of denim-and-leather, but Justice requested something sexy. Jeans didn't seem like the right fit, not on his birthday.

We stop in front of the door with a huge laminated *Justice Cross* sign.

The voice that comes from the dressing room after a knock is clipped and noticeably unhappy. "Not right now, boys!"

I look at Dominic, searching for reassurance.

He shakes his head lightly and rolls his eyes. "Don't mind Colby. He takes the job way too seriously."

Holding my breath, I push the door open. The view unveiling in front of me is to die for. Justice is shirtless, straddling the chair, with his right arm wrapped around its back. He's wearing a pair of leather boots and black-coated jeans with zippers across his knees.

I swallow hard. His heat starts to consume me from across the room. He looks wild and delicious, facing the mirror above the table. His eyes are closed, but I can see the reflection of his dark long lashes fluttering against the white paint on his cheeks. He is wickedly beautiful with his black hair tied at the base of his neck and his inked skin shimmering in the bright dressing room light, the cross on his back almost glowing.

A young man with blue hair and a brush in his hand looks up from the makeup kit. A toothy smile is tossed my way.

"Am I interrupting?" I ask, stepping into the room. The noise from outside fades away.

Justice snaps his eyes open and shifts on his chair. A smirk toys with his lips. "Not at all, baby. Come in."

"Sorry I yelled, love," the blue-haired man says apologetically. "We're so behind it's not even funny."

"Would you give me a few minutes, Colby?" Justice asks.

"Of course, but don't forget we need to be done by nine," the makeup artist warns him on the way out.

The door slams shut, finally giving Justice and me some time alone.

My entire body trembles as I cross the room. I'm not sure whether it's because I haven't really eaten since breakfast or because I'm nervous being near him when he's like this, when he's in his element, when he's the performer, when he's wearing the mask.

"You look very sexy," I babble.

"You like?" His hooded eyes follow me in the mirror.

"I must confess I'm jealous. Colby is a catch. I hope he isn't going to try and hit on you like your previous makeup artist." I'm surprised cracking a joke about his past dalliances doesn't bother me.

"He has a boyfriend." Justice laughs, relaxing on the chair.

I stop in front of the makeup station and glance over the kit and the brushes. Hopefully Colby won't be too pissed at me for borrowing some of his tools.

"You look beautiful." Justice reaches for my dress, his palm running over my lower back.

"Thank you." I stare at the reflection of his eyes in the mirror in front of me, pick up one of the tiny brushes, and spin around to face him.

He drags the chair across the floor and snakes both arms around my waist. His body is tense, just like mine.

"Do you mind?" I ask, running the brush over the side of his cheek that hasn't been finished yet.

"Colby will probably be furious." Justice chuckles, his hands roam around my back.

I have no shame. "I've done some paint jobs before, Mr. Cross." I rub my finger across the patch of his skin that's already been worked on. He's shaved. His face is clean and smooth.

"I saw. I think you're pretty awesome, van Gogh." He grins.

I bring my hand to my mouth and lick the substance off my finger.

"Don't do that. It tastes like crap, babe."

"It tastes like you," I whisper, stroking his hair.

"I can ask Colby to fix it up after the encore if you want me to fuck you with the makeup on." He smirks, palming my ass. His hot breath fans against my chest.

"You've got a very dirty mind, Mr. Cross." I stare down at him, my heart starting to beat faster. The anticipation of seeing him onstage is killing me.

"I'll be anything you want me to be, baby," he whispers, running his hands up my back. The tips of his fingers burning my skin through the soft fabric of my dress. "I have something for you too." His tone is serious now. "But I want to give it to you after the show. When we're alone."

"You didn't have to get me anything else." I swallow hard, my legs unsteady, the makeup brush about to slip from my hand. "It's *your* birthday."

"I wanted to." He gets to his feet and backs me up against the makeup station. "I'm sorry we didn't get to spend much time together." He slides his hand to the back of my head. "I'm sorry I'm so fucking busy. I'm sorry today's a fucking mess."

"It's okay." I shake my head. "I understand. You can't control these things."

He inhales sharply, his cheek touching mine. "The venue didn't let any guests in until after seven. We had to push back the meet and greet. We'll be doing it after the set."

My heart sinks to my stomach, but I try not to show my disappointment. "What time will you be done then?"

"It'll be fast. An hour maybe. Dominic will arrange a car to take you to the hotel so you can pack while you wait. You still have the keycard from my room?"

I nod.

"Don't leave tonight." The despair in his voice is turning me inside out. "Please. Stay another day."

"You know I can't. Rayna will hate me for skipping out on her baby shower."

"There's something else…" His voice trails off. He pulls back a little and looks me in the eyes. A deep frown knits his forehead.

"What is it?"

"Rachel's here."

I still in his arms, contemplating whether telling him that I've met her is something Justice needs to hear from me.

"She's with Zander," he goes on. "I think they're seeing each other." Even the makeup can't conceal his panic. His eyes are like two raging volcanos. "I didn't know he was going to fly her in. I swear."

"It's fine. I saw her at the lounge," I finally say, grabbing his chin and pulling him to my mouth, his makeup sticking to my fingertips and my cheeks, maybe even my dress. I'm not sure. I'm too busy kissing him.

Of course, Colby is pissed once he gets back. The vein throbbing furiously in his neck gives away his displeasure.

The tour manager grabs Justice shortly after nine, the same time Dominic shows up to escort me to my booth. A security guard joins our procession on the floor. The lights in the arena go off the moment we reach our section.

"Don't worry. They won't start for another five or ten minutes," Dominic reassures me, taking my elbow and leading me up the stairs. For the first time since I left the hotel, I hate that I'm wearing high heels. It's going to take me some time to get used to dressing sexy for a man like Justice.

The view from the VIP booth is breathtaking. The whole floor is right in front of me, a sea of people below my feet. Their whispers of anticipation stir something in me, something forgotten and buried away. It's been a very long time since I participated in an event this grand, and the thought of being a part of this madness electrifies me even more. My chest swells with emotions. Excited, I snap a few photos and text them to Rayna.

My heart starts to race when the long airy sound of an organ fills the arena. It's met with the deafening roar of the crowd. The blue spotlight dancing across the stage is followed by the thick clouds of fog. Zander is the first one to come out. He's tall and gorgeous with longish dirty blond hair and a suggestive grin. I saw him briefly before the soundcheck without his mask. We didn't get to talk, but it took me three seconds to figure out he was a charmer. His costume is all black, slick and simple. It almost doesn't fit his personality. He waves at the fans and takes his spot behind the kit, the cameras feeding his every move to the huge LED screens on both sides of the stage.

The guitarist, Tyler, enters next. He's mysterious and reserved, his outfit is modest just like Zander's, his hands rest possessively on his guitar, face serious. The audience rages again, clapping, whistling, and screaming his name. Their voices all mesh into one, full of enthusiasm and elation.

The bass player, Cruz, whose lovely wife I had the pleasure of chatting with earlier, takes his spot on the right side of the stage seconds later. The three of them reel in the madness on the floor first, teasing the fans. Their masks ominous and a little disturbing. They are a strange combination of glamorous and forbidden, impossibly beautiful in their own twisted way.

The lights onstage go off again. The darkness devours everything but the roar erupting from the restless crowd. This time it's so loud I have to cover my ears. Glancing over my shoulder, I meet Dominic's gaze. He's smiling at me from ear to ear, probably for the first time since I met him.

The arena explodes with the screams.

My stomach spasms when I look back at the stage. I'm not sure what exactly I'm feeling. So many emotions surge through me all at once it's hard to separate them. Justice is magnificent. He moves slowly and graciously with the spotlight shadowing his every step. The way his torn-across-the-chest t-shirt clings to his body leaves nothing to the imagination. His tight jeans are too low on his hips. He's pure eye candy and the crowd is crazy for him. They plunge against the barricade, pushing forward, their hands thrust in the air, their eyes locked on him. The line of security in the pit starts forcing the front rows back. I've never seen people throwing themselves at another mortal being the way these fans throw themselves at Justice.

The music blasting through the arena rips me to shreds. It invades every cell in my body, vibrating through me, breaking me apart and putting me back together, but differently. Gluing the parts of me with something else that's not pain.

I'm so overwhelmed by everything happening onstage that I can't seem to follow the show. It owns me completely. I've heard all the songs before. God knows how many times I've stalked Justice on YouTube mentally preparing myself for the real deal rock concert, but this experience is nothing like watching him on the screen of my laptop. Justice is sexy and gorgeous, his voice deep in my head, his smile flashing at me from the LED screens sends tingles down my spine.

He works the crowd effortlessly, like the god he is. And oh my! These people worship him. Because to them he probably is.

When the song comes to an end, the cameras pan to the floor. The glowing faces of the fans fill up both screens, freezing on one of the girls riding her friend's shoulders. The crowd roars in approval when she lifts up her tank top and flashes the camera and then the stage.

I laugh at her boldness. Given the amount of alcohol people consume at the shows like this, I can see why she would want to scribble "Fuck Me, Justice" on her breasts. He *is* hard to resist, especially when he sings.

I know part of me should be jealous, but before I determine how exactly I feel about a teenage girl undressing in front of my man, the camera pans back to the stage and follows Justice. The crowd is waiting for his reaction.

He stares down at the floor, the devilish smirk toys with his lips. Beads of sweat trickle down his cheek and his neck. He's playing the audience for a few moments, torturing them before finally giving them what they want.

"That's very good. I like it." His voice, deep and smoky, fills the arena while his hand is pointing at the topless girl.

The crowd cheers.

I'm waiting for him to crack one of his sexual jokes, but he does something entirely different. Not exactly sex-drugs-and-rock-and-roll material.

Throwing another glance at the camera, he whispers into the microphone, "I don't know if my girlfriend will be up for it. Let me ask." The light murmur echoes through the arena. "She's right there." The spotlight dances across the field of heads and lingers on our booth for a brief second, blinding me.

"But Tyler's single. Right, Tyler?" Justice goes on.

Thunderous laughter erupts from the crowd. The guitarist plays along, tossing a few picks and some smiles at the fans.

By the time the show reaches the encore, I'm an emotional mess. I cry during "Amber". I cry like a fucking baby. I cry because the music is haunting. Because I know he wrote it for River, for a boy he'd never met. Because the song reminds me of how lost I once was and how happy this man has made me. My mascara starts running, my chest hurts, and my body desperately wants a hug. Dominic has to help me walk. There's so much happening in my head and around me that when we finally make it backstage, I don't even remember about the meet and greet and the fact that I need to go back to the hotel and pack.

Dominic takes me to the dressing room. Justice has already showered and changed into a fresh pair of ripped jeans and a plain black t-shirt. People are crowding him with their cell phones, pleading for selfies. This goes on until he orders everyone out. It's just him and me left in the room.

"Dominic will get us a car." He moves closer and slides his hand to the back of my neck, his thumb rubbing circles into my skin. "I'll take you to the airport myself."

I want to tell him how much I loved the show and how much I don't want to leave, but he knows all these things. Instead I tell him something he doesn't know.

"My son would have loved it." My voice is barely above a whisper because Justice is stealing all the oxygen in the room. "He would have loved you too."

"We need to go, Justice." A knock on the door interrupts us.

"Sorry." His fingers slip in between mine gently, his hand hot against my skin. The fact that I still have to share him, even after the show is unnerving. He stares at me for a few moments and walks me out of the dressing room. We stroll through the walkway, surrounded by his faithful flock, and his hand possessively travels to the small of my back. His minty scent is all over me. His voice still humming deep in my head.

We stop next to the stairs leading up to the lounge where Tyler and Cruz are waiting for us with their entourage.

"Where's Zander?" a man in a Motorhead jacket cries out.

"Coming," a gruff voice belches out from our group. I see people in the upstairs area fidgeting, their curious eyes darting back and forth. They're waiting to meet the band.

"Where the hell is he? Someone call him. I said fifteen minutes. Not fifty." The Motorhead jacket guy looks like he's about to have a heart attack. "Let's go, folks."

"I'll see you at the hotel, baby," Justice whispers, kissing me on my lips.

He is like a magnet. People swallow him when he enters the lounge.

I spin around and head for the exit, my eyes trained on the wall, my body still reeling in the post-show bliss. Zander and Rachel, engaged in a wet kiss against the wall, enter my line of vision when I reach the end of the walkway. Zander detaches himself from the woman and starts moving in my direction. He's is just as attractive up close as he is in the band's videos. Sly grin, curly thick hair, ripped chest.

"Finally!" He opens his arms. The gesture's so charming, I have no choice but to let him hug me. "You look stunning. Sorry I didn't get to talk to you much earlier. Today's schedule was all fucked up. I hope you enjoyed the show."

I'm taken aback by his friendliness. For someone who doesn't know me, he sounds genuinely kind. "The show was amazing," I say, awkwardly shuffling my feet. My toes want out of these killer shoes.

"You should come hang with us after the meet and greet."

"Thanks for the invite."

"Gotta go mingle for a bit." He winks at me and charges for the stairs. Charismatic. Polite. Full of sunlight. *Not the kind of guy who'd pick up his friend's leftovers.* Speaking of which, Rachel is still in her spot, frozen. She draws a pack of cigarettes from her purse and nods at me.

"Want one?"

"Thanks. I don't smoke," I say, mustering up a smile. Part of me is still struggling with liking her. She hasn't done or said anything that would make me hate her, but at the same time, she isn't someone I'd want to be friends with. Enemies neither.

"Good for you." Rachel sucks in a loud breath through her teeth and follows me outside onto the loading dock. "I've been trying to quit for five years."

"Sorry to hear that."

"Fucking hard when you're surrounded by people who smoke like chimneys." She snorts, tucking a loose strand behind her ear.

"I know." My eyes sweep over the screen of my phone. The mist starts turning into a persistent drizzle.

"Right." She puts one of the cigarettes in her mouth.

"Hey, listen. You don't have to be nice to me—" My voice trips. "I know you and Justice have history."

She stares at me long and hard with a rapt expression on her pretty face. "Don't tell Zander. I really like him."

The bright lights of the limo slowly pulling up to the dock is my cue to go.

"Of course not," I say, waving at her. "Goodnight."

"Goodnight. Nice meeting you." She gives me a curt nod as I hop into the back seat.

The traffic around the venue is horrible. We circle the arena for nearly thirty minutes. By the time the streets finally clear out, we hit another checkpoint jam.

I'm starting to panic when I realize that the car hasn't moved an inch in the past ten minutes.

"Do you think there's another way around?" I ask the driver carefully. "I'm really, really late."

"No, ma'am. Doesn't look like it."

"Can we turn around?"

"Can't do it here, ma'am. Jumping into ongoing traffic is a bad idea."

We wait some more until the traffic in the right lane eases up. I'm on my phone, composing a text message to Justice when the limo starts changing lanes. The crashing noise comes out of nowhere. It cuts through the sound of rain beating against the roof of the car like a hot knife through butter. My phone slips from my hands from the impact, my body flying across the car. Panic and shock paralyze my insides. The faint sound of my bones snapping followed by the sharp pain in the back of my head is the last thing I remember before the dark consumes me.

42 JUSTICE

I BARELY MAKE it through the meet and greet. For the first time in my life, I despise the people who spend their hard-earned money on a chance to hang out with me. The guilt for feeling this way still eats at me, but the horror that grips me the moment I see Rachel talking to Hazel dominates every single cell of my brain, erasing all the desire to stick to my obligations.

I hate the screamfest inside the lounge. I hate the fans trying to touch me, but most of all, I hate Zander for flying Rachel in this weekend. Out of all the dates of the tour he had to fucking pick this one. Why not Paris or Barcelona?

On the way to the car, I dial Hazel's number at least a dozen times. I'm fucking terrified when she doesn't pick up the phone. My emotions are all over the place, blood pounding behind my ears, chest aching. I feel like the time just slipped through my fingers. We're supposed to be back at the hotel, just the two of us. Instead, I'm wasting precious minutes wrestling insane traffic and shitty weather.

The moment we pull up to the hotel, I jump out of the car and charge for the elevator, ignoring a small group of kids who assault me with their cell phones near the back entrance. I love my fans dearly, just not tonight. Dom's footsteps echo somewhere in the back of my head as my feet carry me through the lobby.

Hazel's not in her room, nor in mine. Her things are still unpacked. I stride over to my luggage and dip my hand into the pile of clothes to make sure the ring is still where I hid it earlier.

"She's not here?" Dom's voice drifts at me from the doorway. He steps into the room, his eyes darting back and forth.

"No," I snap, shoving the box with the ring into my pocket and heading over to Zander's suite. I don't know if he's back. We left the arena separately. He could have taken the after-party anywhere, but my mind is grasping at straws wondering where Hazel is.

The look on his face when he opens the door is a mix of confusion and wonder. "Where's the girlfriend?" His slanted grin indicates he's been hitting the bottle.

His suite is loud and crowded. It smells like liquor, leather, cigarettes, and an expensive fragrance. Exactly how it would smell with people getting their party-like-a-rockstar freak on.

Ignoring the greetings of Zander's guests, I walk over to Rachel and say, "What did you tell her?"

She cocks her head, eyes like two daggers, blazing. "I don't know what you're talking about."

"Don't fucking lie to me." I grit my teeth. "I saw you two talking. What did you tell her?"

"Dude, what the fuck?" Zander's hand lands on my shoulder.

"What did you tell her?" I repeat the question, my eyes still on Rachel. The music pounding in the background is making my head throb.

"Nothing," she deadpans.

My blood begins to boil.

"Dude, what the fuck is your problem?" Zander attempts to pull me aside but I shove his hands off me and stand my ground. I need fucking answers. The sick part of me wants to strangle them out of Rachel, but I'm in a room full of people. The last thing I need is for everyone to figure out Zander is picking up my leftovers. Right now, I hate him a lot but not enough to hurt him like that.

"You need to chill, Justice," she says with a straight face, not even a fucking flinch.

"You heard her. Fucking relax," Zander growls, grabbing me by my t-shirt.

This time he's not messing around. His grip is firm and deliberate, his jaw clenched.

Dom emerges from the crowd before all hell breaks loose. "Justice, come on." He drags me out of the suite against my will, whispers following us to the door.

In the hallway, he gives me the news. "I just got a call from the University Hospital. Hazel was in an accident. We need to go."

I pinch the bridge of my nose and squeeze my eyes shut, Dom's words slowly settling in. A chilled-to-the-bone feeling of dread roots me to the floor, and my chest stiffens. The melody seeping from Zander's suite is off The Gates of Hale's debut album. As if my uncle is laughing at all my failures right now.

"Justice?"

I scramble for my phone and dial her number again. It goes straight to voicemail.

"You hear me?" Dom growls.

"Yeah."

I don't really remember anything on the way to the hospital except for the Cartier box squeezed in my palm. The soft, smooth, and warm feel of it. Like her hand. And the rain. Lots of it. Beating against the roof of the car. Serenading me.

The hospital is cold and gloomy with blinding fluorescent lights everywhere and dirty blue chairs lined up against the empty white walls. There's a lingering scent of the end in the air. Rotten and sinister and nauseating. The doctor doesn't come out to see us until after four in the morning. I stand there staring at him and shaking while Dom does all the talking. I can't understand anything he's saying. It's not even the accent. His speech is just a jumbled medical-terminology mess. My hand, thrust into my pocket, is still squeezing the Cartier box. I'm wondering how I got here and why they won't allow us to see her. Part of me desperately wants to believe it's a mistake and the woman isn't Hazel.

"As soon as we know more, we'll give you an update." The doctor gives us a curt nod. "Please stay positive."

"What the fuck do you mean stay positive?" I whisper. My voice feels rough and foreign. It's all starting to come down on me like a ton of bricks. I glance over at Dom as if he has the answer. He looks distraught and tired, his eyes red.

"Her brain activity seems to be normal"—the doctor's eyes sweep over to me—"but there's no saying when she's going to wake up. All we can do is wait and hope she decides to come back."

She decides to come back?

"How the hell is it up to her? You're the fucking doctor." I grit my teeth.

"Sometimes it's up to a patient, Mr. Cross. Like I said, the human brain is a fascinating thing." He tilts his head and gives me a sympathetic smile, the kind people give you when there's nothing else left to say.

"When can I see her?"

"As soon as we run a few more tests."

I feel sick to my stomach after the doctor leaves. The floor beneath me starts shifting.

"I'm going to call her parents," Dom says with an acidic look on his face.

I don't remember how I make it to the restroom. The trip down the hospital hallway is just a vague memory, filled with the fuzzy voices of medical personnel and the nonstop buzzing of my phone. My body isn't really in sync with my brain. The whooshing sound of blood pounding behind my ears makes me dizzy. I can feel my whole body vibrating in the wake of the upcoming storm.

I stagger into the restroom, slam the door shut, and lean against the stall for support. There's a blur in my eyes. *Tears.*

"Fuck," I groan, sliding down to the cold floor. "Fuck. Fuck. Fuck."

Nausea twists my stomach. I can't fucking breathe and I can't fucking think. I sit there, still and terrified, trying to understand what to do next. Until the impatient knock on the door drags me back to reality.

I find Dom in the waiting area.

"You need to call May. And you need to call Samantha." I descend into the chair next to his and pull the hood of my sweatshirt over my head before someone recognizes me. My fingers tap-dance across my jeans.

He turns to face me, fear and panic in his eyes. "Are you sure?"

"I'm not doing the rest of the tour."

"I think it's best we wait for an update," he retorts.

"She's in a fucking coma, Dom," I snap. Tears well up in my eyes again. "What do you think is going to happen when she wakes up? You think she's just going to magically heal over the course of two days and take a fucking plane back to Los Angeles?"

"That's not what I'm saying. Canceling all the dates is not smart. We're contracted with venues all over the world. This is a potential lawsuit in the making. Besides, this is not just you. You're in a goddamn band with three other people."

"Then get the lawyers on the fucking phone and do your fucking job," I mutter, wiping off the hot tears spilling down my cheeks.

The silence that falls between us is suffocating. Part of me understands why he wants to wait, but part of me doesn't care about the tour and the band anymore.

The nurse escorts me to see Hazel shortly after Dom makes the call to L.A.

"Can I please have a moment alone?" I ask when we're at the door.

"Certainly." The nurse nods, her accent thick and distorted.

I wait till she's gone, turn off my phone, and enter the room. My eyes move from one object to another, searching for something that's not there, a sign of her being awake, but she's not. Her body looks small and thin hooked up to monitors and the IV drip. There are tubes everywhere, so many I can't even make out her face. Her head is covered in bandages, as is her right arm. The first rays of crisp morning sun seeping into the room through the window blinds dance across the white hospital blanket that's on top of her.

My chest tightens when I walk to the bed. The machine's beeping is an endless roar in my head. She was so fucking alive in my arms last night. Bright and hot like a timeless flame. I stare at her for a while, then pull up a chair and settle down.

"Come back to me." My voice is small, almost nonexistent. Meant only for her.

My hand shakes when I draw the Cartier box from my pocket. Fear and confusion rattle my insides. There's this new, horrifying feeling of being at a point of no return soaring through the air. The same one that took over me once before. The night Chance died. Right after the paramedics came. Their gray faces said it all.

I study the ring for a few moments, wondering how she would react. Would she be surprised? Shocked? Threatened? Happy? Her hand is lifeless and cold when I finally slide it onto her finger, and I hate that she doesn't smile back, that she doesn't see me, that she doesn't even fucking flinch.

I hate it that I'm here and she isn't.

43 HAZEL

THERE'S a certain beauty in death.

Death strips you of all the pain, the suffering, and the ambiguity of life.

Death doesn't feed you with empty promises and leave you hanging.

In a way, I've been secretly wanting for it to come and summon me. Just like it summoned my four-year-old baby boy.

Mommy?

His voice is bright and happy, without the weight of disease.

"River?" My heart beats like crazy, my legs are wobbly. A familiar warmth floods every cell in my body. The same warmth I felt the first time I held him in my arms. Calming and pure. That's when I knew I was meant to be his mother, that he'd been sent to me from heaven, a little angel with the biggest eyes ever. And I was going to love him until the end of eternity. If not in life, then in death.

"River, honey?" My tongue feels thick and heavy. "River?"

My eyes flutter open, drinking in the bright, blinding light at the end of the tunnel.

Mommy...

A soft gasp escapes the back of my throat.

Mommy...

I can still smell the stench of the burning rubber and hear the screech of crashing metal, but the only sound that really matters is the voice of my four-year-old son, a voice I haven't heard in over two years. Sweet and fuzzy like the first hug he ever gave me and every single one after that. Every kiss, every word, every touch, even every tear.

"Mommy's here, River," I call out into the void, fisting the light fabric of my milk chocolate brown dress. I can hear my pulse thump-thumping in the back of my head and my heart thrashing wildly in my chest. I can even hear my own thoughts.

Fear and excitement swirl in my stomach as I spin on my heels and stare into the distance. The other end of the tunnel is bright and cozy. The small silhouette of my son's body drawn against the curtain of light pulls me in like a magnet. My feet start moving on their own, shuffling through the loose gravel. Soon I find myself running, cold wind whipping my hair and the skirt of my thin dress.

My voice is rough, almost unrecognizable. "River...Mommy's here...Mommy's here."

The emotions are starting to choke me. His tiny figure becomes clearer with each step. He's wearing his light gray Tommy Hilfiger hoodie and his dark blue Levi's jeans I bought him for his fourth birthday. His small hands are clutched under his chin, his face serious, lips pressed together. His big amber eyes gaze at me, smiling secretly.

"What are you doing here, Mommy?" he asks, tilting his head.

"Hey, baby." I'm at a loss for words when my hands reach out to him. He's so small. So delicate, like a dandelion caught up in the wind. All I want is to hug him and tell him that everything will be okay, that he doesn't have to be here all alone. "Mommy isn't going anywhere anymore." My knees sink into the sharp gravel. "I've missed you so much." Tears threaten to spill any second now as I pull him closer and wrap my arms around his fragile body. The sweet smell of bubblegum shampoo swamps my insides when I inhale his scent. Every part of me is on fire, ready to explode with joy. My heart is bursting into millions of sparkling pieces, creating dozens of magical fireworks in my chest.

"I miss you too, Mommy," he murmurs into the folds of my dress, his hands locked behind my neck.

There's a long pause filled with an eerie silence. I'm too scared to let go of him, scared that if I do, he'll disappear again. "Mommy isn't going anywhere. Mommy loves you so much." My voice is barely above a whisper. "Mommy's staying, baby." There aren't enough words in the whole universe to express what I feel, not enough hugs and kisses to make up for the lost time.

"It's not scary..." River mutters. Releasing his grasp, he looks up at me through his lashes and pulls his bottom lips between his teeth. "It's not scary, Mommy."

"Of course it's not. I'm here now," I say, fisting the sleeves of his hoodie. My eyes can't get enough of him. The color on his face is refreshing. He looks good, healthy, even without his hair.

"You don't have to stay, Mommy," he says, running his tiny hand across my cheek. "I'm okay."

"Don't say that. I'm never leaving you again."

River tilts his head, his eyes staring past me into the distance, and the corners of his mouth curl up. "If you stay, you'll never get to meet Faith, Mommy." He smiles shyly, and his fingers pull on the strands of my hair. He always did that when he was a baby.

"I'm not going to leave you." My chest stiffens and the long-overdue tears finally break, rolling down my cheeks and burning my skin.

"Don't cry, Mommy. It's okay...I'm okay...really." His soft voice trembles. The moisture in my eyes blurs his features, but the lingering scent of bubblegum shampoo is still there, luring me in toward the light, toward an eternity of peace with my son.

"I'm okay, Mommy. You don't have to stay," River whispers again.

Wiping off the tears with my fingers, I shift to face the other end of the tunnel, the one I came from, the one where the light is just as bright as here. The gravel scratches my knees and as the cold wind messes up my hair, shivers start taking over my body. Part of me wishes for it to be just a hallucination, something my delusional mind has made up. There's no way I can possibly choose between him and my son. It'll always be River. It'll always be my little boy.

Taking a deep breath, I rub at my eyes again, hoping the vision will disappear, but when I draw my hands away from my face, Justice is still there—on the opposite side of the tunnel. Aiden is by his side, his small hand clutched around his father's large one. He's taller than I remember. His hair is longer too, almost past his shoulders, just like his daddy's.

My stomach spasms in response. Having this man love me was the best thing that happened to me after River.

"Hazel?" His voice is smooth and deep. "Come back to me." It's not simply a request. It's a desperate plea, transformed into a midnight serenade, calling me out, wanting me there with him and his son...and the little girl with the golden hair he's holding in his arms.

"It's okay, Mommy." River's whisper washes over me in a sweet lullaby. "It's okay. You're okay."

You're okay.

You're okay.

You're okay, Hazel. Don't move. Don't move, baby. It's just oxygen.

You're fine. I'm here.

Suddenly, I'm paralyzed. I can't feel my body, but I can still see the light. It's bright and sterile, somewhere above my head. Blurred images of moving silhouettes enter my line of vision—some women and a man. Their agitated voices blast through my head like a grenade. There's so much fussing around me that it makes me want to go back to where I came from, to the dark calm. The noise finally subsides and the women, who I now see are nurses, leave me one-on-one with the man.

The heaviness in my chest is like nothing I've ever felt before. There's a whole lot of fog inside my head. And it's replaced all my memories.

I blink a few times, and his face starts to swim into focus. He's got an amazing smile, wide and enchanting.

"You've been in an accident, baby. You're okay," he says, grasping my hand, his fingers sliding in between mine. They're long and warm against my skin and send small electrical currents into my arm.

I drink him in slowly, my heart racing in my chest for some

unknown reason. I sense we have a history. The desperate look in his eyes says he isn't just a friend.

"It's going to be okay. The doctors did good," he whispers, bringing my hand to his mouth. His lips brush against my scratched knuckles, and the ring on my finger shimmers under the stream of bright light. "You just need plenty of rest. Your parents are flying in today."

My parents? Flying? Flying where? Where am I? A light spasm clutches my stomach. The little hammer, pounding in the back of my head, ups its game. I swallow hard and try to articulate a sound, but the plastic tube in my mouth prevents me from producing anything but a low grunt.

"I'll get the nurse. Hold on a second," he says, getting up from his chair.

I blink in response, watching him exit the room. My mind tries to scramble together the pieces of what used to be my life, but for now, they're just fuzzy images. No names, no places, no dates. And it pisses me off that I can't get this puzzle right.

The nurse is adamant about removing the tube. She leaves to consult the doctor first. I lie there still and quiet, staring at the man by my bed. I think about my dream. I think about the children I saw. I think about the little girl. I think until the pain in my head is too much and I close my eyes.

A few hours later when the nurse finally removes the tube, I make another attempt to speak. Which fails miserably, but I keep trying.

"Don't strain yourself." He moves his chair closer and reaches for my face. "The doctor said you'll have some difficulties with speech at first. It's typical for patients with head trauma." His knuckles brush my cheek. His touch is featherlike but it almost feels like too much. So intense it scares me. "You just need a few days. You have a broken arm too, but it's healing nicely. And it's your right one, so you'll still be able to paint when you get out."

Paint? Am I a painter?

I swallow hard and push the words out, "H-how long h-have you—?"

"Two days."

"H-how?" My tongue doesn't seem to be able to sync well with my brain.

"It was an accident. Some truck hit your car on the way to the hotel."

"Hotel?" I whisper.

"I'm sorry you missed your friend's baby shower." His hand squeezes mine gently.

"Don't...r-remember."

"You don't?" He tilts his head, his smile faltering but only for a fraction of a second. His eyes staring down at me are big, gray, and terrifyingly beautiful.

I shake my head, my vocal cords painfully sore.

"Do you remember your name?"

There's a huge lump in my throat. My head is starting to hurt again. The life I've lived is like an enigma, a puzzle of sorts. The pieces are all there, just out of order, and I don't know how to put them back together.

He's waiting for me patiently while I take my time to sift through the incoherent visuals filling my brain. I keep thinking about it until the word that feels right pops into my head. "Hazel?"

"Yes." There's bliss in his voice. "What else do you remember?"

My chest stiffens as my brain latches on to another image. "My son."

"Yes, that's right. River." The man nods, his hand still clutching mine.

"N-not here?" I'm not certain if this is a question, because the hole in my heart tells me my little boy has been gone for a while and I've learned how to live with it.

"I'm sorry, baby," he whispers. "What about my name? Do you remember my name?" His long fingers start rubbing circles into my palm.

I still from his touch, my body numb. The images of us are dancing inside my head, blurry and dark. Some very dramatic and some very expressive.

"It'll come to you. You hit your head really hard, van Gogh. It's okay if you don't remember."

"I do," I force out.

"You remember my name?" He shifts in his chair, bringing his body forward.

"Picasso."

A soft laugh escapes the back of his throat. "Okay." He leans over me and kisses the part of my forehead that's not covered in bandages. "You remember how much I love you?" His minty breath fans against my face. His lips are warm and familiar as if they belong on my skin.

I'm tired and not sure I can produce any more words. Instead, I just nod and stare at him for a minute, mustering up one last question before the medication pulls me back into a hazy slumber.

"Just relax, baby," he says, raking his inked hand through his long hair. "It'll be okay in a few days."

I open my mouth and whisper through the dull pain in my throat, "Are we…married?"

There's a hint of a smile on his face, and his warm palm cups my cheek. "Not yet, baby. We can be if you want to, though."

I nod again, ignoring the black holes in my memories. He makes my insides feel like I'm riding the wildest roller coaster ever. All while I'm still in a hospital bed. Why on earth would I not want to be married to him?

"You just rest now, van Gogh. It'll be fine. I promise."

And I believe him.

44 JUSTICE

Day seven.

I'm not sure why exactly I need to keep track of how much time it's been since Hazel was admitted to the hospital, but I feel like it's important. Not for me but for her. The progress she's made with her speech is amazing. Her memories are all slowly coming back too. The black holes rattling her mind are insignificant, nothing to worry about according to the neurologist Dom chased down and brought in all the way from Berlin.

Getting one of the top brain trauma specialists in the world to agree to postpone his vacation was a nearly impossible mission but Dom accomplished it. I didn't care how much it cost or what it took for us to get this particular doctor to London. The only thing that mattered was him being here, doing his magic.

The dull noise coming from the neurology wing kicks up a notch when I sit down on the lonely leather bench in the middle of the glass walkway that connects the trauma center with the outpatient clinic. My body and mind are past their sane limits of exhaustion, and all I want is for this nightmare to be over so that I can take Hazel back home. Wherever that is. Just not here.

Yesterday was my first night back at the hotel, an honest attempt to catch up on some sleep. Part of me didn't want to leave the hospital, but my gut told me to give Hazel some time with her parents. The Tanners weren't very thrilled to find their only daughter hooked up to a bunch of monitors while wearing a sixty-thousand-dollar ring she has no memory of receiving.

You can't seem to get this respectful-and-proper-boyfriend shit right, Justice. The better-man crap is just not going to happen.

The hysterical screams accompanied by fierce banging on my suite's door woke me up around three this morning. Some high sixteen-year-old teen sneaked into the hotel to make sure the rumor going around the internet about me being hospitalized due to some freaky backstage accident after our one and only UK show wasn't true.

It took three security guards and a night shift manager to get the little maniac off the floor.

I snap myself out of my delirium and fist my phone that's tucked in the side pocket of my sweatshirt. Aiden's fizzy voice is still loud and clear in my head even though we FaceTimed over an hour ago. He wouldn't stop talking about his upcoming trip to Disneyland—a very unlike-Nikki activity with our son. I'm sure this was either her lawyer's or her publicist's idea. Right in time for the untimely demise of my public image due to pulling the plug on the band indefinitely.

The sound of footsteps approaching me from afar grows louder, their echo ricocheting off the glass walls.

"Hey, man." Zander's voice, low and gruff, fades into the chilled air filling the empty walkway.

My gaze shifts from the glass that's wet from the never-ending drizzle to his face. "I thought you flew back to L.A. last night." My statement sounds more like a question since I'm not certain why he's still here. The remainder of the tour has been canceled. Cruz, Tyler, and the rest of the road crew took off yesterday because the label was getting fidgety.

"Wanted to stick around for a couple more days." Zander clears his throat and thrusts both hands into the pockets of his leather jacket. "To make sure you're good."

"I'm good." I run my palm over my face and close my eyes for a few seconds to shut off the numb pain in the back of my head.

"You don't look good. You sleeping at all?"

"Yeah," I lie.

The truth is, even if I want to, I just can't. Dom and May have been doing a stellar job keeping the enraged fans all over the planet at bay, but the aftermath of last week's disaster has started to unravel my private life. Last night's incident wasn't the only one. Three days ago, some kids slipped in to the trauma department. One of the nurses caught them two rooms down from Hazel's.

"Her parents still here?" Zander asks, settling on the bench next to me.

"Yes." Dom set Clair and James Tanner up with two first-class tickets and a suite in the hotel down the street from the hospital. That still doesn't make me feel like less of a shit when her mother looks at me.

"Corrine here too?"

"You know how my sister is." I shrug. She refuses to leave London until Hazel's cleared to fly back to the States. Which may not happen for a few weeks.

Zander stares into space. The reflection of our slumped silhouettes in the glass across from us sketched across the flickering picture of nighttime London takes me back to the exact moment Chance died in front of me in that hotel room back in Texas. I can see myself watching him shooting up H and joking about it. Fifteen minutes later he was dead.

"Look." I swallow hard and brush my fingers against the cold leather of the bench as if it's going to make me less nervous. Real-talk time. "I know we haven't been on the same page about the band for a while and I know you're pissed."

Zander cuts me off before I get to finish my sentence. "Yeah. I'm fucking pissed, man, because you don't tell me shit. Not because you fucked up the tour." He shifts to face me. "I'm your fucking brother for life and if you're going through something, you come to me. You talk to me. You hear? Whether we're on the same page artistically or not. You understand?"

I sit there motionless, listening to the soft sound of rain and muffled hospital noises until his words finally start settling in. They sting and they hurt a little, but for the most part, they make me want to tell Zander the truth.

And that's what I do. "Sometimes I feel like I sold my soul to the devil for this. For being on the covers of magazines, postcards, CDs, and other crap. The band has consumed everything good I had in me. In us." My voice is weak and hushed. "It's made us into its puppets. And now it's time to pay up and it's taking us out one by one."

"You need to stop reading all those philosophy books." Zander scoffs, stretching his legs in front of him.

"There's gotta be another way to keep doing what we're doing."

"I thought you didn't want to?"

"Not right now. But once Hazel is better. It's all I know. Doing anything else makes no sense. I just don't want it to be fake anymore." My confession doesn't elicit any reaction from Zander. He's quiet for a moment, gaping at me like he's never seen me before. There's a small group of medical personnel marching by, two of the younger nurses tossing us suggestive smiles.

"What do you want it to be?" Zander asks when they're gone.

Any other music but the kind that killed my best friend. Only, the bitter words don't make it out. Because, in a way, it wasn't the music. It was all three of us. "Something different. Something less dangerous."

"You know what?" He slams his heavy hand against my back like a true drummer, almost crushing my spine. "Don't worry about it. Just do what you gotta do. I'm still your friend, even if we're never going to share a stage again."

"Thanks."

"Don't stress over the band business right now. The insurance is handling it. We'll talk when the time is right."

"Okay." I want to elaborate, to give him more than that one word, but my tongue doesn't move. At this point, I truly don't know if we're ever going back to what we used to be musically.

Getting a hint, Zander gets to his feet. "I'm gonna split. My flight is tomorrow. You let me know if you need anything, alright?"

"Sure. Thanks," I mumble, watching him walk off in the direction of the elevators.

After a few more minutes of studying the cityscape of London, I head back to the trauma department.

Hazel's mother catches me right outside the room. Her fingers lock around my wrist and she draws me away from the door.

"There's something I need to talk to you about." She doesn't use my name. She hasn't used it once ever since they arrived.

"Of course." I obediently follow her to an empty waiting area; my heart is racing a million miles a second. This is probably the most intimate Clair Tanner has been with me since we've met and the sudden change of behavior terrifies me.

Concern shadows her face as we settle on the couch in the corner near the window where no one can hear us. She gives herself a few seconds before finally speaking up.

"I wanted to thank you for getting Hazel the medical attention she needs. Doctor Müller is amazing. We really like him." She draws in a tremulous breath. The sight of the wrinkled tissue she's been fisting in her hands folded on her lap makes me anxious. I'm pretty sure I'm in the loop with what's going on with Hazel medically, even though the immediate family technically gets the news first, but the stern look on her exhausted face causes something in my stomach to twist.

"It's no problem at all. She should have the best doctor." *She should have the best everything.*

Clair Tanner is a stunning woman. Refined and elegant. Just like my own mother, she's aged well. I can clearly see where Hazel gets her looks and her spunk.

Releasing the tortured tissue, Clair rests her small palm on my shoulder. "Hazel's last two blood tests are showing high levels of hCG."

I blink slowly, trying to understand what this means, but my mind draws a blank. This is a term I'm not familiar with. Even though these past few days have been very educational. In a scary way.

Clair's hand is still on my shoulder when the chilling words leave her mouth. "There's a good chance Hazel is pregnant, Justice."

My chest tightens. A whirlwind of different emotions from confusion to terror rushes through me.

Clair's voice is a muddled echo in my head when she goes on. "I'm going to assume you're the father since you've been the only man in her life for the past seven months."

I want to scream *are you insane, woman?* Because if Hazel is really pregnant, of course the baby is mine. But the temporary paralysis taking over my body messes with my vocal cords and other parts of me responsible for proper communication.

"Justice?" Clair calls out, withdrawing her hand. "I want you to know we don't expect anything from you, but Hazel doesn't have insurance."

I swallow down the lump in my throat and force out the first question that comes to mind. "Does Hazel know?"

"Yes. The doctor already spoke to her about it earlier."

A cold shiver zips down my spine.

"She'll tell you herself when she feels it's the right time." Clair's gravelly voice is barely a whisper. "It's too soon to say for certain anyway. It could be just some abnormality in her blood."

Yes, the abnormality that happens when you don't use a condom, I think, examining the erratic thoughts filling my aching head. The best way to describe my current condition is probably to compare myself to a bug crushed by a massive cement block someone threw at me without a proper warning. "You don't have to worry about insurance," I say, fidgeting in my spot. My body is finally starting to come out of its stupor. Every part of me shakes.

"Like I said"—Clair tilts her head—"we don't expect anything else from you as long as you help our daughter get back on her feet, but you need to understand there might be risks considering her current condition."

I inhale deeply. "I heard you."

"Thank you." Clair rises up from the bench. "You do understand why I'm telling you all these things? I know you're very fond of our daughter and I appreciate you trying your best, but both of you have barely gotten your divorces finalized. Promising her certain things right now because she isn't well might not be the best way. Please, don't give her false hope."

The tightness in my chest is so painful that each breath is a fucking struggle. "I'm not."

"You should get some real sleep."

I watch Clair walking off in silence while panic and fear are spiraling through me like a twister. I need some sort of privacy, at least for a few moments, to sort through the mess in my head, but my body refuses to move again. The sharp smell of the hospital clinging to my clothes and my skin is starting to suffocate me. Numerous scenarios rushed through my head the moment I bought Hazel the ring, but none of them included us having a baby. I pictured her sweet, bright, and tender. Sometimes naked. I didn't picture her pregnant with my child. I just couldn't. That was always the dark, forbidden territory I wouldn't allow my imagination to wander off to.

At first, the idea of being a father again horrifies me because having another baby wasn't part of my plan when I thought of marrying Hazel. This is just as much of a surprise as Aiden was. But watching him grow has been the biggest joy of my fucked-up life. He's the one creation I'm proud of. So proud it's hard to put it into words. It's a warm fuzzy sensation in my heart that keeps me going.

I'm not sure how much time passes before the initial shock of the news wears off, but my head is still a hot mess when I return to Hazel's room. Coming to a halt in front of the door, I take a few seconds to get my shit together. My palm is cold and sweaty when it curls around the handle.

Hazel's in bed, propped against the pile of pillows. Her head is slightly turned, she's staring at nothing in particular, but the intensity of her gaze speaks for itself. There's an iPad on her lap. She's attempted to get back to reading, but so far it's proven to be challenging.

Her father's occupying a chair in the corner. His piercing gaze locks on me when I step into the room, and every cell in my body can feel the air between the three of us shifting. I brush my hands over my jacket to get rid of the dampness on my skin and silently take my spot on the opposite side of the hospital bed.

Hazel snaps out of her daze and looks at me. There's panic in her eyes.

"How are you feeling?" My voice is rough and low and I can't make myself say more than that because James Tanner's stare is like a screwdriver, drilling a hole in me.

"Could you give us a second, Dad?" she requests, setting the iPad aside.

He takes his time getting to his feet. His sharp eyes sweep over the room full of flowers and freeze on me. "I'll be outside."

He's definitely not in my fan club, which is a pity since the tradition requires to get his approval in order for me to marry his daughter. I guess I fucked up here too.

"Please, Dad." Hazel insists, tilting her head.

James Tanner clears his throat and exits the room.

The silence between us is thick and a little disturbing. Her eyes are like wildfire, burning right through my skin to the very bone. I reach for her hand and slip my fingers in between hers, and the Cartier diamond feels rough against my skin.

"Justice." She tightens her grip. The way my name rolls off her tongue makes me shiver all over. I don't understand why five minutes ago I was questioning the validity of my decision to marry her. I still want that despite what Clair Tanner and everyone else may think.

Hazel pulls her lower lip between her teeth and takes a deep breath. "The doctor said there's a chance I might be pregnant."

My heart is running a fucking marathon because hearing this from her is different. Terrifying and beautiful.

"Say something," she whispers, shaking.

I bring her hand to my mouth and kiss her knuckles. "I love you. I don't know what else to say, baby." Because I'm truly lost.

A labored sigh escapes the back of her throat. "Look at me." Her chest starts heaving. "I'm not ready to do this right now."

"I'm looking at you, and you're fucking beautiful."

A sardonic smile touches her lips. "I'm in a hospital bed, trying to learn how to read again."

"You're doing really good. Your brain function is almost back to normal. Your arm is going to heal in a month or two. The doctor says you'll be out of here next week. We'll get you a private nurse when we're back in L.A. Dom is already looking for someone. When the baby comes, we can get a nanny to help you out if you want. It's going to be fine." I scoot over to the edge of the chair and brush her hair away from her cheek. "We're going to do this together. I'm going to be with you every step of the way."

"You don't have to marry me just because I might be pregnant, Justice," she counters. "Or because you want to stick to your word. I understand why you said it back then. You wanted to make me feel better while I was out of my mind. That's not why people get married. People get married because they want to share a life together."

"Hazel?" I palm her cheek and let the warmth of her body comfort me while my mind is putting together the right words. "Listen to me. You're not pushing me away this time. I'm not going anywhere. Just because you're not well right now doesn't mean this is how it's going to be for us from here on out." My voice is a ragged whisper. "We don't do well when we're apart, baby. You know it."

She nods.

"Do you remember how amazing we were?"

She nods again.

"I'm marrying you because I want to share my dysfunctional life with you. Because you make it better. You make me and everything around me better."

Despite the hurricane in my brain and the tightness in my entire body, saying these words out loud feels right. It's an exquisite sensation I've never felt before. New and overwhelming, but in a good way. An epiphany. As if my entire existence, besides Aiden, has been a dull bore until right now.

Hazel inches forward on the bed and snakes her arms around my neck. Her cast hard and cold against my skin. Her fingers skim through my hair as she presses her cheek to mine. I love that she doesn't shy away from touching me, that she craves intimacy even after everything she's been through this past week—the endless blood tests, the physical therapy, and the lengthy conversations with dozens of doctors. She is so fucking determined to make it out of here.

"Do you really want a baby with me?" Her mouth near my ear, she trembles against my body while waiting for an answer.

My chest expands as I draw a deep, shaky breath. "It'll take me some time to get used to, but yes. Especially with you."

For a while, we just sit in silence, curled into an awkward human ball. Our tangled embrace is warm and soothing and it reminds me of my first time meeting Aiden. He was tiny and very quiet and the world around me stood still when I held him in my arms. It was one of those rare moments when I knew exactly who I was and where I was going. Just like I know now.

"You're sure you want a baby? Because babies aren't always fun," Hazel asks again.

"Yes. I'm aware. I already have one." I smile, pressing my lips to her cheek. "Let me see your hand." The taste of her skin on my lips is intoxicating. Exquisite and so familiar.

"Why?" she coos, nuzzling my shoulder.

"Because I'm going to take this back," I explain, pulling the ring off her finger. "It's a do-over."

She stills in my arms but doesn't say anything. Her face is so close I can taste her on the tip of my tongue, the faint flavor of coconut and vanilla along with all her hidden fears. The fears I'm going to take away.

Her delicate hand, still rested in mine, looks bare without the ring.

I play with it for a second before putting it back. "Will you marry me, baby?"

"What did you just say?" She stares down at the diamond returned to its rightful spot.

"Will you marry me so that we can raise our child together?" I repeat the question, stroking her hair. The warmth flooding my chest spreads to my stomach.

"You may need to say it a few more times until I stop forgetting." She bites back a shy smile. "Temporary loss of short-term memory due to head trauma."

"I see what you're doing there, van Gogh." My lips capture hers in a soft, slow kiss, our first real one since the accident. Fervent, promising, with a hint of wild. "It's not going to be easy, but we're going to get through this and every other storm coming our way," I whisper against her mouth. "Remember, it's us against the world."

"Us against the world," she repeats, kissing me back.

EPILOGUE

The Deviant Tour Dates are Rescheduled for 2019

12/3/18 By Associated Press

The band's publicist and the label confirm that after the abrupt cancelation of all The Deviant's fall tour dates, the thirty-six rescheduled shows are going to be the final shows the band will play together under The Deviant moniker.

In his recent interview with *Rolling Stone*, Zander Shaw, the drummer of the band, opened up about the struggle behind the decision to split up and the future plans.

. . .

I think a break was long overdue. We just never addressed the fact. I know the fans are a little disappointed because they weren't expecting for us to retire this soon, but I know they're also excited to see what we're going to do next. I'm not sure when it's going to happen, and I'm not sure if we're going to do it together or separately. But it's something that all of us have considered for a while now, and I think we really need it.

In a statement posted on social media, the band says they are "saddened by their decision, but the change is necessary."

Shaw didn't comment on his bandmate's marriage. However, sources close to the band confirm singer Justice Cross and his girlfriend Hazel Tanner secretly tied the knot last month. The ceremony took place in their residence in Santa Barbara.

The Deviant is best known for energetic live shows and attention-grabbing imagery used during their performances and in music videos. The juxtaposing of religious symbols and explicit sexual content in their music, along with a history of drug and alcohol abuse among the band members early in their career, has earned the band a controversial reputation in mainstream media.

———

THE END…OR NOT QUITE.

Thank you so much for reading my very first book baby Rapture. While Justice and Hazel's love story has come to an end, you'll get to see more of them in Deliverance—Zander's story.

If you enjoyed this book and have a second, please consider leaving an honest review. It would mean the world to me.

Want to meet another rock & roll idol Frankie Blade?
You can read his story for FREE in digital format here:
https://BookHip.com/XJBSSW

AMBER LYRICS

Will you pray with me
For those who can't speak?
Will you let me be
The peace you seek?

Will you walk by my side
Through the valley of shadows?
Will you help me decide
Between dark and chaos?

I'll burn, I'll drown, I'll live or die
For you
I'll go through hell as long as you wait for me
On the other side
I'll break myself apart
I'll burn, I'll drown, I'll live or die
For you, for them, for him, for her,
For everyone who's cast aside

For everyone who's weak
I'll be strong

Will you give me escape
When I ask for one?
Will you keep me awake
As I wait for the sun?

Will you grant salvation
To those undone?
Guide to the final destination
All those on a run?

I'll burn, I'll drown, I'll live or die
For you
I'll go through hell as long as you wait for me
On the other side
I'll break myself apart
I'll burn, I'll drown, I'll live or die
For you, for them, for him, for her,
For everyone who's cast aside
For everyone who's weak
I'll be strong for them

I'll burn like a magic spell
I'll burn for all to remember
I'll burn brighter than hell
I'll burn like fire the color of amber

ACKNOWLEDGMENTS

I'd like to start by thanking my Mom. Even though you aren't here to share this with me, you are my biggest inspiration because you always told me to follow my heart, always encouraged me to practice all forms of art no matter what they were, be it dancing, drawing, or writing.

I'd also like to thank my Dad. Although you know only three words in English (*hello my baby*), you still give the best business advice ever.

I'd like to thank my sister Galina. Thank you for listening/reading to my endless rants about my books and my characters.

I'd like to thank my first round of beta readers: Katia, Laura, Anne. You had to deal with a horrible pile of shit of a first draft.

Thanks to my second round of beta readers: M Putaway, Sam, Roopa, and Rebecca.

Thanks to my awesome beta reader Amanda. You helped me make Justice a better man.

Also, huge thank you to my writing buddies: Jason, Mandy, and Jacklyn. Thank you for encouraging me to keep going.

Thank you to my editors Megan McKeever and Loredana Elsberry Schwartz for helping me get this manuscript in shape. Now I definitely remember that the word "makeup" doesn't require a hyphen.

A big thanks to amazing R.C. Craig for reminding me that contractions are a girl's best friends. Your help has been invaluable.

Thank you to Robin Hill. Your help means the world to me.

Make sure to check out her Waiting for the Sun duet.

Thank you to Judy at Judy's Proofreading. I'm the queen of funny typos. I'm sure you noticed.

Thank you to Margarita for all things piano and stage performance.

A huge shout-out to Anthony. Thank you for helping me create amazing cover. You rock as Justice.

Check out his music at www.mursic.com and look up his other band Neon Coven on Apple Music and Spotify.

Thank you to my friends Gene and Chip for answering my really random questions at the most inappropriate times of the day or night.

Also, a huge thank you to my friend Shanda. You bring sunshine to my life when you visit.

Thank you to my friend Shauna. We've just met, but you've already done so much for me. Thank you to my amazing street team. Girls, you rock!

I hope I'm not forgetting anyone. Please forgive me if I do. Know that my gratitude is endless.

Thank you so much to all those taking a chance on this book.

And finally, a huge thank you from the bottom of my heart to all my favorite bands who created the music that inspired me to write this.

Music, without you, I am nothing.

ABOUT THE AUTHOR

N. N. Britt is a Los Angeles-based music journalist and photographer whose photos have graced CD covers, promotional posters, t-shirts, and billboards. When she is not writing or drinking coffee, she is probably reading or attending a heavy metal show.

www.nnbrittauthor.com